SOMEONE TO TRUST

Plucky Lucy Linden supports her widowed mother and little brother, selling firewood and toffee apples on the streets of Liverpool. Her uncanny ability to be in the right place at the wrong time gets her noticed by a young policeman, Rob Jones. At first Rob is amused by her exploits, but when he learns how tough life is for Lucy, he decides to keep a watchful eye on her – much to her annoyance. When Lucy's uncle returns from the war with a tendency to lash out and some alarming connections with the IRA, her attitude to Rob changes dramatically...

SOMEONE TO TRUST

SOMEONE TO TRUST

by

June Francis

Magna Large Print Books
Long Preston, North Yorkshire,
BD23 4ND, England.

British Library Cataloguing in Publication Data.

Francis, June
  Someone to trust.

  A catalogue record of this book is
  available from the British Library

  ISBN   0-7505-1688-7

First published in Great Britain in 2000 by
Judy Piatkus (Publishers) Ltd.

Published in Large Print 2001 by arrangement with
Judy Piatkus (Publishers) Ltd.

Magna Large Print is an imprint of Library Magna Books Ltd.

Printed and bound in Great Britain by
T.J. (International) Ltd., Cornwall, PL28 8RW

With love to John, whom I met in a 'Picture Palace'. And those like us, who found their escapism – thrills, tears, laughter, romance and adventure – via the magical Silver Screen.

Acknowledgements

I would like to thank Bob Harrington and the Beacon Archives Group, as well as Hugh McKinley, Elsie Shimmin, Gladys Thomas, Mrs E Conroy, Dolly Lloyd, Mr John Hewitt, Ron Simmons, Mrs Hull and Dot Gallagher, for helping me with my research. It was much appreciated.

Although I have done my best to get my facts right there were times when I needed to use a little poetic licence. Court 15 mentioned in the book existed, but due to so much of old Liverpool having been destroyed by bombs or rebuilt by the City's Corporation, I had to use what I knew of other courts to describe it. If I've got it wrong, please forgive me.

Chapter One

Lucy ran as fast as her legs could carry her along Great Homer Street, trying to shut out the sound of breaking glass and the shouts and cries of men, women and children fighting over clothes and boots looted from shattered shop windows. There was no one to stop them on this August bank holiday weekend of 1919 because the Liverpool bobbies were on strike. The sky was overcast and thunder rumbled in the distance. The air was hot and clammy, and perspiration ran down her flat chest beneath the well-washed, too-tight calico bodice of the secondhand navy blue frock her mam, Maureen, had purchased from Paddy's Market last year. Lack of regular nourishment caused her to look younger than her twelve years but helping to support their small family had matured her in other ways.

She raced past the North Star pub, clipping the kerb with a pram wheel. A drunk sprawling in the gutter reached up to touch her skirts, causing her to swerve to avoid him. She almost lost control. The boarded-up window of Mr Bochinsky's draper's shop came up to meet her and she put out a hand to ward it off. One of her plaits, fastened with string, hit her in the face and for a moment she could not see where she was going and grazed her cheek on the sooty brickwork of a wall.

Her brother Timmy yelped and dropped the pair of boots clutched against his chest to cling grimly to the sides of the orange box attached to the wheels in which he squatted on unsold bundles of firewood. Fruit and vegetables bounced several inches in the air before landing between his booted feet, braced against the inside corners of the box. Boots which were too large for him, boots which had once belonged to a relative, boots split across the toes and with the sole coming away from the uppers. They squashed an apple.

'Yer going too fast, our Luce,' he cried. 'Yer'll have us over!'

'Shut up! We're nearly there,' she panted, swerving to avoid a disreputable-looking woman with a bulging shawl bundled against her chest with goodness knows what concealed inside it. 'Think of Mam's face when she sees what we've got!'

She pushed the cart along Bostock Street, a thoroughfare of mixed housing and shops built in Victorian times. Some dwelling places had cellars and attics and had been turned into lodging houses; others were simply two ups, two downs or parlour houses. Between the Methodist Mission Hall and Mr Moore's lodging house was the entrance to Court Number 15 where her grandmother's home lay.

Lucy's pace slackened as they came within sight of the passageway next to the Mission Hall. Of the youths who normally hung about beneath the gas lamp in the evenings there was no sign. No doubt they were busy among the looters.

10

There was a gnawing anxiety in Lucy's chest as she began thinking of her gran. She went past the ash bins and the privies shared by the court dwellers, careful not to get a wheel jammed in the gutter running through the centre of the court, carefully steering round the cast-iron drinking fountain in the middle. The foul air hung heavier here than out on the streets, trapped as it was on four sides by buildings. The lower half of some of the houses had been whitewashed in spring but was already dingy with the soot from thousands of chimneys. She thought of her grandmother, lying in the stifling hot room under the eaves, and remembered the sound of her breathing that morning when she'd stood outside the old woman's room, listening to the doctor telling her mother that Gran didn't have long to live. Lucy was convinced if they had not had to move from Everton Heights then her grandmother would not be on her last legs now.

Three steps led up to their front door, which stood ajar. Lucy placed both her arms round her brother and hoisted his skinny frame out of the box. With his help she managed to drag the orange box on wheels up the steps and indoors.

'Is that you, Lucy?' called her mother, a soft Irish lilt in her voice.

The girl took an orange from the box and gazed upstairs. 'Yes, Mam! Can I come up?'

'No, best not!'

'But I've got something for Gran,' said Lucy, holding the orange to her nose and sniffing it with a pleasure that bordered on the ecstatic. 'It'll make her better.' She began to ascend the

11

rickety, dark stairway.

Timmy took an apple and followed, clipping her heels. 'It'll make her better,' he echoed, his golden hair glowing like a halo in the darkness.

'Have the pair of you got cloth ears now?' Their mother Maureen's slender outline loomed at the top of the stairs, arms outstretched to either side of her, forming a barrier. 'No further,' she said firmly. 'Your gran's not up to visitors.'

'But we're not visitors, we're family,' said Lucy, mouth drooping at the corners. 'She'll want to see us and know what we've done.'

'She won't know you, you eejit!' Maureen shook her auburn curls. 'Besides the priest's with your gran right now – but maybe I'll come down a moment and see what you've got.'

The priest! thought Lucy. What was she thinking of having a priest in the house when they hadn't set foot in St Anthony's since last Christmas?

'We've loads,' said Timmy, beaming up at her. 'Loads and loads.'

'Loads of pennies?' Maureen lifted him and hugged him tightly. 'My, you're the spitting image of your daddy.'

Watching them both, Lucy felt an ache in her chest, remembering the days following the sinking of the *Lusitania*. Every German-sounding shop had been smashed and raided. She'd been bewildered by the violence as she had been dragged through the streets by her mother to the shipping office. The sight of the mourning women, black shawls pulled over their heads as they wept and wailed for husbands, sons and brothers had left an indelible impression on her. Maureen had behaved no differently and yet a short while later when Lucy's paternal grandparents had visited and suggested she accompany them to Cobh in Ireland, where her husband Lawrence's recovered body had been taken for burial, she had refused to go with them.

'So how much money have you made?' asked Maureen now, smiling. 'I spent ages chopping wood last night. I hope you've sold all the bundles?'

Lucy avoided meeting her mother's eyes, scratching at a patch of scurvy at the corner of her mouth, thinking swiftly.

'Don't do that! You'll have it bleeding,' said Maureen, frowning.

The girl laced her hands in front of her and pinned on a bright smile. 'You said we needed fruit, Mam! Well, we've brought you some. Fruit'll make it better, you said. So we've oranges, bananas and apples. Isn't that good?'

Maureen drew her chin in against her neck, squinting at the apple Timmy was tapping against her collar bone. 'And where did you get them from?' she said softly.

'We didn't steal them, Mam!' Lucy's voice was scandalised. 'But hardly anyone's buying firewood today. Everybody's on the streets. The fruit was rolling all over the pavement and in the gutter.' She took a potato from the box. 'See! Spuds as well!'

'And I've got a new pair of boots, Mam,' shrilled Timmy, almost squeezing the life out of her as he wrapped his arms round her neck.

'They were in the gutter, too!'

Maureen's lips tightened as she freed herself from her son's embrace. She put him down and tapped a foot on the cracked linoleum at the bottom of the stairs. 'Is it that my children are thieves?' she asked in a soft, silky voice.

'No, Mam!' Lucy shook her head wildly. 'We didn't take anything out of the shop windows!'

'Keep your voice down! The priest's upstairs,' hissed Maureen. 'You certainly didn't pay for any of this stuff. Is it that you're saying it dropped from heaven, my girl? That it's a gift from God?'

Lucy seized on the idea, although as a family they'd had little to do with the church since her father was killed, but they had Scripture in the elementary school she attended so she wasn't completely ignorant where religion was concerned. Her eyes gleamed. 'Didn't teacher tell us only last week that it says in the Bible that God provides for the poor and hungry?'

Her mother was silent a moment then the slightest of smiles lifted the corners of her mouth. 'Who'd be a mother trying to bring up her children these days? Put those back in the box and go wash your hands. Take Timmy with you and we'll talk about it later.' At that moment the priest called her name and she hurried upstairs.

Reluctantly Lucy dropped the potato and orange in the box and, taking her brother by the hand, passed through the kitchen to the scullery which had no window or outside door because there was no backyard. She lit the candle stuck to a cracked saucer with melted wax before

14

whipping the cloth from a bucket of water which stood on the draining board next to a shallow stone sink.

Carefully she poured water into an enamel bowl. Then with a piece of rag she washed her brother's face and hands, drying them with a rough towel. She washed her own hands and face before standing on a stool and taking a comb from a shelf. She replaited her hair which, when newly washed, had the glow of a freshly dropped conker – but that didn't happen often because soap was in short supply in this household. Then she set about bringing some order to Timmy's tangled curls. 'There,' she said at last, pleased at the result. 'I think we'll do if we have to face the priest.' And she blew out the candle.

Two hours later the children were seated with their mother at the table in the kitchen. Maureen was dividing three oranges into quarters. She then divided them into eighths. 'Too large and they'll sting your scurvy,' she murmured, sharing out the pieces equally on a large plate, cracked and brown in places from the heat of the oven.

Lucy was feeling dreadful. She had wept when her mother broke the news that her gran was dead; she hadn't thought she'd be able to eat due to feeling so sick, but she'd had no food since breakfast so was feeling half-starved. 'Can we start, Mam?'

The woman's green eyes rested on her daughter's tearstained, freckled face. 'Why is it you have freckles? You'll never be a beauty like me if you don't grow out of them. Not that you appear to be growing at all. At your age I already

15

had curves and everyone thought me a beauty. I had lovely white skin and roses in my cheeks... That's Irish air for you. Sometimes I wish Mammy and Daddy'd never left our home in County Cork and brought us to Liverpool.' There was a catch in her voice.

Lucy felt that sinking feeling that came over her every time her mother said that kind of thing. It made her feel ugly and she despaired of ever being attractive to boys.

Maureen sighed. 'No, I'm not the girl I used to be.'

Lucy knew this was her cue. 'You're still beautiful, Mam.' She had lost count of the times she had said those words.

'No, no, no!' Maureen rose from the table and went to gaze at her reflection in the fly-spotted mirror which hung over the fireplace. She had a heart-shaped face the same as Lucy but her skin these days held an unhealthy pallor. 'I'm only a pale imitation of the girl I used to be. I'm not getting the good food I used to eat in Ireland and I'm not breathing that clean fresh air.'

'You enjoyed the spare ribs and cabbage from Maggie Block's.' Lucy's stomach rumbled just thinking of that mouthwatering dish.

'That was over a week ago.' Maureen returned to her seat, picking up a segment of orange. 'But perhaps we can spoil ourselves once I've my hands on the burial money.' She paused to eat the fruit before adding, 'You must never take what doesn't belong to you, children ... but seeing as how we don't know which shop this fruit came from we can't return it. Now eat

16

slowly – never rush a treat – and when I get the burial money we'll give a penny to the ex-soldier with no legs.'

'What about the boots, Mam?' asked Timmy, gazing up at her hopefully.

'You can't keep them.' There was regret in her voice.

Her son's face fell.

'Don't look like that!' Maureen reached out and touched his cheek. 'They're far too big for you, Timmy.'

'But I'll grow into them, Mam,' insisted the boy. 'I've never had boots that fit me.'

She laughed. 'It'll take you six years to grow into them boots.'

'You can pawn them at Dalglish's,' said Lucy eagerly. 'And with the money you can buy him a better secondhand pair and still have some money over.' She turned to her brother. 'That's OK with you, isn't it, Timmy?'

The boy nodded vigorously as he sucked noisily at a slice of orange.

Maureen raised neatly arched dark red eyebrows: 'You've got it all planned, have you, my girl? And how do I explain to Mr Dalglish how I came by a brand new pair of boots?' She picked up the offending items: lovely, brand new, un-cracked leather with steel caps.

'Say they fell from heaven, too?' said Timmy with relish, wriggling in his seat.

Lucy hid a smile but was unsure how her mother would take that remark. She was relieved when Maureen laughed. 'I shouldn't have said that. The trouble with you children is you're apt

17

to remember the things I'd rather you forgot. Eat your orange now. It'll do you good.'

'Poor Gran!' sighed Lucy. 'I wish she could have tasted this orange.' Her eyes filled with tears and she couldn't hold them back. They trickled down her cheeks and into her mouth to salt the orange. 'Why did she have to die? I've only one gran left now and I never see her.' She sighed, only able to hazard a guess as to why her other grandparents had not been in touch since her mother had refused to go with them to Ireland. It could be simply down to Maureen's having been unable to pay the rent on the larger house up near St Edward's College on Everton Heights so being forced to move in with her parents a few doors away. Maybe Lucy's other grandparents hadn't been told the new address. Only then hadn't her mother's father been killed in an accident, and her Uncle Mick, Maureen's younger brother, gone off to war? It wasn't until the end of hostilities, when Maureen lost her job in munitions and Gran became ill, that they'd moved again, to this dingy little house which they all hated. Still, at least they had a roof over their heads and due to the firewood round were managing to pay the rent.

Maureen's hands stilled. Then almost feverishly she said, 'Now you mustn't be wishing your gran back. She's gone to her rest.'

'It isn't easy, Mam, when yer sad,' said Lucy, wiping her face with the back of her hand.

'Don't I know it! Didn't I lose your daddy and my daddy in the last five years? And when I was your age I lost two brothers and a sister to the

18

fever! The only people I have left now are our Mick and you two.'

Lucy would have liked to have mentioned her father's parents but decided it would be a waste of time; still, she would never forget the day her father had taken them all on a train to the other side of the country to show his baby son to his parents before sailing away on the *Lusitania*, never to return.

There was still a vivid picture in Lucy's mind of a white-painted house with ruby velvet curtains gently moving at the open windows. The sea breezes had been so strong, her father had laughingly said they could blow you all the way across the North Sea. There had been a grandfather who'd smelled of fish and had a ruddy face. He'd given Lucy a whole shilling. And there was a plump lady with soft brown hair whose worried eyes were forever resting on her son. Even so she'd a smile for Lucy and had cuddled her new grandson. She had baked slabs of sticky ginger cake for them.

Lucy's Irish gran on the other hand had made sweets and toffee apples and sold them to the queues outside the theatres and new picture palaces. It was she who had built up the firewood round which Lucy had taken over when Gran became too ill.

Maureen put a hand to her head and her eyelids drooped. 'Anyway, that's enough talk, my girl. There's things to do. In the morning I'll be needing to make the funeral arrangements. I'll write a letter to our Mick right now and you can post it for me. Maybe it'll hasten his demob.'

19

'It's mad out there on the streets, Mam,' said Lucy, reluctant to face the crowds again.

'Tush, girl! Don't be fussing. You'll be fine.'

Lucy wondered how her mother could be so sure but knew it was a waste of time arguing. She went and found Timmy and herself a banana to share.

Lucy leaped off the step and raced across the court and through the passageway as fast as she could. The air felt hotter and heavier than before and thunder rumbled nearby. The sooner it rains the better, she thought, easing her clinging skirts away from her legs as she raced along Bostock Street in the direction of Scotland Road. She kept her eyes on the crowd milling about several lorries on the other side of the street. Trouble, she thought, and tiptoed past, watching the soldiers leaping from the rear of the vehicles to be met by a hail of stones and half-bricks. She could hear a man egging on the troops to have a go at him. To her relief no one was taking a blind bit of notice of her so she quickened her pace and reached the pillar box on Scotland Road without hindrance.

It was on her return that she met trouble head on. The crowd had spilled out of Bostock Street, falling back before the soldiers who were now wielding the butts of their rifles. Lucy decided there was nothing for it but to make a wide sweep and return home by a different route which would bring her to the junction of Stanley Road and Scotland Road where the Rotunda Theatre was situated. As she ran she could hear the shouts and jeers of the crowd. Then came the sounds of rifle fire.

As Lucy reached the main road she slowed down, having to step carefully over debris and broken glass, then she became aware that more soldiers were spilling out from the Rotunda Theatre and realised she could be trapped between the fleeing crowd and the reinforcements if she didn't get a move on. She raced across the road, her eyes on the soldiers, only to catch her foot in a tramline. She went flying, landing on her hands and knees.

As she struggled to rise a man fell over her, cursing and swearing. He picked himself up and ran on. The next moment she was buffeted from either side and knocked flat again. She tried to get up only to have her wrist seized. Roughly, she was dragged to her feet.

'Gotcha!' The soldier's grip was like iron.

'Let me go!' said Lucy through gritted teeth. 'I haven't done anything wrong!'

'They all say that, love. Pure and white as the driven snow you'd have us believe.' It was a young voice but powerfully attractive with a hint of Welsh in the Liverpool accent.

'But I *am* innocent!' said Lucy, struggling to free herself.

'All you slummy kids say that. You'd think we were born yesterday!'

She bristled, trying to see his face, but his head-gear threw it into shadow. 'I'm not a kid!' she hissed. 'And how dare you call me a slummy? We're poor but respectable.'

'Skint and desperate more like! I've heard it all

21

before, love, so you might as well save your breath. You'll have your chance to state your innocence at the Juvenile Court in the morning.'

That did it! Lucy panicked and bit his hand as he began to drag her in the direction of Athol Street bridewell. He swore. 'That's BH, girl – you'll regret it.' His sinewy fingers gripped her wrist tighter so she lashed out with her foot and felt the steel cap of her boot catch him on the shin. His breath hissed between his teeth and his grip slackened long enough for her to wrench herself free and scarper. She tore up William Moult Street, experiencing a peculiar exhilaration as well as fear, expecting at any second to hear the thudding of his heavy Army boots behind her and feel his hand on her shoulder.

She darted up a back entry and stopped to catch her breath. There was a stench of decaying cabbage leaves, rotten fish and cats' wee. For a moment she was reluctant to go any further because the way forward was so black. Then, almost as if she'd prayed for light, lightning flashed across the sky, turning the entry into day. She ran, only to be plunged into darkness seconds later. Thunder crashed overhead and the rain came.

By the time Lucy arrived home she was soaked to the skin. Weary as she was, she paused to sit on the front step and remove her boots in case there was something nasty on them. She stumbled into the house and found her mother dozing in front of a fire that was almost out. Shivering, Lucy sank on to the rag rug.

Maureen started awake and blinked at her.

'What took you so long? You're soaked to the skin!'

'It's pouring with rain, Mam – and there's a battle going on worse than the Somme! Guns ... rifles going off and everything. A soldier got me but I escaped.'

Maureen stared at her daughter as if scarcely able to believe what she was saying. 'What d'you mean, got you?'

Lucy explained, watching anger kindle in her mother's eyes. Maureen jumped to her feet and, hugging herself, began to pace the floor. 'What kind of world is it when the British Army fights its own people? Is this what my husband died for?'

Lucy was silent, hoping her mother wouldn't work herself up into a state. They were big questions she was asking, but what was the use of asking *her* at this time of night and after the day she'd had? 'Can I put more wood on the fire, Mam?' she asked.

Maureen stopped her pacing and sighed. 'What's the use of that? Best save it to sell in the morning. We'll go to bed. You'll soon get warm once you're alongside Timmy and me.'

It was true Lucy did get warm, but not immediately. And she would have given a lot to have had a cup of tea made for her and to have toasted her cold toes in front of a blazing fire.

Lucy felt she had hardly slept when she was awakened by a thunderous knocking. Surely it couldn't be morning already? There it was again and she could hear voices down in the court.

Maureen turned over, dragging the blankets with her, leaving Lucy's half-naked body exposed to the air. The hammering came again and she forced herself into a sitting position. 'Mam, I think there's someone at the door.'

'Tell them to go away,' muttered Maureen, not moving.

Reluctantly Lucy got out of bed.

'What's going on?' said Timmy sleepily.

Lucy did not answer but went over to the window. The rain had stopped and when she pushed up the lower sash the air felt cool and reasonably fresh. She glanced down into the court and saw soldiers. They were using rifle butts to hammer on doors and even as she watched one smashed in a door panel. 'Mam! Come quickly,' she shouted. 'It's the soldiers and they're going to smash our door in. Shall I go down and let them in?'

Maureen groaned and with a weary gesture threw back the blankets and got out of bed, leaving Timmy in his vest, curled up like a kitten on the edge. Silently she padded over to the window, only to let out a shriek when she saw what was happening below. She turned on her daughter. 'This is your fault, Lucy! You've brought this on us!' she hissed. Then she stuck her head out of the window and yelled. 'Don't you dare go bashing my door in, soldier! I'm coming down.'

She slammed the window shut and whirled round to face her daughter. 'Well, don't just stand there, my girl! Do something! Hide those things you stole while I get dressed and answer the door.' She was visibly trembling. 'Pass me my frock first!'

Lucy picked up the garment from the floor before darting over to the chest of drawers and pulling on the bottom drawer that had a habit of sticking. She tugged hard and fell backwards with the drawer as it came right out.

'Will you stop messing about and get dressed!' cried Maureen. 'He'll have the door in in a minute.'

'I'm moving as quickly as I can.' Lucy snatched up the black dress she'd worn for her grandfather's funeral. It was far too small for her now but she knew beggars couldn't be choosers and the frock she had worn last night was hanging damply on the washing rack in the kitchen.

Her mother faced her, frantically doing up her buttons. 'If he breaks my door down, I don't know what'll happen to us! And he'd better not find those stolen things 'cos if we're fined it'll be prison – I won't be able to pay! Now hurry up and hide them!'

'I'm moving, I'm moving,' cried Lucy, forcing the frock over her hips. 'Perhaps I should bring them all upstairs? The soldier's bound to search downstairs first!'

'Yes, do that! Then get back into bed and pretend to be asleep.'

Lucy didn't waste any time but collected as much of the fruit and veg as she thought looked surplus to their normal expenditure, which was most of it, and carried it upstairs, wondering where was the best place to hide it. She went into her grandmother's room and stowed it under the

25

bed. Then she hurried downstairs again and carried up the boots, passing her mother on the way down. She was calling to the soldier that she was just coming.

Lucy paused in the doorway of her grandmother's room and then, with a giggle bubbling inside her and an apology to the old woman on her lips, she hid the boots. Shivering slightly, she went and stood at the top of the stairs to listen to the conversation being carried out on the doorstep. It was the familiar inflection to the soldier's voice that caused her to shoot back into the bedroom and dive under the blankets.

'What's happening?' muttered Timmy, his eyes blue slits.

'It's a soldier. Pretend to be asleep.' She was conscious of the sound of his heavy boots as he climbed the bare wooden stairs. They seemed to shake the whole house. The giant's words from 'Jack and the Beanstalk' ran through her head: *Fe-fi-fo-fum. I smell the blood of an Englishman*. Suddenly she had an insane desire to laugh. He was outside their door. She could hear her mother saying indignantly. 'This is a disgrace. My children are in bed. Do you have to wake them?'

Lucy closed her eyes tightly. The door opened and she could sense the soldier standing at the foot of the bed, gazing down at them. Her heart was beating wildly and she wanted to put a hand over it to calm it down. Was it him? Was it him? Would he recognise her?

'Out, kids!'

Neither of them moved but Lucy couldn't stop

her eyelashes from fluttering.

'You're not fooling me. Now get up!'

Lucy opened her eyes and was unable to tell whether it was last night's soldier or not. He looked to be about twenty with a firmness about his jaw that boded no good for those who might attempt to put one over on him, but there was something about his mouth that suggested he might not be as tough as he made out. She wondered if he'd actually seen any action at the front. She knew there were those who'd had romantic ideas about valour and fighting for one's country and had lied about their age. He had very noticeable black eyebrows which seemed to be able to move independently. One was raised like a humped caterpillar right now. He also had a scar next to his left eye which disappeared beneath his hairline. He didn't give any sign of recognising her but maybe he was a good actor.

She and Timmy scrambled out of bed to stand next to their mother. They watched the soldier tweak the blankets with the barrel of his rifle so that they fell over the foot of the bed, revealing absolutely nothing. Lucy smiled. That was one in the eye for him. He indicated with his head that they should climb back in but Lucy sat on the bed next to her mother as he went through the flimsy chest of drawers only to reveal the paucity of their contents.

He left the room. Quickly Maureen and Lucy followed him next door where her grandmother's body lay. As he gazed down at the corpse Lucy was watching him intently. His eyes rested on the outline of the boots beneath the bedcovers, exactly where the old woman's feet should be, and there was a woodenness about his expression that told them he wasn't fooled.

'Died with her boots on, did she?'

Lucy could not help it. Her lips twitched. Maureen cleared her throat. 'And why not?' She drew herself up to her full height and tilted her chin. 'Young man, it's only yesterday she passed to her rest. I'll be taking them off her today.'

'No, missus. I'll be taking them off her now,' he said, pulling back the bedcovers and removing the boots.

Lucy protested. Those boots would have brought them some desperately needed cash. He looked at her. 'Your gran, was she?' The Welsh inflection in his voice overrode the Scouse this time but Lucy could not detect any sympathy.

'That's right. But what do you care?' she spat, folding her arms across her chest. 'Do what you came for and get out of our house!'

His eyes hardened. 'Watch what you say, kid!' He turned to Maureen. 'Are you a widow?'

'That's right. My husband sacrificed his life for king and country. And my daddy was a member of the police force – a lot of good it did him!' She sounded bitter.

He made no comment but bent and picked up something from the floor. As he did so he glanced under the bed before straightening up. Lucy and her mother stared down at the apple in his hand. He polished its red skin on his sleeve and bit into it. Maureen blurted out, 'You'd take the food out of my children's mouths now, would you?'

'You be grateful I'm only taking the boots and one apple and not arresting the pair of you!' He stared at Lucy and there was a look in his grey eyes which left her in no doubt he was the same soldier whose hand she had bitten last night. So why wasn't he arresting them now?

She and her mother followed him downstairs. He went into the kitchen, gazing about him before entering the scullery. He emerged, shaking his head. 'God, what a dump!' He threw the apple core on the ashes in the grate.

Lucy glanced at her mother and saw two bright spots of colour in her cheeks. The girl burned with resentment, too. 'We don't live here by choice, you know, but because the government's slow in providing Mam with a pension.'

He frowned. 'There's no need to tell me that. What I said is no reflection on your mother or yourself – but you don't want to end up in the juvenile courts so keep your nose clean. No more pilfering! I know it feels like there isn't much justice in the world but you've got away with it this time. Next time you mightn't be so lucky and could end up getting out of here only to end up in a girls' reformatory. You don't want to be separated from your mother and your little brother, do you?'

Lucy reddened. 'I hear you! But you've got me all wrong.'

Her mother poked her in the ribs. 'Not another word, girl,' she muttered. 'Don't push your luck.'

'Aye. You heed your mam,' said the soldier, and left the kitchen.

Maureen hurried after him but Lucy ran

upstairs. She was almost in tears, angry with herself for failing in her attempt to help her family. She found Timmy waiting at the top and he seized her sleeve. 'He didn't find them, did he?' His tone was anxious.

'The boots? Yes, he did.' She heaved a sigh of regret.

'Your sister isn't very good at hiding things.' Maureen's voice floated up the stairs. 'Let this be a lesson to you both. Our Lord doesn't approve of thievery.'

Goodness. That visit from the priest must have stirred her conscience, thought Lucy, and called down, 'But he pardoned one when he was on the cross, Mam!'

'Don't you get smart with me, Luce,' warned her mother. 'I think you've done and said enough for one day. Now downstairs! At least we've an early start on the day so we'll get through everything. You light the fire.'

'Shall I peel us some tatties as well?' asked the girl eagerly. 'There's a bit of dripping in a cup on the shelf that Aunt Mac gave us. I could make scollops.'

Maureen's mouth relaxed. 'Why not? Scollop butties. That sounds good. I'll see to the fire. You hurry to the bakery now. The bread'll be warm. But don't go eating the jockey if there is one.'

Her mother had to be joking, thought Lucy, running quickly downstairs. She was starving! The jockey was a bit of bread thrown in with a loaf if it wasn't the exact weight. It was just the right size to stave off early-morning pangs of hunger on the way home.

More soldiers were knocking on doors in Bostock Street as Lucy made her way to Great Homer Street. She thought of the one who had told her to keep her nose clean. It was OK for him to say that, she thought. There was nothing half-starved about him! The Welsh did OK for themselves. Strict chapel most of them and a large number of them lived up on Everton Heights. No boozing for them and they kept their noses to the grindstone, so she'd heard her gran say.

Tears itched at the back of her eyes just thinking of the old woman. She was going to miss her gran's warm, comforting presence. On the money front, too, they were going to miss her old age pension which had helped keep a roof over their heads. The girl gnawed on her lip, wondering how they were going to survive until her Uncle Mick came home.

Chapter Two

'What's taken you two so long?' grumbled Maureen, glancing away from the black crêpe-draped mirror.

Lucy flopped into a chair and yawned. It was three days since the riots and the peace on the streets was an uneasy one. Special policemen had been drafted in to work alongside the battalion of Welsh Fusiliers billeted at the Rotunda but they weren't the only soldiers. There were loads of others, as well as battleships in the river. There had been plenty of arrests despite some looters having rid themselves of their ill-gotten gains by dumping them in the gardens near St Martin's church.

'Well?' said Maureen, raising her eyebrows.

'There was a huge queue at the cooperage because we were late getting there.' Lucy muffled a yawn. She had not only delivered firewood that morning but helped her mother clean the house from top to bottom and visited Aunt Mac's (she wasn't a real aunt, just a neighbour from Everton Heights whom she'd known since she was born, who'd been given the courtesy title). 'By the way, Callum's home from the Army so I asked him to the wake as well.' Callum was Aunt Mac's son.

'Good girl.' Maureen turned back to the mirror. 'Holy Mother! What do I look like? A clown! That's what I look like,' she said, sounding exasperated. 'A clown!'

'What's a clown?' asked Timmy, leaning against Lucy's chair and gazing up at his mother.

Lucy grinned, remembering being taken to a circus by her Yorkshire grandparents in Bridlington. 'They have big red false noses and wear wigs and paint their faces white. They make yer laugh by acting daft.'

Maureen whirled to face them again. 'So my daughter thinks I'm a figure of fun?' she said tartly.

'No, Mam,' said Lucy hastily. 'And I didn't mean it the way it sounded. You're lovely. Even with flour on your face you look lovely.'

'So you can tell I've flour on my face?'

'But you know yer have because you put it there.'

Silence. For a moment Lucy thought her mother was going to spit nails at them but instead she laughed. 'Now that's the kind of thing your father'd say. He'd say there was no way of getting round the truth. So I look lovely, do I?'

'Of course you do,' chorused the children.

'Black suits me, does it?' Maureen ran her hands down her body, fingers lingering on her hips. 'I'm a little on the skinny side but I've still some shape.' She smiled at them. 'Sorry for sounding cross but I'm a bit on edge. Go wash your hands and faces, and change into your black frock, Lucy. There'll be no tea because there's bunloaf and cheese and crackers for the wake. You can have some as soon as you're ready. Now hurry! Folk'll be here soon.'

Bunloaf and cheese and crackers? Oh, goody, goody! thought Lucy, wondering nevertheless how she was ever to grow curves if she didn't get proper food. And even when she did get some it wasn't much because she made sure Timmy got a good share of it. She was almost permanently hungry and would have much preferred a bowl of steaming scouse to the cold food that lay on the table, but she did not complain and went in search of the hated black frock.

Half an hour later people began to trickle into the house bringing with them bottles and glasses. As the level of liquor in the bottles sank, spirits rose. Older people reminisced about Ireland in the days when the dead woman was a child and soon the talk turned to Home Rule and the tardiness of the British Government in sorting things out. Some said there would be trouble soon if they didn't get a move on.

Timmy escaped to his favourite hiding place under the table and Lucy decided to go with him. There had been enough comments made about her appearance to hurt. Someone had even teased her about being one of the little people. She took some food with them and kept an eye on what was going on by lifting the tablecloth every now and again in between telling her brother some of the stories of Ireland her gran had told her when she was his age. So it was she saw Callum arrive and not long after that noticed him tying a piece of string to her grandmother's hand where she lay in her open coffin. The other end he tied to the doorknob. When the next caller opened the door the hand of the corpse rose as if in greeting. The gesture was met with gales of laughter and Lucy felt certain her grandmother would have enjoyed the joke.

Maureen certainly had. She was talking animatedly to its instigator. Callum was a man you couldn't help noticing. Big and muscular, he was wearing a green tie and a pompom trimmed tartan beret on his nut brown hair. There would certainly be trouble if he met any of the Orange-men from up Netherfield Road way, thought Lucy, pricking her ears as he and her mother came over to the table.

'So when d'you think Mick will be home?' asked Callum.

'God only knows,' replied Maureen, twisting a glass between her fingers. 'But I'm praying it'll be soon because we're on our uppers and I'm hoping he'll find himself a proper job and not be messing about like he did before he was called up.'

'But what'll you do in the meantime?' asked Callum's mother, Aunt Mac.

'We wouldn't let her starve, now would we, Ma?' said Callum.

'Of course not. We'll help where we can.'

'I appreciate that,' said Maureen. 'I know I can't carry on living on air.'

'We've all tried it,' agreed Aunt Mac. 'But you just go down and down like a pricked balloon. You only have to look at your Lucy – there's not a pick on her and nobody'd guess she'll be thirteen soon and leaving school.'

Maureen bristled. 'Don't you be worrying about our Lucy. She'll be OK. I'll be finding myself another job now Mam's gone. Let's change the subject. How about giving us a tune on that fiddle of yours, Callum? I'm sure Mammy'll enjoy "When Irish Eyes Are Smiling"?' Maureen fluttered her eyelashes at him.

He took her hand and kissed it. 'Sure, and aren't yours like a morn in spring, darlin'!' he said gallantly.

The next moment music flooded the room and people began to sing and some to dance. Lucy enjoyed both and she and Timmy emerged from beneath the table and joined in the fun.

The following morning Lucy woke bright and early. She slid out of bed and went over to the window. Lifting the edge of a washed out curtain she could just about see blue sky above the roofs of the opposite houses. 'Mam, it looks like it's going to be a lovely day for the funeral,' she called.

Maureen groaned. 'Am I wanting to know that when my mouth feels like sandpaper and my eyes like they've fishing weights dragging them down? Get me a drink of water, girl, and see if there's a Beecham's powder in the box downstairs.'

Lucy donned her dress and boots and hastened to do her mother's bidding. There was a broken glass on the draining board and the water bucket was empty. She put on an apron before picking it up and leaving the house. The court area was deserted except for a rat nibbling at some offal. She picked up a stone and threw it, catching the rodent smack on its backside. It shot away behind the ash bin. She hated rats. She turned the tap on the drinking fountain and, cupping her hand, drank thirstily before sluicing her face and drying it on her apron.

When the bucket was full she left it a moment to go to the privy. Here was something else she hated. Without fail, every time she went into the stinking place she wished they were back in their old house with their own lavatory.

As she emerged from the privy her gaze fell upon a girl in a grubby, torn frock and bare feet, struggling to carry away *her* bucket of water. 'Stop, thief!' cried Lucy, darting over to her and seizing the handle of the bucket. 'Give me that back right away before I clout you one!'

'You prove it's yours!'

36

Lucy's eyes flew wide, her eyebrows arching beneath her fringe. This girl and her brother and mother had only moved in the other day and Lucy didn't know their names. 'You've got a nerve! You know it isn't yours. I left it there while I went to the privy.' Lucy pulled with all her might and water slopped over the sides of the bucket, drenching her apron and feet. 'Now look what you've done,' she said wrathfully. 'These are me funeral clothes.' She clouted the girl on the arm and managed to yank the bucket out of her grasp.

The girl cringed before her. 'I'm sorry! I didn't know it was yours, honest,' she wailed. 'But ours has a hole in it.'

'Then you should take it to the ironmonger's. He'll put a patch on it.' Lucy gripped the handle of her bucket tightly. 'Anyway, I've got to go in. It's me gran's funeral today.'

'I'm sorry about yer gran,' said the stranger, poking a finger through a tear in her frock. 'I didn't know her but I believe she used to make lovely toffee apples.'

'Shut up!' said Lucy fiercely, her own eyes filling with tears at the memory of how her gran used to allow her to dip the apples in the hot toffee. Without another word she hurried indoors.

Remembering what her mother had said about needing a Beecham's powder, Lucy found the last one in the cardboard box that served them as a medicine chest. She mixed the powder with some water in a cup and carried it upstairs.

Her mother was lying supine beside Timmy

who was sucking his thumb, eyes closed. 'Here yer are, Mam. Yer going to have to get moving,' said Lucy.

'What is it?' muttered Maureen, and without opening her eyes eased herself into a sitting position. Her auburn hair hung in tangled ringlets about her clammy face.

'The Beecham's you asked for.'

Her mother's expression eased. 'Ah, you're an angel. Give us it here!'

Lucy placed the cup in her mother's out-stretched hands and went back downstairs to light the fire before going out again to the bakery, knowing that as soon as Maureen got up she'd be demanding a cup of tea and fresh bread.

A couple of hours later the coffin bearers arrived with the undertaker. The hearse was parked in Bostock Street: a fancy black one with shining brasswork, and drawn by two jet black horses. Lucy admired the whole set up, remembering her granddad had been given the same kind of send off. 'That's cost you a bob or two, Mam.'

'Sure it has but I couldn't not give my mammy a good send off even if we have to go hungry for the next six months,' said Maureen, loud enough for the other court dwellers to know that there was no money left over from the insurance going begging. She had Timmy by the hand and Lucy walked sedately by her side, following the coffin bearers, who had a bit of a struggle squeezing through the narrow passageway beside the Methodist Hall to the open street.

Lucy felt uncomfortable on entering the

church. It was bright with stained glass and statuary and she remembered her gran putting herself into debt to purchase Lucy a white silk frock for her confirmation here. If it hadn't been for her mother working in munitions they would still have been in debt today. She remembered the days when her father was alive and there had been new clothes for her every bank holiday and at Christmas.

The requiem mass seemed to go on forever and when it was over Lucy knew she still had to face the burial in Ford cemetery to the north of Liverpool. To her relief and surprise, though, when they stood outside church Maureen said, 'You and Timmy don't have to come to the cemetery, Lucy. We'll be going to an inn out there for a bite to eat and a drink. You can stay here.'

'What about food for us, Mam?' asked Lucy, hoping her mother wouldn't drown her sorrows in drink as she had last night.

Maureen sighed and from her handbag took an engraved silver match container. She shook out two silver threepenny bits. 'Here! Don't spend it all in one shop,' she said with a hint of a smile.

Lucy thanked her, wishing she could trust her mother to be sensible with her own money. 'I've never seen that before,' she said of the matchbox, lifting her skirts and placing the coins in a pocket in her drawers. 'Where's it from?'

Maureen tapped the side of her nose. 'Shall we just say your gran kept some secrets even from me. But there's not much where that came from so make the most of it. Now, scram!'

Lucy seized Timmy's hand and raced out of the

gates before Maureen could change her mind and ask for the money back. She was brought up short by a voice. 'Where are you off to in such a rush, Lucy Linden?'

She gazed uneasily at the youth standing on the corner of Newsham Street with the girl who'd tried to steal her bucket. Lucy avoided him when she could. Now she was hoping he wouldn't cause trouble because she'd hit his sister. 'I'm not going anywhere in particular,' she said, trying to sound nonchalant. 'Why d'you want to know?'

'We're meeting our cousins. They live up by Our Lady Immaculate's,' said the girl, hopping about on one foot. She had on a pair of down-at-heel shoes. 'D'yer want to come? We're meeting them at the Pit on Mere Lane. It's good up there with swings, a shaddle and everything.'

Lucy said warily, 'Why are you asking us?'

'We feel sorry for yer, with your gran dying,' said the youth, looking mournful as he picked his nose.

Lucy didn't want his pity but Timmy tugged on her hand. 'I'd like to go on the shaddle, our Luce.' A shaddle was a kind of seesaw.

Her face softened. 'It's a bit of a way, a lot of it uphill.'

'It's better than going home.'

Lucy agreed and, besides, the Pit was up on Everton Heights. It would mean crossing Netherfield Road where every twelfth of July the Orangemen marched along, banners flying, pipes, drums and squeeze boxes playing, defying those who wore the Green who responded by throwing a few bricks and picking fights. She didn't have much time for either side. Her father, nominally C of E but who had gone along with Maureen's wishes and married in her church, couldn't understand how, if they were all Christians, they could hate each other so much. Lucy agreed with him.

'OK, we'll come with you,' she said, 'but say "Truce" first. Which means you won't be sneaky and hit me when I'm not expecting it.'

The youth grinned. 'I'll say "Truce" if it makes yer happy. Truce! Truce! Truce! Now, race yer to the top of Newsham Street!' He took off.

The other three ran after him. Lucy knew she had little chance of catching up with him but had to try; he wore short trousers and a sleeveless pullover and she was hot in the calf-length black frock and so he won, swaggering about afterwards as if he'd won a prize.

Eventually they came to Netherfield Road where there were several shops boarded up. A tram clanged by and there was a rumble of cart wheels and the clip-clop of horses' hooves. A carter called to a man standing in the doorway and women with small children clinging to their skirts gossiped on the pavement. There was a smell of hot tar and horse manure, the scent of hops and yeast from a nearby brewery and the oily undertone of ground nuts wafting up from Bibby's soap manufacturers down by the docks.

The four children paused a moment, waiting for a break in the traffic before darting like swifts across the road. On the corner of Havelock Street stood the John Bagot Fever Hospital. Lucy remembered her mother bringing her here with

41

Timmy, in a panic because his chest was bad and she thought he would die.

'We go up here,' said the youth, indicating Havelock Street.

Lucy did not need telling. She gazed up the cobbled street which rose almost perpendicular to where St George's cast-iron church stood on the crest of the hill. On one side of the street was a handrail. She skipped over to it, followed by the others, and bringing her skirt through her legs, took a safety pin from her collar and pinned it to the fabric at her waist. Then she swung by her hands, before turning herself upside down and hanging by her knees. It was fun and the others followed suit. Then the youth went and spoilt things by tickling her under both arms when she changed her position.

Lucy's hands slipped from the bar and she fell to the ground, grazing both her knees. 'You eejit!' she cried, turning on him, her hazel eyes glinting. 'What did yer do that for?'

'To pay yer back for hitting my sister,' he said, thrusting his face close to hers. 'I didn't hit yer so I haven't broken the truce. Now, the pair of yer, get moving. We're supposed to be going to the Pit.'

Annoyed with him, Lucy almost turned back then. Instead she flounced off, unpinning her skirt as she went. By the time she reached Northumberland Terrace she was out of breath and collapsed against St George's churchyard wall. She did not linger long but instead went inside the church grounds and took off her boots so she could feel the grass beneath her feet. It was soft as a feather cushion. She twirled round and round before flinging herself down and closing her eyes. The world spun around her and she felt herself going with it.

For several minutes nobody spoke. Then she said, 'Look at those clouds. I'm going to pretend I'm floating across the sky just like them.'

'Yer daft,' said the youth, getting to his feet and walking towards the church.

Lucy did not care what he thought but she got up, remembering the view from the church steps was well worth seeing. She held her face up to the breeze, letting it cool her hot cheeks. Then she looked down on the slanting roofs of hundreds and hundreds of sooty-bricked houses trying to spot where Court 15 was situated, but it was impossible. She let her gaze wander to the Mersey and out to the bar and the estuary where she could see a dredger, and a liner accompanied by a pilot boat, heading for the Irish Sea. 'I think I can see New Brighton,' she said.

'Where, where?' cried Timmy, running over to her.

'Over there.' She hoisted him up into her arms so he could get a better view, wishing she still lived up here. She remembered her gran telling her about the local toffee shop, which had been famous for its Everton Toffee. Now Barker & Dobson had bought the recipe and were churning the toffees out by the million and exporting them worldwide. Sometimes she dreamed of owning a shop and, just like the cottage in 'Hansel and Gretel', it was made of all kinds of sweets.

'It's lovely! It's all lovely,' cried the other girl, startling Lucy out of her dream. She flapped her arms. 'I'm a bird and I'm going to fly up in the sky and over the sea.' She ran round and round in an ever-widening circle. Timmy struggled to get down and a moment later was chasing after her.

'Yer look as daft as she did before,' said the youth, giving Lucy an unfriendly look.

'I think it's fun,' said Lucy, her eyes glinting. 'I'm going to be a bee so I can buzz and sting and get you back for tickling me and making me graze my knees.' She darted at him and pinched his arm. He yelped and landed her a smack.

'You're all crackers,' said a voice behind them. 'And you don't belong here. This is our territory.'

Lucy whirled round and stared at a lad who stood before them whittling a stick with a pen-knife. He wore dusty brown corduroy shorts and a grubby blue shirt open at the neck, had a shock of sooty black hair and a tanned face. He was not alone but with two other youths.

'Who are you?' she said warily.

'I know who I am,' said the boy. 'Name's Owen Davies.' He dropped the stick and pushed himself away from the church wall with a quick thrust of his hips. 'And I know what you lot are.' Before Lucy could step back he pressed the point of his blade against her bodice. 'You're Irishes and you don't belong in this churchyard.'

'I was born in Liverpool and my dad was from Yorkshire so you leave me alone!' Lucy was frightened but trying not to show it. She darted a look at the youth who'd led them up here. Why didn't he do something?

'We'll go,' he said, backing away. 'It wasn't me who wanted to come in here. It was her. She's daft.'

'You're a liar!' cried Lucy indignantly.

Owen's knife hand dropped and he turned on the youth. 'Is that right? You're a liar?'

He reddened. 'Yer not believing her, are yer? She's a girl and yer know what girls are. *They're* the liars. Anyway I'm not looking for a fight.'

'You're a coward then?'

The colour in the youth's cheeks spread to cover his neck. 'I'm not! Besides, you've a knife and me mam's told me not to get into fights.'

'So you're a mammy's boy,' sneered Owen, clicking the blade shut and tossing the knife to one of his mates.

Lucy's eyes brightened. Any other time she wouldn't have liked the idea of boys fighting but these two – the one who'd tickled her and caused her to graze her knees, and the other who'd threatened her with a knife – she hoped they punched the hell out of each other. 'Up the Irish!' she said mischievously.

The youth lunged forward and swung a punch, grazing Owen on the side of his jaw. The next moment the boys were grappling, lost their balance and were rolling about on the ground, still pummelling each other.

The girl who stood next to Lucy shrieked and darted forward. 'Stop it! Stop it, Bert! Mam'll have yer if yer go home with yer trousers all torn!'

'Leave them alone,' said Lucy, dragging her back. 'Let them kill each other. It'll teach them a lesson.'

'What the hell d'you think you're doing?'

Lucy glanced in the direction of the voice and could not believe it was *that* soldier again. He was hauling the two boys up and shaking them like a greyhound would a hare. 'Owen, what has your mother told you about fighting – and here on church property, too?'

'I'm sorry, Mr Jones! You won't tell her, will you?' The boy was all supplication and apologies now. 'I swear I won't do it again – honest.'

'She'll have your hide if you do. Or worse than that!' He released both lads. 'Now beat it if you don't want to feel the back of my hand.'

Owen and his mates scarpered in the direction of the front gateway. Bert, followed quickly by his sister, went the other way, round the bulk of the church to the gates on St Domingo Road which led to Mere Lane and the Pit. Lucy made to go after them but the soldier moved to block her way. 'What are you doing up here?' He sounded exasperated.

She thought of asking him what it had to do with him but changed her mind. She might get another lecture on justice and the law and the penalties for misbehaviour. 'I used to live up here.' She cocked her nose in the air. 'We had a better house then. My dad earned a fair screw.'

'What was your dad before he was killed?'

'A ship's purser. He was a Yorkshireman but met Mam when he came ashore here. He was a Proddy. We lived near St Edward's College. Only first my dad was killed and then my granddad was attacked coming home one night up from Great Homer.'

46

'The one who was in the police force, I take it?' He sounded interested.

She nodded. 'He came from Cork in Ireland but came over here thinking he'd earn more money and perhaps the hours would be shorter and conditions better.'

'Bet they weren't, though.'

She nodded. 'Mam and Uncle Mick were round my age then. I was brought up with a proper respect for law and order so you're wrong about me, you know.'

He didn't argue but asked where her mother was. 'Why isn't she keeping an eye on you?'

'I'm not a kid!' Lucy's eyes flashed and she took a step back from him. 'I'll be leaving school at Christmas. I work now. One day I'm going to be rich and live in a big house.'

He grinned. 'Oh yeah!'

'Yeah!' she said defiantly. 'Anyway, I'm going now.' She turned her back on him and called her brother, thinking it was blinkin' tough luck on her the way this man kept turning up like the genie in 'Aladdin'.

Timmy slipped his hand into hers as they walked down Havelock Street. 'Are you really going to be rich one day, Luce?'

'Of course!' She smiled down at him. 'But right now I'm planning on buying sherbet dabs and toffee whirls at O'Donnell's. We deserve a treat.'

But when she got to the sweet shop and felt in the pocket of her drawers for the money it had gone. 'Oh, no!' she groaned, realising it had probably dropped out when she'd swung on the railing despite having pinned up her skirt. Timmy

47

burst into tears when she told him what had happened and Lucy felt like crying herself. Instead she squeezed his hand and dragged him in the direction of home.

It was as they passed the cinema with its glazed white tiled frontage that a poster caught her eye. It wasn't the advertisement for Charlie Chaplin's latest film which drew her gaze but a handwritten notice stuck to the poster, saying: CLEANER WANTED. APPLY WITHIN. She remembered what her mother had said about finding a job and ran the rest of the way home, but it was too early for Maureen to have returned from the cemetery.

Lucy sat on the front step, fretting, knowing that jobs could be taken almost immediately after being advertised. She had to do something. She left Timmy playing in the court and rushed back to the cinema. She found the glass plate door open and stepped inside the foyer.

There were two men standing talking there. One was the pianist, Barney Jones, known to all the kids who attended the Saturday matinee as Uncle Barney. And the other was *that* soldier! She could scarcely believe it and almost walked out again but at that moment Barney looked up and smiled at her. 'What is it you want, lovey?'

Scarcely daring to hope, Lucy approached the two men. That Owen up in St George's had called the soldier Mr Jones. Could he be related to Barney who was so popular? He was always cheerful, and handsome into the bargain. He had wavy fair hair and lovely teeth. Her mother had likened him to Douglas Fairbanks who swash-buckled his way across the silver screen. But poor

Barney could never swashbuckle because he wore a built-up shoe so you always knew when he was coming. Thump, thump, thump! Lucy had not seen him for a while, not since her gran had been taken ill, but she trusted him to hear her out. Though she would have much preferred it if Soldier Jones could have disappeared in a puff of smoke.

Even so she spoke up. 'The job that's advertised – it's not what my mam's used to but we need the money.'

'You're Lucy Linden,' said Barney, his light blue eyes twinkling. 'You've a lovely mother.'

She smiled, knowing how pleased Maureen would be when she told her that, and thought that was why everybody loved Barney – because he remembered names and could put them to faces and say nice things. 'Thanks.'

'I remember she lived near us when her family first came to Liverpool.'

'You're right again!' Lucy glanced at the soldier, hoping he'd noted her story had been verified. Everyone knew Barney had a large house up on St Domingo Road which he shared with his younger brother's widow, not that anybody Lucy knew had ever met her. Everyone knew, too, that he had several other houses and was part-owner of the cinema and only played the piano because he loved music and making people happy. Not that he ever talked about these things, everybody just knew.

'Fancy that,' said the soldier, an expression in his grey eyes that convinced Lucy he knew what she was about. 'Give her mother the job, Barney.

49

She needs it.'

'I didn't realise you knew the family, Rob?' said the older man, surprise in his voice.

'I searched their house the other morning. They could do with a break.'

'It's true,' said Lucy, nodding her head vigorously. 'We're broke and desperate. Mam hasn't been able to work since Gran took so bad. We're hoping Uncle Mick'll help us out when he gets demobbed but we've no idea when that'll be.'

Barney placed a hand on Lucy's shoulder and, lowering his head, said in her ear, 'Tell your mother to be here at ten in the morning with a bucket, brushes and polishing cloths. I'm sure she'll get the job.'

Lucy felt so grateful she could have kissed his boots. Instead she just thanked him and danced out of the cinema, barely able to contain herself until she got home.

Her mother had still not returned and Lucy had to be off to the cooperage in search of wood offcuts to chip. Not that she depended on offcuts alone but cadged orange boxes and crates from the various other businesses round about.

When Maureen eventually came rolling home she was in no fit state to make sense of anything Lucy said. She went upstairs and was fast asleep when the girl took her a cup of tea so Lucy didn't bother waking her but got on with chopping wood. Timmy helped her bundle it and load the cart. They were hungry, only having eaten a couple of sugar butties. Fed up with her mother's thoughtlessness, Lucy went through Maureen's pockets and found two pennies, four farthings and a florin. She took the florin and left the house with her brother.

The fish and chips tasted marvellous and were consumed in St Martin's Gardens so the gorgeous smell wouldn't linger in the house and give them away.

The following morning after Lucy had finished her firewood round she bought a Beecham's powder, mixing it when she arrived home and taking it up to her mother. Despite having slept heavily there were dark rings beneath her lovely eyes and wisps of auburn hair clung to her sallow cheeks. 'Never again,' she groaned.

Lucy sat on the bed. 'Mam, you've got to get up. I've a job for you at Barney Jones's cinema.'

Maureen almost dropped the cup. 'You've what?'

'I thought it was too good to miss! Dead handy for you, not half across the town like some of them who have cleaning jobs.'

'OK, OK! You don't have to convince me.' Maureen put a hand to her head as if it needed holding on. 'Although cleaning isn't what I'd have chosen if I had any choice – which I don't until our Mick comes home.'

'Then you'll have to move yourself. You'll need to take a bucket and cloths and things.'

Maureen stared at her and her eyes were sharp as she punched her daughter lightly under the chin. 'Did you spend those threepences I gave you? Only I'm a bit short.'

'We were hungry, Mam. I've done my round and I've put the money in the jar.' But for the very first time ever Lucy had kept some money back, determined to build up a little nest egg for her and Timmy. Threepence a day, that was all, but she remembered her grandfather saying that if you looked after the pennies the pounds would take care of themselves.

'You're a good girl.' Maureen's voice sounded more cheerful as she drained the cup before climbing out of bed.

Lucy watched her as she dressed, wanting to trust her but not convinced that if life got tough her mother wouldn't weaken. If she did Lucy had to be prepared. She was determined she and Timmy would not go hungry again.

Chapter Three

Maureen got the job. A few days later Lucy watched her mother fastening a sacking apron around her waist before going to work. The girl picked up the galvanised metal bucket containing clean floor cloths, a scrubbing brush, a packet of washing soda and a block of green soap, as well as furniture polish. She hung it from her arm as her mother reached for the sweeping brush resting against the kitchen wall. 'I'll come and give you a hand, Mam.'

'You might as well, seeing as how you're not back at school yet. And as a reward you can take Timmy to the matinee on Saturday.' One of the perks of the job was that Maureen received a pair of complimentary tickets for two evening performances and two for the kids' matinee.

Maureen took one last look at herself in the mirror and so did Lucy, wishing not for the first time that she'd inherited her mother's looks, but she still had freckles and looked about ten. Both of them then went over to Timmy who was resting on the sofa with a blanket over him. He'd started with a summer cold last night and both mother and daughter were worried about him, mollycoddling him because they didn't want it to go to his chest. 'Now you be a good boy,' said Maureen. 'If you need anything, go next door.'

Timmy nodded, gazing at the pictures in a book that Lucy had brought him from the library. His mother and sister kissed him and left.

The weather was unseasonably foggy. It hung over the area like a damp Army blanket, catching at the throat and causing them to hurry. Outside the cinema a ladder was propped up against a wall where a youth was sticking a poster proclaiming what was showing that week. It was the first time that Lucy had seen him here and to her dismay she recognised him. Putting her head down, she followed in her mother's wake, hoping that he had not recognised her.

'Morning, girls!' Mrs Malone, the other cleaner, greeted them. 'How's tricks with you this miserable day?' She did not wait for an answer but continued talking. 'I had a bad start. I broke me broom handle. Talk about bad luck!'

Lucy glanced at her mother who had already got down to work and was dusting the backs of the seats as she hummed 'The Londonderry Air'. Lucy looked back at Mrs Malone. 'You believe in

53

luck?' The girl genuinely wanted her opinion. Was there such a thing as luck or was everything ordained by God? Which surely meant you didn't have a say in what was going to happen to you.

'To be sure I do. See this?' The woman pulled a purse from a pocket in her long skirts and opened it. There wasn't much by way of money inside but she drew out a bit of tissue paper and opened it carefully. 'There's me lucky four-leaved clover, come all the way from Wicklow.'

Lucy stared at it dubiously. 'D'you really believe it brings you luck?'

'I found it, didn't I? Amongst thousands of three-leavers. If that isn't luck for yer, I don't know what is.' The older woman cackled, showing gaps in her rotting teeth.

Lucy couldn't help agreeing with her. 'But d'you believe in some people being lucky and others bringing bad luck?'

'Aye, I do, girl. Yer meets them all over the place. Everything goes wrong for some folks. If a slate falls off their roof, it hits them. If there's a hole to fall down, they come a cropper. And yer can bet if their lads are playing football in the street, they'll smash a window.' She winked at Lucy. 'Yous ready to get cracking with that brush? There's a ton of orange peel just waiting for you.'

As Lucy swept between the rows of seats she glanced up at the screen, remembering *The Perils of Pauline,* a series of hair-raising adventures which had helped keep some of the kids off the street and out of trouble at the cinema. Soldier Rob Jones should be pleased about that, she thought. Had she been lucky or unlucky the way he'd turned up in places where she'd least expected him? He'd certainly stopped the two youths in their tracks up on the Heights, and it was possible he'd helped convince Barney to give her mother this job, too. But what about that other youth sticking up the poster outside? If she wasn't mistaken that was Owen Davies. Was he someone who'd landed a job because of the soldier's or Barney's championing? He was in what some would regard as Irish territory but Lucy wasn't about to challenge him. If he kept himself to himself when they chanced to meet, that would suit her. She paused for a moment in her task, leaning on her broom.

'What's this? What's this? Extra staff?' said a familiar voice.

Lucy glanced at her mother who swept Barney a smiling glance from beneath her eyelashes. 'You're not minding Lucy, Mr Jones? She's a good worker and offered to help, not expecting any payment.'

Lucy wished heartily she would receive some payment but guessed the takings wouldn't run to hiring three cleaners as well as a doorman, cashier, two usherettes, a projectionist and his assistant, and of course Barney himself. He was dressed as smartly as ever, in a dinner jacket and white tie. It suited him. His hair glistened like a newly minted sovereign and when she looked at his shoes, which somehow denoted status in her mind, they were highly polished. She wondered why he had never married. Of course some women would be put off by that built-up shoe but he had money, a handsome face and a pleasant disposition to go with them.

'How old are you, Lucy?' he asked, taking a silver cigarette case from an inside breast pocket.

'Almost thirteen.' She couldn't hide the pride she felt, considering herself almost grown up.

'Good Lord! You don't look it. But then your mother doesn't look old enough to have a daughter that age either.'

'It's a silver tongue you've got, Mr Jones,' murmured Maureen, sending him another of those slanting glances from beneath her eyelashes.

Lucy, whose spirits had sunk at his words, wondered whether she should practise that look. It just might get her somewhere. 'I need to eat more,' she said aloud, thinking at the same time how proudly her mother carried herself. It was easy to forget she was wearing a sacking apron and occupied in the lowly task of polishing the backs of seats.

'You'll grow, girl,' said Mrs Malone reassuringly. 'I've seen it happen time and again.'

'Well, I can't stand here chatting, pleasant as it is,' said Barney with a smile, rubbing his hands together. 'You get on with your work, girls, but perhaps I can make it a bit more pleasant for you. Music while you work, hey?' He clumped down the aisle to the piano situated at the front of the auditorium.

Soon music flooded the place and Lucy's feet itched to dance. She sang along to 'Oh, You Beautiful Doll', but soon Barney was ringing the changes and a tinkling melody put her in mind of

56

a snowy street and a young woman with a baby in her arms. Lucy shivered, knowing that if the mother couldn't find shelter then they would both die. The tempo changed, became rousing, full of excitement. It swept her along and she was flying away along the Mersey and out into the open sea. Then once more the music changed, was sweeter, and she felt as if her insides were melting, yearning for ... exactly what, she didn't know.

'My, that's romantic,' said Mrs Malone in a dreamy voice.

A few more moments of indescribable sweetness then the music stopped.

Lucy felt bereft. 'Don't!' she cried, dropping the brush and rushing down the aisle. Her eyes glistened because she had truly been moved to tears. She gazed in fascination at Barney's long slender fingers, two heavily stained with nicotine, resting on the black and white keys. 'How do you do it? I wish I could make people see pictures in their heads and feel so different.'

'Don't be disturbing Mr Jones with your questions, girl!' Maureen's voice was half amused, half exasperated as she hurried down the aisle after her. 'It's the last time you'll be helping me here. What a carry on!'

Lucy met her gaze. 'Didn't you feel it? Didn't the music touch you, Mam?'

'Of course, it was lovely,' said Maureen, placing a hand on Lucy's shoulder. 'But how's Mr Jones to concentrate on his playing when you go on like this?'

'It's all right, Mrs Linden,' said Barney, taking

his smouldering cigarette from an ash tray on the piano. 'She's doing me good. Matching up to pictures is exactly what the music is supposed to do. Tell me, Lucy, about some of your pictures?'

Warmed by his interest, she said, 'I was flying, up over the Mersey. I was with the seagulls, following a ship out to sea.' She held out her arms and pirouetted.

Maureen shook her head. 'Don't you be encouraging her, Mr Jones. You're kind to take notice of her but I'm needing her feet firmly on the ground. Flying indeed! She'll be wanting lessons next.'

Barney smiled but asked Lucy was she in an aeroplane?

The girl's eyes twinkled. 'Oh, no! Although I'd love to have a go – just like Perilous Pauline.'

He laughed.

She grinned and did a spin, holding out her arms. 'It was lovely.'

'Enough!' Maureen frowned and seized one of Lucy's plaits. 'You'll have to excuse us, Mr Jones.'

Lucy gritted her teeth, putting up a hand to ease the pressure on her scalp as her mother dragged her away from the piano by the hair, up the aisle and out into the foyer. 'Let go, Mam! What did I do wrong?'

'You were flirting! Not thirteen years old and flirting with a man more than twice your age! That's a dangerous thing to do.'

'I *wasn't* flirting!' Lucy couldn't believe the way her mother was going on.

'You were flattering him, making a fuss of him, amusing him! There's men who like young girls...'

58

'What's wrong with that? I'd rather be liked than hated.'

Maureen let out an anguished squeal. 'You're getting to that age, Lucy, when it could be dangerous! If a man was to start putting his arm around you, kissing you ... or ... or putting his hand up your skirts, you promise me to run.'

Lucy felt a tide of hot colour flood her neck and face. 'But Uncle B–Barney wouldn't do that!'

'I should think he wouldn't,' said Maureen sniffily. 'He is a gentleman.'

'Then what's the fuss about?' Lucy was bewildered.

'You're practising on him. You're getting to that dangerous age as I said.' Lucy opened her mouth, wanting to know more about the dangers attached to her age, but Maureen held up a hand as if to ward her off. 'Enough! You have far too much to say for yourself. Get home and see how Timmy is.'

Lucy flounced out of the cinema, really annoyed with her mother for making such a show of her and treating her like a child in front of Uncle Barney. She'd never be able to look him in the face again after all that talk of kissing and hands up skirts!

She was still feeling a bit like that when her mother took them to the pictures the following week. Timmy sat beside Lucy at the end of a row so he could get to the toilet quickly. Sometimes during matinees children were so reluctant to miss the excitement they wet themselves. Her brother, like the rest of the audience, was soon caught up in the drama on screen, played out for them by Lillian Gish. Lucy admired the actress tremendously. She was small like Lucy herself, with a fragile beauty but spunky with it. Lillian could cope with anything, be it storm, flood, war or family troubles.

Soon Lucy forgot Barney was playing the accompaniment. Despite a girl behind her reading the words on the screen aloud Lucy was not distracted. It was an emotional scene and the music set the mood beautifully. The cruel father of the heroine had just hit her and flung her to the floor. An angry murmur ran through the audience. They were all with her. But the tables were soon turned on the evil monster and our heroine ended up in the hero's arms. A cheer went up as THE END flickered on the screen and the gas lamps were turned high.

'Is it finished, Luce? Do we go home now?' asked Timmy, wriggling in his seat. He asked this every time without fail and every time she said the same thing.

'The projectionist is changing reels for the next film. It's a Harold Lloyd short. You'll remember him. He's funny.'

She was about to get up and take her brother outside to the lavatory when Barney came clumping up the aisle. Her escape route was blocked. He rested his hand on the back of Timmy's seat and flashed his wide smile. 'Hello, Lucy. Mrs Linden!' He inclined his handsome head. It was hot in the cinema and Lucy noticed beads of sweat on his brow. 'Did you enjoy it?'

Maureen spoke before Lucy could get a word in. 'When the day comes I don't get pleasure from the films and your playing, it'll be a sad day indeed.'

Lucy could only agree and ask him to excuse her and Timmy. She was still within earshot, though, when she heard him ask if her mother had had news yet from Mick.

There had been none. Last they'd heard he was in Russia, fighting the Bolshies. But as things sometimes happen, within days a letter arrived, explaining he had been wounded, was in England and now on his way to a hospital on the outskirts of Manchester. Maureen and Lucy would have liked nothing better than to go and visit him there but he'd said they weren't to bother. He'd been shot in a place he'd rather not mention and when he was fit for company he'd be coming home.

The news excited Lucy but she wondered what he would make of the house they were now living in. They'd still been up in Everton when he'd gone off to war. She remembered her uncle being a regular visitor at their house then. He'd played at wild animals with her, growling and pretending to be a lion. She would run away screaming with delicious excitement. When she was seven he'd taught her to play cards: Snap and Rummy. More often than not they'd played for farthings and he'd sub her and let her win as well. She really looked forward to seeing him again. When the next letter arrived saying he was being invalided out of the Army and would be home for Christmas, she couldn't wait.

Mick arrived one stormy evening. Maureen fussed over him, ushering him to the best chair in front of the fireplace. A freezing draught whistled under the front door, lifting the rag rug. Lucy shoved an old coat against the door in an effort to keep the cold out. Uncle Mick was looking about him with a frown. 'You have come down in the world, our kid.'

'I know,' sighed Maureen. 'Times have been tough.'

'That's a miserable-looking fire.' He rested his head on the back of the chair. 'Don't be tight with the coal, Mo.'

'We haven't got much to be tight with. I'm saving the last half hundredweight so we can have a lovely blaze over the Christmas holiday.' Maureen placed a stool nearby for him to put up his feet. 'Lucy, help your Uncle Mick off with his boots while I see to the tea.'

Lucy knelt, smiling up at him. He was a ginger top and had freckles just like her. No longer was he lean and wiry but had put on weight, probably due to his stay in hospital. He returned her smile, gripping the wooden arms of the chair and thrusting out his foot. 'I've money. We'll have a good Christmas. More coal definitely. I'm thinking I'll go down to the pub later.'

Maureen smoothed his hair back from his brow. 'You won't go drinking all your money away?' she said in a teasing voice. 'Jobs aren't that easy to come by and you might have trouble getting work straight away.'

Lucy remembered her mother telling her Mick had gone to sea a couple of times when he was a kid but had given it up, saying it was a rotten, hard life. She remembered him having worked in one of the warehouses down by the docks, too.

'I'll get something,' he said confidently. 'And don't be acting like me mam, doing that to me hair. I'm a man now.'

'Tell us what Russia was like, Uncle Mick?' said Lucy, tugging at his boot. It came off suddenly and she toppled backwards.

'Easy, girl!' he laughed, looking down at his foot. There were holes in his sock. 'You'll darn these for me, Mo?'

'Lucy'll do it for you. Perhaps you'd like her to take the jug and bring you a pint back from the North Star? She could take two jugs and you could buy me one as well?'

He shook his head. 'I'd rather go out. I want more than one pint. I'll go up to the Mere and see if any of my old mates are still alive, find Callum and have a crack. Does he know you're drinking? I'm surprised at you. That man of yours never did for all he went to sea. I don't know why you ever married him.'

Maureen frowned. 'Don't start, Mick. Larry was a good man and Daddy didn't say anything against him. Liked it that he had a bit of money and was sober and upright. As for me drinking ... I don't much, but if you'd been through what I've been through the last few years, *you* might have started drinking, too. Now take that other boot off and come to the table and get this scouse down you.'

'You know nothing about suffering,' her brother said, scowling. 'You should have been at the front. I tell you, girl, it's a miracle I survived.'

Timmy, who had been silent until then, chimed

up now. 'Will you tell us about Russia?'

'Found your voice, have you, lad? Decided not to be frightened of me?' His uncle grinned. 'I'll tell you what Russia's like: snow as thick as you're tall. Icicles as long as me arm. And a waste of bloody time us being there! What do I care about the bloody Russian aristocracy? They've kept the workers down for years, just like the English kept us Irish. The Bolshies are winning and up the revolutionaries, I say.'

'Things are changing here, Uncle Mick,' said Lucy, thinking there had been enough fighting on the streets of Liverpool. 'Women over thirty have the vote. They'll help to get a Labour government in.'

Mick shook his head. 'You don't understand what I'm getting at, girl.' He dug his fork into a potato. 'But now isn't the time to go into it. Christmas!' He gazed across at his sister. 'Remember the goose Mam used to buy? We'll have one this year. She always swore the grease was good for our chests. You said young Timmy suffers like I did. You can buy other goodies, as well.'

Lucy thought, Things are going to change now he's home. She looked at her brother and they both let out a whoop of joy.

It was late Christmas Eve. Lucy stood in the queue in Limekiln Lane, waiting to put the goose in one of Skillicorn's bakery ovens. The bird had cost almost as much as a week's rent but her mother had said it would be worth it because it would feed them for days. Lucy's mouth watered, imagining a slice of breast moist and succulent on her tongue.

'Well, well, look who it isn't!' said a boy, coming alongside her.

She dropped the goose, recognising him by his shock of black hair as the youth who'd threatened her with a knife, in the grounds of St George's and whom she had last seen pasting a poster outside the cinema. She went down on her knees and managed to get her arms under the goose and to struggle to her feet. Now Owen was standing in front of her and the queue had moved up. 'D'you mind?' she gasped. 'That's my place.'

'I'm not taking your place.' He thrust his face into hers. 'Do I look like I've got a chicken up me sleeve? Anyway, how would you stop me if I did? You're a midget.'

'I'd bloody stop you, lad,' said a woman behind Lucy, thrusting an arm the size of a ham between them. 'I'm wanting to get to mass, so beat it!'

He stepped back a few paces. 'Keep your hair on, missus. I was just passing.' He turned to Lucy. 'I believe your mam works at the cinema where I do? My mam's a cleaner, too, and my dad was killed in the war. I never thought you and me would have something in common.'

'So what?' she said, sticking her nose in the air, wishing he would go away.

He shrugged. 'So what about that lad you were with that I had a fight with at St George's? Any competition?'

She wondered what he meant by that. 'His family did a moonlight flit.'

Owen looked pleased. 'I'm the projectionist's assistant now. So next time you're watching a film, think of me working behind the scenes, helping lift them heavy reels. I have to fetch them, too, wheeling the handcart to the filmshop and pushing them all the way home 'cos I'm not allowed on the tram. They can catch fire easy, you know!'

'Fancy! You'll have me crying next.'

'I will if you speak to me like that again and you haven't got your bodyguard with you.' He cocked his head in the woman behind's direction before walking away.

Lucy told Mick and her mother about him when she arrived home. 'What d'you think of him, Mam, threatening me like that? It makes me wonder why Barney Jones helped him get that job.'

Mick glanced up from the newspaper. 'He fancies you, Lucy. Any lad who'd stop and talk to a girl in a queue of women must.'

'Don't be putting ideas into her head, Mick,' said Maureen, putting down the flat iron. 'She'll be thinking soon enough about boys without starting this early. I'll speak to Mr Jones about the lad. I don't know if he's the right sort to be working at our place.'

Mick snorted. 'You make it sound like Lord Derby's estate! Leave the lad alone. If his mother's cleaning then maybe there isn't much money coming into their house and that's why he got the job.'

Maureen's face brightened. 'You're right. He does seem a nice lad. Our Lucy's probably misunderstood him.'

Lucy felt really indignant about that but decided it was no use saying anymore.

Christmas passed pleasantly. There were even presents. Lucy received a pair of gloves from her mother and a skipping rope with bells on from Mick. She kissed him and told him how pleased she was that he was home. 'Aye,' he said, frowning. 'But I don't know if I'll be staying, Lucy.'

That news dismayed her as it did Maureen. 'It's your not having a job, Mick. You must try. What about Collins' on Vauxhall Road. I believe they're going into the electrical goods market.'

'OK!' he said, frowning. 'I'll give it a go.'

But Mick didn't get the job. There were no vacancies. Next Maureen suggested he try the police. 'Those that went on strike never got their jobs back. I know they've taken more on but some don't last. Remember what Dad said?'

'Yeah, I do,' said Mick with a sneer. 'It's a tough job but someone has to do it. Well, it's not going to be me, our kid.' And he stood up and walked out.

'Couldn't Callum help him get a job?' asked Lucy, looking up from her darning.

'Aunt Mac said he's in Ireland. God only knows what he's doing there,' muttered her mother. 'Anyone can see by reading the news-paper there's going to be trouble, the time every-thing's taken to be sorted out over there. I just wish Mick wouldn't be so bloody awkward. He's eating us out of house and home and his money's all gone.'

'Perhaps you could have a word with Uncle

Barney, Mam?' said Lucy. 'He might have friends with influence who'd take Mick on.'

Maureen gnawed on her lower lip and made no comment. Lucy could only hope she would ask the pianist.

A week later Mick received a letter from the British American Tobacco Company. One of the biggest factories in Liverpool, it was situated on Commercial Road down near the docks, backing on to the Leeds-Liverpool canal. He was taken on but had to be vaccinated against smallpox before he started.

'It was horrible,' he said to the children. 'The doctor had this pronged thing and scraped my arm until it bled. Then he put the cowpox vaccine into it. It doesn't half hurt!'

Mick's arm continued to hurt – and didn't Maureen, Lucy and Timmy know about it! He was like a cat that had caught its tail in the mangle. Eventually the wound healed and he started work. He complained occasionally that the room where he worked was dusty and hot, yet he came home smelling sweetly of the spices and perfumes that were put into the tobaccos. He smoked like a chimney and developed a hacking cough, which kept them awake half the night, but the money was good and the rent arrears were paid off.

Lucy celebrated her thirteenth birthday in March and left school. As jobs were scarce and her mother did not want her going into service and she already had the firewood round, Maureen suggested she make do with that. Although perhaps she should try and build it up.

Spring arrived and as Lucy made her way down to Vauxhall Road, she sang the latest song from the music hall. At last she came to Farrell's cooperage. It was a huge place, producing casks and barrels for all kinds of substances: turpentine, whale oil, creosote and pitch, cotton, palm oil, syrup and molasses, not to forget barrels for beer.

Timber was being unloaded from a cart, on the side of which was painted G. GRIFFITHS, TIMBER MERCHANT. A line of children waited outside the sawmill and Lucy frowned. How had she come to forget the schools had broken up for Easter? By the time she reached the front of the queue there would only be the smallest of offcuts, of no use for chopping into firewood. This hadn't happened since her gran had died.

She decided to try somewhere else. Making a choice was not easy. There was another cooperage on Richmond Row up near Paddy's Market in a district known as Sebastapol but she remembered her gran warning her not to go there. The girl shivered, recalling the warehouses and buildings towering above the mean, narrow streets where women with painted faces stood on corners or hung out of windows, shouting down to seamen. Suddenly she had a brilliant idea. What about the Griffiths who delivered wood here? She would try there.

Lucy did not delay but hurried past the seedcrushers and oil refineries, tallow, paper and coal merchants on Vauxhall Road, eventually turning left and heading up Roscommon Street where the Rossie Picture Palace was situated, once two large houses but now knocked into one. She hurried past rows of stables. This was where the teamholders and carters of the district were located and she wished she had the time to stop and stroke the grey horse which stood in a cobbled yard, eating hay from a manger on a wall. Next to the stables was a glassmaker's. Several men sat in a yard, cheeks puffed, blowing glass into shape. Lucy stared, fascinated, as jars and bottles were cooled in heaps of sand. She carried on, heading for St George's Hill. It was not as steep as Havelock Street but even so she was hot and sticky by the time she arrived at Griffiths' timber yard, which was situated a few minutes' walk from St George's church.

The yard appeared deserted but then she heard the clip-clop of hooves and the next moment a young man, jacketless and with his shirt sleeves rolled up, came out of a stable with a woman and a girl who was leading a horse. Lucy scrutinised them as they approached and realised with a sense of shock that the man was Rob Jones, the soldier who'd searched their house. Instantly she felt less sure of herself, knowing she looked far from her best. She placed her hands behind her back and gripped the handle of the cart firmly.

'Can I help you?' said the woman, who had a long bony face.

'I–I'm after offcuts. I'd appreciate them if you have any?' She glanced at Rob, who looked even younger out of uniform. He appeared to be in a mood because the eyes that met hers were stormy. 'It's Lucy Linden, isn't it? On the cadge, kid?'

Lucy flinched, hating the way she must look in her grandmother's old cut-down coat and with her hair damp with perspiration. 'Something wrong with that, Mr Jones?' she said truculently.

'Did I say there was?' He turned to the woman. 'Give her some, Aunt Gwen. She's in as much need as your other lame ducks.'

Lucy was not amused. 'I'm no bloody charity case!' she protested in a trembling voice. 'I work for my living. I chop offcuts into firewood. If you want me to pay for them, I will!'

The three of them stared at her as if shocked and, realising she'd used a swear word, Lucy blushed and fled with her cart bumping along behind her, heading for St George's Hill.

That was a big mistake.

Chapter Four

She lost control of the cart going downhill. It swerved into the road and she tripped over the kerb, losing her grip on the handle. The cart bounced straight in front of a horsedrawn coal wagon. The horse reared between the shafts, front legs flailing. The driver swore fluently, fighting to regain control of the beast. Lucy ignored him, thinking only of the cart and what its loss would mean to her. She shot after it, barely aware of a steam lorry hissing its way up the hill.

The hand against her back which sent her

flying on to the wet cobbles came as something of a shock. Even worse was having the breath almost squashed out of her as someone landed on top of her. The steam lorry hissed past within inches of them.

A moment later the man's weight was taken off her and she was jerked to her feet. He seized a handful of her coat and lifted her off her feet so that she was eyeball to eyeball with him. 'You're choking me!' gasped Lucy.

'I should think I am. You could have been killed!' yelled Rob Jones. 'Don't you ever look where you're going?'

'It–It wasn't my–my fault!' she stammered.

'That's what kids always say! "It was his fault, mister, that I broke the window!"' Rob mimicked a child's voice.

'I–I didn't see the lorry!'

'You're not blind, are you?' His grey eyes appeared almost charcoal and she couldn't detect any sympathy in them.

'I was thinking of me cart! I'm sorry if I upset you.' Oh, why didn't he let her go? The traffic had come to a standstill and everyone was staring at them.

'I accept your apology.' Rob opened his hand and she fell to the ground. She watched him hurry over to where the traffic was building up behind the coal cart. He began to give orders as if he knew what he was about.

She forced herself to look away and glanced round for her cart but it was nowhere to be seen. Her heart sank and she ran over to Rob and seized his arm. 'I've lost my cart! I need it to do my firewood round!'

He shook her off and said exasperatedly, 'What d'you expect me to do right now? Stop middering me, girl, and go home!'

'But what about my customers? I need it! Mam'll kill me!' she cried despairingly.

'I doubt it.' He turned his back and waved on the traffic.

Lucy had an urge to drum on it with her fists but winced as she curled her fingers into her palms. She looked down at her hand and noticed an open wound with bits of grit stuck to it. She felt sick, aware how close she had come to death, and stumbled towards the pavement. Several minutes passed before she felt well enough to walk home.

It seemed to take her ages to complete the journey and she was weary by the time she arrived to find her brother sitting just inside the doorway, his skinny arms clasped about his hunched knees. He looked fed up. 'You've been ages, Luce!'

'Have I? Is Mam in?' Feeling as exhausted as an old woman, she lowered herself down beside him.

'Where's your cart?'

'I've lost it.'

He gasped. 'What are you going to do? Mam'll have a fit.'

Lucy sighed. 'Maybe she won't. She'll understand when I tell her what happened.'

She got up and went in search of her mother, finding her in the kitchen, bending over the fire. The smell of barley soup almost made Lucy forget her troubles.

'So you're back,' said Maureen, glancing over her shoulder. 'You've been long enough.'

Lucy said in a trembling voice, 'Mam, I lost the cart and I was nearly killed.'

Maureen dropped the ladle in the soup and took hold of her arm. 'How? You're not hurt?'

'Not much. I'm sorry, Mam ... about the cart.'

'Well, I'm glad you're not badly hurt. We can find another cart. What happened?'

Words poured out of Lucy. Eventually Maureen held up her hand, palm up. 'Enough!'

But Lucy hadn't finished. 'I'll do me best to find some new pram wheels. I shouldn't have any trouble getting an orange box.'

'Will you stop babbling on about pram wheels and go and wash your face and hands? Get something on that graze and then come and have your supper.'

Lucy did as she was told. It was painful washing her palm but after it was done and she'd covered it with a clean piece of rag she was almost light-headed with relief. That steam lorry could have crushed her bones and flattened her like a pancake if it hadn't been for Rob Jones. She felt calm now, drowsy even as she sat at the table. Her mother placed a steaming bowl in front of her. 'You say the soldier who searched our house seems to be related to the woman in the timber yard? You also think he's related to Mr Barney Jones – is that right?'

Lucy nodded.

'Then I don't see why our Mr Jones can't help us with this. I'll ask him about this timber yard and I'm sure he'll see we get those offcuts the woman was about to give you. So stop worrying about tomorrow's money. I'll go up after supper and speak to him about it.'

That sounded fine to Lucy but there was only one thing wrong. 'I've still got no cart, Mam. How am I going to deliver the firewood?'

Maureen didn't look too concerned. 'I'm sure we'll think of something. Where there's a will, there's a way.'

Lucy supposed she could always carry the firewood on her back. As long as her mother was right and Barney could get her the offcuts.

Maureen left the house almost as soon as they had finished eating, telling her to see to Mick when he got in. Lucy washed the dishes and then sat on the sofa with Timmy curled up beside her and told him fairy stories. His favourite was 'Jack the Giantkiller'.

An hour passed and there was still no sign of Mick or Maureen. Then there was a knock at the door and Lucy went to answer it. A man dumped a sack just inside the doorway. 'Courtesy of Mr Jones,' he said. 'All chipped and ready to bundle up.' Without another word he walked away.

Lucy was amazed that Barney had worked so fast. Fancy having the wood chipped for her as well! She untied the raffia fastened round the neck of the sack just to make sure the man was right and brought out a perfectly chopped chip of wood. Warmed by such kindness, she dragged the sack indoors.

It was late when Maureen arrived home and Mick was still not in. Lucy told her about the wood and her mother smiled. 'Quick work. Lead me to the fire, kids. I'm ready to collapse.'

The three of them snuggled up on the sofa together and for a moment nobody spoke. Then Lucy said, 'What did Barney say when you asked him about the offcuts, Mam? Was he related to the woman?'

Maureen rubbed her chin on the top of Timmy's head. 'Yes. That soldier is some kind of cousin. Mr Barney Jones actually said, "If I can help somebody as I pass through this life, Mrs Linden, then my life has had some meaning." Isn't that a lovely thing to say, Lucy?'

'Lovely!' She brought her face closer to her mother's and realised she'd been drinking. Not a lot but enough, it seemed, to put her in a very good mood. 'Have you been to the pub, Mam?'

Maureen hummed to herself as she gazed into the fire. 'I met Callum on his way here and he took me for a drink.'

That news didn't please Lucy – and where was her uncle? 'Mick isn't home yet,' she said.

Maureen frowned. 'Is he not? I wonder where he is.'

They were soon to find out when he staggered home, drunk as a newt. Maureen managed to get out of him that he'd lost his job but it was not until the following lunchtime when he managed to drag himself out of bed that they discovered why.

Lucy had just returned from St George's Hill, having gone there in the forlorn hope she might find her cart but it was nowhere to be seen. It had taken her twice as long to do her round, carrying the wood on her back. She had to find another cart, but right now her mother was more interested in finding out why Mick had been sacked.

'The foreman didn't like my colour,' he said belligerently.

Maureen groaned and put a hand to her head. 'You eejit! Fancy telling him you were Irish!'

'You don't think he could tell that for himself?' said her brother sarcastically.

Maureen's eyes flashed fire. 'You can talk perfectly good English when you want. Daddy saw to that.'

'Daddy, Daddy! We should have stayed in Ireland where we belonged,' he roared.

She seized his arm but Mick shook her off, his expression sullen. 'I was only there on sufferance anyway. I'm not ashamed of what I said. Ireland has a right to be a republic. There's countries in Europe who've been given their independence since the war. England agrees with that right enough – and yet the time they're taking over giving Ireland hers! I've a good mind to go and join in the fight.'

Lucy stared at him, wondering what fight he was talking about. Then her mother spoke up. 'Don't be stupid! You survived the war but don't be thinking you're indestructible. Keep your opinions to yourself and try and get another job.'

'OK! OK!' he shouted, banging a fist against his knee. 'I'll do it your way.' Getting up, he stormed out of the house.

There was silence for several minutes after Mick had left then Maureen told them to eat

77

their jam and bread. They had just finished when there was a knock at the door. Lucy went to open it but there was nobody there. Then she noticed her cart at the bottom of the steps. Delighted, she dragged it up before looking round for whoever had returned it.

'A bobby brought it,' called a girl by the drinking fountain.

Here was a puzzle, thought Lucy. Could Barney have bothered the police about finding her cart? It would be just like him. She went inside to tell her mother and Timmy that at least something had gone right that day.

Mick did get himself a job but it was illegal. Lucy found that out when Timmy revealed that while he'd been playing football on the lockfields with his uncle, a man had asked to put on a bet. 'He was an Irish,' said her brother. So, thought Lucy with a grin, Mick was a bookie's runner. She told her mother who grimaced. 'Daddy would have had a fit – but so long as he doesn't get caught, and hands over some money to me, that's all I care.'

It appeared that Mick did both because he and Maureen seemed happier in the weeks that followed.

Summer brought a mammoth crane to the docks and Maureen, Lucy and Timmy were not the only ones wanting to look and marvel at the size of the thing. That summer bank holiday Mick had given them some money and they queued up for the New Brighton ferry. The crane, bought by the Mersey Dock Board, had been intended for the Czarist Russian Admiralty but the revolution had overtaken matters. Lucy thought of her uncle and what he'd said about revolution and Ireland and hoped he wouldn't get involved in the fighting that was going on over there.

They boarded the ferry and watched the crew casting off from the upper deck. 'Lucy, there's that Irish!' said Timmy, shooting out an arm and pointing at the landing stage. 'He's there with another man and they're arguing. His name's O'Neill.'

Lucy's gaze followed his pointing finger and she spotted the two men. Faintly she caught the sound of their voices. 'You're crazy, Shaun. I don't want anything to do with your daft scheme. You could get the family involved and I won't have it.'

'You believe me such a fool, Danny? I've more sense than you've ever given me credit for. I've found someone to help us and a new meeting place. No one will ever suspect...' The younger man laid a hand on the older one's arm but he shrugged it off and walked away.

Now what was that all about? wondered Lucy.

Timmy smiled at her. 'See. He's a friend of Uncle Mick's. I've seen him more than once.'

Lucy did not like the sound of that but soon forgot about it when they reached New Brighton. It was a bit of a job finding space on a beach that was crowded despite the overcast sky, but the tide was on its way out, exposing more sand, and soon Lucy and Timmy were digging like fury, intent on building the biggest sandcastle on the beach. It was his suggestion to make a moat and the pair of them went down to the water's edge to fetch water despite Lucy's feeling certain it would be a waste of time unless they lined the bottom of the moat with pebbles. She soon discovered that was a complete waste of time, too, So they went crabbing instead. But come time to go home, Timmy refused to free his crabs. 'I want to take them home,' he insisted.

'You can't. They'll die,' said Lucy, taking the bucket from him and running with it towards the water edge.

He let out a yell and chased after her but she had longer legs and he soon gave up. She set the crabs free and then stood listening to the hush of the waves as they formed lacy patterns on the sand. She gazed across the river to the sprawl of Liverpool; with its slums hidden it looked quite different.

'Cruel sister,' said a voice tinged with amusement.

Lucy spun round and stared at the young man in black corduroys and jacket. His cap was tilted so that it rested on the back of his dark head and she recognised him immediately. She felt the blood rush to her cheeks and for a moment wanted to run away, then had second thoughts. What was she scared of? And besides, she owed him her life. 'I never thanked you,' she muttered.

'For what?' There was a quizzical expression on Rob's boyish features.

'That time on St George's Hill ... you saved my life.'

'Oh, that!' He grinned. 'You got your cart back OK?'

'Yes, thanks. But there was a bit of a mystery

about that.' She hesitated, wondering if he knew anything about it. 'I opened the door and there it was! Apparently a policeman brought it. I thought Uncle Barney might have spoken to them, but he says not.'

'So what's the mystery?' Rob's eyes twinkled. 'It's what policemen do – find things and see they're returned to their proper owners.'

'I suppose so.' Lucy began to walk, swinging the bucket in her hand, feeling a little shy of him. 'I was really glad to have it back. That morning I'd carried the wood round on my back. It nearly broke.'

He stared at her and there was a tiny crease between his eyebrows. 'Amazing! Why didn't your uncle help you?'

She looked up at him. 'You've heard about him?'

'Your mam talks to Barney. Are you glad he's home?'

Lucy thought about that. 'Things are easier in some ways,' she murmured, 'but the house feels overcrowded. Timmy's growing but Uncle Mick doesn't want him in his room. Mam says I'm growing too, but I can't say I've noticed,' she commented candidly, glancing down at herself.

Rob stopped and placed a hand on her head then swept it across to just below his chest. 'I think you have. Give yourself another six months and you might be up to my chest.'

Lucy laughed. 'I doubt it! You're so tall. Taller than Uncle Mick and Barney.' He seemed about to say something but at that moment Lucy realised how close she was to where her mother and Timmy were sitting. Immediately she wanted to get rid of him. She felt awkward, uncertain how Maureen would react to her being in this man's company. 'I have to go. It was nice meeting you again,' she said politely.

'I'd like to say hello to your mam again.'

'Why?' said Lucy bluntly.

'Because of Barney. His sister-in-law's interested in her and so is my aunt.' Rob gave her a bland smile. 'She's interested in you, too. You've met my aunt. She owns the timber yard and said if you want more offcuts, you're welcome.'

Lucy wasn't sure how to take all this information. She hoped the two women didn't see her family as charity cases. She hated that idea.

Maureen looked up at them. 'Who's this?'

'I'm Rob Jones. A distant cousin of Barney's.' He held out his hand.

Maureen smiled and shook it. 'You're the soldier who searched our house. I must admit, I wouldn't have known you. Amazing what a uniform can do for a man,' she said drily.

'I don't know whether to take that as a compliment or not, Mrs Linden. But it's a pleasure to meet you and your daughter in more congenial surroundings,' he said, returning her smile.

Is he being smarmy or what? thought Lucy, wishing he would go away now he was flirting with her mother. A drop of rain fell on the girl's face. She looked up and was surprisingly glad to see slate-hued clouds piling up overhead. 'We'd best get off home, Mam,' she said hastily.

'Want a hand carrying your things?' offered Rob, addressing Maureen, much to Lucy's annoyance.

She thanked him and soon they had joined the mad dash to the pier where queues were already forming. On the ferry Timmy fell asleep and it was Rob who carried him off the boat when they reached the Pierhead, covering the boy with his jacket. The rain sheeted down and they were soaked long before they reached the house. He followed them indoors.

They all stopped abruptly at the sight of the two men sitting at the table. Lucy recognised her uncle's guest as the younger of the two Irishmen whom Timmy had pointed out at the Pierhead.

Mick pushed back his chair and stood up, his eyes on Rob. 'Who's this?'

'Tush, Mick. Don't sound so unfriendly. He's related to Mr Jones,' said Maureen, taking off her hat and shaking it. She turned to Rob. 'Thanks a lot for your help.'

'No trouble.' He put the boy down and, without looking in the men's direction again, left.

'He's forgotten his jacket,' said Maureen.

'Take it to him, Lucy. I don't want him coming back,' said Mick.

She hurried after Rob, leaping off the steps and shouting his name just as he was about to disappear up the passage. She had a feeling he wasn't pleased to be stopped but he walked back towards her and took his jacket. 'Thanks.' He hesitated. 'D'you know who that bloke is with your uncle?'

She was surprised by the question. 'I think his name's Shaun O'Neill.' Rob thanked her and walked away.

The room was quiet when Lucy re-entered the

83

kitchen. Her mother had placed a chair in front of the fire and was hanging her coat over it. She said abruptly, 'I'm thinking it's time your visitor was going, Mick. We'll need to dry our things and get something hot down us before we catch colds.'

Shaun stood up, smiling at her. 'It's all right, missus. I'm on my way.'

'I'll see you out,' said Mick hastily.

As soon as the two men had left the room, Maureen said to Lucy, 'I don't like him. He's got shifty eyes.'

'I think he's up to no good, Mam. Timmy pointed him out to me at the Pierhead. He's a punter. But it's not that which bothers me. I overheard him speaking to another man about some mad scheme and him having found someone to help them and a place to meet. I'm thinking it's Uncle Mick he's found, and this is the house he meant.'

Maureen's eyes flashed. 'It'll be some mad caper to make money, I bet! He's always liked a gamble, our Mick. That's OK if you've got the money to throw away, but we haven't. I'll have a word with him when he comes back.'

She had more than one word. Mick just sat there, elbows on his knees, looking downcast. 'You've caught me out, Mo. You're right, I have been gambling. I owe money and there's a bloke after me. I'm thinking that maybe I'll have to get away. To Ireland maybe. He's not going to follow me there.' Maureen and Lucy stared at him in astonishment. 'I know what you're thinking,' he said swiftly. 'That there's fighting going on there.

But I'll maybe go to Cousin Dermot's farm. It's peaceful there and I'll help him with the animals and stay out of trouble.'

Maureen seemed satisfied. 'I'll miss you, Mick, but I'd rather you were safe from the money-lenders.'

Two days later they went and waved him off and everything settled down to just the way it had been before he'd come back from the war. Lucy briefly considered taking up Rob's aunt's offer of offcuts, but thought that as he probably worked for his aunt at the yard, the less chance she had of seeing him the better. There was something about him that disturbed her, made her feel restless and even more dissatisfied with her lot than she was already.

Lucy was feeling particularly fed up one day when she arrived home to find her mother had a visitor. She had burst into the house ready to air her grievances only to stop short at the sight of Callum seated in the best chair, wreathed in a haze of pipe tobacco smoke.

'Where've you been?' said Maureen, frowning as she looped a curl behind her ear and wiped her sweaty face with a cloth as she stood over the fire, stirring a pan. 'I was ready to send out a search party.'

'A big queue at Farrell's again. I think I might have to go up to Miss Griffiths' yard after all.'

'Who's she?' asked Callum.

'She's sort of related to Barney Jones,' said Lucy.

'And who's he?' said Callum absently.

Lucy looked at her mother. 'Don't be staring at

me, girl,' she said sharply. 'Why should I be interested in Mr Jones's relatives – or him for that matter?'

'But you and he are friendly, Mam,' said Lucy, surprised.

Maureen gave a tinkling laugh as she removed the steaming, blackened pan from the fire. 'Tush, girl! That doesn't mean I'm interested in his family.'

Callum looked mildly annoyed. 'Is he the fella that plays the piano at the cinema at the top here? He's a Protestant, isn't he? I would have thought you'd have had enough of them with the one you married, Maureen? Not that I've anything against the Welsh but I hope it's nothing serious, darlin'?'

'Didn't you just hear me say I wasn't interested in the man?' Maureen's colour was high as she bustled over to the table with the pan and a ladle. 'But he's kind and gives Timmy and Lucy sweets.'

'Doesn't come visiting here then?'

'As if I'd allow it,' she said with a toss of her head. 'Are you going now you've had your say? The children will be wanting their suppers.'

He got up, knocking his pipe out on the fireplace. 'It's a flirt you are, Maureen, just when I thought we were getting on fine.'

'Of course we were getting on fine,' she said hastily. 'But enough said. Your mammy'll be wondering what's keeping you. Thank her for her offer and tell her I'll think about it.'

'Sure and I will.' Callum reached for the tammy on the mantelshelf. 'But I'm hoping you're being straight with me about this piano player?'

Her expression hardened. 'You're pushing your luck if you still want to be made welcome here, Callum McCallum. I'll not be answering to you. Now out of my house! My children need feeding.' She turned her back on him, spooning scouse into bowls.

As soon as the front door slammed behind him, Maureen rounded on Lucy, holding the ladle aloft, a wrathful expression on her face. 'Why did you have to go and mention Mr Jones, yer eejit? Callum won't be forgetting him now. He's that on edge I'm even scared to talk to the neighbours!'

'Why's he on edge? And why's he so worked up about Barney Jones?' said Lucy, her eyes on the dripping ladle, thinking about what Callum had said about Maureen being a flirt. 'You told Callum that he's only–'

'I told, I told!' Her mother whacked the table with the ladle and Lucy nearly jumped out of her skin. 'What I told him wasn't true! I'm very fond of Mr Jones and I don't want anything happening to him while we're away in Ireland.'

'Ireland?' Lucy's heart leaped. 'We're going to Ireland?' Her voice squeaked.

'That we are! I have to see our Mick and I'm to take you two with me. We won't be away long. Only a couple of days.'

'Where's the money coming from?'

'Our Mick sent it.' Maureen's tone was abrupt. She sat down at the table. 'Come on, get your suppers and forget about this for now.'

'What about my round? I can't let my customers down,' protested Lucy.

Her mother put a hand to her head and groaned. 'So many things to think about. I'm sure we can get someone to do it.'

'Who?' said Lucy. 'Who can we trust?'

Her mother dropped her hand and began to eat. 'Perhaps young Owen'll do it. He doesn't have to be in work until half-ten.'

Lucy did not like that idea at all. 'Owen Davies! Remember what I told you about him at Christmas – and Uncle Mick seemed to think he fancied me! I don't want to encourage him.'

'Don't be silly. When did you ever have anything to do with him? Unless – have you been going into the projection room and asking questions about how things work? It's not feminine to take such an interest in machinery.'

'No, Mam.'

'He's a nice lad. Always polite.' Two-faced, thought Lucy. 'I'll ask him,' said her mother. 'He can go up to that Miss Griffiths' yard for offcuts. He doesn't live far from there. In Daniel Street, I believe. His mother's a widow. She cleans the liners when they dock. You'll have to write down the addresses for him.'

'Right,' murmured Lucy, still not happy with the idea but knowing she had no choice but to fall in with her mother's plan if she wanted to go to Ireland. She realised something else. 'We can go and visit Dad's grave!'

'Aye, that's true,' said Maureen, looking sad. 'I've never been able to face it before. Of course his parents never forgave me for not going with them that time.' Her eyes filled with tears. 'I

88

loved him though they didn't believe it. Thought the marriage was a big mistake.' She dabbed at her eyes with the hem of her pinafore.

'Is that why we've never heard from them or seen them since?' said Lucy.

Maureen did not answer and Lucy put down her spoon and leaned across the table. 'If we visit Dad's grave we could write and tell them we've been. Then they'll forgive you and maybe invite us to live with them so we can be a proper family.'

Her mother looked at her as if she'd gone mad. 'The last thing I want is to live with *them! We'll get by without their help, thank you very much! Now eat your dinner. There's a lot to be done before we go to Ireland.'

Chapter Five

Lucy gazed at ships great and small as they left the open sea behind and steamed past Roches Point which marked the harbour entrance to the port of Cobh. It was a short distance from the city of Cork, on the south-west coast of Ireland. A natural deepwater harbour, it was the first and last European port of call for the transatlantic liners. Only eight years ago the *Titanic* had departed from Cobh to continue its ill-fated maiden voyage.

Seagulls wheeled overhead. There had been a downpour a short while ago but now the sun was peeping out from behind the clouds. Lucy gazed

89

across the waves towards a granite spire which pierced the sky above slate-roofed houses. A carillon of bells sounded sweetly across the water and it was as if she'd been touched by magic. She thought of the tales her gran had told her and wondered if the 'little people' really did exist.

'That's the noon bells,' said Maureen, her arm round Timmy who was sitting on the ship's rail. 'We'll be landing soon. I was your age, Lucy, when we left here and Daddy filled my head with dreams of how wonderful everything would be when we reached Liverpool, but nothing turned out how I expected.'

'What's Cork like, Mam? It's a funny name for a city.'

'It comes from the Irish, *Corcaigh*. Which means "marshy place". The marshes have long gone but there's still the River Lee. It twists and turns, almost encircling the city centre, and there's that many bridges you feel like you're forever crossing the water. There are some lovely shops on St Patrick's Street.'

'But we're not staying in Cork?'

'No.' Maureen looked disgruntled. 'I've never been one for the countryside. Still, it won't be long now before we see Mick. He'll be waiting for us on the quay and I'll be glad to make sure he's all right.'

Lucy wondered why he shouldn't be but didn't ask. She was trying not to worry about anything. Especially Owen Davies doing her round.

But Mick was not on the quayside and they found themselves in the uncomfortable position of feeling they'd been forgotten as the minutes ticked by and there was still no sign of him. Maureen began to show signs of impatience. 'I knew it! I just knew he'd be late,' she said, tapping her foot on the pavement. Lucy wondered how she'd known that when she'd said she was convinced he'd be on the quay waiting for her.

Suddenly there was the sound of horses' hooves and they gazed hopefully at the pony and trap that was heading in their direction. It stopped alongside them and a man, broad-shouldered and dressed in a shabby tweed suit, a broken nose in his weather-beaten face, called to them, 'Is it Maureen and her children now?'

'Cousin Dermot?' A smile flooded Maureen's face.

'Aye! That's me.' He twinkled down at her. 'You're looking bonny, woman. And what nice-looking children.'

'Don't you be trying to softsoap me,' she said, laughing. 'Where's that brother of mine? Digging potatoes or milking cows?'

'Neither, woman. He's off on some business in Cork. Yer'll be climbing aboard now? I'm wanting to get away from here.' He glanced in the direction of some men across the way, dressed in khaki and black. 'Up with you all! I'm not wanting the Tans to get too good a look at me.'

Lucy did not ask why not but climbed into the trap with Timmy while her mother sat on the seat beside Dermot. He clicked his tongue, flicked the reins and they were off through the rainwashed streets. Nobody spoke. Lucy could tell from the way her mother held herself that something was bothering her, but it wasn't until the port and the coast were left behind and fields of golden wheat, flowering potatoes and grazing cattle surrounded them on either side, that Maureen broke the silence.

'I didn't expect to see the Tans so soon.'

'And aren't they all over the place, the arrogant buggers?' Dermot retorted. At her reproving look he added meekly. 'If yer'll excuse me language?'

She cleared her throat. 'The violence is as bad as the newspapers say then?'

'You're not to be worrying yerself. You'll be in and out of here before yer know it.'

'I will that, but even so I worry. I don't want our Mick getting himself involved.'

Lucy pricked up her ears but kept her gaze fixed firmly on the distant rounded hills, chin resting on her arms against the side of the cart.

'You have Callum's letter?' asked Dermot.

Maureen reached into a pocket and took out an envelope. She waved it under his nose before returning it to her pocket. 'I don't know what he's got to say to our Mick that's so secret it couldn't be sent through the post.'

'Letters can go astray, woman, and Mick thought you'd be glad to come over with it and see how he's getting on.'

'I am,' she agreed. 'That younger brother of mine has caused me more worry than both my children!'

'You mustn't worry. Mick says he can take care of himself.' There was a trace of irony in Dermot's voice which made Lucy think he doubted the truth of this.

They turned off the road into a stone-infested,

pot-holed, dirt track which terminated at a farmyard with a dung heap to one side and hens peck-pecking in scrubby grass and dirt. Smoke trickled from the chimney protruding from a thatched roof. The house was whitewashed and long and single-storeyed.

The front door opened and several more hens and a pig came squeaking and squawking from its dark interior. Timmy laughed and pointed. 'Animals! I like animals.'

A woman with a tanned, wrinkled face stood in the doorway, carrying a galvanised pail and gazing up at them. She rattled off a string of words Lucy couldn't make sense of but Dermot responded in the same language as his mother ambled over to him.

'Down, children!' ordered Maureen. 'And don't forget the bag, Lucy!'

Flies zoomed in on them as they made their way to the house and hurried inside. Lucy stood staring about her. Somehow she'd expected something grander from the way her mother had spoken about her home in Ireland, but still this place was homely enough with well-worn furniture and a huge open fireplace, resembling a cave. There were shelves holding crockery and food jars of this, that and the other, and a sack of flour on the floor. Under a window was a sink with a pump and on the sills of both windows were statues: one of St Francis of Assisi and another of the Madonna and the Holy Child. A scrubbed table twice the size of theirs at home stood in the middle and a couple of doors opened off the room.

The old woman entered and said something in English but with such a strong Irish brogue that Lucy couldn't understand her. She beckoned to the children with a smile and began to slice bread. They'd had little to eat since leaving Liverpool and wolfed down the bread and butter, washing it down with buttermilk.

'That'll put some flesh on your bones, my girl,' said their mother, getting up and speaking to the old woman in the Irish.

She scurried over to the fireplace, taking down a heavy frying pan. A flitch of bacon was lifted from a hook on the ceiling and several slices cut from it. Salt crystals clung to its smoky brown skin and soon the delicious smell of frying filled the room. Lucy's mouth watered. Perhaps it wasn't going to be so bad staying here after all.

But when the bacon and eggs came they were swimming in fat and she wasn't so sure then. Still all that fat might give her some curves so she ate the lot, mopping up the grease with bread.

Afterwards Maureen settled herself on the sofa with a newspaper and suggested the children go and explore. But they had scarcely reached the outskirts of a wood just beyond the farm buildings where a couple of pigs snuffled in the grass when there was the sound of a motor engine. 'Perhaps that's Uncle Mick,' said Timmy.

They raced back as quickly as they could and were just in time to see an open tourer roaring away along the dirt track. They watched until it was out of sight then, hearing voices coming from the house, went inside.

The room appeared to be full of men. Mick was

lying on the sofa, groaning. His shirt was unbuttoned and his trousers undone. There was blood. Lots of it. Dermot's mother was frantically rooting in one of the table drawers, while Maureen was over by the sink, working the pump.

The children ran over to her. 'What's happened?' whispered Lucy. 'Has Uncle Mick been in a fight?'

'Aye, the eejit! I'm hoping it's not as bad as it looks.' Maureen sounded angry. Her face was pale and tense, her eyes dark with worry. 'I'm starting to believe we've a jinx on us. Now, out of my way.' She lifted the enamel bowl out of the sink and carried it over to the sofa.

Lucy and Timmy followed her over to the sofa but were told to stay back. Lucy felt rebellious, wanting to help, thinking that if she'd been a few inches taller they wouldn't treat her like a child. She noticed one of the men had a bloodstained rag fastened about his head and another held his arm as if it hurt.

The water in the bowl soon turned red. 'Ugh! It makes me feel sick,' said Timmy, and ran outside. Lucy supposed she should keep an eye on him and went to stand in the doorway. For a moment she watched him stalk a hen, smiling when he swooped upon it. It squawked and fluttered away and he fell on to his knees. A man spoke in the room behind her, asking Dermot whether he had any whiskey.

'I was saving it for when the doctor comes. He'll be needing to dig the bullet out.'

'Mick nearly did for us all,' rasped another

voice. 'It was pointless starting shooting once Mayor McSwinney was arrested.'

'Mick can't be trusted to show sense. That's what being in the British Army's done for him. He doesn't know how to be invisible in a crowd.'

'Shut up!' said Maureen fiercely. 'Have a heart. If you don't have anything useful to say, get out!'

'We had to leave our bikes behind when we stole the car,' grumbled the first voice.

'More fools you then,' she muttered. 'I don't know what you're all thinking of, leading my brother into trouble. He came here to get away from it and to have some peace and quiet.'

There was a moment of deathly silence. Then one of the men said, 'Now who's the fool? I'll be going. Mother will be wondering where I am.'

Lucy moved away from the doorway to lean against the outside wall of the house. The rough whitewash was scratchy beneath her back but she did not heed it, watching the men disappear round the back of the outbuilding, wondering who Mayor McSwinney was and why he'd been arrested and whether Uncle Mick's being shot was his own fault. What if he died? She told her brother not to wander off and went inside the house.

Maureen appeared to have staunched the bleeding but her uncle's face was twitching, eyes tightly shut and teeth clenched. 'Couldn't you give him some whiskey?' she said. Dermot shook his head. 'He'll be needing it later when the doctor comes. Tea! We'll have some tea.'

It was a couple of hours before the automobile reappeared with the doctor and all that time

Mick had been moaning and groaning. 'Where's that bloody whiskey, Dermot?' he rasped now.

A bottle was produced and the wounded man gulped down a tumbler before gasping and falling back against the cushion.

Dermot noticed Lucy watching and gave a faint smile. 'Outside, girl. This isn't going to be a pretty sight for a child.'

'I'm not a child,' she said impatiently. 'Mam, can I help?'

'You can help by saying a few prayers,' said Maureen tersely. 'My God, you can never trust a man to keep his word or stay out of trouble.'

'I'm not very good at praying,' muttered Lucy. She'd have much preferred to play at nurses and staunch the blood.

'Shame on you,' said Dermot sternly. 'Go and try hard.'

Lucy went outside and asked God to take away Mick's pain. After that she said a few Hail Marys. There was a gasp, a groan, a scream and after that silence. Was he dead? she wondered and went back inside.

Her uncle's eyes were shut but she noticed his chest was rising and falling. The doctor was washing his hands. Maureen was sitting at Mick's feet, a glass in her hand, her face paler than ever. Dermot was drinking out of the whiskey bottle. 'Will we be staying here longer, Mam? He'll need nursing, won't he?' said Lucy.

'Ha! Your mam doesn't have to do that. The old woman will see to him,' said Dermot. 'She's best off home – and you two as well. When Mick can stand on his feet, we'll see you get him back.'

Lucy thought it didn't sound like she and her mother and Timmy would get to visit her father's grave this visit. She was disappointed but glad at least that Dermot seemed to think her uncle wasn't going to die.

She and Timmy spent the night with her mother and the old woman in a double bed. It was a bit of a squash and Lucy didn't sleep a wink. The next morning Maureen told Lucy she and Timmy were to go to mass with the old woman and say a few more prayers for Mick. She would stay and help him write a letter to Callum.

They walked miles to the nearest village of Innashannon and Lucy ended up with painful blisters. 'I suppose there's no chance of us visiting Dad's grave today?' she asked when they arrived back at the farmhouse.

'There's no time for that.' Maureen's face was strained and Lucy knew this was not the time to argue with her.

It had all been a bit of a disappointment really, she thought. No shops to look at and definitely no leprechauns. The same for the banshees, though, which was a relief.

Going home took longer than getting there because there was no liner leaving for Liverpool that day so they were taken to Cork and put on a train for Dublin, there to catch the regular ferry which sailed from Dun Laoghaire to Liverpool. By the time they disembarked at Liverpool on Monday morning they were fit to drop.

But Maureen had work to go to – Aunt Mac had filled in for her on Saturday. She only had time to pick up her brushes, polish and cloths.

She was about to go when Lucy noticed there was no sign of her cart and asked her mother to tell Owen to bring it back. 'Of course he'll bring it back!' She almost snapped Lucy's head off. 'You just take Timmy to school. Explain why he's late. Then light the fire and see to the washing.' She hurried out.

Lucy knew her mother was tired and worried about Mick. She was herself but there was nothing they could do for him right now. That would have to wait until he was fit enough to come home. And when he did, she thought, that would be when Maureen would give him a piece of her mind. She just hoped her mother wouldn't forget, in worrying about Mick, to ask Owen Davies for her cart.

'Your cart?' Maureen's voice was vague.

'My cart, Mam,' said Lucy impatiently. 'I can't collect offcuts and deliver without it. Remember what I had to do last time I lost it?'

Her mother blinked at her and forced a smile. 'Owen said you weren't to worry. He'd do your round.'

'And you agreed to that?' Lucy was dismayed. 'What are you thinking of, Mam?'

'He said it was hard work for a little girl like you, and it's true.'

Lucy couldn't believe what she was hearing. 'I've managed fine since Gran died,' she said fiercely. 'We need the money! I knew I couldn't trust him. Who does he think he is? I'll speak to Uncle Barney about him.'

'You can't be bothering Mr Jones. He's having

a little holiday. Has gone to Wales.'

Damn! thought Lucy.

'You know what I've been thinking, Luce. I could do with finding myself a husband,' said Maureen in a vague voice.

Lucy wasn't interested. 'Did he say where my cart was, Mam?'

'Griffiths' yard.'

Right! Lucy didn't waste any time but shot out of the house and sprinted in the direction of Great Homer Street.

As she entered the timber yard she could hear the whine of a mechanical saw coming from one of the buildings. Now where could Owen have put that cart? She gazed about her at the piled up planks of timber and walked round for a while. A man glanced her way and asked what she was looking for.

'A cart.'

'We don't make carts here, luv. But if you ask at the office Miss Jones might be able to help you out with the name of a business. She's in the office.'

'Not that kind of cart,' said Lucy impatiently. 'It's–' She broke off, deciding maybe this Miss Jones was the right person to speak to.

She knocked at the door that said ENQUIRIES and was told to enter. To her surprise and irritation Rob's aunt wasn't there. The only person in the room was a girl sitting at a typewriter, hitting the keys one finger at a time. 'Hello!' said Lucy loudly.

'Damn!' The girl tore the paper out of the typewriter and scowled at her. 'What d'you want?'

'I was looking for a Miss Jones.'

'I am Miss Jones.' She got up and came round the desk and looked Lucy up and down before leaning against the desk and folding her arms. 'Haven't I seen you before? We don't get many girls coming in here.'

It was then that Lucy recognised her and wished she could be so confident, but perhaps she could if she dressed as smartly. Miss Jones was wearing a black pinstripe skirt, the palest of pink blouses. Her hair was done up on top of her head and kept in place by two large decorative combs. 'Yes!' Lucy spat out, deeply envious of the other's appearance to the core of her being. 'I've come for my cart.'

Unexpectedly the girl chuckled. 'The orange box on wheels? You're welcome to it, lovey. But I thought Owen had taken charge of it now?'

'That's what *he* thinks,' said Lucy, tossing back her hair. 'My gran built up that round and I'm not going to give it over to him.'

'Good for you! There mightn't be much of you but Napoleon was only a small bloke and look what he did.'

Lucy wasn't interested in Napoleon. She wanted to get her cart and be out of this place before Owen arrived. She reckoned he must dash up here in his break between the afternoon and evening performances. 'If you'll tell me where it is...'

'I'll show you.' Miss Jones led the way out of the office and round the side towards the stables.

'Is Miss Griffiths your aunt?' asked Lucy as a thought struck her.

101

'That's right. I'm Dilys. You've met my brother Rob.' She glanced at Lucy and grinned. 'His bark's as bad as his bite, you know, but he doesn't bite people often.'

Lucy felt the colour rise in her cheeks. 'He told you I bit him?'

Dilys nodded, still smiling as she opened a door and they went inside. There was a strong smell of horses and hay but the stable was empty. The cart stood just round the corner inside and Dilys pulled it out. 'Here you are. I'll get your sack filled up for you.'

Lucy thanked and followed her. She was soon on her way, taking her time as she went down Havelock Street. It was after she'd crossed Netherfield Road that she ran into Owen. He took in the situation immediately and before she could prevent him he'd gripped the cart handle and wrenched it from her. 'I said I'd do it!'

'I don't want you doing it! Give me it back, Owen Davies, or you'll regret it!' Lucy put both hands on the handle and tugged.

He laughed. 'Nice try, little girl, but you're no match for me.'

That 'little girl' infuriated her and made her all the more determined not to let him get away with it. She gritted her teeth as he prised the fingers of her left hand from the handle and pushed her away. 'Choppin' wood's a man's job, not a girl's!' he taunted. 'Now be a good kid and get lost.'

But she wasn't going to give up. 'You're not a man – you're a shirt button!' She shoved him with her bottom and got another grip on the handle. 'If you don't give it to me it'll be the worse for you. I'll go for the police.'

'You do that. Who d'you think they'd believe – me or a little slummy?' mocked Owen, forcing back the fingers of her left hand. Lucy gasped but resisted all his efforts to shift her right hand. Then, bringing down her head, she bit him. He yelped and let her go and just the same as she'd done once before she ran, thinking how mistaken Uncle Mick had been in believing this youth fancied her.

Owen gave chase and would have caught her if Lucy had not noticed they were being watched. She screamed. 'Help! Help! This boy's after me and won't leave me alone!'

'What's he done to yer, girl?' called one of the onlookers.

From the depths of her memory Lucy trawled up an answer that would get them firmly on her side. 'He put his hand up my skirt!'

'Oh!' gasped a woman. 'The dirty little swine!' She advanced on Owen and hit him with her shopping bag. The force of the blow knocked him sideways. Lucy could not help it – she laughed. 'And that!' said her saviour, and hit him again as he rose to his feet. He staggered back and Lucy saw the murderous expression on his face. The laughter died on her lips and she scarpered.

'What's up with you?' asked her mother when Lucy collapsed on the sofa.

'You don't want to know, Mam, but I'm back in business. I got my cart and offcuts so I can get chopping.' Maureen gazed down at her and Lucy noticed the strain in her face. 'You OK?'

Maureen picked up the axe and ran a finger

over its sharp edge. 'I'm sick of men telling me what to do!'

Lucy dismissed Owen from her thoughts and sat up. With part of her mind she noticed water dripping from the washing on the drying rack on to her mother's hair. 'What's happened?'

With a smouldering expression on her face, Maureen took a piece of wood from the sack and stood it on its end on the floor. She brought the axe down, splitting the wood straight down the middle. 'That Callum! He had the nerve to tell Mr Jones I was spoken for while I was away.'

Lucy barely caught the words because she was staring at her mother in admiration. 'Golly! That was a clean cut!'

'It's more than "Golly", girl. I'm really annoyed!' She brought down the axe again and chopped one of the halves clean in two. 'I don't know what I'm going to say to Mr Jones when he comes home from holiday. He'll take some convincing it was only Callum's wishful thinking. I don't want to marry a carter! I want to go up in the world.'

Lucy did not know what to say to that. Her mother was an attractive woman but the girl found it hard to accept that someone rich like Barney would want to marry her. He seemed to admire Maureen greatly but surely that wasn't enough of a reason for him to take her from the slums. She was Catholic, too, and surely he'd consider the difference in religion seriously? 'What are you going to do?' she murmured.

Maureen brought the axe down again. 'Never you mind! You get cutting bread. I've some brawn in and it'll be tasty melted on toast.'

Realising she wasn't going to get any more out of her mother, Lucy did as she was told before going and calling Timmy in for his tea. It was just at that moment that Owen limped into the court. His shirt was hanging out and he looked the worse for wear. She dragged Timmy inside and slammed the door shut swiftly. But Owen must have seen her because he lifted the letter box and shouted through it: 'When I've finished with you, Lucy Linden, no bloke'll want to marry you.'

'I don't want to get married!' she shouted back. With the door between them she gained Dutch courage. 'I'll earn my own money. Most lads are good for nothing anyway!'

'What's all this shouting?'

Lucy spun round. For a moment she debated whether to tell her mother of Owen's threats, but she'd want to know the reason why he'd made them and Lucy was embarrassed to say that she'd accused him of having had his hand up her skirt. 'Nothing,' she said, attempting to look innocent. 'Is the toast OK?'

'It's fine. Hurry up and get bundling the wood. I thought we'd go to the pictures to cheer ourselves up.'

While admiring the daring-do of John Gilbert, and giggling over the antics of Buster Keaton, who could sit in an automobile and have all the wheels fall off without moving a muscle of his face, Lucy was able to forget Owen's threats. Later, though, as she lay in bed, she felt uneasy, guessing the reckoning would come. If only her father were alive or Mick were here Owen would not have dared threaten her, and neither would their little family have needed her firewood money so desperately.

The following morning Lucy set off on her round. She came to the first house and, lifting the knocker, rat-a-tat-tatted on the door. It was opened by a man in his shirt sleeves and she could hear a baby crying. He looked surprised to see her. 'Hello, luv. I thought you were in Ireland?'

'I got back yesterday.' Lucy smiled and held out a bundle of firewood.

He shook his head regretfully. 'Sorry, luv. We've already bought some from the lad. He said you were still away.'

Lucy's smile faded. She felt sick. 'He lied to you! He—He's after my round!'

The man looked sympathetic. 'Sorry, luv. It's a dirty trick but he got here first. I'll chase him tomorrow if he gets here before you.'

Dismayed and angry, Lucy walked away to try her next customer and met with the same tale. It was a similar story with the next three. She didn't bother after that, realising Owen had a head start on her even at this early hour. She felt cold inside and at a loss what to do. She might tell her mother about it, but would Maureen do anything in the strange mood she was in? Lucy realised it was up to her. As far as she knew Owen didn't have a cart. It would take him longer to get round. She decided to skip the street she was on and run to the last lot of houses on her round and hopefully beat him to it.

Lucy did that and managed to sell to all her customers in that street and warn them about Owen before coming face to face with him on Great Homer Street. The thoroughfare was already busy with women queuing up outside their favourite bakeries. Tobacconists and news-agents were competing for the business of people going to work. So she felt it was reasonably safe to give vent to her anger. 'You sneak, Owen!' she said, shoving the cart against his legs.

'Ouch! I'll get you for that!' He lunged at her but Lucy darted back.

'You just try it and I'll scream blue murder again! You've robbed me!'

'No, I haven't.' The light of battle was in his eyes. 'I've worked for what I've got.' Again he tried to get to her but she dodged aside, pulling her cart instead of pushing it, and managed to keep it between them. But Owen was not about to give up and dumped his sack in the cart. 'It's the early bird that catches the worm and my mam needs the money just as much as yours.'

'I wouldn't argue with that but you've already got a job.' Lucy's voice trembled. 'Yer've no right to take what's mine! My gran built that round up.'

'So what? She's dead! And how are you going to stop me?' He managed to seize the cart's handle and wrench it out of her hands. He ran.

Oh, no, not again! thought Lucy despairingly, and raced after him as he weaved his way along the pavement between people. Owen kept looking back to see where she was so did not see the policeman and ran headlong into him. The bobby seized him by the ear. 'What's the rush, boyo? You're a danger to the public, racing along the pavement like that!'

'Lemme go! I'm sorry, Constable, but I've got to get home to me mam? She's sick!' Owen wriggled to free himself.

'He's a liar!' gasped Lucy, coming up to them. 'He stole my cart!'

The policeman looked down at her and Lucy stared and blinked, recognising the face beneath the helmet. She could scarcely believe it was Rob Jones. He shook his head and let out a deep sigh. 'Well, if it isn't Lucy Linden of Court 15. Perilous Pauline has nothing on you, kid. I thought you'd given Owen the cart? Now you're saying he stole it. Shall I lock him up?'

Put Owen in prison? She stared at this boy who was getting to be the bane of her life, and wished he could be locked away and the key thrown in the Mersey, but he was frantically signalling a message with his eyes and she thought of his mother and the fright she'd get if a bobby came knocking at her door. 'I just want me cart back. I think he only meant to borrow it,' said Lucy.

'I did, I did,' put in Owen, eager to agree to anything she said, it seemed. 'We're friends, aren't we, Luce? I was just messing about.'

'Friends, hey?' said Rob. 'Now there's a surprise.' He released Owen with an abruptness that took the youth by surprise so that he fell over the cart. 'Don't let me catch you careering along this pavement again or I'll have you before the magistrate. Now beat it!'

Owen shot off. Lucy was about to follow him

when she was stopped by a hand on her arm. 'You've forgotten something.' She looked up at Rob, anxious to get away. 'Your cart.'

It struck her then it might have been he who had returned it when she'd lost it on the hill. She smiled. 'Thanks.'

Sedately she walked away. It was only when she arrived home that she realised Owen had left his sack in her cart. The corners of her mouth lifted. He'd reaped the rewards of more than half her round. Well, she'd take his bundles of wood as just payment and tomorrow she would make sure she got a head start on *him*, just in case he tried something else on her.

Chapter Six

Lucy decided to make up the deficit in her firewood money out of the threepences she'd been saving in a drawstring bag she'd made from a scrap of cloth and which hung inside her skirt from a button.

The following morning her first customer told her he'd been offered firewood a farthing cheaper than she charged by the lad who'd delivered the other day so he'd bought at that price. Lucy was hurt as well as angry. 'I thought you'd tell him where to go!' she cried, stepping backwards off the step.

'Sorry, luv!' The man sounded like he meant it. 'But a farthing a day is nearly twopence a week and I've six mouths to feed.'

'I can add up,' she muttered, and turned on her heel and went next door, hoping that at least they had stuck by her, only to be told the same thing. Stubbornly she continued on her round, hoping to find at least one person who'd remained loyal to her and was relieved to find several. She was so grateful she felt compelled to lower her price to match Owen's. She realised by the time she arrived home that she was going to have to tell her mother what had happened.

Lucy poured out the whole story but Maureen didn't seem to realise the seriousness of what her daughter was saying. 'Well, that's clever of him,' she murmured, putting on her coat and picking up her cleaning implements.

Lucy was furious. 'Clever? It's downright sneaky!' She seized her mother's arm. 'I've only got a shilling to give you.' This time she had Maureen's full attention. 'So what do I do? Lower my prices to less than his to win them back?'

'But that would leave us with hardly anything,' said Maureen, frowning. 'If only our Mick hadn't been such a eejit as to get involved in Ireland. Now Callum wants me to go back there with an answer to Mick's letter. I've told him I'm not a carrier pigeon. That man – he's a dreamer! Got no sense. The things he says to me, you wouldn't believe.' She sat down, gazing into space. 'I've told him I'll go one more time to see how our Mick is but that's it.'

Lucy was exasperated. At the moment she didn't care about Mick. 'Stick to the point, Mam.

My round! What am I going to do about Owen?'

Her mother pulled a face. 'I don't know what we can do. He's surprised me. I wouldn't have thought he'd be so unkind to you. But give credit where it's due, he's managed to get one step ahead of you, girl. I don't know how we can stop him.' She picked up her bucket and broom. 'I'm going to have to go. You'll have to think of some other way of selling your firewood.' And she hurried out of the house.

Lucy flopped on to a chair, feeling let down. Her gran had worked hard building up that round. She felt sad, thinking of the old woman. Gosh, she'd been gutsy! What would she have done in Lucy's position? The girl sat thinking for a long time and suddenly she came up with an idea.

'Timmy, I need your help.' She took a bundle of firewood out of the cart.

Her brother looked up from chalking on the slate Aunt Mac had given him. The tip of his tongue protruded from the corner of his mouth. 'What is it?'

'Help me take a chip out of every bundle,' said Lucy, her fingers working busily. 'I'll get extra bundles that way and make up the money I've lost. We'll go up to Netherfield Road where they have more money and nobody knows us. You can pull down your mouth and look pathetic. All the woman'll feel sorry for us, and with a bit of luck they might even pay the full whack for a bundle. I'll try that first. If in ten minutes they don't go, I'll knock a farthing off.'

But Lucy didn't have to lower her prices. She

111

sold the firewood without any trouble and for less effort. Thrilled by her success, she decided to carry out another idea she had and bought apples and sugar with the money she'd made from selling the extra bundles. She'd make toffee apples just like her gran used to.

'Well, well, well!' said Maureen, smiling, as Lucy told her what she had done. 'I'd never have believed my girl had so much sense.' She dipped a finger into the lentil soup Lucy had made. 'Your idea knocks spots off Owen's.'

Lucy flushed with pleasure. Her mother wasn't often forthcoming with praise. 'I wish I'd thought of it before. But the toffee apples, Mam? Is it OK for me to make them?'

Maureen nodded. 'Mammy'd be pleased if you did. I can see her now, a smile on her face, gazing down from Heaven on us. You'll need grease-proof paper to wrap them in, don't forget – and sticks!'

Lucy thanked her for the reminder and knew she would have to use some of her savings, but hopefully this way she'd have more money to put away.

'I'll add up how much we spend and then work out what I need to sell them at to make a profit,' she said aloud.

Her mother laughed. 'You do have a brain. But I hope this doesn't affect what you bring in from the firewood?'

'It won't, Mam!' Lucy hugged her, grateful for the words of encouragement.

Later that day it wasn't the only reason she had to be grateful to her mother. Her gran had made boiling sugar and water into toffee appear easy but it wasn't. To get the toffee to set it had to reach the right temperature and Lucy had no way of knowing what that was. It was Maureen who reminded her to drop a teaspoon of the precious mixture into a cup of cold water and if it hardened, it meant the toffee was ready. She made several attempts before getting it right.

Soon there was a row of greaseproof paper-wrapped toffee apples on the mantelshelf. All Lucy had to do now was sell them – and where better than to the cinemagoers who queued up outside the picture palace every night? She voiced her idea aloud to her mother.

'Why not?' said Maureen, looking round from the table. 'You just make sure you get there early, girl.'

Lucy knew she had to get the price right otherwise she wouldn't sell her toffee apples. So she made sure her profit margin was only small, to encourage people to buy.

She sold a plateful of toffee apples at the first performance and with her mother's encouragement returned for the second house. She had sold half her wares when a little woman turned up with a basket of oranges. Her eyes almost popped out of her head when she saw Lucy and she ran at her, swinging her basket. Lucy easily dodged her but was intimidated when the woman came at her again. Even so, she wasn't going to give up. It was a free country and she had as much right as the old woman to be there. But she felt an idiot as the orange woman came at her again and the people in the queue laughed.

The woman was not amused and shrieked at Lucy. 'What d'yer think yous are at, girl? Yous are pinching my customers.'

'It's the early bird that catches the worm,' said Lucy, remembering what Owen had said to her.

'I'll have you and your worms,' yelled the woman. 'Yous are only a kid! Yous should be at home, getting yer beauty sleep. Now scram or I'll get a scuffer. There should be a law against kids your age working.'

'I'm not a kid, I'm thirteen!' cried Lucy crossly. But having no wish to tangle with the law – especially if he came in the shape of Rob Jones, and as she had sold most of her toffee apples, she went home.

Her mother was dozing in a chair and laughed when Lucy told her about the little old woman. 'That'll be old Mary! She's always at the second performances at the top. I'd forgotten about her. Perhaps you should just sell to the early queue, and you can always go to other cinemas.'

So Lucy did that, buoyed up by her mother's encouragement and her own sense of achievement. Her days fell into an agreeable pattern. Occasionally she was surprised by how easily she'd surrendered her round to Owen. She did not know whether Maureen had mentioned what she was doing to him, would prefer it if she didn't in fact, but she wasn't going to lose any sleep over him. As long as she could make money, Lucy felt certain her gran would have understood about giving up the round.

When Maureen eventually went back to Ireland, Lucy and Timmy did not go with her.

Instead they stayed with Callum's mother. Lucy had known Aunt Mac since childhood and was fond of her. She had never had a daughter so welcomed the girl with open arms, taking an interest in everything she did, as well as talking about the old days when Lucy's grandmother was alive and they were neighbours.

Aunt Mac did not think it was right, though, that Lucy should have the job of chopping wood. 'If your Uncle Mick had his head screwed on right, he wouldn't have got himself involved with the troubles in Ireland,' she observed.

Lucy dropped the axe and sat on the back step, wiping her sweating brow with the back of her hand, guessing the old woman mustn't know about her own son's involvement. 'I agree, Aunt Mac, but you can't tell fellas, can you?' The girl closed her eyes against a suddenly blazing sun before it slid behind a cloud once more. For a moment she enjoyed the silence then she began to sing, '"Is the struggle and strife we find in this life, really worthwhile?"'

'You can say that again,' muttered Aunt Mac.

Lucy smiled and sang the next bit. '"I've been wishing today I could just run away, out where the west winds call. With someone like you, a pal good and true, I'd like to leave it all behind..."' Her voice soared. '"And go and find, a place that's known to God alone. Just a spot to call our own."'

'Now that would be nice,' agreed the old woman. '"We could find perfect peace..."'

'"Where joys never cease,"' crooned Lucy, before her voice rose again, '"Out there beneath

115

a kindly sky!"'

'"We'll build a sweet little nest, somewhere up in the West,"' quavered Aunt Mac.

'Big finale,' hissed Lucy.

'"And let the rest of the world go by!"' they chorused.

There was a moment's silence when Lucy giggled and Aunt Mac chuckled. 'We'll never make the stage of the Hippodrome, girl. But I'm glad you're still able to sing and aren't weighed under worrying about your mam and Mick.'

Lucy threw back her head and gazed up at the old woman. She had pure white hair and the few teeth she had left were blackened stumps from eating molasses which her husband brought from Tate's down on the dock road. 'I do worry but it's no use letting it get me down.'

The old woman rested a hand on Lucy's shoulder. 'Finished all your chopping?'

She nodded. 'Ma'll be back tomorrow.'

'I'll miss you.'

'I'll come and see you again.' Lucy hesitated. 'What d'you think, Auntie Mac, about me one day owning my own sweet shop?'

'We can all dream, girl. I remember Wignall's shop. It was Molly Bushell's grandson who had it. She it was who made the first Everton toffees from a recipe given to her by a doctor to help her make money. She had very little and mouths to feed. Who'd have believed her grandson would end up supplying them to the old Queen! If you're sensible and work hard and don't rush into marriage, unless you can find yourself a rich husband who'd indulge you, then why shouldn't

116

your dream come true? I remember...'

The old woman was off, talking about when she'd worked in a boarding house on the dock road which took in emigrants waiting to go to America, and how they were risking all to fulfil their dream. It was exciting but scary as well.

Lucy was thinking about all that Aunt Mac had said when she arrived home the next day after going to the timber yard. To her surprise she was welcomed by singing. Her eyes widened at the sight of Barney, flamboyantly dressed, sitting on their doorstep, built-up booted leg stuck out straight in front of him, cigarette dangling from the corner of his mouth, a folded newspaper in his hand with which he was conducting a group of women and children.

'The Boy I Love' came to an end and the gathering broke up. Women went back to their daily tasks and children began to play, squabbling over stones and pieces of chalk. A couple of girls were playing ball, chanting: 'Ikey Moses, King of the Jews bought his wife a pair of shoes'. Lucy smiled at Barney and he asked how she was and stood up to allow her to get the cart indoors.

Curious to why he was there, she picked up her skipping rope and went out again. He was still outside, leaning against the metal handrail and talking to her mother. Lucy kept an eye on the pair of them, as she began to skip to the accompaniment of 'Salt, pepper, mustard, vinegar', when Callum came whistling through the passageway. At the sight of Barney the whistling tailed off and his expression darkened.

Lucy stopped skipping and went over to her

117

mother. Their voices trailed away as Callum, his bushy brows drawn together in disapproval, approached the step. 'Well, if it isn't Mr Jones,' he said, adding in a tone of underlying menace, 'Sling your hook, matey!'

Barney's smile didn't falter. 'Isn't that a docker's term? Don't they have hooks to pick up goods when unloading a ship?'

Callum scowled. 'Don't try and be clever with me. Clear off! What does Maureen want with the likes of you?' He prodded Barney's boot with his foot and didn't need to spell out what he meant.

Lucy was watching Barney's face and for a split second it was as if a mask had slipped. He's furious! she thought. Then his smile was back again. 'And you think she wants the likes of you?'

'More so than *you*. I can look out for Maureen. You can't! You don't belong here. So beat it!'

'He wasn't doing any harm,' chorused a couple of neighbours.

'Indeed he wasn't! You're a vulgar little man, Callum McCallum, and you don't own me,' said Maureen, cheeks aflame, body quivering as she stood and faced him.

'Calm down now, Mrs Linden,' said Barney, placing a restraining hand on her arm. 'Mr McCallum is indeed a sorry, ignorant creature if he judges a man by outer appearances. But I've met his like before and whatever he says – "Sticks and stones may break my bones but names will never hurt me". I have performed my errand and was just about to leave so I'll go on my way in full confidence that you can deal with Mr McCallum without my help.'

118

'Indeed I can, Mr Jones,' said Maureen, and kissed his cheek. 'You're a real gent.' She turned to her daughter. 'Lucy, see Mr Jones out into the street.'

Lucy hurried to do her mother's bidding but couldn't wait to get back to see what happened next between Callum and her. She waved Barney off as he clumped up Bostock Street then raced back up the passage just in time to hear Callum tell her mother she was a disgrace to her family and religion and wouldn't be allowed to get away with her flirtatious and mercenary ways.

'And how are you going to stop me?' snapped Maureen. 'What's between me and Mr Jones has nothing to do with you. So go boil your head!' She picked up her brush and waved it in his face.

Callum backed off, a comical expression on his face. 'But I thought there was something between us. What about the other week? I love you, darlin'!'

'I must have had one too many. Now go! You're making a show of me in front of my neighbours.'

He went, looking down in the dumps. Maureen waved to her neighbours. 'Show's over!' she said, cocking her nose in the air, and beckoned Lucy inside. 'Well, did you behave yourself at Aunt Mac's?' Lucy caught a whiff of alcohol from her and wondered what Barney had made of that.

'Of course. How's Uncle Mick?'

Her mother's expression darkened. 'Miserable as sin! Sorry for himself! Wanting to be on his feet when he isn't up to it. Just sits there, oiling a revolver. And to top it all Callum had the nerve to write him a letter, telling him about me and

119

Mr Jones! Mick was angry about it. Had the cheek to tell me I was betraying my own kind.' She snorted. 'I was mad, I can tell you. I told him he was a fool and should leave the fighting to those he thinks are "his kind". They're a lot better at it than our Mick is. So he just might come home now.'

'What are we going to do?' asked Lucy, not liking the sound of an angry Mick with a gun.

Maureen sighed and her shoulders drooped. 'You're asking me questions I don't have answers to.' Her voice was low and troubled. 'There's been a big funeral in Cork for Terence McSwinney. Remember he was arrested when we were over there? He starved himself to death. Took him over seventy days to die.'

Lucy's blood ran cold. How could anyone bear going hungry that long?

'His chaplain's saying he's stronger dead than all the living forces of the British Empire.' Maureen glanced at her daughter. 'You understand what this means, Lucy? Now McSwinney's paid with his life for a Republic of Ireland, the fight'll go on until the rebels win – and only Our Lord knows how many lives that'll take. Perhaps it's just as well our Mick is coming home. He's my brother after all and we were close when we were young. I just wish Callum hadn't opened his big mouth!'

It was early in November when Lucy arrived back from the timber yard to find her uncle seated in front of the fire. He had put on weight, filling the seat of the chair. No longer did he look the least bit like the wiry, smooth-cheeked man in the photograph on the mantelshelf. His fox-red hair was close-cropped and his drooping moustache curved into points to either side of his chin. He wore baggy dark blue trousers and a shirt of the same colour.

'You be nice to your Uncle Mick now, Lucy,' said Maureen, placing a stool in front of her brother. 'We've all got to be nice to him to make up for what he's been through.' There was a look in her eyes that signalled, *Do whatever he says, for God's sake!*

'Of course I'll be nice,' said Lucy, trying to drum up some enthusiasm, but she had a headache and was feeling tired. 'Are you glad to be home, Uncle Mick?'

'In this dump?' He rolled his eyes in a way that was reminiscent of her mother and thrust out a leg, thumping his foot on the stool. 'Take off my boots, girl, so my feet can breathe!'

She remembered doing this for him the last time he'd arrived home but she was less keen this time. She sat listening to him talking to her mother and didn't like what he had to say. 'This bloody Mr Jones! You put him out of your mind, sister, or I'll give you what for! I won't have you taking up with another bloody Englishman.'

'Barney's Welsh.' Lucy shot a glance at her mother. He didn't sound very brotherly, not like the old Mick at all.

'That's right.' Maureen stroked her brother's shoulder. 'And I've told you, Mick, there's nothing in it. You shouldn't be taking any notice of Callum. He's just jealous!'

'And has reason from what's he's said. The trouble is, you're a good-looking woman. Maybe I should do something to stop him fancying you...'

'I'm not knowing what you mean, Mick. Mr Jones is a cripple. You can't go hurting him.'

'I wasn't thinking of laying a finger on *him*. I was talking about you, sister.' He reached up and gripped the hand that lay on his shoulder, squeezing it. 'You know what we do to traitors?'

Maureen gasped. 'You're hurting me! And I'm no such thing.'

Lucy paused in what she was doing and glanced at Timmy, who had also stopped what he was doing and was staring at his mother and uncle open-mouthed.

'I'm your brother. You should put me first,' said Mick, exerting more pressure. 'You'll not be seeing him again!'

'Yes, Mick. Anything you say,' Maureen squealed, tears springing to her eyes.

He released her. 'You see you do and we'll get on fine. Just like the old days.' Running a hand over his face and hair, he ordered, 'Now get me something to eat. I'm hungry.'

Lucy would not have believed he could do such a thing to her mother if she hadn't seen it for herself. She should have done something to stop him but he was so strong and heavy. Still, maybe it wouldn't happen again. She could only hope so.

He glanced down at her and smiled. 'Are you having a struggle there, girl?'

'A little, Uncle Mick. They're such big boots.'

Lucy gave a final tug, the boot came off and she toppled backwards. Again, just like before. But he didn't laugh this time, just told her to stop messing about.

'Perhaps you'd like her to run up to the pub with the jug for you?' said Maureen.

'Yes. She can do that.' Mick surprised Lucy by touching her cheek gently with one finger. The red hairs on the back of his hand tickled her skin. She couldn't make him out and felt confused. 'Get them to fill it with best bitter.' He took a coin from his pocket and flicked it in her direction.

She caught it deftly. 'What about your other boot?'

'Your mammy can do it. You be off, and take your brother with you.'

Lucy didn't argue but took the chipped blue jug and left, followed by Timmy. They had not closed the front door behind them when she heard her uncle say, 'That boy's getting to look more like his bloody daddy every day. I hope you're not spoiling him?'

'He's my only son and has no father. Who else is there to spoil him but me?'

'He shouldn't be getting spoilt at all. I'm thinking that maybe I should stay on here. The boy needs a man about the place. He's got to learn that life won't do him any favours.'

'So – you're not going back to Ireland?'

'Didn't I just say that?' growled Mick. 'Dermot wanted rid of me anyway. There's things I can do here.'

'You mean get involved in–'

'Keep your mouth shut, sister! D'you want the neighbours knowing our business? Is the front door closed?' There was the sound of heavy footsteps.

Lucy and Timmy fled.

Neither of them spoke until they were through the passage and into Bostock Street. 'I'm frightened, Luce,' whispered Timmy, hunching his narrow shoulders and slipping a hand into hers. 'I don't like him.'

'You mustn't be frightened,' she said firmly. 'And what are you whispering for? He can't hear you.'

Her brother's blue eyes expressed doubt. 'How d'you know? He might be magic.'

'Don't be daft!'

'It's not daft. Sir has eyes in the back of his head. He's always telling us.'

Lucy smiled. 'That's just to make you behave when his back's turned. If Mam doesn't see Uncle Barney, things'll be OK.' Goodbye dreams of having him for a stepfather, she thought. Although what about Mam's job? More often than not she saw him when she went in to clean.

'Uncle Mick doesn't like me because I look like our dad,' muttered Timmy, kicking at a stone.

Lucy knew he was right but felt a need to reassure him. 'It probably isn't that at all. The way he goes on about Mr Jones, I think he's jealous of him. We just have to be nice to Uncle Mick like Mam said.'

But it wasn't easy to be nice to their uncle because he wasn't nice to them. Not that they saw a lot of Mick despite his not making any effort to find work. He made the excuse that the wound he'd incurred in Ireland was still giving him trouble, but that did not stop him from going out and not coming back until late at night. And when he was home, more often than not he was oiling or polishing his revolver, which made them all uneasy.

One day Mick seized Timmy by the throat as he passed his chair and held the gun to the boy's head, barking, 'Your money or your life!'

Timmy shrieked, 'I've got no money, Uncle Mick! Don't kill me!'

Maureen yelled at her brother to stop frightening the boy and Lucy sprang forward and seized her uncle's arm and tried to break his grip. Mick laughed and pushed first Timmy away, then Lucy. 'I'm only playing with the lad. He's a cissy.'

'He's not! Anyone would be frightened if they had a gun held to their head,' said Lucy, trembling as she hugged her brother.

'That's true, Mick,' said Maureen, eyes wide with fright. 'Why don't you try and get yourself a job? The money you gave me when you first came home is running out.'

His face froze. 'Are you complaining, sister? You know I've got work.'

She swallowed. 'I meant proper work! Not being a lapdog to that O'Neill fella, getting yourself involved in things you're best staying out of. I need regular money from you, Mick. If it weren't for my job and Lucy's, we'd be in the workhouse.' Inexplicably Mick did not appear to have remembered Maureen worked at the cinema where Barney Jones played the piano. 'It's not right, us keeping you. You're eating us out of house and home.'

'Stop moaning, sister! I'll get you money.' He glared at her and took up a scrap of black velvet cloth and carried on polishing his gun, whistling a marching song through his teeth.

Maureen left him and went upstairs. The children followed, not wanting to be alone with him. Lucy sniffed as they came to the landing. 'What's that smell?'

'Don't ask!' said Maureen wearily. 'And there's no need to be following me. Mick won't hurt you. He's just being a tease, that's all.'

'He's not nice,' muttered Timmy, leaning against a wall. 'I'm scared he might hurt you again, Mam.'

Maureen laughed lightly. 'He won't. Now I've work to do. You go out and play.'

'What about my making sweets, Mam? Remember we said we'd try coconut ice? Did you get ingredients?'

Her mother's mouth tightened. 'And how can I be doing that when we're needing more coal and extra food? You're going to have to forget selling toffee apples and sweets for the moment. Now go out and play!' She went into the bedroom and slammed the door.

Worried and disappointed, Lucy went downstairs with Timmy and out of the house. Should she spend her own money on ingredients? But if she did that her mother would immediately want to know where she'd got it from and Lucy was determined to keep her secret hoard. Things might get worse.

When she went to bed that night she realised what the smell upstairs was. Paraffin! She mentioned it to her mother who almost bit her head off. 'Why should we have paraffin in the house, you eejit? You're imagining it.'

Lucy thought she might have imagined it once but not twice. So where was the smell coming from?

Chapter Seven

The next day Mick was in a better mood, joking with his sister and even complimenting Lucy on how well she was doing selling firewood, ruffling her hair and tickling her under the chin. She suffered the indignity, wanting to get a closer smell of him, and was convinced his clothing reeked of paraffin. But what was he doing with that? What was he up to? No good, she'd bet. When she saw the newspaper headlines in the Liverpool *Echo*, Lucy felt sure she was right. There had been arson attacks down by the docks and it was suspected they were the work of a cell of Sinn Feiners in the city.

The following Saturday was a dull damp day and the children were indoors when Mick limped in at lunchtime. He took off his wet coat and hung it on a nail then sat down in front of the low-burning fire. There was a brooding expression on his face and he smelled of drink. After a single glance in his direction, Maureen and the children kept quiet.

'That lad should be out playing,' he said abruptly. 'You're turning him into a nancy boy, letting him play with slates and chalk. He should be out with the other lads playing football.'

'The damp's not good for his chest,' said Lucy swiftly, glancing at her mother.

'He needs toughening up. When I was a lad...'

Maureen interrupted him. 'He was out earlier with Lucy, selling the firewood, and came in shivering. Will you be going out again later, Mick? Only...'

'I've just come in! Wanting to be rid of me already? Boy!' Mick snapped his fingers at Timmy. 'Get some coal for this fire. I want it roaring up the chimney!'

'We've hardly got any coal, Uncle Mick,' said Lucy. 'Why d'you think we've got our coats on?'

He glared at her. 'Shut up and sit down! Unless you want to feel the back of my hand?'

Lucy sat down, her body tense, wanting to hit him.

Mick thumped the arm of the chair with his fist, startling them all so much they visibly jumped. 'I'm sick of being told we can't have this and we can't have that. Boy! You come over here and take the bucket and get some coal.'

Timmy, pale and trembling but with a resolute expression on his face, went over to the fireplace where his uncle sat. The next moment the boy was flat on the floor and groaning. Lucy and Maureen started in his direction, only to be held back by Mick's outstretched leg and arm. 'Let the lad get up himself!' he roared.

Lucy's heart was beating so fast with anger and fear she thought it would jump out of her chest. How dare he make them feel like this? How dare he! She watched her brother struggle to his feet and saw that not only was he clutching his stomach but that a lump was forming on his head.

'I–I can't believe you–you just did that!' gasped Maureen.

'It was an accident! The boy's clumsy,' growled Mick. 'That's what comes from staying in and messing about with chalk. Fresh air'll clear his head. Get him out of here!'

For a moment Maureen just stared at him and then she screeched. 'It's cold and damp out there, you eejit! Will you talk bloody sense! Do you want him dead?'

Mick pushed himself up out of the chair and slapped her across the face. The force of the blow knocked her head sideways. Lucy screamed and flung herself at him. He seized her by the arm and threw her so that she landed on her bottom on the floor. It hurt and for a moment she was too shocked to move. Maureen's back was towards Lucy and she could see her mother's shoulders shaking and hear her making a keening noise.

'Stop that! It makes you look ugly!' shouted Mick, his hand hovering above her head. 'Stop it! Or I'll hit you again.'

The crying shuddered to a stop.

Lucy decided to stay on the floor. It felt safer there. She rubbed her upper arm, waiting, not knowing what would happen next. Mick turned his back on them, muttering to himself, feeling with one hand along the mantelshelf. For what seemed like an age nothing happened. Lucy could see a spiral of smoke weaving about his head. Timmy looked at her and in an attempt to reassure him she winked.

His mouth trembled into a smile and cautiously he inched towards her, carefully avoiding his mother's feet. She appeared oblivious of him. As soon as he reached Lucy, the girl took his hand and slowly they backed towards the door, their eyes on Mick. Carefully Lucy turned the knob and pushed the door open with her bottom. She looked at Maureen, not wanting to leave her, but her mother's attention was on Mick. Lucy delayed no longer but left the house.

They stood on the step, trembling. She glanced around the court, marvelling that nobody was rushing out to see what was going on. They were probably all huddled indoors, ears to the walls, having heard the commotion but feeling too scared of Mick to interfere. Perhaps they'd guessed he might have a gun. She didn't blame them for staying out of the way. Suddenly she noticed next door's black and white cat cleaning itself on the step and somehow the ordinariness of the action reassured her. She slipped her hands into her pockets and her fingers curled about something inside one of them. She brought out two tickets for the kids' matinee that day. Timmy had given her them yesterday to look after. Lucy considered herself too old to go these days but the matinee was actually where she'd like to be right now.

Timmy tugged on her arm and looked up at her

with anxious eyes. 'What are we going to do?'

'How does the kids' matinee sound?'

He grinned. There was no need for words.

For a short while in the warm darkness of the cinema Lucy could forget what had taken place earlier. Last week Perilous Pauline had been left hanging from a cliff edge. Now all that mattered was finding out how she was going to get out of trouble. Children cheered as the rope to which she clung managed to loop itself about the stump of a tree halfway down a cliff and stopped her from dashing out her brains on the rocks below. Within a short space of time she was in trouble again and the audience couldn't wait to come back again next week.

The lights went up and Lucy heard the clump, clump of Barney ascending the aisle towards them. 'Hello there, Lucy, Timmy.' He beamed down at the pair of them. 'How's tricks? Getting on with your uncle?'

Timmy groaned and Lucy dug him gently in the ribs, remembering her gran saying that families should stick together, come what may. 'We're getting on fine,' she said.

Barney chuckled. 'Timmy doesn't sound like he is.'

'He says I'm a cissy,' said the boy, jutting out his chin. 'He tripped me up deliberately and punched me in the stomach. He said I need toughening up. I don't like him.'

Barney shook his golden head. 'I don't know what to say. These ex-soldiers! I know what you're suffering, boyo. He's a big man, is he, your Uncle Mick?'

'Fat,' said Timmy, unfolding his arms and making a large circle. 'He frightens me.'

'A bit of healthy fear is no bad thing,' said Barney thoughtfully. He patted Timmy's head, took a couple of sweets from his pocket and gave them one each. 'My regards to your mother. I haven't seen much of her lately but I suppose she's busy now your uncle's home?'

Lucy nodded, wishing she could tell him the truth about Mick, but what could Barney do? She now felt guilty about leaving her mother and hurried home but when they arrived the house was empty. Had her mother gone in search of them? Lucy decided to look for her. She told Timmy to stay in the house where it was comparatively warm, adding that she wouldn't be long.

She did not have to look far, bumping into her mother in the passage. 'Are you OK, Mam? He didn't hit you again, did he?'

'No.' Maureen sounded weary and rested one hand against the wall. Lucy could just about make out the shadow of a bruise on her cheek in the gloom and felt angry. 'Where did you go?' asked Maureen.

'The kids' matinee. I wish we could go to the police.'

'Don't even think about it!' Her mother's voice was alarmed. 'Family's family and you don't go telling tales. Besides, he'd kill us!'

'Do you really think...' Lucy clutched her mother's arm.

'No, no! Take no notice of what I said.' She leaned against Lucy. 'Let's get home before parts

132

of me freeze and drop off.' Slowly they went up the passage and into the house where Maureen reassured herself that Timmy was OK.

In one way Lucy was glad of her mother's refusal to talk about Mick's violent behaviour because that way it was easier to pretend it had never happened. A few days later her uncle came back looking pleased with himself and seemed more his old self.

'You've been going on at me, sister, to get meself a job and haven't I gone and done it.'

'That's marvellous news, Mick!' Maureen uncurled herself from the sofa and flung her arms round him.

'I'm back with a bookie. A different one this time.'

Her face fell. 'What about that moneylender who was after you?'

Mick cut himself a slice of bread. 'I had a bit of luck there. I was told someone set fire to his house and all his books were destroyed. He's left the neighbourhood.'

Now fancy that! thought Lucy. Have I got a suspicious mind or haven't I? She had not forgotten the smell of paraffin on his clothes, which still lingered upstairs too.

Christmas came and there was talk of a cease-fire in Ireland. Mick disappeared for a few days and when he reappeared didn't come empty-handed but carried a basket containing butter and eggs, several bottles of Guinness, a whole leg of pork, and hats and gloves for Maureen and the children, which Dermot's mother had knitted 'specially for them.

'Things are looking up,' said Maureen, setting the bright green tammy at a flattering angle on her auburn curls. 'Now that suits me, wouldn't you say, Mick?' She flashed him a saucy smile.

'Aye, you're looking a picture.' He swept her into his arms and danced her round the kitchen. After he'd left Maureen laughing and gasping for breath on the sofa, he dragged Lucy up and danced her round the room as well. She was bemused. Was this smiling, charming man one and the same as the one who'd hit her mother, flung herself to the ground and punched Timmy in the stomach?

They had the pork with sage and onion stuffing for Christmas dinner and Maureen and Mick were all smiles as they reminisced about their childhood.

On Boxing Day they went to Aunt Mac's. There was music, dancing, singing and much talk of Ireland becoming a republic. The conversation became heated and there would have been a fight if Uncle Mac hadn't threatened to knock a few heads together.

The church bells had not long welcomed in 1921 when Lucy arrived home to find Mick pacing the floor, a brooding expression on his face because apparently negotiations between the government in London and the leaders in Dublin and Belfast were not going smoothly. Six counties in the North wanted to remain part of Great Britain.

Lucy set about chopping wood. Mick flung down the newspaper, watching splinters go flying as she brought down the axe for the umpteenth time. 'What the hell's the girl doing?'

'You know what's she's doing, Mick,' said Maureen, glancing up from her sewing. 'You've seen either Lucy or myself chopping firewood for months now. You'd know what she was about if you took any notice of what's going on in this house, instead of being out with Callum and that Shaun, drinking and plotting.'

'Don't speak to me like that, sister!' he roared, thrusting his face in hers.

Maureen shrank back in her chair. 'I'm sorry, Mick, but I thought you'd have noticed.'

'I have bloody noticed! I've noticed she's making a mess of the floor.'

Lucy stared at him. 'I've got it on some newspaper. We've no yard where I can do it.'

'You shouldn't be doing it here.' He jerked the axe from her hand. She yelped as the handle burned her palms then watched as he brought down the axe with all his might, only for it to dig so deeply into the wood that he couldn't wrench it out. He tried but the shaft broke off and the wood with the axe head stuck in it flew through the air, catching Timmy a blow on the side of the head. He screamed and clutched his ear.

'Shut up, boy!' Mick lunged at him. Timmy ducked and covered his head with his hands but the blow never landed because suddenly Mick was doubled up, clutching his groin.

Timmy lowered his arms. Maureen dropped her sewing and went to him. Blood was running down the side of his face. 'See what you've done to him, you eejit!'

Mick swore. 'What about me? It's me wound.'

'Tush! You and your bloody wound.' She lifted up her son and licked the blood from his ear.

'Uncle Mick nearly chopped me head off, Mam.' He snuggled into her, darting his uncle a look of loathing.

'I wish I bloody had!' muttered Mick. 'Has no one any sympathy for me? Here, Lucy, come and help me up to bed. I'll have to lie down.'

She hesitated, not wanting to help him.

'Come on, girl! This is your fault.'

How's it my fault? she wanted to say, but didn't dare. Reluctantly she went over to him and he laid his arm about her shoulders. His size and weight swamped her and as they climbed the stairs she felt as if her back would break. But the breath was whistling between his teeth and she presumed he really was in pain.

She helped him lower himself on to the bed and was about to turn away when he said, 'Don't go! A teensy-weensy flesh wound, that's all Timmy's got. I caught a bullet in my groin and the doctor lost count of the stitches I needed when they sewed me up. Yet not a sound passed my lips. What d'you think of that, Lucy girl?'

'You're brave,' she said diplomatically, remembering his screams when the doctor had dug out the bullet.

'Nothing brave about it, girl. Pride! That's what it was.' Uncle Mick shifted himself on the bed until his head rested against the pillow and thrust one foot at her. 'Do the honours!' She hesitated but he frowned and said, 'What are you waiting for? I'm not going to bite you.' But you could kick me, she thought. Nevertheless she began to unlace his boot.

'I've got a scar as long as your arm,' he boasted.
So what?

'You don't believe me?'

'Of course I believe you, Uncle Mick,' she said,
trying to hurry with the laces, only to end up
tying one tighter.

'Damn me if I don't show you, girl!'

She looked up, startled. Already he was sitting
up and had begun to unfasten his flies. His boot
slipped through her fingers and fell with a thud
to the floor. She felt trapped, certain her mother
wouldn't approve of him taking his trousers off in
front of her. 'I don't have to see it, Uncle Mick. I
do believe you!' she said hastily.

'It's all right, Lucy, you won't be seeing anything you oughtn't to see.' He bared a hip,
holding his clothing carefully and moving it little
by little until she could see the scar that ran from
his hip bone into his groin.

It repulsed her, reminding her of a tapeworm
her grandmother had shown her in a bucket
once, having told Lucy she'd starved it out of her
insides because it had been eating her food
almost as soon as she'd swallowed it.

'You don't like it, do you?' He laughed. 'Touch
it!'

She shook her head and, turning, fled from the
room, almost falling downstairs in her haste to
reach her mother. She felt an overwhelming rush
of affection and relief when she found Maureen
sitting in a chair by the fire with Timmy on her
knee. She went over to them, put her arm round
her mother's neck and pressed her hot cheek

137

against hers. Maureen looked at her askance. 'What's this? He didn't hit you?'

Lucy shook her head, too choked to speak.

'It's always there, waiting to erupt,' said Maureen, a catch in her voice. 'It's our history. So much oppression and violence, so much passion and dreaming. It's no wonder he's the way he is, what with fighting for the British and then fighting against them. Then his wound and the frustration of no decent work or a fit house for us to live in.' She eased Timmy off her knee. 'I'd best go up and see him. You bundle the wood you've chopped, Lucy.' She vanished upstairs.

Within moments the children heard raised voices. Lucy's fingers shook as she fastened the wire round the wooden chips.

Her mother reappeared, eyes shiny with tears, but when she spoke her voice was normal. 'Your Uncle Mick's nothing but a baby!' She picked up the axe and tugged it free of the wood and ran a finger along the blade. 'See, Lucy, this is blunt. Ask the ironmonger to sharpen it and have a new shaft fixed. Mick said he'll do all the chopping in future. It's not fit work for a girl your age, he says. It'll give you calluses and a man likes a girl to have soft hands.'

Lucy thought of the scene upstairs and it struck her there was only one reason why her uncle should care whether her hands were soft or not. A chill ran down her spine. She was determined never to be alone with him again.

Chapter Eight

Lucy watched her uncle wielding the axe and thought there was something strange going on. If Mick's war wound was as painful as he'd made out a while ago, how was he able to chop wood? Not that she was going to complain about him taking over because she still sold the wood, though she would much rather make sweets, but that was out of the question at the moment.

Times were hard and Lucy's conscience was bothering her. Maureen was behind with the rent, although she was managing to pay a little off the arrears each week. It was only the thought of her uncle benefiting from her money that kept Lucy silent about her savings. As it was they were dwindling because straight after school every day she swore Timmy to secrecy and took him to Maggie Block's where they drank mugs of steaming cocoa and gobbled down eggs on toast or a few spare ribs or cooked hearts in gravy. She comforted herself with the thought that money wasn't much good to you if you didn't live to spend it.

There had been lots of deaths that winter. So many were suffering hardship as more men joined the ranks of the unemployed. There was widespread dissatisfaction over conditions and pay and the broken promises of the government about improved housing. The land fit for heroes which had been promised the homecoming troops had not materialised, and neither had Home Rule for Ireland.

Mick straightened, putting a hand to the small of his back. 'You can pick this lot up and tie it into bundles.'

Lucy nodded, bending to gather the chips of wood together. She felt a hand on her bottom and shot up, scattering wood all over the place.

Her uncle grinned. 'Sorry, Lucy girl, but I couldn't resist it. You've got a lovely little bum.' He picked up his coat and walked out of the kitchen.

With trembling fingers she crouched to pick up the wood, gauging how many chips she needed for a bundle and tying it with wire. Her stomach was quivering and she was furious with Mick for scaring the life out of her, just when she had begun to put behind her that episode in the bedroom.

By the time the cart was loaded she had calmed down and was even a little scornful of that small, scared girl inside her. She was fourteen now and had grown two inches. After all, didn't her mother occasionally send her on the way with a pat on the bottom? Even so she hated her uncle doing it, not after wanting her to touch his scar.

He did not come home that evening, but the next day when Lucy and Timmy were hurrying back from Netherfield Road they took a short cut up a back entry and saw him with another man. He was handing over a parcel to Mick and what looked like money and a note. If it had not been for the parcel Lucy would have presumed he was a punter, but they didn't hand over parcels. She was so busy glancing over her shoulder at them that she ran into someone. 'Sorry!' she gasped, rubbing her chest which was already feeling sore that day.

'That's OK,' the man murmured and brushed past her, not sparing her a second glance.

Lucy stared after him. If it had not been for the voice she might not have recognised Rob Jones in that shabby suit and cloth cap. He had been un-shaven, too, and altogether looked like he didn't have two farthings to rub together. Could Constable Jones possibly be in disguise? Could he be after her uncle for breaking the law by taking bets? Or had the police got wind of his being involved in something far more dangerous? She thought of Mick's gun and was worried. Should she warn the policeman or would he already be aware of such a possibility? And how would her mother feel if Mick were arrested and put in prison? Despite his occasional bouts of violence and cruelty he was her brother and, as she had said in the past, family was family. Lucy decided for the moment to keep quiet.

When she returned from the timber yard it was to find the fire was out. She checked the coal cupboard because there should have been enough there to make up a fire but it was bare. Where was her mother? Had she gone to queue up for some? Lucy chopped some wood and got a fire going to welcome her home when she arrived.

Maureen looked none too happy when she came in. 'Holy Mother! What a lousy day it's been!' she said, dragging off her tammy. 'Run upstairs, Lucy, and put a match to the fire in Mick's room.' The girl stared at her. 'I know what you're thinking,' said her mother, looking gloomy. 'I told him we couldn't afford to have a second fire in the house but he...' She paused and took a deep breath. 'You know what he's like.' She threw a box of matches at her daughter. 'He's got some friends coming and wants to be private.'

As soon as Lucy entered Mick's room she could smell paraffin. She closed the door, not only to shut out the draught coming up the stairs but so her mother wouldn't hear her rummaging around. Not that there were many places to look. She got down on her knees and peered under the bed and there was the parcel and a can of paraffin.

She would have liked to open the parcel and see what was in it but didn't dare. Instead she went over to the fireplace and struck a match. It took another two for the paper to ignite but soon there was a nice blaze going and she went downstairs.

Half an hour later Mick arrived home with Shaun O'Neill and Callum. The latter looked un-happy as he glanced at Maureen but she ignored him. Lucy saw his mouth tighten as he followed the other two upstairs.

Two days later there was an explosion in St Domingo Grove and a house was destroyed. Lucy could not help noticing that it was the same number as Barney's house on St Domingo Road. She thought of pointing that out to her mother but as it was believed that the explosion had been caused by a gas leak Lucy decided that it could be just a coincidence. Besides she wasn't feeling well and her mother might get all upset and cause a scene.

It was the following morning that Lucy found blood on the sheet. Maureen sighed. 'This is the first time you've bled?'

Lucy nodded, gazing down at the stain on the multi-darned sheet and then at the blood trickling down her leg. She knew this had happened to other girls who were younger than herself but had only a vague idea what it meant.

Her mother went over to the rickety chest of drawers and took out a handful of rags. 'This is going to happen every month and it means you're turning into a woman. So no teasing or flirting with the lads,' she said firmly. 'You keep your distance or it could lead you into mortal sin.'

Lucy nodded. Her belly ached and so did her chest but she smiled because here at last was a physical sign that she was growing up and was no longer a 'little girl'. If only she could grow a few more inches!

'Here, take these.' Maureen thrust the rags into her hands, along with a couple of safety pins. 'Fasten them inside your drawers. You'll have to boil them up in a pan afterwards because you'll have to use them again. My mother was right when she called it the curse.'

'The curse?'

'God's curse on Eve for tempting Adam in the Garden of Eden. Although God only knows why Adam couldn't have said no.' She shrugged. 'But

143

there you are, we women always get the blame. I only wish I could tempt Mr Jones into marrying me, but at the moment I'm keeping him at a distance. I don't want any harm coming to him.'

'Mam! That explosion in St Domingo Grove...' Lucy said earnestly. 'You don't think it was Uncle Mick or Callum?'

Maureen sat down on the edge of the bed, her face taut. 'I did wonder but I hope to God we're wrong. Anyway, there's nothing we can do. You bind yourself and keep yourself pure. When you marry there'll be times when you'll look upon the curse as a friend. Now, strip off that sheet. It'll have to be soaked and the sooner the better.' Lucy did as she was told, uncomfortable but with a new awareness of her own femininity.

The three men met again some weeks later. Maureen had popped next door and they were upstairs. Timmy suggested hiding under the table from them in case they came down again. 'I could be Jim Hawkins hiding in an apple barrel on the good ship *Hispaniola,* and you could be the mate.'

Lucy was quite happy to fall in with her brother's plans. She had the curse again and didn't want to go out.

They had been there half an hour when the men came downstairs. Immediately Lucy and Timmy fell silent.

'They must have gone out,' said Mick. 'I thought I heard the door go.'

'Never mind that. Are we decided?' said Shaun. 'I can trust you to see to this? So far you've made a mess of things by blowing up the wrong house.

I thought we'd get that bobby. It makes me question whether you're the right person to be helping Mick with this task, Callum. You're not used to explosives.'

'I didn't want to do it,' he muttered. 'I just thank God, nobody was killed. I'm not cut out for this game.'

'You're in now. You can't be getting out,' said Shaun, a menacing note in his voice.

A bobby! thought Lucy, with a shiver. Could that be Rob Jones? She must tell her mother and see what she thought.

An hour passed and Maureen still had not come home. The gas had gone out but Lucy used one of her precious pennies to have light to read by. She sent Timmy to bed. Another hour passed and she had just decided to give up on her mother and go to bed herself when the door opened and Mick appeared.

'Hello, Lucy girl, you back?' He stood there swaying, one hand against the door jamb, a fatuous smile on his face. 'Our Mo still out?' The girl felt angry he could get drunk when they had so little so ignored his question. 'Cat got your tongue?' He walked unsteadily across the room towards her.

Lucy was scared, remembering him touching her bottom. 'She–She's just gone the privy,' she said in a rush, holding the book to her chest.

His expression froze. 'That's a lie! I've just been in there meself.' He put a hand on her book but she hung on to it, using it as a shield. There was a tussle and his fingers brushed against her breast. 'My, my, you're growing there,' he

145

muttered. 'You'll soon be a woman, girl, and the fellas'll all be after you like wasps round a jam pot.' He brought his face close to hers and his nose and mouth appeared enormous. 'Will you like that?'

'I–I don't like you t–talking like that, Uncle Mick. Please don't damage the book. It's from the library.'

'Put it down then and give me a hug. Let me have a feel of you! I won't hurt you. I'm lonely, girl. You don't know how lonely!' His voice trembled.

Lucy didn't care if he was the only man in the world, she just wanted him to go away. He tore the book from her grasp. 'What's up with you? There's no need to be frightened of me.'

But there is! she thought, too terrified to move. He ran his hands down her arms. 'Lovely skin. Young, firm flesh. If you'd seen the stinking, rotting corpses I'd seen when I was at the front you'd know what a treat this is.'

'Stop it, Uncle Mick! Please stop it! You're drunk!' She lifted her voice, remembering suddenly how thin the walls were and that her mother was only next door.

'I'm not drunk, girl.' He stroked her neck. 'Lovely little throat you've got. I've strangled a man. I bet you didn't know that. It's so easy, girl.' He put a finger against her windpipe. 'Just one little press, that's all.' She tried to cry out but the words wouldn't come. He smiled. 'But I wouldn't do that to you. You're my niece and I love you.'

There was a sound at the front door. 'Is anybody still up?'

Lucy had never seen Mick move so fast. He lumbered upstairs and the girl sank on to a chair as her mother entered the room. She looked pale. 'You OK?'

Lucy nodded. Her mother hugged her but neither of them mentioned Mick's name. Maureen kept her arm round her as they went upstairs.

In the week that followed Lucy made sure she was never alone in the house with her uncle. Then another explosion down by the docks was reported in the *Echo* and Mick didn't come home the following day. That evening Aunt Mac came to visit them. Her wrinkled face was strained and there were tears in her eyes. It took her some time to speak but when she finally managed it they could hardly understand her, so upset was she. 'Callum's gone missing. I don't know where he is,' she mumbled, dabbing her eyes with a damp rag. 'I knew he'd been up to something.'

'He's a fool, just like our Mick,' said Maureen, white about the mouth. 'He's got himself involved in Ireland's troubles.'

'I think he wanted out,' burst out Lucy, feeling terribly sorry for Aunt Mac. 'It's that Shaun O'Neill who's the ringleader. Without him, Callum and Uncle Mick might have kept out of it.'

'You don't think they've been arrested?' said the old woman, her voice quivering.

Maureen bit her lip. Lucy glanced at her. 'We'd have heard, Mam.' Those words seemed to comfort both women and soon afterwards Aunt Mac went home.

The following evening Lucy's eyes were drawn to a newspaper boy's placard: SENSATIONAL THEFT. She handed over a precious penny for an *Echo* and read what it had to say. Then she ran home with the newspaper to her mother.

'Read this, Mam,' she said excitedly, thrusting the *Echo* at her. 'D'you think Mick and Callum could be involved?'

Maureen shushed her and began to read. 'A group of men with Irish accents stole passports and liner tickets from a boarding house in town. They claimed to be members of the police force to gain entry to bedrooms.' Her voice trailed off and she carried on reading in silence before lifting her head, hope in her eyes. 'It says that a wireless message was sent to the liner in question, which was on its way to America, but it had stopped off at Cobh on the way and the men escaped.'

She sank on to the sofa. 'Thank God for that! Now if the pair of them have any sense they'll stay in Ireland and we'll have a bit of peace.'

It was as if a weight had been lifted off them.

A month passed with no word from Mick and Lucy could only be thankful for that. Aunt Mac did receive a letter from Callum. Apparently he was staying with some cousins and had a job and was keeping his nose clean. Lucy hoped for the old woman's sake he was telling the truth.

Summer arrived, and although it was still a struggle to make ends meet Lucy was much happier than she had been six months ago. Once again she had the task of chopping wood but she would rather that than have Mick back.

Sometimes she would see Owen on the way back from Griffiths' yard, carrying a sack on his back. He would look her up and down as if assessing what lay beneath her frock. Lucy had finally developed curves and had grown three inches in height and he seemed less inclined to throw insults at her.

When she arrived home one night it was to find her mother sitting on the step, a letter in her hand. She looked so upset that Lucy could only think that maybe her uncle was dead. 'Is it from Ireland?'

'No, Liverpool.' Her voice trembled. 'Mick's back! Go and get me a pencil, girl.'

Lucy hurried indoors and realised as she took a pencil from off the mantelshelf that her own hands were shaking. *Dear God,* she prayed, *please, don't let him come here!*

She watched her mother write on the back of the envelope. 'I'm wondering if he's right in the head, coming back,' she muttered. 'Especially as he seems to think it was me that put the police on to him. Me! His own sister! I haven't seen any policemen hanging round here, have you?'

'No,' said Lucy, but she was thinking of Rob Jones in disguise. He certainly seemed to have the knack of losing himself in a crowd.

'Mick wants to know if this place is being watched. How the hell am I supposed to know?' Maureen looked down in the dumps as she handed the envelope to Lucy. 'Take this to Maggie Block's refreshment house.'

'Do I have to?' Lucy wished her uncle on the other side of the world.

149

'Now don't get yourself all worked up,' Maureen said impatiently. 'He can't do anything to you at Maggie's. Honestly, I wonder at his brains. He calls me a traitor yet tells me where he is.'

Reluctantly Lucy took the note and left. Her stomach was churning unpleasantly despite her mother's words.

She could not immediately see Mick on entering the crowded portals of Maggie's refreshment house so waited just inside the door and took a second look around. The room was full of men and the smell of sweat and tobacco mingled with that of scouse, ribs and frying sausages. Her nerves jumped when she spotted Shaun. He had his head together with another man and as if he sensed her eyes upon him he looked up and she realised it was her uncle. Mick had shaved off his moustache and looked completely different. He beckoned her over and reluctantly Lucy squeezed her way between chairs to where they were sitting.

Shaun caught hold of her arm, pinching her skin. 'What is it you're wanting, girl? Your mammy send you to spy on us, did she?'

Lucy tore herself free and looked at Mick. 'I've got a message from Mam,' she said sullenly.

He smiled and patted his knee. 'Come and sit here, Lucy, while I read what she has to say.'

You must think I'm daft, she thought, handing him the note but keeping her distance.

Shaun leaned across the table towards Mick and she thought how unattractive he was, face covered in pimples. 'What does she say?' he asked.

Mick read slowly and his smile vanished. 'She says I'm an eejit! That I'm seeing spies up the chimney when all there is is soot because it needs sweeping and it's caught fire a couple of times with her having to burn wood and paper, having little coal because the miners aren't happy with their wages!'

Shaun looked incredulous. 'Your sister's crazy!' Then he frowned. 'Unless it's code?'

'She's having me on, that's all. She's angry with me.' Mick crushed the paper in his hand, his face like thunder. 'I'll go and see her and tell her what's what.'

'As long as you're careful, Mickey lad,' growled Shaun.

'Don't you start giving me orders! I'm sick of it!' Mick glared at him. Then he bent and picked up a parcel from the floor. 'Here, girl, you carry this. Go ahead! I'll catch you up.'

Lucy was relieved to get away and ran, wanting to reach her mother before she saw either of them again. She had reached the passage leading to the court when Mick came up behind her and dragged her to a halt. She froze and stared at him with the fascinated gaze of a frog caught in the hypnotic stare of a snake, watching as he took a coin from his pocket. 'What can you tell me about these Joneses your mother knows? One's a piano player and one's a policeman. Two Ps. You can have this shilling if you give me the right answers.'

Lucy found her tongue. 'I don't want your money!' she cried, struggling to free herself. 'You're up to no good.'

151

Mick's expression turned ugly and he hit her in the face. 'Tell me the truth! You're a spy for them, aren't you?'

Fury erupted inside her and her eyes flashed fire. 'I wish I was! Yer an eejit, coming back here! They'll get you and put you in prison and it'll serve you right! Carry your own parcel!' She heaved it at him. He yelled in alarm and caught it just before it hit the ground.

Lucy took to her heels, not in the direction of home but away from it. She raced up Bostock Street, slackening her pace only when she lost herself amongst the crowds in Great Homer Street. She thought of going to Aunt Mac's but decided her uncle might think to look for her there. So she crossed the road and headed for Griffiths' timber yard. Only when she passed through the gates did she feel safe. She was exhausted and sank down on a heap of piled up planks, holding her face up to the sun.

'Lucy! What's wrong with your face? Has someone been hitting you?'

She opened her eyes and saw Dilys and did not know what to say. Her jaw hurt and so did her mouth.

'Do you want to speak to my aunt? She's at home today but I could take you there.'

Lucy opened her mouth but no words came. She wanted to see Rob but realised she was scared that if she did, Mick might not only kill her but him as well.

Dilys's face softened. 'Come on! I'm taking you to my aunt and I think you should speak to Rob as well.' She took Lucy's arm and helped

152

her up. She protested then but the other girl only said, 'I'm not taking any notice of you. You need help.'

This time Lucy did not argue but went with her out of the yard and along Mere Lane past the Picture Palace. 'You don't have to talk about who hit you to me but you shouldn't let them get away with it,' said Dilys.

Lucy glanced at her. 'I'm surprised at you saying that,' she said through swollen lips. 'I thought you'd say, "Vengeance is mine, saith the Lord. I will repay!" I know you're a churchgoer – that you sing in the choir at St George's – because Barney Jones told my mother.'

'You'll know my brother's a detective then if you know something about me?'

Lucy nodded. 'My grandfather was in the police force, too.'

Dilys looked surprised. 'And my father was but he's dead. He was beaten up during the riots in Liverpool in 1911 and his insides were damaged that bad he died from his injuries.'

'Mine went down with the *Lusitania.*' Lucy thought it was no wonder Rob Jones had given her a lecture on the pitfalls of going off the rails that morning he'd searched their house.

'My mother died when I was born,' said Dilys with a sigh. 'You're lucky still having yours – but Aunt Gwen's been good to us. She's mam's sister and wanted Rob to work in the timber yard, but once he came out of the Army he had his heart set on following in Dad's footsteps.' She paused. 'Here we are.'

They stood in front of Miss Griffiths' house in

153

St Domingo Grove. It had three storeys and its roof was gabled. A couple of doors away there was a gap in the row of houses. Lucy stared at the crater and remembered that conversation between Mick, Shaun and Callum. Suddenly she wanted to run but Dilys was leading her up a path and round the side of the house into a back garden. The other girl pushed open the kitchen door and there was Miss Gwen Griffiths with another woman, short and plump. The smell of baking wafted towards them.

'I've brought you a visitor,' said Dilys, squeezing Lucy's arm gently. 'She won't tell me who's hurt her but she might talk to you.'

'Come in, lovey,' said Miss Griffiths, opening the door wide. 'What can I do...?' She stopped abruptly and took hold of Lucy's chin with a gentle hand and turned it up to the light. 'My dear, who's done this to you?' The concern in her voice was almost Lucy's undoing. Her eyes filled with tears and there was suddenly an enormous lump in her throat. 'There now!' The woman's arms went round her. 'You have a good cry. Then we'll talk about it.'

Those last words were enough to cause Lucy to pull herself together. 'I can't talk about it,' she said in a choking voice. 'He might do something to you.'

'Who's he, lovey?'

Lucy was silent. Why had she come? Mick was family. He would kill her if he knew she was here, and her mam wasn't going to be too pleased either.

'If you don't want to say anymore I can't make

you, but I can put some witch hazel on that bruise – and a cup of hot sweet tea won't go amiss, would you say?' She turned to her niece. 'Take Lucy into the big kitchen. I'll be with you in a minute.'

Lucy followed Dilys into a larger room where a fire burned in an open fireplace. They both sat down on a cretonne-covered sofa. Lucy glanced about her. The room seemed full of old solid furniture which was strangely reassuring. Some of the tension seeped out of her.

Hot sweet tea and strawberry jam and cream scones helped make her feel even better. 'Now tell me what happened, lovey?' said Miss Griffiths, after Lucy had finished eating and she was dabbing witch hazel on the girl's face.

Before Lucy could speak, a man's voice said, 'What's going on? What's she doing here?'

Lucy scrambled to her feet and gazed at Rob standing in the doorway. He was dressed in the same clothes as last time she'd seen him and she wondered if perhaps he was still after Mick and had been keeping an eye on Maggie Block's, knowing it was a place where her uncle and Shaun O'Neill met sometimes.

'Rob, just the person we want!' said his aunt, sounding relieved. 'Just look at this poor girl's face.'

Before Lucy could draw back he did what his aunt had done and took her chin between strong fingers to tilt her face towards the light. 'Who did this? Or do I need to ask? I think I'd best see you home.'

'No!' Lucy pulled away from him. 'He might...'

155

Her voice trailed off as she saw the anger in Rob's eyes.

'Stop protecting him!' he said fiercely. 'This thing has gone too far. Time to sort it out, lovey.' He took hold of her arm. 'Shall we go?'

Chapter Nine

'Your mam's gone out,' called a neighbour, who was sitting on her front step. Lucy dragged the key on the string through the letter box with trembling fingers. 'She looked in a right state and little Timmy was like a zombie. I asked her to come in here but she wouldn't.'

'Is anybody in the house now?' asked Rob.

The woman shook her head. 'He went off – maybe an hour ago.'

'We are talking about Mrs Linden's brother?'

The woman hesitated, then nodded. 'I'm sure it was him. I recognised the way he walked. He's got to be stopped. It's not as if he was her husband.'

Relieved to know Mick was not in the house, Lucy pushed open the door. Rob held her back as she made to go indoors. He called over to the woman, 'Have you been here all the time since he left?'

'I went in for a few minutes, that's all.'

So her uncle might have nipped back, thought Lucy, fear rooting her to the spot. Rob went ahead of her and she forced herself to follow him.

All was quiet. He went into the kitchen and scullery before taking the stairs two at a time. She dogged his heels, scarcely able to believe he could get up them so silently, remembering the sound of his Army boots the last he had been here. Perhaps he was hoping to catch Mick asleep if he was upstairs – but what if he had heard them talking and was waiting for them, revolver at the ready?

'He has a gun!' Lucy whispered.

Rob nodded, signalling she should go into the bedroom where he had found her and Timmy the morning he'd searched the house. She hesitated but he bundled her inside and closed the door. Lucy sank on to the bed. Her face was throbbing and her pulse racing but she was only there a few minutes before he called her.

He stood on the tiny landing, cradled a cardboard box as gingerly as if it was a newborn baby. 'This little lot could blow you sky high once put together. I'm taking it with me to police headquarters. You'd best come along, too, Lucy. I'm sure you could help us with our enquiries.'

'He'll kill me!' she whispered, quaking at the thought of Mick even laying a finger on her.

Rob looked at her with a mixture of concern and anger. 'I won't let him. Now, let's get out of here.'

'You know he'll be back! He'll be back for that!' Her voice sounded shrill in her own ears.

Rob didn't answer but started down the stairs. He had just reached the bottom when the front door opened and Mick entered.

He saw them immediately and dragged his

revolver from a pocket. Rob lunged forward, the box still in his arms. Lucy could only think he intended to ram Mick against the door with it. Her uncle's reactions were swift, but not having the space to bring up his gun and aim at Rob, he caught him a blow on the side of the head with the butt of the gun instead. The younger man sank to his knees, still clutching the box. Mick hit him again and Rob collapsed on to the floor.

Then it was as if everything was happening in slow motion as Lucy watched her uncle take the box and place it carefully on the torn linoleum. He lifted his head and stared at her. Slowly he brought up the gun. He wouldn't! she thought, but another voice in her head said, *Run!* There was only one way to run and that was up. She stumbled up the stairs, recalling there was a lock on her uncle's bedroom door. She flung herself inside but her hands were shaking so much she could not turn the key. Mick forced the door open and was inside the room, looming over her.

Something seemed to disintegrate inside her brain. 'Don't touch me! Don't touch me! Don't touch me!' she screamed, hammering at him with her fists. 'You're evil! Evil! Evil!' More by luck than intent she knocked the gun from his hand and it went spinning across the floor.

Mick swore and hit her across the head with his fist. There was a ringing in her ears but still she fought him. He was laughing now, trying to pin her arms to her sides. He lifted her easily and flung her on to the bed. 'God, you're a wildcat,' he said, sounding excited. Then he dropped on the bed beside her. She managed to roll off it and reached for the gun. It was heavy, far too heavy for her to hold with one hand. She prayed like she had never prayed before and the words of the Lord's Prayer rang in her head ... *deliver us from evil! For thine is the kingdom...* She managed to get her other hand under the barrel and pointed the gun at Mick.

To see fear and surprise on his face was as good as a plate of spare ribs and fried cabbage. Lucy wanted to say something like, 'Say your prayers, Uncle Mick!' but her mouth had gone dry. She had seen many a cowboy kill a baddy on the films. Bang! Bang! It should be easy but it wasn't. Her hands started to sweat.

Suddenly Mick laughed. Reaching inside a pocket, he took out cigarettes and matches. 'Holy Mary, girl! Don't be pointing it at me like that. It could go off.' He lit a cigarette.

Lucy was furious with herself for not having the guts to pull the trigger but still she did not put down the gun.

He frowned. 'I hope I'm not going to have to force you to give it up, girl.'

He reached across the bed towards her. It was the wrong thing for him to do. Her fear and anger escalated and she hit him across the head just as she had seen him hit Rob. Mick fell, his head hanging over the edge of the bed. The cigarette dropped from his fingers and rolled under the bed.

Cautiously, she reached out to touch him. With a 'whoosh' flames leaped up from under the bed. Lucy shot back, clutching her arm, and dropped the gun. There was a strong smell of paraffin and she realised what must have happened. She had never seen a fire take hold so swiftly. Her first instinct was to run, and then she looked down at Mick.

Unconscious, without that wicked glint in his eyes, he was no longer a monster. For a second she remembered the uncle who had laughed and played with her when she was a child. She went round the bed, thinking to grab him by the feet and drag him off the bed, but already the heat was intense.

Water! She rushed out of the room, clutching her blistering arm, and went downstairs. Rob was still slumped at the bottom. She would have to move him to get past. She seized hold of his shoulders and tried to shift him, but he was too heavy.

She shook him. 'Rob, wake up! Wake up!' Dear God, she hoped he wasn't going to die. She shouted louder: 'Rob, you've got to help me!'

He groaned but didn't open his eyes and so Lucy climbed over him and ran through the kitchen and into the scullery and struggled back with the water bucket. It was tremendously difficult trying to lift it higher as she stepped over him again. Some of the contents slopped over the rim. He came to with a start, gasping as the water fell on his face, and looked up at her with befuddled dark eyes. She rested the bucket on a stair. 'The bed's on fire! Mick's unconscious! I've got to try and save him!'

Rob was staring at her as if she wasn't making sense. She decided to try one more time to get him upright. Keeping one hand on the bucket to prevent it from overbalancing and placing her opposite shoulder beneath his armpit, she managed to drag his arm round her neck. She heaved and despite his wobbly knees enabled him to get to his feet. 'What happened?' he muttered.

'I've just told you,' she gasped. 'Can you stand up on your own now?'

He nodded, leaning against the wall, but didn't look too good. With a sinking heart Lucy decided he wasn't going to manage the stairs and, gripping the handle of the bucket with both hands, began to climb the stairs. The smell of smoke and paraffin was overpowering. She could taste it on her tongue and began to cough.

'Lucy, where are you going?' croaked Rob.

She was unable to answer as she coughed and coughed in an attempt to rid her mouth of the noxious smoke. Her head began to spin but she hung on to the bucket as it tipped and water drenched her feet. She was seized from behind and, staggering and swaying, kept from falling by the hands that held her elbows with a rigidity that lent her strength.

When they reached the bottom of the stairs, Rob took the bucket from her and with his arm round her shoulders, forced her out of the house. It was such a relief to be in the open air! Her chest heaved as she struggled for breath.

'You're going to be OK. Just keep on breathing in, out, in, out. Don't give up, lovey.' Rob's voice was urgent.

She wanted to drift but did as she was told. Besides, something was worrying her, stopping her from floating away on that nice soft cloud. Where was her mother? She wanted her mam. She should have been here, protecting Lucy. But hadn't the policeman said he'd protect her? He had let her down! Mick could have killed her. Yet it was Detective Rob Jones who had carried her out of the house.

'I'll have to leave you a minute,' he said.

She could hear shouts, sense panic all around her. Someone mentioned the fire bobbies. Fire! Something horrible had happened. A picture flashed into her mind but she didn't want to think about it so closed her eyes tightly in an attempt to banish it. Slowly, as she began to breathe more easily, she let herself drift.

Lucy could hear voices. She couldn't make out what they were saying but that didn't matter. The pain in her arm was less severe and she was content just to lie there, having lost track of time, with no idea how long she had been in the hospital. She knew her mother had been to see her, remembered her sitting by the bed, holding her hand, tears running down her face. Neither of them had spoken a word. In fact Lucy had not spoken since she had been half-carried out of the house.

The ward door opened and there was the rustle of starched cotton and the firm tread of regulation shoes which stopped beside her bed. Lucy kept her eyes shut, knowing once they opened whoever it was would demand something from her. A Scottish nurse kept asking for a smile and a hello but that meant making an effort.

162

Lucy breathed in the scent of Devonshire Violets and knew it was prim and proper Sister Taylor.

'Miss Linden, I know you're awake so there's no use pretending. It's out of hours but you've a visitor. Maybe you'll find your tongue to speak to D.C. Jones.'

Lucy made no sign of having heard but her heart rate accelerated and she listened hard for the sound of his footsteps. The chair creaked next to her bed and her own heartbeat drummed in her ears.

'Hello, Lucy. How are you, love?'

At the sound of his voice muddled images flashed through her mind: tripping over tramlines, Gran lying dead, strong teeth crunching into an apple, a steam lorry and being pushed out of the way. Then there was someone on the floor ... a man lying huddled in the lobby, blood making his hair sticky. Something dark hovered on the edge of her consciousness. It swooped in like a raven. Fire! Lucy gasped, almost choking with fear. She coughed and coughed, then managed a scream.

An incredulous laugh and Rob said, 'My God! My voice has never had that effect before.'

A sob broke from her. It had been real, all too real! The fire, and Mick slumped unconscious on that burning bed. She had done that to him. She was a murderess, but bloody hell! He'd deserved it in some ways.

'Hey! There's no need to cry,' said Rob. His grey eyes were kind and sympathetic as he placed his hand over her small one lying on the bed-cover. 'I'm not here to midder you. I just wanted to see how you were.'

Lucy did not know what to say. Had he really just come to see how she was? He was a detective and they detected.

'I hate seeing girls cry. Although our Dilys can turn the tears on like a tap when she wants her own way. Did it when we were kids every time she wanted to escape the blame for something. It always worked because Da was daft with her.'

'I'm not crying,' said Lucy, scrubbing at her face with a corner of the sheet.

'So it's rainwater coming from your eyes then?'

She looked at him and surprisingly he crossed his eyes. A giggle rose like a bubble in her throat.

He grinned. 'That's better. You mustn't let things get to you.'

'It's OK for you to say that,' she protested, pulling the bedcovers up to her chin. 'You didn't go through what I've been through!'

He protested. 'My head was split open! Your uncle could have killed me.'

'He was going to do horrible things to me so I hit him on the head with his gun after I'd knocked it out of his hand,' Lucy babbled. 'He'd still be alive if I hadn't done that.' Rob stared at her and there was no longer anything remotely funny about him. Lucy's mouth felt dry. 'Does that make me a murderess?' she whispered, the blood like ice in her veins.

He cleared his throat. 'They could have you up in court for manslaughter. You could claim it was self-defence. Even so, you'd go to prison.'

All other sounds in the ward seemed to fade away and they were alone, just the two of them,

164

cut off from the rest of the world. Lucy wondered what it was about Rob that had drawn that confession from her? 'You're frightening me,' she croaked, her eyes fixed on his worried face.

'There's no need to be. I'm just warning you of the consequences of repeating what you've just said to anyone else. I didn't hear it. Understand, Lucy? I didn't hear what you said. Everyone's convinced he was having a nap and died in the fire.'

'Poor Uncle Mick,' she said raggedly. 'What turned him into a monster? He used to be such fun. A couple of years ago I thought that when he came home everything would be marvellous. We'd get out of that hole and Mam'd be happy. Instead . . .' She stopped and swallowed. Tears ran down her cheeks.

Rob took her hand and squeezed it. 'You have to try and forget what happened,' he said firmly. 'I know it won't be easy but at least you won't be going back to that house. It's a wreck. So, in a roundabout way, he got you what you wanted.' Rob released her hand and leaned back in his chair. He folded his arms and forced a smile. 'I don't mean to sound callous so let's change the subject. Anything else you'd like out of life?'

She rubbed her eyes and after a few moments managed to say, 'Lots of money and peace of mind.'

He ignored the latter half of the sentence. 'Money's important to you?'

'I like to eat and I'd love to wear clothes like your sister's. I did manage to save some money once but me and Timmy got hungry.'

165

'I guess you're fond of your brother.'

'Of course.' Her eyes widened. 'What a question!'

'You'd want to keep him safe. Yourself and your mam as well.' His words puzzled her.

'Why do you ask?'

He hesitated. 'Shaun O'Neill. Do you know where he's hiding?'

Her smile faded. So that was why he was here. She'd been daft to think he'd be bothered about a kid like her. 'No,' she said shortly. 'And I don't want to know either.'

'He went to your house.'

'But I had nothing to do with that! I'm no criminal!' She realised what she had said and the colour drained from her cheeks. Of course she was! She was responsible for Mick's death and she wanted to weep again. 'Go! Please go,' she whispered. 'I don't feel well.'

Rob sighed, his hands clasped between his knees. 'Don't look like that, kid. I don't want to upset you but I have a job to do. I know rebels like O'Neill and their cause can hold an attraction for families like yours. I can understand love for one's country but he's trouble, so if you know anything about him, tell me.'

'Is that an order?' She felt all strung up. 'Is that a "tell me or else I'll throw you in prison"?'

He scowled at her. 'No, it bloody isn't! I just thought if you had a childish fancy for Shaun O'Neill and favour his cause, you should rid yourself of it.'

'I haven't! He has spots and shifty eyes and is as mean as they come.'

'That's all you can tell me about him?'

Lucy shrugged. 'What else is there to tell? I don't know where he is.'

'Right.' Rob looked disappointed as he stood up. When he next spoke his words surprised her. 'Has your mother told you where she and your brother are living now?'

Lucy shook her head. She hadn't given it much thought. She waited for him to tell her but all he said was, 'I'm sure she'll enjoy informing you. 'Bye, Lucy. Hope you're out of hospital soon. My aunt and Dilys wouldn't mind you calling on them. They think you've got guts – so do I. See you.'

He replaced his cap and she watched him stroll up the ward like he didn't have a care in the world. Yet they shared a terrible secret and her freedom depended on his keeping his mouth shut. But why should he? He was someone who believed in law and order. A man who upheld the ten commandments. *Thou shalt not kill!* The thought of Mick caused such a heaviness within her breast it was a struggle to hold back the tears. Her head began to ache.

She glanced at the chair where Rob had sat and only then did she notice the box of chocolates on the seat. His gift confused her. Why had he done that? And why was he prepared to let her off scotfree? She could only believe that maybe he liked her, just a little. She burrowed down in the bed, wishing he hadn't come, realising that she wanted much more from him.

'Lucy, darlin'! Give us a kiss!' The strain of the

167

last few weeks showed in Maureen's face as she clutched her daughter's hand. 'Sister said you'd spoken at last. Pity it had to be to a policeman. Questions, questions! But I played dumb and I hope you didn't tell him too much?' her mother said brightly. 'Anyway, it's all over now. Callum's out of it in Ireland, but God only knows where that fella O'Neill is – that's what they want to know. Seems he's been involved in some protection racket with our Mick. They weren't after him just because of terrorist activities at all.'

Lucy wondered why Rob hadn't told her that but maybe he thought he'd said enough to her. Crazy, she thought, and tried to put Shaun and Rob and Mick out of her mind, but the latter two continued to lurk there on the edge of consciousness. 'Can I go home, Mam? And where is home these days?'

Her mother smirked. 'Now that would be telling and I'm not doing that – not just yet. You'll just have to wait and see ... but I think you'll be pleased. We all hated that horrible, unhappy, dingy house. I never had any luck from the moment I went to live there. Hopefully our luck's changed now.'

Lucy remembered a conversation she'd had once with Mrs Malone in the cinema about luck. She just hoped as a family they'd done with bad luck and from now on things would only get better.

Lucy linked arms with her mother as they walked through the gates of Stanley Road Hospital and turned in the direction of the Rotunda Theatre.

Her legs felt wobbly and her head a bit peculiar. She'd had too much time to think in the gap between Rob's visit and her mother's. Even Lucy's dreams had been haunted by visions of Uncle Mick, screaming at her to rescue him from the flames. Yet in reality he had done no such thing the day he'd died so horribly.

Even now, outside in the fresh air, Lucy was asking herself whether he had felt anything as the flames had licked his body? She tried to imagine what it must have felt like and it was as if thousands of goosebumps covered her skin.

'You shivered then. Someone walk over your grave?' asked her mother with a smile. 'You can't be cold. It's a lovely day. Perhaps it's nerves. You've been through such a lot. Maybe you'd like to talk about it?'

'No!' said Lucy baldly. 'I want to forget it.'

'That policeman said you were a heroine.'

'Did he?' She gave her mother a startled, almost horrified, look.

'He said you really tried to save Mick's life.' Maureen sighed and the corners of her mouth drooped. 'I never did like having that paraffin in the house.'

'No,' murmured Lucy, with an overwhelming urge to tell the truth. That she had tried to save him but only because she was responsible for his being unconscious. She told herself it wouldn't serve any useful purpose. Her mother would certainly not turn her in to the police, but she would see her with different eyes. Besides, if Lucy told the truth she would have to tell Maureen what Mick had said, and had in his

169

mind to do with her, when he threw her on the bed, and that would upset her mother further. No, it was best to stay silent.

Lucy had no sooner come to that decision than she began to ponder on whether she should go and confess to a priest – seek absolution and rid herself of her burden of guilt. After all, wasn't that what priests were for? But she hadn't been to church for ages and maybe he'd try and persuade her to give herself up to the law. She would have to go over and over it again, telling them what had happened in the bedroom when she had hit Mick. She hardened her heart. No, he had betrayed her trust. Had had to be stopped because otherwise he would just have carried on hitting them all, and he could have killed someone with those explosives. She had done the right thing. Even so she felt depressed, part of her grieving for the man her uncle had once been.

She felt a tug on her arm and realised Maureen had paused in front of a shop window displaying women's fashions. Lucy gazed wistfully at a nifty model in jade green with black spots, and remembered what she'd said to Rob about money and what he'd said to her. Give herself a few years and hopefully she wouldn't know herself. And neither would he. She'd like to show him how good she could look then. Although maybe it was best if she kept her distance from him. Would she ever be able to look at him without thinking that he was the only person in the whole world who knew she had been responsible for her own uncle's death? She sighed. Wording it like that felt just as bad as using the

M word. M! Murder! Money! She had to make some money and leave this area. To get away from the memories. Everything boiled down to having money.

'One day,' said her mother, without Lucy saying anything.

The girl glanced at her and forced a smile as they carried on walking. After a few minutes Lucy could sense tension within her mother as if she was working herself up to say something. Dear God, make it not be about Mick, she thought.

'I found an extra money pouch in your clothes,' said Maureen. 'There was five shillings in copper in it. Where did it come from? Did our Mick give it to you?' Her voice shook.

At the mention of her uncle's name yet again Lucy wanted to screw herself up into a ball and hide in a hole. 'No!' she cried. 'I wouldn't touch his money. He offered me a shilling to tell him more about Barney and Rob but I refused it. I've been taking threepence out of the firewood money every day since Gran died. I was scared when you started drinking! Felt I couldn't depend on you. I didn't want Timmy and me going hungry.'

'Well!' Her mother took several deep breaths and there was a surprised look in her eyes. 'You sneaky thing! I should be angry about that, but I'm just glad it wasn't our Mick that gave it to you for services rendered.'

Lucy stared at her, guessing what she was talking about. There were two spots of colour high on Maureen's cheekbones. 'Forget what I

171

said. I can see you're innocent of that and I'm glad, girl, very glad.' She leaned towards her daughter and kissed her cheek. 'I loved Mick. He was my brother and I loved him, but I'm glad he died before he completely destroyed every warm feeling I ever had for him. A man needs a woman. If our Mick hadn't gone off to war – if he had found himself a wife – maybe he wouldn't have gone off the rails. I just pray that God'll forgive him. I pray and pray.'

Lucy felt as if she had a lump in her throat as big as a marble and lowered her head, gazing at the pavement. She pretended to concentrate on avoiding cracks in the pavement.

'You, Lucy, will save yourself for your husband, I'm sure of that. You're a sensible girl.'

'I don't want a husband,' she murmured. 'I think they could be a lot of trouble. I'll make my own money!'

Maureen laughed. 'I wish you luck, girl! I really do. Some men can be a pain in the backside, but we can't live without them.' She turned into Great Homer Street and headed for Everton Heights, much to Lucy's surprise.

Eventually her mother stopped in front of a four-storey house on Northumberland Terrace, not far from St George's church. A flight of steep steps led to an open front door which was flanked on the right by a bay window. There was a basement below and two storeys above. A toddler was sitting on the bottom step, playing with a pullalong wooden horse on wheels.

'This house belongs to Mr Jones,' said Maureen, almost bursting with pride and pleasure. 'I can tell you, Luce, he's come up trumps. As soon as he knew I was homeless he found me a place here. It's split into apartments. Imagine the rents coming in!'

Lucy could easily do that but hoped her mother wasn't getting herself all excited for nothing. She presumed they also were being charged.

'We're on the top floor which is a bit cheaper than down below,' said Maureen, climbing the steps. 'He wanted the one on the ground floor for me but his sister-in-law insisted on moving the old couple from upstairs down into the empty one. I'm sure she only did it so he couldn't come calling because stairs give him trouble with his gammy leg.'

Lucy, who was counting the steps (there were nine), thought it was nice of the sister-in-law. A man mightn't have thought of the difficulties old people have climbing stairs.

From behind a door came the plaintive wailing of a violin. Lucy wished they'd liven the tune up a bit. She was beginning to feel excited about the move, despite the smell of cooked cabbage and fish on the landing. There was also a hint of gas and something more unsanitary in the air.

'There's a lavatory on the floor below ours and one in the yard,' whispered Maureen, panting a little as they came to the top floor. 'It beats sharing a privy.' She inserted a key in the lock and pushed open a brown-painted door.

Sunlight flooded the patch of linoleum where they stood and the heaviness in Lucy's heart lifted as she walked inside the room. The furniture was new, or at least new to her. Had her

173

mother been able to rescue anything of theirs from the burning house? Then she saw on the mantelpiece above the fireplace several photographs. She hurried over and recognised the one of her parents on their wedding day, and herself as a seven year old with Timmy as a baby taken in a studio in Church Street. There was also the one of Mick in Army uniform. She couldn't take her gaze from that one. It was as if his eyes were reproaching her. She wanted to slam it away in a drawer.

'I'd like to remember him that way,' said Maureen, sitting on the sofa with a relieved sigh. 'What do you think of the place? Not bad, is it?'

Lucy glanced at the pale blue walls and then up at the high ceiling with its three-lamped gaslight and knew she had to start putting on the act of her life, pretending something she did not feel for her mother's sake, or they'd all end up miserable. 'It's so bright and roomy. It's great!' She went over to the window and gazed out, careful not to lean on the arm which had been burned.

Instantly she was reminded of the day she had stood on the steps of St George's church. The sea! She could just about see the sea. 'It's lovely! Really lovely.'

'I knew you'd like it.' Her mother sounded delighted. 'Although it has its drawbacks. There's the climb, and the kitchen's downstairs which we have to share. That has a gas stove, but I've been cooking on the fire up here. It's not what we're used to – no oven – but I've managed.' She grimaced. 'The other drawback is – herself! Mr Jones's sister-in-law. She doesn't approve of me.'

'What's she like?' Lucy feigned interest.

'No beauty! And won't see thirty-five again.'

Lucy turned away from the window and sat beside her mother. 'I bet she's jealous of your looks.'

Maureen lifted a hand and stroked Lucy's hair. 'She's from Lancashire but met Mr Jones's brother when he was stationed in the South of England before going off to France. She was visiting her sister who has since died. She must have been years older than him, but perhaps he was looking for a mother figure.'

'Will I get to meet her?'

'She collects the rents. Unusual a woman doing it but Barney said it's because of his foot.'

Lucy wondered why he hadn't got a man but perhaps he didn't have to pay his sister-in-law. 'Are you managing the rent OK, Mam?'

Maureen nodded and gave a sigh. 'I'll manage better, though, once you're back on your round again. Your cart's in the little room next to this one. And that reminds me.' She stood up. 'I'll have to get moving. I've work to go to.'

'At this time of day?' said Lucy, surprised, following her out of the room and into another which contained a double bed and a tallboy. She raised her eyebrows. 'Where's this come from?'

Maureen looked embarrassed. 'That bobby Rob arranged it for us. Some benevolent fund. I wanted to refuse but Mr Jones said the boy meant well.' She took out an overall.

Boy? thought Lucy. He was a man! But she did not want to think of Rob. He knew too much about her, was too old for her – and so she was

175

never going to get married. Suddenly Lucy noticed the overall her mother was wearing. 'Have you changed your job?'

Maureen smiled. 'I have. By the way, if you want something to eat while I'm out, there's food in a cupboard in the little room next to the front one. Our dishes are there, too, and there's a cupboard on the landing for coal. I don't need to tell you to be careful when cooking on that fire.' She stared at her daughter intently, then surprised Lucy by placing a hand on her cheek and stroking it. 'I'm glad to have you back. The keys are in the door.'

Her mother had worked fast, thought Lucy, following her to the door. 'Where's this job?'

'Cinema in town that Mr Jones has an interest in. He's got rid of the other. I'm not a cleaner anymore.' Maureen smiled and went out before her daughter could ask what the new job was.

She took the keys from the door and decided to go in search of her cart. She discovered the axe inside it and wondered who'd had the sense to rescue it from the burning house.

It was noisy trundling the cart down two flights of stairs. A door opened at one point and a balding man popped his head out and told her to stop making that racket. She pretended not to have heard. When she reached the front steps and bump-bumped the cart down them as well, she promised herself not to go up those steps and stairs again. She would find the back door and do her chopping in the yard, leaving the loaded cart there.

Miss Griffiths was in the office when Lucy

arrived at the timber yard. 'Hello, lovey! It's nice to see you.' She gazed across the desk and there was sympathy in her eyes. 'You ready to start work already? You've no colour in your cheeks. What you need is to convalesce. Lots of lovely fresh sea air! The sort you get holidaying on the Welsh coast.'

'That sounds nice,' said Lucy politely. 'But we haven't got that kind of money.'

'Money! Money!' Miss Griffiths made a noise in her throat. 'What's the use of having money if you can't help people with it? I'll write a note to your mother and see what she says. I've family you can go to. As for your chopping wood into chips, my girl, I think it's best I get one of the men to do that. We don't want you tiring that sore arm of yours when you've only just come out of hospital.'

Lucy had known Miss Griffiths to be a kind woman but felt a bit uncomfortable at this overwhelming concern, but she couldn't turn down the offer and so it was she returned to Northumberland Terrace with the note burning a hole in her pocket. A holiday in Wales! Would her mother agree to that? She had never had a proper holiday before. Neither had Timmy. Thinking of her brother made her realise her mother hadn't mentioned where he was. It was still the school holidays so she presumed he was out with his friends somewhere.

She did not have to wait too long to see him and he was obviously glad to see her, surprising her by giving her a hug and asking after her arm.

'It's still sore but it's getting better.'

'Can I have a look?' His eyes were alight with interest. 'Mam said some of your skin had burned off.'

Lucy laughed. 'You're a real ghoul, you are!'

'But I've never seen skin coming off.' He bent his head so that his nose almost touched her arm. 'What's underneath? Blood?'

'Some. But you have more skin underneath. It's still a bit of a mess and I have to keep it covered so I don't get septicaemia. If I did, that could be me gone,' she said, attempting to make a joke of it.

'You mustn't get dirt in it then. I don't want you to die.' Timmy's expression changed. 'I'm glad Uncle Mick's dead, though,' he said frankly, straightening up and sliding his hands into his trouser pockets. 'They said you tried to save him. You must have been mad, it nearly killed you.'

For a moment she couldn't think what to say to that but eventually all she could do was agree with her brother that she must indeed have been mad. Her spirits felt a bit lighter. After all, she *had* risked her life trying to save Mick's.

Lucy did not get to give her mother the note from Rob's aunt until the following morning. Maureen had not come in until way past midnight but at least the girl knew now what her job was in the new cinema in town. She was a waitress. Sometimes Barney also worked at the same cinema, playing the organ, although more often than not they had a full orchestra in residence. It was a real classy place.

As it happened Barney and his sister-in-law were in the house when Lucy handed over the note to her mother who immediately took it downstairs to consult Barney about what she should do.

'Eeeh! I never in all my born days heard anything like it!' said Winnie, the sister-in-law, gazing down her long nose at Lucy. 'What's she wanting a holiday for? Work, that's what the girl needs to help her forget her aches and pains.'

'We're not all as strong as you, Winnie,' said Barney, shaking his head and smiling at Lucy. 'She's lost all her colour.'

Lucy beamed at him, thinking she could depend on him not to have changed, to be kind to her. She could smell his hair oil helping to dispel the cooking odours coming from the kitchen as they stood in the lobby.

'I think it's really generous of her to offer,' said Maureen, her eyes luminous as she gazed at Barney. 'I don't like to say no.' They were all standing in the lobby.

'Can I go as well?' asked Timmy.

'Eeeh! *You're* not ill, lad!' said Winnie, snapping her teeth together. She was dressed in black and her clothes had last been fashionable during the war. She had a wart on her chin and bristling brows hooded deep-set eyes. Not surprisingly she was known as Winnie the Witch by the tenants.

'He is prone to chests,' said Maureen, gazing at her son anxiously. 'It would really do him good to have a holiday.'

'I haven't heard him wheezing,' objected Winnie.

Maureen coloured. 'That's because I look after him, but a nice trip to the seaside or the country would set him up for the winter.'

'She's right there, Winnie!' said Barney, grinning. 'You're forever lauding the country air.'

'Eeeh, I should have stayed there,' she sniffed, 'but when I married your brother I felt it my duty to come here and look after your ailing mother. With all my family dead I'd nowt to keep me there but if my opinion doesn't count, I can easily up sticks and leave.'

'No, no, there's no need for that,' said Barney hastily, placing an arm about her shoulders, causing both Maureen and Lucy to glance at each other in surprise. 'We need you here. I don't know what I'd have done without you since Mam went.'

Winnie looked mollified and patted his hand. 'I hope you mean that, lad. Right! I've a suggestion to make.'

'What's that, lovey?' Barney's expression was attentive.

'Why doesn't Mrs Linden take her daughter to Llandudno by steamer on her day off and the girl can be picked up from there? The lad can go with her for the outing. The sea air will blow his pipes clean through. It'll be as good as a tonic.'

Lucy thought it a good idea though her mother looked none too pleased. Again Barney enthused. 'Marvellous idea, Winnie! It'll do Mrs Linden good, too.' He turned to Maureen and beamed at her. 'It will, you know!'

'Oh, yes, it's a grand idea!' Her smile was fixed. 'But perhaps your sister-in-law can tell me how I'm going to pay for the tickets? Not that I wouldn't sacrifice everything I have for my son. I'll maybe pawn the bed and we'll sleep on the floor.'

'Eeeh, woman, you're being right daft! I'll find you the money,' said Winnie, sounding suddenly enthusiastic. 'There's plenty of charities that'll cough up for an outing for those that can't help themselves. In fact, I'm sure I'd be able to get enough money for you and the lad to have a holiday as well! I can put forward a good case, what with your house burning down.'

Lucy was thrilled. What was wrong with her mother that she didn't like Winnie? The girl would love their company rather than being on her own with strangers. She glanced at her mother's tight expression and hoped she wouldn't let her dislike of Winnie and hurt pride get in the way. But before Maureen could say anything Winnie made for the front door, oblivious to any offence she might have given.

Lucy thought her mother was going to explode when the door closed but Barney must have foreseen such an eventuality because he seized her hands and said hastily, 'Her intentions are good!'

'She has no idea how to handle people,' said Maureen, her voice shaking. 'If she knew what it was to be in my shoes... My family once had a position in the world. As you know, Mr Jones, I haven't always been poor.'

'You must forgive her. She came here with my brother and within days she'd taken charge of the whole household. "A right bossy piece" Mam called her.'

'Well, she's not bossing me and mine about,' said Maureen, removing her hands from his grasp. 'Anyway, how can I take anything she says

181

seriously when she changes her mind like a weathercock?'

'She realised there was something in what you said. Please, Mrs Linden – Maureen – don't be upset.' He seized her hands again. 'You know how fond I am of you. I don't like it when you get upset.'

Lucy was relieved that this time her mother left her hands where they were. 'I'm thinking that maybe she wants to get rid of me for a few days,' said Maureen stiffly. 'She doesn't like it that you take a kindly interest in me and mine.'

'No, no! It's not that. She's a little bit too possessive, maybe. Likes to mother me. But that's all it is, lovey.'

There was a long silence. Finally Maureen said playfully, 'You don't think she's jealous of me then?'

'If she is, can you blame her? It's lovely you are!'

Maureen's chest visibly swelled. 'I was thinking I was losing my looks. I was thinking I'm not getting any younger. It really upset me, the fire and our Mick's death. I felt it aged me ten years.'

'Never! But if you're feeling like that then a week in Wales will do you a world of good.' Barney squeezed her hand between both of his and, raising it to his lips, kissed the tips of her fingers. 'And I'll make you a promise now to take a day off and come and visit you.'

Much to Lucy's relief those words changed her mother's mind. All they had to do now was wait for Winnie to come up trumps and provide the money.

Chapter Ten

The sun shimmered on the river as Lucy and Timmy raced ahead of their mother down the floating roadbridge to the Pierhead. It took some skill, avoiding the vehicles which queued for the luggage boat that would take them across the river. There had been talk for years of a tunnel being built under the Mersey because of such tail-backs but it had yet to materialise. Timmy was so excited he hardly stopped talking, continually asking questions about Llandudno which Lucy could not answer. In the end he ran back to Maureen, who was carrying the suitcase Barney had loaned them, but she only replied, 'Wait and see.'

Being patient was not easy for either Lucy or Timmy. This was a real holiday, unlike the brief one they'd spent in Ireland. As soon as they were aboard the steamer Lucy led the way up to the top deck so they could gaze at the ships being loaded at the docks. At Seaforth the new Gladstone dock had yet to be completed. Seagulls screeched overhead, dipping and gliding. Dredgers were busily employed in keeping the channels from silting up between the sandbanks.

Once past the bar they were out in the Irish Sea and a stiff breeze got up, whipping Lucy's hair about her face. The salt-laden air was fresh, even a little on the chilly side, making her feel as if she was being doused in cold water, having her sins washed away. It made her feel clean all over. Surely God would forgive her? She hadn't meant Mick to die and after all it was the fire that had really done for him. She hadn't been responsible for paraffin being stored under the bed.

'I think I'll go down below,' said her mother. 'You'll keep your eye on Timmy, Lucy?'

The girl nodded and looked round for her brother. He was kneeling beside an elderly woman, stroking her dog and chattering away to her with all the chirpiness of a sparrow. Lucy smiled, thinking that this holiday was just the ticket to get them all on their feet, ready to face the future. She had to forget the past. She started concentrating on what they might do in the days ahead: building sandcastles and paddling in the sea; eating big meals for once instead of skimpy ones. Funds had been provided for full board in a guest house for a whole week. They'd even been given pocket money.

Lucy had been amazed by the speed with which everything had happened. As a result of Winnie's interference the plan to send Lucy to Miss Griffiths' relatives had been dropped. A trust fund which had been set up to provide holidays for overworked mothers and their children had paid for a family trip instead. Even so Barney had given a florin to Lucy and a sixpence to Timmy. They had thanked him profusely. Aunt Mac had also been generous, providing Lucy and Timmy with secondhand outfits from Paddy's Market. 'We can't have you looking like scruffs and shaming us,' she'd said gruffly. Even the weather promised to hold fair for them.

Now Lucy gazed dreamily at the Welsh coast, thinking of dragons and castles. A young man came and stood a foot or so away from her and she found herself weighing him up. Was he the dependable type? You just couldn't go by looks, she thought sadly, thinking of the young Mick in the photograph on the mantelshelf. Once more her heart felt leaden. She forced herself to concentrate on the view. A moment later the young man was joined at the rail by a young woman. So much for thinking he might start chatting me up, thought Lucy wryly.

But soon she found herself listening with interest as he extolled the attractions of each seaside resort on the North Welsh coast: Rhyl ... Abergele ... Colwyn Bay ... Llanfairfechan, near Conway with its castle and bustling harbour. There was no doubting the man's love for his homeland and she remembered what Rob had said about such patriotism. Her emotions were confused whenever she thought about him, which was too often for her peace of mind. She had not seen him since he had visited her in hospital and in a way that was a relief for how could she look him in the face with him knowing what he did about her? Why couldn't she have kept her big mouth shut!

At last they reached their destination. Llandudno was situated on a wide sweep of a bay. Barney had told them it had once been a fishing village but was now the largest of the Welsh resorts. They disembarked at the pier to find the son of their landlady waiting with a horse and trap to ferry them and their luggage to the guest house on Mostyn Street.

He winked at Lucy and she thought a flirtation might be in order but when he spoke his Welsh accent was so strong she knew they would have difficulty understanding each other. He was much too young for her anyway. She preferred a real man, and again found herself thinking of Rob and Mick and what constituted a real man.

As they bowled along her mother compared the place to Liverpool. There had been no scruffy, bare-footed youths fighting to carry their bags, such as you'd find at the Pierhead, and the air was sweet, smelling of sea and countryside. It seemed another world, just like Ireland had.

No sooner were their belongings unpacked and they had washed their hands and face in the flower-sprigged bowl in their room than a gong sounded below.

'What's that?' Timmy had wrapped himself in the lambswool rug on the floor and was pretending to be a sheep.

'It's telling us it's time to eat,' said his mother, smoothing the lace collar on her black frock as she gazed at her reflection in the dressing-table mirror.

The trip from Liverpool had taken just over two hours and lunch was about to be served. Lucy couldn't wait.

The landlady served fish caught only that morning, boiled potatoes and green peas, and there was to be pudding as well. The sea air had put a real edge on Lucy's appetite and she ate the lot. Feeling stuffed to the gills by the time she'd finished, she decided if every meal was going to be as good as this one then the holiday would be perfect.

It *was* perfect. There was the occasional sea mist in the early morning but it was nothing compared to the fogs which could envelop the streets of Liverpool come winter. It soon evaporated and the sun shone.

Every morning after breakfast Maureen insisted they walk around the shops or along the promenade but afterwards they spent most of the day on the beach. Lucy helped Timmy build sandcastles as best she could with one hand, her arm still being sore, but most of the time she lazed in the sun, reading Florence Barclay's *The Rosary*, reputed to have been read and wept over by every housemaid in the British Isles. She could see why and would have preferred a happier read but it was a library book and there was no way she could change it on holiday.

The highlight of their week was the two whole days, not one, which Barney spent with them. He took them up the Great Orme on the railway where they could see right across the sea to Anglesey. They also went to the Pier Pavilion Theatre. Maureen sparkled in his company, laughing as she hadn't done for a long time. Lucy noticed that finally they'd dropped the formality of surnames and were on first-name terms. They held hands as they walked along the promenade and Lucy knew that all that was needed to make this holiday utterly unforgettable was for him to pop the question.

Whether he did or not Lucy was not to know

but she guessed he must have said something promising because after his departure her mother sat staring into space with a tiny smile playing round her mouth.

Two days later they caught the steamer back to Liverpool. The next day was Sunday and to Lucy's surprise Maureen suggested they attend St George's church. Lucy stared at her, thinking Dilys and her aunt would be there. Perhaps Rob, too. Could she depend on him not to have mentioned what she had told him to his sister? 'I'd rather not,' she muttered.

Her mother frowned at her reflection in the mirror as she twisted a curl round her finger and patted it into place. 'I want you with me. I won't have the nerve to do it without you.'

'Then why do it at all?' Lucy clasped her shaking hands together. 'You're a Catholic.'

Maureen made an exasperated sound in her throat. 'Use your commonsense. You like Barney, don't you? I'm sure, like me, you'd find it comfortable living under his roof. I'm sick of struggling to make ends meet and waiting for Callum to show sense. Wasn't it lovely having that holiday in Wales? Wasn't it grand when Barney was with us? I'm thinking if I go to his church he'll see there's nothing to keep us apart. I've even thought of sending Timmy to St George's school. It would make sense with us living so near.'

'Even so,' said Lucy, picking up the Sunday paper, 'I'd rather not go.'

Maureen slammed a fist down on the table. 'You'll do as I say! This could change our lives.

So get yourself ready.'

Lucy backed down, hoping to get in and out of church before anyone could speak to her.

It was obvious their presence at St George's pleased Barney. Lucy could see no sign of Rob, and was relieved; but Dilys and her aunt were there and so were Owen and his mother. They were all members of the choir and she had to give them their due, the singing was glorious. Afterwards she was unable to escape swiftly because her mother made a beeline for Barney. At the same time Dilys and her aunt spotted Lucy and expressed their delight to see her, asking how she had enjoyed herself in Wales and what she was doing in their church.

Lucy realised her fears were unfounded. 'It was lovely,' she said, returning their smiles. 'And Mam liked the Welsh so much she decided we had to come here and listen to you singing.'

'Can you sing, Lucy?' asked Dilys eagerly. 'You should join our choir.'

Lucy was alarmed, knowing if she was roped into the choir there was no getting out of coming to church every week. Rob was bound to come some time and she was best avoiding him. She told them her singing was only fit for the cat's ears, which made them laugh. Then Owen came up and asked what was so funny. Lucy hastily excused herself and left. Things had gone better than she had expected but that didn't mean that next time they would, too. Her own guilt had weighed heavy on her when it had come to the general confession. Yet it was so easy to confess your sins and be absolved in the Protestant church. No need to squirm alone in the confessional.

Her mother was not pleased when Lucy made no move to get ready for church the following week. 'I want you with me. This isn't easy for me, you know! I'm doing it for you and Timmy.'

Lucy wondered if that was true but accepted her mother's words at face value and once again gave in and went with her. She did not feel so bad the second time, especially as the sermon was about forgiveness and Jesus being like a shepherd, caring for his lost sheep. The thought comforted her. Sometimes she felt very lost and alone.

Money was still a problem in the Linden household. By asking around Lucy managed to find herself an evening job, cleaning offices down by the Pierhead, and what with that and her firewood round she managed to start putting a little aside again most weeks.

She had wondered why Rob had not been in church but put it down to his working long hours because of his job. His being a plain clothes detective reminded her of her grandfather talking about the time there had been uproar in Liverpool when a chief constable had first introduced plain-clothed policemen to mingle in pubs and clubs in an attempt to cut down on drunkenness and gambling. She presumed that was still part of a detective's job on a Saturday night.

So the months passed and Lucy and her mother became familiar faces at St George's. Lucy caught sight of Rob only twice during that time and he vanished before any words could be exchanged between them. She wished she knew what he made of their being there but did not like to ask Dilys. There was only one person who didn't appear pleased to see them and that was Winnie. Lucy waited for her mother to break the news to her that Barney had popped the question, but waited and waited in vain.

In December it seemed like the troubles in Ireland had come to an end at last when a treaty was signed in London making Ireland a free state. Michael Collins, the leader of the IRA, said that it would give the Irish people the freedom to win freedom. Lucy wondered if Callum would come home to Liverpool and wished Barney would make a move but Christmas came and still Maureen didn't wear his ring.

Early in 1922 Barney took the whole family to the pantomime at the Rotunda Theatre. Lucy thought, This is it! He's asked Mam to marry him and they're going to break the news to us. But that proved to be wishful thinking.

When they arrived home from the pantomime her mother threw herself into a chair and sat with her chin in her hand, gazing moodily at the embers of the fire. 'The man's dithering! It's that Winnie. He doesn't want to upset her, but it's time he told her to go. The trouble is he's just too nice for his own good.'

Lucy agreed. But what could they do? She herself often felt restless, as if she was marking time, waiting for something to happen in her own life that would rid her of her guilt. She had started to make sweets again but standing out-side picture houses at this time of year and then cleaning offices, just like selling firewood on the streets, was no picnic and certainly not a quick way to get rich. But then, most people in Liverpool didn't have enough food to keep body and soul together and she knew she should be thankful for what she had. Times were hard and the ranks of the unemployed were growing every day.

One day Lucy felt drawn to her old area so made her way down to Bostock Street. She had not been there since the fire and as she came out of the passage into the court a couple of women glanced her way. One smiled and asked how she was. 'OK. I never thought I'd miss this place and...' She glanced about her and knew she'd been mad to come. Perhaps she'd come to lay a ghost. She still had nightmares about that day her uncle had died. She gazed up at the remains of her old home. Its walls were blackened by smoke and the window frames and door were completely gone. She went and climbed the steps.

'Yous be careful, luv!' shouted one of the women. 'Some say it's haunted. Don't yous be going inside unless yer want it to come crashing down on yer!'

Haunted? Lucy felt a prickle at the back of her neck. She could hear the wind whistling down the chimney. Was that her uncle screaming at her to save him? She heard what sounded like footsteps and didn't hang around but beat a hasty retreat.

By the time she reached Northumberland Terrace she had calmed down, only to come face to face with Owen.

He was wearing a suit and looked reasonably smart. 'Well, if it isn't Lucy Locket, all alone for once, getting grown up and beginning to look good.'

'You can stick your compliments,' she said, with a toss of the head. 'I still haven't forgiven you for pinching my round.'

'That's old news.' He lit a cigarette and blew smoke in her face, causing her to step back. 'I did you a good turn. I've seen you selling your wood and your toffee apples. I broke the mould, made you think of other ways to make money. I have thought, though, maybe you and me should go into business together.'

She screwed up her face and looked at him incredulously. 'Business? You and me? You have to be joking! I wouldn't trust you as far as I could throw you.' She turned and walked away.

He followed her and seized hold of her wrist. She struggled to free herself but he yanked her other arm and pulled her round to face him. 'Now listen to me, I'm serious.'

He looked it, too, but if he thought she was going to get involved in anything to do with him he'd have to think again. 'I don't want to listen! Let me go!'

Suddenly a voice Lucy recognised said, 'You heard the girl! Let her go!' A hand caught Owen on the side of the face and knocked him off balance. Callum stood gazing down at him. 'Scram before I catch you another clout, me laddo.'

Owen got to his feet and glowered at him. 'You had no right to do that. Who are you anyway?'

'It doesn't matter who he is,' said Lucy with a grin. 'You just beat it.'

Owen's eyes met hers. 'You'll regret turning my offer down. See you in church.' He swaggered off.

Lucy turned to Callum and her expression changed. 'What are you doing here?' she said, thinking the last thing she wanted was him coming between her mother and Barney again.

Callum tucked his hands into his pockets and smiled down at her, rocking backwards and forwards on his heels. 'Now don't be like that, Luce. Didn't I just play the knight in shining armour and rescue you from that lad's attentions?'

She could not deny that. 'What d'you want?' Her voice was a little friendlier because she had changed her mind. Maybe a bit of competition might egg Barney on to make a move in the direction of marriage.

'To see your Mam, of course. If you'll be so good as to show me where you're living now.'

She was unsure of her ground here. 'I'm not certain Mam'll want to see you.'

'Aw! Your mammy doesn't know what she wants. Her middle name should have been Contrary. I know she's still seeing that piano player and going to his church. Ma's not pleased about that.'

Lucy bristled, not liking to hear Barney being referred to in such a way. He was much more than just a piano player. 'And if she is, what's it to do with you? You've been in Ireland for I don't know how long and we've got on very well

194

without you. They've made us very welcome.'

Callum scowled. 'Don't cheek me, girl! I'm telling you, she'll be happier with me than him. It's only his money she's after.'

Lucy did not believe her mother was solely after Barney's money. He was a lovely man and much better looking than Callum, who had a long nose and bushy hair and terrible taste in clothes.

'Believe me, girl, I'm telling you the truth!' he said, sounding exasperated. 'I love her and want to marry her. Now show me where you live.'

Lucy came to a decision. Her mother should see their old friend, if for no other reason than to tell him he was wasting his time.

'I won't go away, girl,' said Callum, smiling grimly. 'I'll dog your footsteps.'

'OK! I'll take you up there,' Lucy said abruptly. 'But don't you go middering Mam.'

He grinned and ruffled her hair. 'You're a sensible girl, Lucy. You'll see, she'll be glad you did.'

But when they reached the flat it was to find it empty. 'I'll wait,' said Callum, going over to the window and gazing out. 'Nice view. Belong to him, does it? I tell you, Lucy, I don't like it. I don't like his being her landlord at all. He'll take advantage. She should have gone and lived with Mam. The trouble is that piano player has filled her head with fancy ideas that'll take her away from her own kind. She'll be better with me.'

'How can you be so sure about that?' Lucy sat on the sofa. 'Maybe you were thinking of taking her back to Ireland?'

He took his pipe out of his pocket and fiddled

195

with it. 'I'd thought of it, yes. But there could be more trouble there and I wouldn't want anything happening to her. It's safer here. Now, how about a cup of tea?'

Lucy stood up. She wouldn't mind a cup herself but the fire needed a match to it and so she decided to go downstairs. 'I'll be back in a minute.'

'If you see your mother, tell her to hurry,' Callum called after her.

Lucy was on her way back up and had almost reached their landing when she heard her mother talking to one of the other tenants on the ground floor. She called down. 'Mam, Callum's up here!'

The voices stopped and the next minute Lucy heard Maureen's footsteps on the stairs. The girl waited for her to catch up with her. 'Callum, you say?' Maureen's face was pale and her eyes uncertain.

Lucy was about to explain what had happened when he appeared in their doorway, pipe in hand. 'Darlin'! I thought I heard your lovely voice.'

For a moment Lucy thought her mother was going to say something welcoming. Then she said in a strange high voice, 'What are you doing here? I told you I didn't want to see you again. You're smoking, too! I hope you've put that match out properly? You'll have heard about the fire and our Mick.'

'Sure and I did!' he said reproachfully. 'That's why I've come. I thought you might be glad of me company. You need a real man in your life.'

'And that's what you think you are?' said Maureen wrathfully. 'Well, I'm building a new life for myself and I don't want to be reminded of the old one.' She brushed past him and went into the flat. Lucy followed, closing the door behind her.

'You mean, you've still got your eye on that Barney Jones's money,' said Callum scornfully.

Maureen drew herself up to her full height. 'I am not after his money. You've no right to say that!'

'I'll say what I like, woman. There's something fishy about him. He's supposed to own several houses and yet he plays the piano at a picture house. What man of property would do that?'

For a moment Maureen looked taken aback but she soon rallied. 'He's a musician through and through. He has to play! Couldn't live without music. Besides, it gives him great pleasure to make people happy.'

'He could make *me* happy by leaving you alone.'

'And you could make *me* happy by going away!' Maureen turned her back on him and looked at Lucy, a helpless expression on her face.

Callum went over to Maureen and placed one hand on her shoulder. He whispered something in her ear. She shook her head and shrugged his hand off. 'Lucy, pour that tea! I'm parched,' she ordered.

The girl did as she was told, glancing up every now and again at the two adults. Her mother sat at the table on which she had placed her shopping bag. Callum seated himself opposite her. 'You need to think twice, darlin', before you do something you might regret. What kind of man is he anyway? He'll never take you dancing.'

'He may be a cripple but at least he's a gentleman,' she flashed back, startling not only Callum but Lucy too. 'You'll bring me nothing but grief and I've had enough of that. Mick beat us, you know. He hit us again and again. I'd never have believed him capable of such things if I hadn't been on the receiving end of them. You call yourself a proper man! Where were you when I needed you? Off playing games in Ireland. Now leave me alone, Callum.'

'I never knew he hit you! Why didn't you speak out?' He sounded devastated.

'He was my brother, a dear brother. How could I betray him?'

'Even so, you should have told me. I'd have knocked his block off for you. But I never dreamed...'

'No. Neither did your mother or father,' she said wearily. 'So is it really surprising I want to marry a different kind of man altogether from the ones I was brought up with? A cultured man, one who doesn't drink but loves music and books.'

'I like music and books, and I'd never hurt you, darlin'!' he said hoarsely. 'I don't know what got into Mick sometimes. But I'm not like him.' He reached across the table towards her and pressed his lips against hers. The kiss seemed to go on for a very long time.

Watching them, Lucy's heart beat painfully. All this talk about Mick was making her head ache. If Callum did come back into their lives he would be a constant reminder of her uncle, whereas Barney and Mick had been strangers.

198

Callum stood up. His eyes were bright and there was a flush on his cheeks. 'I'll leave you now. Give you time to think about what I said. I'll be back, though, because I care about you, Maureen. I really do care, darlin'.'

Lucy stared at her mother as the door closed behind him and saw that her eyes were swimming in tears. She went over to her with a refilled cup of tea and put an arm round her shoulders. Maureen rested her cheek on Lucy's arm for a minute and then she rose and left the room, carrying the cup.

Lucy did not know what to make of it all. What would her mother do? How did she really feel about the two men? Did she love either of them? She talked about wanting a different kind of man but was that a good enough reason to marry? Lucy just didn't know. What did it take to make a good marriage? Her own parents' had involved Maureen spending weeks at a time without her husband when he was at sea. But one thing she felt certain of was that her mother would be much safer with Barney. Callum was much too volatile. If only Barney would make a move and ask Maureen to marry him! If only there was something Lucy could do to force his hand. Then she had a brainwave.

'My, my, girlie! You're looking nice.' Barney beamed at Lucy who had a new frock on.

It was green and navy blue and she had made it herself from a pattern in a magazine, with material she had bought in the market. Really she should have been wearing black because of the death in their family but despite the guilt she felt, she had very mixed feelings about mourning the man Mick was before his death.

The frock had not been difficult to make. Hems were getting shorter and styles were simpler, often just straight up and down with no waist to speak of. It seemed a shame because Lucy had spent so much time when she was younger worrying about developing curves. The long sleeves had been the most difficult part but she had to have them to hide the puckered skin on her arm left by the burn.

'You're growing into a lovely young lady. You'll soon be having all the young men chasing you and won't want to be bothered talking to an old has-been like me,' said Barney, sounding mournful though there was a twinkle in his eyes.

Lucy smiled. 'You're not an old has-been! You're worth a dozen of any of the boys I know.' She hesitated, linking her arm through his. 'I wish you'd say something really nice like that to Mam. She's just had a visit from Callum and he's made her real mopey.'

Barney's smile froze. 'Has he now?' he said softly. 'I'm sure the police would be interested in his being back in Liverpool.'

'No! No bobbies!' Lucy was alarmed. That wasn't what she'd wanted at all and she had to think quickly. 'That would only rouse Mam's sympathy for him. And besides, I don't know if they've really got anything on him. At the moment she's cross with him but he says he loves her. He wants to marry her and perhaps might even whizz us all off to Ireland now things have quietened down there. We'd never see you or Liverpool again – and that would be terrible.'

'I can't have that!' Barney pursed his lips. 'I'll have to do something.'

Lucy looked at him with hope in her eyes and egged him on a little further. 'You'll have to move quickly. Mam's getting tired of working so hard. I'm thinking she might weaken and say yes to Callum.'

'No!' He hit his open palm with one fist. Then he smiled and, leaning towards Lucy, put his hands to either side of her head and smacked a kiss on her forehead. 'Don't you worry, girlie, I'll sort something out. I haven't played for and watched all those films without learning a thing or two!'

Reassured, Lucy stopped worrying.

A week passed and Barney still appeared to be doing nothing but she told herself she could trust him. He had said she was not to worry so she mustn't. He would come up trumps.

Callum had called three times but so far her mother had refused all his offers of marriage. Nevertheless, Lucy couldn't help remembering the way Maureen had reacted to his kiss. Come Friday Callum turned up at the flat again. Maureen was at work and Lucy was just about to leave for the timber yard. He said he'd wait. She didn't like leaving him alone in the flat. Winnie was due round for the rent and Lucy tried to persuade him to leave. Callum proved stubborn and was still there when Winnie knocked at the door.

Lucy opened it and Winnie came right in. On

201

seeing Callum she stared at him with obvious disapproval. He was wearing his green tammy and a checked tweed jacket, puffing away at his pipe and filling the room with noxious fumes. 'Eeeh! I never in all my born days saw such a hat on a man,' Winnie said, her eyes almost popping out of her head.

'Then it's time your life had a bit of colour in it, missus,' said Callum good-humouredly.

'My life's been colourful enough, thank you very much.' She folded her arms beneath her bosom and hoisted it up. 'I recognise you from my brother-in-law's description. I don't know how you dare to show your face round here.'

He growled, 'You want to watch what you say, missus. What I do is none of your brother-in-law's business – or yours! The bobbies have nothing on me they can prove.'

Winnie glared at him. 'Eeeh! You've got a nerve, speaking to me like that. Pride comes before a fall so you want to watch yourself or you'll be in trouble.' She clutched her large handbag to her.

He bristled from his overgrown eyebrows to the fist that clenched the stem of his pipe. 'Are you threatening me, missus? Because if you are...' He waved his pipe at her.

'Are *you* threatening *me?*' Winnie stepped back as if alarmed. 'You can make what you want of what I've said, but I'm serious. I don't want you hanging round here. I'm going now, I've got what I came for. But I'm telling you, I'll be having words with Mrs Linden about the company she keeps. Good evening.' And with those words she stalked out of the flat.

'She's got a bloddy nerve!' muttered Callum, ramming his pipe back in his mouth. 'People like her need shooting.'

'It's no use swearing at me,' said Lucy, amused that the two of them should have taken such an instant dislike to each other. 'She isn't all bad. She's done some good things for us. But perhaps you should go. Mam won't be home for ages.'

He nodded. 'Maybe I'll walk along to that place where she works and wait for her.'

'Mr Jones might be there,' Lucy warned.

Callum made no reply and she watched him go downstairs before fetching her cart and setting out for the timber yard.

The wind had risen, threatening to snatch her hat from her head. As she passed the pub on the corner of Mere Lane two men crossed the road in front of her. They were talking loudly. She stopped abruptly and shrank back against the wall of the pub, recognising one of the voices. She kept perfectly still until they were out of earshot and then ran all the way to Griffiths' yard.

Dilys was there but Lucy was less pleased to see Owen. She waited for him to make some smart alec remark but he ignored her. She didn't know whether she was relieved or not. In a way she found her confrontations with him stimulating but for now she chose to act like he wasn't there. She went over to Dilys who was talking to one of the workers outside the saw mill and waited for her to finish her conversation.

'What's Owen doing here at this time of day?' demanded Lucy.

Dilys looked surprised. 'What's with your tone

203

of voice? Has he been doing something to annoy you?'

'Nothing apart from the usual,' said Lucy with a shrug.

For a moment she thought Dilys was going to question her about that but instead she said, 'He's working here part-time. He's left the cinema, says he wants to work outdoors, but I reckon he was late getting in once too often because of his firewood round so he came here, knowing what a soft touch my aunt is. His mother's having trouble with her knees and it could be she'll lose her job on the liners. Anyway, that's enough about Owen for one day.' Dilys smiled. 'How are you? Why don't you come to my aunt's one day and we can have a good gab?'

Lucy was pleased with the invitation but uncertain about accepting it. She had managed to avoid coming face to face with Rob since he'd visited her in hospital but if she started visiting his aunt's house then surely it wouldn't be long before they did bump into each other. So she made the excuse that at the moment she couldn't set a date for getting together, but she couldn't resist asking after him.

Dilys grimaced. 'He's after promotion because there's this girl...'

'You mean, someone wants to marry him?' Lucy was dismayed and surprised at herself all at the same time.

'I'm presuming she does. Although it's really him who's fallen for her. She's a real beauty. Jet black hair, magnolia skin and deep blue eyes ... as well as a figure that takes some beating. Not that

204

Aunt Gwen or I want him to marry. Aunt thinks he's too young. As well as that she likes having a man about the place. It makes us feel safe.'

'Depends on the man,' said Lucy, thinking of Mick. 'Your aunt's forgiven your brother, then, for becoming a policeman?'

'Yes.' Dilys smiled. 'Like Owen, Rob can turn on the charm when he wants. I like a bloke to have charm but I'm wanting someone tall, dark, handsome and rich, as well. What d'you say?'

Lucy smiled. 'I agree with you,' and then realised Rob Jones and Owen fitted the tall and the dark and neither of them was bad-looking. 'Although I'd almost decided never to get married.' She forced a laugh before hurrying away.

It was dusk by the time she arrived home and found Timmy sitting on the front step eating a jam butty. 'Where've you been?' he mumbled through a mouthful of bread. 'Mam's been home but she's gone back to work. She wanted to talk to you. She was panting and gasping. Said we'd be lucky if we didn't lose the roof over our heads.'

Lucy sat on the step beside the boy, wondering if this had anything to do with Callum. Perhaps Winnie had spoken to Barney and told him about Callum's being at the flat? Maybe Barney had decided to move them so Callum couldn't find them. She hoped that was all it was. She rose and went inside to prepare their supper, impatient for her mother's return.

Maureen was late getting home, very late. It was well past midnight and Lucy was dozing in a chair.

'You shouldn't have waited up,' said Maureen. She looked drained and slumped down.

'What's up? Is Barney moving us because of Callum calling here?'

Maureen moistened her lips and made a couple of attempts at speaking before finally managing to whisper, 'Winnie Jones is dead. She's been murdered!'

Chapter Eleven

Lucy sprang to her feet. 'But she was here only a few hours ago!'

Maureen took a handkerchief from her pocket and wiped her eyes. 'That's the trouble. She was here at the same time as Callum. Then they both turned up at the cinema and there was an almighty row. I don't know how Barney managed to stay calm but he did and the shouting was mainly between the other two. In the end Callum stormed off. I think what made him extra angry was that Barney wouldn't be provoked into losing his temper. Winnie followed almost on Callum's heels. Barney was a bit worried about her so he didn't hang around after the second house waiting to get the tram with me but left immediately.'

'So how did you find out she was dead?'

'I called at their house. It's out of my way, I know, but I was all on edge after the row. There were things she said that didn't make sense to me. I wanted to get a few of them sorted out. Instead I – I–' Maureen lowered her head.

Lucy knelt in front of her and covered her hand with hers. 'Take your time, Mam.'

'Barney'd just found her when I got there. He said the front door was open when he arrived home. She'd been shot.'

'Shot!' Lucy was shocked to the core and crossed herself frantically as if to ward off evil. 'You're not believing it was Callum?' She was wondering how could they be involved in such a thing again! Also thinking of Aunt Mac and how she'd feel about her son being accused of murder.

'Who else could it be? The hot-blooded eejit!' cried Maureen, and dissolved into tears.

'But...' Lucy had been about to say, *Why should he kill her?* But people did kill others in the heat of the moment and he'd said that people like Winnie needed shooting. Of course anybody might say such a thing and not intend doing anything of the sort. But he was hot-blooded and had been in such a state over her mother and Barney. Lucy knew what it was like to be frightened out of one's wits. 'What happened after you spoke to Uncle Barney?' Her voice trembled.

'He asked me to go for the police while he stayed with the body.'

'Did you see them?'

Maureen nodded. 'They asked me if I'd heard anyone else making threats against her. Barney'd already mentioned Callum. I did put it to them that with her being a rent collector someone might have followed her, knowing she had money on her.'

Lucy's heart lifted and she looked at her mother with hope in her eyes. 'That makes more sense. Was the money gone?'

'Yes. But Barney said Callum could have taken it.'

Lucy could believe some things of Callum but not that he was a thief. 'Do you think they'll arrest him?'

'They were sending a bobby round to Aunt Mac's.'

'Oh, poor Aunt Mac!' Lucy could not stay still any longer but paced the room. 'I hope the shock doesn't kill her.' She stood staring out of the window. The houses opposite were all in darkness except for a single light in a bedroom.

'Of course it won't, eejit!' Her mother lifted her head. 'She's strong! Although none of it'll make sense to her.' Maureen's eyes grew round with dismay. 'They'll probably blame me. Say it was my greed spurred him on and that I drove him mad with desire! But Callum's a grown man and he should know how to control himself.'

Lucy remembered the kiss she'd witnessed between the two of them. Not much control there.

Maureen put a hand to her head. 'Oh, Lucy, what am I going to do? I can't think straight for the pain in my head.'

'I'll make you a cup of tea.'

'It's Guinness I need, girl. Guinness!' she wailed.

'I'll put plenty of sugar in the tea.'

A sob broke from her mother and Lucy put her arms round her. It was as if she was the adult and

208

the other the child. Maureen clung to her, weeping. Lucy felt dreadful, not knowing what to say to comfort her.

After staying awake into the early hours Lucy eventually fell asleep so heavily she did not hear the church bells the next morning. It was Timmy who woke her. 'There's a man who says he's a policeman at the door. I think I've seen him before,' he whispered. 'He's asking for you.'

'Me?' Lucy sat up in bed, scared, and looked for her mother but the space she'd occupied was empty. 'Where's Mam?'

'She's gone out.'

'To church?'

'I dunno. She wasn't dressed for church and didn't say where she was going.' Timmy scratched the back of his neck. 'What's going on, Luce? Mam looked terrible.'

'I'll tell you later.' She scrambled out of bed, wondering where her mother could have gone. Aunt Mac's? Barney's? 'Where've you put the policeman?' She was wondering if it was Rob and what he wanted with her.

'I didn't let him in. Although I've remembered now who he is. It's D.C. Jones. I said you were in bed and I had to wake you first.'

'You did right,' said Lucy, taking a deep breath and thinking Rob wouldn't like being kept waiting outside.

She shooed her brother out of the room then buttoned on a frock. She would be sixteen next birthday and wondered whether Rob would notice any difference in her. She'd eaten his chocolates and they'd been delicious. He must be on her side if he'd not only kept silent about what she had told him but given her chocolates as well. But what did he want with her now? She couldn't think straight, her thoughts all mixed up, remembering snatches of their conversation in the hospital. She had to keep him on her side. Lucy ran a comb through her chestnut hair which swirled about her shoulders as she flung the door open.

Rob was not in uniform. He looked tired, leaning against the door jamb. 'Morning, Lucy. I'm sorry to disturb you but I wonder if you could spare me a few minutes?'

Now it was time to be nice to him she found herself remembering the girl Dilys had mentioned and feeling stroppy. 'It's Sunday, you know, the day of rest.'

One dark eyebrow shot up. 'I know what day it is and I'm sorry to disturb you,' he said with heavy irony. 'May I come in? As I'm sure you know there was a murder la–'

'Hang on.' She was aware of Timmy listening and turned to her brother. 'Go and look for Mam.'

He wasn't pleased. 'But I want to hear what he has to say. What's this about a murder?'

'I'll tell you later.' Lucy pushed him out of the flat, beckoned Rob inside and closed the door. 'So why me?' she said defensively. 'I don't know anything about it.'

'Perhaps not.' He moved over to the fireplace and stood on the rag rug, glancing about him. 'This is better than your last place.'

She ignored the remark. 'Of course I know

nothing about the murder! Just because I used violence once doesn't mean I make a habit of it!'

That eyebrow rose again expressively. 'Now who's being stupid? And what did I tell you about my never having heard that? Now, you were the only witness to an incident which took place here yesterday between Callum McCallum and Mrs Winifred Jones. Barney and your mother both say Mrs Jones alleged he waved a gun about and threatened her in this room.'

The thought flashed into Lucy's mind that here was the perfect way to get Callum out of her mother's life, and for a second she wavered between telling the truth or landing him in trouble. Then, shocked with herself for even thinking such a thing, she blurted out, 'That's a lie! And you won't get me to change my mind about it!'

'I want the truth, Lucy.' There was a warning note in Rob's voice. 'You hesitated. How do I know you're not just saying that because Mc-Callum's an old family friend? It's natural you'd want to defend him, but I need to know the truth.'

Lucy snorted. 'It's not natural at all!' She moved behind the sofa and gripped the back of it. 'I'd rather he was out of Mam's life. I want her to marry Barn – someone else,' she amended hastily. Rob looked at her and the expression on his face baffled her. 'I'm telling the truth, cross my heart!'

Did he believe her? Several seconds passed before he nodded. 'So what was it he waved about when Winnie was here? Or did he wave anything?'

'His pipe. He smokes like a chimney.'

'You'd swear to its being a pipe in court?'

Lucy would rather not but if Callum's life depended on it then she would. How could she let him hang? It would break Uncle and Aunt Mac's hearts. 'Yes!'

Rob surprised her by giving a satisfied nod. 'I didn't think McCallum did it but there's some who'd be happy to pin it on him. It doesn't make sense to me, his killing her. Barney, on the other hand, believes it makes perfect sense. He's convinced McCallum intended the bullet for him as soon as he came through the door and hit her by mistake.'

Lucy's eyes widened. 'But that's stupid! It would mean Callum needed glasses and a hearing trumpet. You can hear Barney coming from halfway down the road. Clump, clump! That's how that boot of his goes.'

Rob smiled. 'Smart girl! It's still possible that the killing *was* a mistake. An ex-soldier, maybe, down on his luck like so many. Frightened of being caught in the house, he might have fired blindly when she entered.'

It sounded so plausible that Lucy found herself believing in that desperate ex-soldier. She felt a deep sympathy for him, and for Winnie. 'He'd have kept the gun for a souvenir,' she murmured. 'I know Uncle Mick kept his although he...' She stopped abruptly, remembering the day he'd died. The palms of her hands were sweaty all of a sudden.

Rob's eyes met hers and he said roughly, 'Stop it! Try and remember that you saved my life by

212

bringing me round and you tried to save his. I never did thank you for saving mine.'

His words chased the shadows away and made her feel wonderful. She could feel a pulse beating at her throat. 'You've saved mine twice. I hope there doesn't have to be a third time.'

'You'll need to stay out of trouble then.'

For a moment she hesitated. 'I saw Shaun O'Neill the other day.'

'Mind if I sit down?' Rob did not wait for her reply but seated himself on the sofa. She thought he looked slightly pale. 'Want to tell me where you saw him?'

Lucy sat beside him but kept a few inches between them in case her mother came in. 'I can't tell you much. He was talking to a man near the Mere Bank pub. I was scared stiff, to tell you the truth. I don't know why he makes me feel that way.'

'He's a violent man and probably reminds you of your uncle. But you mustn't let fear override your commonsense, Lucy.'

'He could be staying in this area somewhere. That's what I'm frightened of.' Her voice was barely audible.

He lifted his head and there was a hard light in his eyes. 'We'll get him, don't you worry.'

She followed Rob to the door, wanting to ask for that in writing. He looked down at her and smiled, then surprised her by touching the tip of her nose with one finger and repeating, 'Don't worry.' He closed the door behind him.

Lucy thought, I really will try not to. She went over to the fire and put a match to the newspaper

213

and stayed on her knees on the rug, watching the wood catch and listening to the familiar crackling as it sent out sparks, thinking of the girl whom Dilys said wanted to marry him. How much did he love her?

The door opened. 'So what did you tell him?' Her mother's voice sounded breathless. There were dark circles beneath her lovely eyes and lines about her nose and mouth. She looked older than she had twenty-four hours ago.

'Where've you been, Mam?' cried Lucy, going over to her. 'I've been worried.'

'Never mind that! What did you tell the copper?' She took hold of Lucy's arms and shook her.

'The truth! That Callum didn't threaten Winnie with a gun. It was his pipe he was waving about.'

She waited for the strain to vanish from her mother's face as the words sank in but all Maureen did was laugh. 'It doesn't prove he didn't have a gun! He was dead jealous of Barney and that could be reason enough for him to do something stupid. Anyway I went round to Aunt Mac's to see if Callum was there and warn him but the house is being watched. I just hope to God that the eejit has had the sense to get out of Liverpool by now or he'll hang!' She hugged herself. 'How dare he put me through what I've been through these last hours? I'll never forgive him.'

'I don't think they've got him yet. And I don't believe he did shoot her. You've known him a long time, Mam. You should have more faith in him.'

Maureen's eyes flashed. 'I had faith in our Mick. How can you have forgotten what he did to us?'

Yes, how could she? thought Lucy, squaring her shoulders. She had done right getting rid of him. But Callum? She still remembered him saying how glad he was that nobody had died when he'd accidentally blown up the wrong house.

Maureen held her hands out to the fire and her voice was hard when she spoke. 'I'll not think of him again. Barney'll need comforting and looking after. I'll give him a little time to pull himself together and for the police to leave him alone – a few days should do it – and then I'll go and see him. You can come with me – help persuade him that he can't live without me.'

Lucy followed her mother into the darkened room where a fire sent shadows flickering round the walls. It was morning but wooden shutters cut out the daylight. Barney sat slumped in an armchair in front of the fire. Maureen tutted. 'You need some light in here, darlin'!' She hurried over to the window and flung the shutters wide.

Lucy had never seen such a change in a man in such a short space of time. Everything about him drooped: his shoulders, his moustache. He had bags under his eyes. Even the wave in his hair seemed to be affected. His hair hung in an untidy fringe on his forehead and about his ears. She went over to him and placed a hand on his arm. 'I'm really sorry, Uncle Barney. If there's anything we can do to help we will. Won't we, Mam?'

215

'That goes without saying.' With a thrust of her hip Maureen eased her daughter away from her position by his side. Lucy went round the other side of the chair as her mother pressed her cheek against Barney's. 'There now, darlin'! What you need is looking after now that dear, dear woman who cared about you so much has gone.'

'I can't believe it!' He lifted his raddled face to them. 'She meant well. She always meant well. I'm going to miss her.' A deep sigh escaped him.

'Of course you'll miss her. She did a lot for you, but I can do just as much.' Maureen perched on the arm of his chair and drew his head against her bosom.

'No! No!' His muffled voice sounded alarmed and he forced his head up and seized one of her hands and one of Lucy's. 'I don't want another Winnie. I just want you living with me so we can be a happy little family.'

'That's all I want, too,' said Maureen, pressing her lips against his mouth and removing her daughter's hand from his grasp at the same time. 'We won't let anyone come between us ever again.'

'You know what they actually hinted at?' His tone was fretful as his eyes went from mother to daughter. 'That it could have been me.'

'That's terrible!' said Lucy, shocked and indignant. 'What had you to gain?'

'Exactly!' he said promptly. 'But Rob explained to me that when there's a murder family members often come under suspicion. Anyway I gave the police the name of her solicitor and of course I'm not mentioned in her will. She left what she had to a cousin, so that soon changed their minds.'

'I should think so, too,' said Maureen indignantly. 'The very idea!'

Barney looked at Lucy. 'I know you said it wasn't a gun McCallum was waving about but he could have gone home for one.' He gave a rueful grin. 'I'm hoping he's had a fright and has run off and won't come after me. I can't scarper like able-bodied people can.'

Maureen stroked his cheek with the back of her hand. 'Callum might be all kinds of a fool but he's not a complete eejit. He'll get to Ireland and stay there.'

'You think so?'

'I'm sure of it. He'll have to accept that he's lost me to you for good.'

Barney nodded, looking much happier. 'Even so, I'm going to have extra bolts put on all the doors. It's a sad state of affairs when a man can no longer feel he's king of his own little castle.'

'It's a terrible thing but I think you'll see I'm right,' said Maureen.

He perked up even more. 'I hope so. But we can't rush into marriage, lovey. We have to observe the proprieties and there's things need sorting out.'

Maureen said she realised that and, turning to Lucy, suggested she went and did whatever she had to do while she and Barney discussed the future.

Lucy decided to go and visit Aunt Mae to see if she could find out if she'd had any news of Callum, but although she was asked inside the

217

house it was immediately obvious that if the old woman knew where her son was, she wasn't cracking on.

'I feel like I can't trust your family anymore,' she said, looking Lucy straight in the eye. 'My boy's innocent. This is all your mother's fault for playing hot and cold with him. I don't want either of you coming round here again.'

Lucy was hurt and felt she had to fight back. 'Callum isn't completely blameless,' she said fiercely, banging on the table. 'Where was he when she needed him?'

Aunt Mac did not answer. Her back was ram-rod straight and her expression uncompromising. Lucy stormed out of the house, near to tears.

Later that day when Maureen came home from work Lucy told her about the visit. 'That's that then!' said her mother, tight-lipped. 'I'm not going to lose any sleep over it.'

'What about Shaun O'Neill?' said Lucy, placing a cup of tea in front of her.

'What about him?' said Maureen, sounding surprised.

Lucy had thought long and seriously before deciding to tell her mother about her recent sighting. 'I've seen him not far from here. It could be nothing but I thought I'd better warn you, just in case.'

'In case what? *He* killed Winnie?' Maureen gave a hollow laugh and sipped her tea.

Lucy laughed. 'Yes. It's a daft idea, I know.'

'Unless you think...' Maureen's eyes widened '...that it wasn't Callum who intended shooting Barney but Shaun mistook her for me in the dark. Callum and our Mick probably spoke about me and Barney ... and I've got a thing or two on Shaun.'

Lucy was alarmed. 'Don't get carried away, Mam. I don't believe that at all. He just makes me feel uneasy and I told you because he might try and get money out of you.'

'Money? You have to be joking?' Maureen threw back her head and laughed and laughed.

Lucy joined in but she wasn't joking. Barney had money and maybe Shaun O'Neill might try a bit of blackmail if he got to hear Maureen was going to marry Barney.

'I think we can forget that,' said her mother, wiping her eyes when she'd sobered down. 'And I'm going to forget him, too. Things are going our way at last, Luce, so don't go and spoil them by you letting your imagination run away with you.' She reached up and brought Lucy's head down to kiss her cheek. 'We'll be moving into Barney's big house and there'll be money for nice clothes and you can have some fun at last.'

'I'm looking forward to it,' said Lucy, hugging her back.

But none of these things happened overnight and Winnie's murder remained unsolved. A couple of vagrants were arrested on suspicion, having been seen in the area, but they were soon released due to lack of evidence. Whoever the killer was they had got off scotfree.

The wedding was arranged to take place at Christmas and at the end of summer Barney suggested Maureen and Lucy do something to brighten up his house. 'I'm tired of browns and greens and duck egg blue but I can't be going round shops and warehouses choosing paints, wallpaper, fabrics and the like. Get the shops to send all the bills to me and don't forget...' he smiled at them both '...I want my two best girls knocking everybody's eyes out at the wedding. So send me those bills as well.'

Barney's house, situated on St Domingo Road, faced on to the Corporation's Electrical Supply Works in Cobb's Quarry and was similar in some ways to the house on Northumberland Terrace, although the front garden was longer and there were more steps going up to the front door. It was on the crest of a hill, so you went down into the kitchen, which was the warmest place in the whole house due to its huge range.

A door led out from the kitchen on to a large rear yard from which you could reach Devonshire Place where there was a children's recreation ground. The other basement room contained a copper, a sink and a mangle. On the ground floor was a parlour and a music room, which contained a piano, shelves of books and music, a roll-topped desk and an enormous buttoned leather chair in which someone Lucy's size could easily curl up and be lost. On the floor above there were two bedrooms and a bathroom and above that two attic rooms. One housed the maid.

'Can I have the other one?' asked Timmy, eyes shining as he glanced up at the sloping ceiling with its skylight.

Maureen looked at Barney, who'd struggled up the stairs with them. 'Why not?' he said, a nerve twitching beneath his left eye. 'This used to be my room. Timmy'll be out of the way up here.'

'You were put all the way up here?' said Lucy. 'How did you manage the stairs?'

'That was the way my father wanted it. I was damaged ... imperfect.' There was an angry light in Barney's eyes.

'That's terrible! How did you turn out as nice as you have?' said Lucy.

He smiled and jingled the money in his pockets. 'I'm no angel, Lucy. And what's the use of worrying about it now? It was a long time ago and they're all dead, but I'm still here? Let's go down.'

Maureen and Barney were to have the large room at the front of the house and of course Lucy was to have the rear one, which pleased her because it looked down the hill and on to the greenery of the recreation ground.

Maureen and Lucy persuaded Barney to have electricity installed in all the main rooms of the house and they delighted in switching the lights off and on, off and on. The novelty of instant light at the touch of a switch took some time to wear off. Timmy and the maid had to make do with candles. Walls were painted peach and cream and sunshine yellow, but the main bedroom and parlour were adorned in floral printed wallpaper, which made everyone feel they had wandered into a garden. Then mother and daughter had an enjoyable time going to Lewis's in the town centre to buy bedding, as well as fabrics for new curtains.

But the highlight of the weeks preceding the

wedding was the choosing of material for Maureen's wedding outfit and Lucy's bridesmaid's frock: ivory satin for the bride and peach for the bridesmaid. The dresses were made up in a shop on Scotland Road. Lucy thought her mother had gone completely crazy when she chose satin shoes to match their dresses.

'It's a waste of money,' she whispered in Maureen's ear. 'Can you see me flogging firewood or sweets outside the pictures in these? Or cleaning? I'll never wear them again!'

'Of course you will! You'll be giving those jobs up, Luce, once I'm Mrs Barney Jones.' Maureen's eyes gleamed as she stood and gazed at her own neat ankles reflected in the mirror. 'If I'm to be a lamb to the slaughter, I might as well be dressed for it.'

Lucy's heart sank. 'I thought you *wanted* to marry Barney?'

'Of course I do!' said Maureen sharply, whirling round to face her. 'We're having a fine time of it, aren't we? You don't think I'm a traitor to my own church and kind, do you?' Her eyes seemed to bore into Lucy's.

'Of course not! If you love him, does it matter? He's a good man. A generous man.'

'Exactly! Who wouldn't love a man like that?' Maureen's smile dazzled Lucy. 'You need your hair cutting and styling. We'll go to Hill's in Ranelagh Street.'

So Lucy's hair was cut, shampooed and set with perfumed lotion. Afterwards it curled like a gleaming chestnut cap about her small head.

'Earrings!' said Barney, eyes shining with

pleasure when he saw the finished product. 'Maureen! She must have her ears pierced – and you, too. Diamonds for you, pearl drops for our little bridesmaid.'

Lucy gasped. She hadn't believed Barney was *that* rich.

The wedding was to take place in St George's church at Barney's request. He had also asked in a teasing voice whether Maureen minded the women of the church preparing the meal afterwards.

Maureen had not answered immediately. From her seat on the large leather chair in the music room, Lucy, who was reading Charles Dickens, had held her breath. Then her mother had smiled and nodded.

From that moment on it seemed no time at all before the wedding day dawned and mother, daughter and son were dressing in their finery to go to church.

Lucy and Timmy, he in a sailor suit, followed Maureen up the aisle. It was one of her dreams come true, thought Lucy. St George's church, with its slim cast-iron pillars soaring into an intricate tracery which held up the Welsh slate roof, was the perfect setting and Barney looked so handsome in a charcoal grey lounge suit. How could her mother not love him? thought Lucy, warmed by her own affection for him. Yet she was anxious for Maureen. Her face was so pale it seemed possible she might faint.

They arrived in front of the chancel and stood alongside Barney and his best man. Lucy had not given a thought to whom that might be and almost fainted herself when she caught sight of Rob, looking very serious. Dear God! she thought. Would she have to dance with him? She tried to imagine that austere face breaking into a smile as his dark head bent over hers. 'A waltz, Lucy?' he would say. She couldn't waltz. The only dancing she knew was prancing around in something that resembled an Irish jig. She would like to learn to dance properly. Some of the new ones that were reported in the papers might make their way across the Atlantic from America. She wondered if Dilys danced.

The service started and Lucy was aware as she took her mother's bouquet that Maureen was shaking like a navvy with a drill. Lucy wanted to say something reassuring but it was too late.

The choir led the congregation in 'Lead me, o thou great Jehovah!' that powerful Welsh hymn to the tune of 'Cwm Rhondda'. It was so moving it made Lucy's toes curl in their satin shoes. She thought what a shame it was that Aunt Mac, who loved a good singsong, wasn't there but she strongly disapproved of what Maureen was doing. Despite its being a lovely service, it was a relief when it was finally over and her mother was married to Barney.

The wedding breakfast took place in the mission hall on Mere Lane. Miss Griffiths and some of the other women from the church had had the arranging of it and the food could not be faulted. There were hams and tongue, sausage rolls and pies, mince pies and cakes. To drink there was tea, ginger beer or lemonade. There was only one speech and it was very much to the point. Barney said what a lucky man he was, not only in getting himself a beautiful bride but in gaining a family in one fell swoop. He ordered the guests to enjoy themselves and that was it.

After most of the food was consumed there were games for the children and the adults, and singing. Such singing that it threatened to lift the roof off. It seemed to Lucy as if the whole church was there, or at least the Welsh Choral Society to which all the Joneses belonged. She need not have worried about waltzing or foxtrotting. There was some dancing but it was the square kind where a man shouted out the steps. Owen had the nerve to ask her to be his partner and she would have refused if he hadn't seized her hand and swept her into a set. She made a complete mess of it, dosy doe-ing when she should have been swinging round and round. She collapsed in helpless laughter and only then did she become aware of Dilys glowering on the sidelines.

Lucy immediately suggested Owen should dance with the boss's niece and pushed him in her direction. She herself was glad to sit out and drink lemonade and watch other people. Then she spotted Rob dancing with his dark-haired beauty and felt such a stab of jealousy that it almost stopped her breath. Oh, to look that good, to be that height and age, to have a man unable to take his eyes off *her* face. She swallowed a sudden lump in her throat and told herself not to be so daft. What did she want with Rob? She would never be able to forget he knew her secret. And could even the best of men be depended on?

He surprised her by coming over towards the

225

end of the evening. 'So, what do you think? Will they be happy?'

Lucy felt thrown on the defensive. 'Of course!' Her eyes challenged him. 'Do you doubt it?'

'They've several barriers to cross but if they love each other...' He paused and smiled at her. 'You've got what you wanted, anyway.'

'I'm very fond of him,' murmured Lucy, gazing across at her stepfather.

'Yes, I've noticed,' said Rob drily, and walked away.

Lucy watched the girlfriend claim him. She'd been told her name was Blodwen Morgan and she worked in a shipping office as a secretary.

Later that day, after Lucy and Timmy had seen their mother and Barney off on the train to Llandudno for a week's honeymoon, they went back to their new home. As Lucy took off her wedding finery and gazed at her reflection in the oval mirror on the chest of drawers she could still see in her mind's eye Rob's face. She did not know why she felt this tug of attraction where he was concerned. It was a waste of time. She thought of Barney and how he'd wanted herself and her mother looking like fairy princesses down to the rings in their ears. Now *he* was the kind of man she could look to if she wanted the next dream on her list to come true – and she was not going to wait long before broaching the topic with him.

Chapter Twelve

Lucy looked across at her mother as they carried the steaming bedding on a sheet of wood from the copper to the sink. They dunked the sheets and pillow cases into cold water. 'Did you ever dream, Mam, when you married Uncle Barney, we'd still be doing this kind of thing?'

Maureen rested a hand on the rim of the sink as she eased a strand of damp hair behind one ear. She looked tired. 'I did sometimes dream of being waited on hand and foot but Agnes is all that husband of mine came up with as a help.'

The all-purpose maid chuckled. 'I'm doing me best, Mrs Jones, but I haven't ten pairs of hands.' She was rubbing the neck of one of Barney's shirts with a block of Lively Polly washing soap.

'But you're a cheerful little soul and that makes up for a lot,' said Lucy, smiling.

'Tell me the truth, are you happy here, Agnes?' asked Maureen.

'Love it,' said the widow woman enthusiastically. 'Since Father died, and having no chick of my own, I've been that lonely.'

'Well, I'm glad you're happy. And how about you, girl? Are you happy being at home?' Maureen looked at her daughter.

Lucy shrugged. 'It beats standing on street corners and getting up in the dark to sell firewood during the winter but now spring's arrived I'm thinking I'd like to be doing something else. A different kind of job.'

It was over a year since the wedding and so much that was good had happened that she felt ungrateful for feeling the way she did but she was seventeen and wanted more out of life than being at home, helping her mother and the maid. But Barney had hit the roof when Lucy had suggested carrying on working.

'Aren't I providing for all your needs?' he had thundered.

His anger had surprised her and as Maureen had immediately taken his side and said she wanted Lucy to stay at home because she enjoyed her company so much, the girl had backed down. But she missed earning her own money, and really was still working but not getting paid for it, although Barney was generous in so many other ways.

'What? Don't start that again, Luce!' groaned her mother. 'Wasn't Christmas wonderful?'

The last two Christmases had indeed been wonderful with an enormous tree in the parlour decorated with tinsel and candles. This Christmas tied to its branches had been lots of surprise presents from Barney for all of them. Tortoiseshell and mother-of-pearl slides for the women's hair, chocolates and sandalwood soap, books and puzzles, gloves and scarves. Under the tree on Christmas morning there had been a bicycle for Timmy and new winter coats trimmed with fur and hats to match for Lucy and Maureen. Dinner had been an enormous leg of pork and a chicken with all the trimmings. There had been a steaming pudding, mince pies and Christmas cake.

Lucy had felt guilty having so much when she knew of people who would be getting very little, so she'd wrapped up slices of cake and posted them through the letter boxes of all the houses in Court 15. Barney had partially eased her conscience by telling her he had given money to the *Echo's* Goodfella Appeal which provided parcels for the poor, but she could only think it wasn't she who had given the money. She had also gone along to Aunt Mac's but there had been no answer. A neighbour had popped her head out of next door, informing Lucy they'd gone to Ireland and she didn't know when they'd be back. She had called several times since but never managed to catch Aunt Mac in. Sometimes she wondered if the old woman was inside listening in silence, waiting for her to go away, and that saddened her.

Barney had also taken them to London. It had been a birthday treat for Maureen. The railways had run special trains to the British Empire Exhibition at Wembley. They had seen the King, whose voice had been recorded for the first time. That had been a thrill but what they'd enjoyed most of all was Liverpool's exhibition in the Wembley Civic Hall, showing the best the city had to offer. There flew the flags of the sixty shipping lines who used the port regularly. To Lucy's surprise, she and Timmy, on wandering off, had met Dilys and Rob who had also gone to see the working models of a Liverpool tram and Stephenson's Rocket.

Rob had explained how the models worked to Timmy and for a moment Lucy had found pleasure in gazing at the man's animated face until Dilys told her that she and her aunt were expecting his engagement to be announced any minute. The four of them had left the building together, pausing outside to listen to the Liverpool Police Band entertaining the crowds. Lucy remembered Rob asking her how things were with Barney and her mother, and whether she was enjoying being a lady of leisure. She told him there was little time for leisure when helping keep clean and tidy a large house and looking after a family. He'd laughed and said that was the trouble when dreams came true: reality wasn't half as much fun.

'Lucy, you've gone off into a dream,' scolded Maureen now. 'Wake up and answer my question. Wasn't Christmas marvellous?'

'Yes,' she sighed. 'But put yourself in my position. Didn't you have a job at my age?'

'Yes, in a tobacconist's, but I was only marking time until I found a husband. Isn't there anybody you like? No young men in church with a decent income?'

'None that I want to marry,' said Lucy. 'And I'm not sure they'd want to marry me, frankly.'

'Why? You're as good as they are,' said her mother indignantly, eyes smouldering.

Lucy squeezed the sheets, watching bubbles form from the Hudson's soap powder and a grimy curd spread over the surface. 'I'd thought of my own sweetshop but now Barker & Dobson are churning Everton toffees and chocolates out by the thousands, I've changed my mind. I'd like to work in the cinema instead.'

'As what?'

Lucy's eyes gleamed. 'Running the place?'

Maureen snorted. 'Tush, girl, you've got a hope!'

'Hope's what keeps people going, Mam.'

'Aye! But you've got to keep your feet on the ground at the same time. Barney's proud of the fact that he can afford to keep you at home.' Her brows knitted.

Lucy remembered how he'd suggested she and her mother join the Bible study group at the church, and the women's group, as well as learning Welsh so they could enjoy its literature and singing. She wanted to please him but it was too much and she wanted to do something that she chose. Her mouth set determinedly. 'I'm going to ask him about the cinema. If he says no I'll turn on the tears. There's not many men can stand to see a woman cry.' She winked.

'You can but try,' said Maureen, easing her back. 'I've a feeling I'm not going to get a bit of peace from you about this until you do. You'll probably catch him in if you run up after we've mangled this lot.'

Lucy found Barney in the music room. He was sitting at the roll-topped desk sifting through some papers. He glanced up and gave her an absent-minded smile. She hesitated only a moment before going over to him. 'Busy?' She kissed his forehead, resting both hands on his shoulders.

'Business.' He patted one of her hands without

231

looking up. 'Is there something you want?'

'Yes, I'd like a job in the cinema.'

He dropped a sheet of paper and it fluttered to the floor. Lucy bent to pick it up but he got to it before she did and placed it back on the desk, covering it with another. He laced his hands on top of the pile and looked up at her, a baffled expression in his eyes. 'Why aren't you happy, Lucy? There are lots of girls, who've come from where you have, would give their eye teeth to be in your position.'

His words annoyed her a little. 'I presume you're talking about the slums? But maybe it's *because* I've been there that I need to do something to earn my own money. Even women from the middle classes are wanting jobs now. The men who would have been their husbands were killed in the war or are unable to work because of terrible injuries.'

'You help your mother and your presence lights up this house and my life,' he said patiently. 'But I suppose you worry about ending up back there in the slums? People can lose money, it's true.'

'Yes!' Lucy pounced on his words eagerly. 'I'm glad you understand. So can you speak for me at the Trocadero? I'd like to work there – and that's your fault, Uncle Barney, because when I was younger your playing made the cinema magic for me. It's still magic! And there's nothing I'd enjoy better than helping bring that magic to other people.'

He looked gratified. 'Well, that's a real nice thing to say, girlie! And I must admit I still get a great deal of pleasure out of helping to create

232

that magic. I enjoy the whole cinema atmosphere.'

Lucy's eyes shone. 'Me too! Whether it's a weepie or a comedy or a *crime passionel!*' She had seen that written on a billboard advertising that week's film outside the Mere Lane Super Cinema. 'I'm caught up in a different world – and what makes it even more lovely is sharing the magic with other people. It gives me a warm feeling.'

He chuckled. 'My goodness, girlie! You should write the cinema advertisements for the newspapers. We'd get loads coming in.'

She leaned against the desk. 'I'd like to run the whole show. Pick the films, choose what people are offered to eat, work in the cash office, have a go at doing everything.'

His expression was almost comical. 'What a dreamer! You're a female. You're not capable of running the whole show.'

'No?' she said with a mischievous smile. 'We'll see. I'll have to work my way up from the bottom. I know it'll take years but...'

'You'll be married before then. Some chap's bound to snap you up,' he said with a sigh.

Lucy shook her head. 'I want my dream. Besides, you've spoiled me for all the young men.'

She thought Barney was going to burst with pleasure. His face turned a beetroot colour and he took her hand and squeezed it. 'Nice of you to say so, lovey. I'm sure I can find you something. There's a vacancy coming up soon for a waitress. One of our girls is getting married. How about

233

that as a place to start?'

'Why not!' she said, having no illusions about how hard the work would be.

'Good. Next step usherette.'

That pleased Lucy but she wanted more. 'How about the projection room after that?'

He threw back his head and laughed. She laughed with him although she was deadly serious. Barney mopped his eyes with a large white linen handkerchief. 'This is real, girlie, not the pictures. That's a man's job. Those reels of film are heavy.'

'I could turn the handle. When do I start?'

He looked down at her hands, inspecting their chapped appearance. 'You'll need to do something about these.'

'I will,' she promised.

'Then I'll speak to the head waitress tomorrow.'

That was good enough for Lucy. She thanked him and almost danced out of the room. She went downstairs and asked her mother did they have any soft wax, glycerine and almond oil left? 'I've got to do something about my hands before I start my new job.'

Maureen sank on to a three-legged stool and the colour drained from her face. Startled and worried, Lucy said, 'I didn't mean to give you a shock.'

Her mother shook her head, then took several deep breaths. 'Nothing to do with you. My legs just went on me. So don't fuss,' she said brusquely. 'Now hang that washing on the rack!'

'Perhaps I shouldn't go out to work,' said Lucy with a sigh, taking a wet shirt out of the basket.

'Don't be daft. I'll be OK. I'm glad you're to get what you wanted.'

But it was to be several months before Lucy really got that.

Her mother had another funny turn at the table later that day. 'Are you all right, lovey?' said Barney, bending over her and patting her face.

'Don't fuss over me!' she snapped. 'And don't call me lovey!' She rushed out of the room.

'Mam had a funny turn this morning,' said Lucy hastily.

'You go after her then. See that she's all right,' said Barney.

Lucy nodded and hurried upstairs. She found her mother sitting in the dark by her bedroom window, gazing out over the front garden. The girl knelt beside her and put a hand on her knee. 'What's wrong, Mam?'

'I'm having a baby.'

It took a few seconds for the words to sink in but as they did Lucy's heart lifted with relief and pleasure. A little brother or sister! That explained everything. How many times had she heard old grannies say that women carrying babies could behave oddly? 'That's wonderful!' cried Lucy, putting an arm round her mother's waist.

Maureen was stiff and unwielding. 'There's nothing wonderful about it at all! I'm worried sick. It could have his trouble,' she said in tragic tones. 'What if it's a girl and ends up having to wear a big boot? This is a punishment for me marrying out of the faith!' Her face crumpled and she burst into tears.

'Mam, Mam, don't cry.' Lucy stumbled to her

235

feet and put both arms round her. 'It'll be OK. She could just as easily take after you and be a beautiful baby ... and to be honest I don't know why you go on about the faith. You hardly went to church after Dad was killed. I remember Gran used to nag you about it.'

'Exactly!' Maureen pounced on her words. 'And she was right. It would have been a comfort to me. I don't feel at home in St George's. It's not what I was brought up to.'

Lucy groaned. 'It's not what I was brought up to either but you can get used to anything if you want. It's in English. Latin's so highfalutin'!'

'I like it. It sounds lovely.'

Lucy thought it sounded dreary but didn't say so. She tried a different track. 'The main thing is that we all try to do our best to live up to what we've been taught is the right way to live. Isn't that what you meant when we took the fruit and the boots that time? I've been angry with God at times, Mam, for taking Dad and all those other men who were killed in the war. But I've also thought those in charge didn't really follow what Jesus taught, did they?'

'Aye. It was all pride and power and greed,' agreed Maureen vehemently, wiping her eyes on her sleeve. 'Even so I'd like my baby baptised into the faith.'

Lucy almost groaned again. Barney wouldn't agree to that and her mother knew it. 'I'd worry about that when it happens,' she muttered.

'Well, who's to know what the future will hold?' Maureen gave a watery smile as she stood up. 'Thanks, love.'

'For what?' Lucy returned her smile.

'You know.' She put her arm round her daughter and hugged her briefly before closing the curtains and switching on the light. She grimaced. 'I'm going to have to say I'm sorry.'

'I'm sure Uncle Barney'll understand when you tell him about the baby.'

Maureen groaned and sat on the bed. 'He'll be *too* understanding. Will swamp me with words and wrap me up in cotton wool.'

'That's what you need. You're no spring chicken, Mam.'

'Don't be cheeky!'

Lucy sat beside her. 'Perhaps I should stay at home? You're going to need help.'

'Don't you worry about me.' Her mother's eyes had a determined glint in them. 'I'll make sure his understanding runs to extra help. A woman coming in daily to cook the evening meal will suit me down to the ground.' And on those words she got up and went downstairs.

The following morning Barney was already up and dressed in his Sunday best when Lucy came into the kitchen. He was reading the newspaper and had a cup of tea near at hand. The newspaper was lowered and there was a broad smile on his face. 'Your mother's gone back to bed. She was feeling queasy because of the baby so she won't be going to church with us this morning.'

'It's good news, isn't it?' Lucy smiled at him.

He nodded. 'We're going to have to look after her. I'll find a woman to do the cooking. Your mother doesn't want you not being allowed to do what you want because of this but I'd like you to

237

wait a bit longer and see how she goes. I'd feel happier if you were with her. You'll have to wait until another vacancy arises.'

Lucy was disappointed but accepted that in this special case her mother's needs came first.

Due to Maureen's not going to church with them that morning Lucy was able to linger after the service. Her mother generally insisted on their rushing back to see to the Sunday dinner. Dilys greeted Lucy like a long-lost cousin but she didn't waste any time in pleasantries, going straight to the point and asked about Rob and his girlfriend.

Dilys shrugged. 'I get the impression she doesn't like the hours he works and the company he keeps.'

Lucy was astonished. 'Shouldn't she have thought about that before getting engaged to him? And what does she mean, "the company he keeps"?'

Dilys looked at her squarely. 'What she calls the "lowest of the low". You're showing a lot of interest.'

Lucy flushed. 'Your brother saved my life. I want him to be happy.'

Dilys seemed to accept what she said and slipped an arm through hers. 'Why don't you come along to my dancing class, Tuesday? It's great fun.'

Why not? thought Lucy. If she wasn't allowed to get a job then she might as well go dancing. She'd get round her mother to lend her the money. When she told Maureen about the dancing class her mother thought it was a good idea and insisted on Lucy's having a new frock so they went into town together. The dress was off the peg in C&A's and made of jade green and cream taffeta, straight up and down and sleeveless. Her mother suggested a pair of long gloves to hide Lucy's scar, which was normally covered up. Whenever the girl saw it she was reminded of the fire. Would she ever be able to forget that day? she thought, feeling tortured by the memory. Her mother looked tired so Lucy decided she would come another day to look for gloves.

It was late-afternoon the following day when she arrived home to be greeted by the most mouthwatering smells coming from the kitchen. A woman she vaguely recognised stood in front of the range, stirring a stewpot. Her mother was sitting in a rocking chair, a smile on her face similar to the Cheshire Cat's. She introduced the woman as Mrs Davies. She gave a reserved smile and Lucy realised this was Owen's mother whose knees had started to give her trouble, forcing her to give up her cleaning job on the liners.

'Something smells good,' said Lucy, nostrils flaring.

'The tenderest breast of Welsh lamb,' said Mrs Davies, holding a dripping spoon over the pan. 'It makes a lovely sweet stew and melts in the mouth.'

Lucy winked at her mother. 'Can't wait. I'll just go up and wash my hands and face and then I'll set the table.'

She found her brother in the bathroom up to his elbows in filthy water. 'Don't you be leaving a tide mark round the sink, me lad, or Agnes'll have you.'

Timmy grinned. 'She likes me. She won't mind.' Even so he pulled out the plug and rubbed at the ring of scum left behind with the edge of the towel. 'What do you think of us having a cook? We've become right toffs, haven't we, Luce?'

'Naw!' She gazed at her reflection in the mirror over the sink as she ran hot water and wondered where most of her freckles had gone. Her skin was almost unblemished and creamy as her mother's once was. 'If we were right toffs we'd be living out Childwall way or Blundellsands and you'd be at boarding school, playing rugby and tennis and the like, not having taken over selling firewood to earn a few extra coppers.' She worked up a lather with the Pear's soap and dabbed a soapsud on her nose. 'You know who the cook is, don't you?'

'Owen's mam.'

'Yes, the lad who called me a slummy. And now *his* mother's cooking *our* dinner.'

'You don't think he'll be here next?'

She shrugged. 'He's got a couple of jobs but if they're hard up it wouldn't surprise me if Uncle Barney gave him work to help them out.'

Lucy discovered how right she was as she came downstairs later that evening, passing Owen on the way. He was carrying coal for the fire in the master bedroom where her mother was resting, reading *Vogue*. Lucy, having changed into the new tube dress, had brushed her hair until it shone. She had rouge for her lips in her bag and planned on applying it once she was out of the house. Despite his obvious admiration for the

240

ladies of the silver screen Barney disapproved of young ladies wearing make up.

As Lucy shrugged on her jacket Owen was descending the stairs. She could tell from his expression she had made an impression but only acknowledged his presence with a brief nod before leaving the house.

There was a spring in her step as she hurried in the direction of St George's church where she had arranged to meet Dilys. Lucy was a little late and her friend was already there.

'Gosh! You look nice,' she said, linking her arm through Lucy's. 'It's hard to believe you're the same girl who came to the timber yard only a few years ago, looking like you didn't have two farthings to rub together.'

Lucy smiled. 'I'm not so different from her inside but I don't think Owen realises that. His mother's cooking for us now. She started today and he was there, too, carrying up coal. I behaved real haughty to him but I have to admire his determination to help his mother keep a roof over their heads.'

'He's been helping in my aunt's garden once a week now the light nights are here,' said Dilys, a fatuous expression on her face. 'She admires his industry, too, finding work when there's so many unemployed. He's got his firewood round...' *My* firewood round, thought Lucy, feeling a prickle of irritation as Dilys ticked off his jobs on her fingers, 'he works part-time at the yard, does gardening, and now he's carrying coal in your house. He'll go far, Aunt says. Don't you think he's good-looking, too?'

241

Lucy acted as if she'd never thought about it. 'Maybe.'

Dilys seemed pleased by her answer. 'Sometimes, just to show him I'm there, I hang around the garden and point out the weeds he's missed. He's a quick learner, though.'

'I know the difference between a dandelion and a daffodil and that's it,' said Lucy with a shrug. 'I think it was Winnie who kept the front garden tidy. Perhaps Uncle Barney'll get Owen to do ours?'

'You should suggest it. Your stepfather can afford it after all.'

Lucy agreed, and changed the subject by asking how much the lesson would cost. Dilys told her, adding, 'You're going to love it. We'll be learning some of the new dances soon that have been taken up by the bright young things in London.'

Lucy had heard about them from Barney who read aloud from the newspaper anything he considered shocking. Her mother had expressed sympathy for them. 'The poor things are all mixed up. What future, have they now their young men are dead because of the war? They have money to squander so they waste it on drugs and drink, trying to forget. They're eejits but they're lost ... lost...' Her voice had trailed off and for a moment she'd looked unhappy.

Lucy was scornful of them. Money, class, education meant they were free to choose how to handle such loss. If they were poor they wouldn't have time to squander but would be fighting for survival.

The dancing class was situated over a shop on

Netherfield Road and was run by a husband and wife team, Betty and Joseph Merton, who were given to demonstrating in flamboyant style exactly how the dance steps should be executed. Fortunately there was a decent number of young men just as eager as Lucy to have a go. In the first instance they tried without music and following the lead of the dancing teachers, then went on to try it to the strains of the piano played by the widowed Mrs Cracker, who wore lace mittens and a hat fashionable before the war which dipped and swayed in time to the music.

Lucy's partner was tall and thin. He had an Adam's apple that due to his nervousness bobbed up and down in his throat like the counter on a Show Your Strength machine at a fairground when the hammer falls. She could not help thinking that at least she had an idea where her head would reach if she ever danced with Rob Jones.

Despite having her toes trodden on several times Lucy enjoyed her evening and told Dilys she was looking forward to the next. 'You could do with a better partner, though,' said her friend. 'It's a pity we couldn't drag Owen along then you could have mine.'

Lucy was beginning to think Dilys had a real pash on Owen. She said dreamily, 'Have you ever seen Rudolph Valentino dance? He's sleek and slinky and holds his partner so close you couldn't get a sheet of paper between them. It shocked me the first time I saw it but the second time it sent a lovely shiver down my spine. I read on a poster he's got animal magnetism.'

243

'I know just what you mean,' said Dilys, beginning to sway. 'I'm dancing down Mexico way with him right now.'

'No, you're not. I am,' said Lucy.

'He reminds me of Owen – dark, a bit of a beast and a good mover,' said her friend, still swaying, eyes closed. 'I'll ask him to come with us next time, definitely.'

Owen refused, saying he couldn't afford the lessons. In the weeks that followed Lucy was glad he had turned Dilys down. He turned up most evenings at their house for an hour or so and would shift furniture, change light bulbs and talk to Barney. Miss Griffiths must have mentioned to Barney about Owen's doing her garden because in no time at all he was digging over theirs as well.

Sometimes Lucy would pause when she did see him and ask how he was doing. Generally he answered in monosyllables but sometimes he forgot himself and asked where she was going or where she'd been. She told him dancing. 'I can guess who got you on to that,' he said, pausing in his task of unscrewing a tap to fix a new washer. 'Miss Dilys Jones. Now *she's* a real eyeful and time'll tell if there's any future for me there. As Mam says, nobody's better than anyone else in God's eyes and Miss Griffiths does rely on me quite a lot now to do jobs for her, Mr Rob Jones being on some course. And other people in her road are always asking me to do things. If it carries on like this I'll be setting myself up in business one day.'

Dilys hadn't mentioned Rob was doing a

course but before Lucy could ask Owen what he knew about it she heard her mother calling her from the bedroom and excused herself.

She found Maureen standing on a chair in front of the wardrobe, clutching her belly, a terrified expression on her face. 'I've got up here and can't get down again and my pains have started and it's not time,' she cried. 'You'll have to get the midwife.'

Lucy didn't waste time asking her what she thought she was doing up there in her condition but called Owen. She did not like leaving her mother, so scribbled a message and asked him to take it straight away to the address on the front and then go and tell Barney what was happening. Then she got her mother into bed.

The next few hours were fraught and in the end, despite all the midwife's efforts, Maureen lost the baby. Lucy wept but her mother lay silently in bed, her face ashen, seemingly in control of her emotions. Unlike Barney who blundered out of the house and did not return until the following morning. He looked as pale and exhausted as his wife when Lucy saw him. She did not know what to say to him but placed a cup of hot sweet tea in front of him and a plate of bacon and eggs. He drank the tea but only picked at the food before getting up and going into the music room. She waited, expecting him to start playing, but there was only silence. It was later that day Maureen began to say that losing the baby was God's punishment upon her.

Lucy shook her head. 'What for? He wouldn't punish an innocent little baby.'

245

'An innocent little baby born in sin,' muttered her mother.

She continued to say it every day, morning, noon and night, like a litany, until Lucy felt like screaming.

She expected Barney to dissuade her mother from such a belief but he seemed to have retreated inside himself and although he still played at the cinema, the piano in the music room remained untouched. He was dour and seldom spoke, only rousing himself enough to give Lucy the announcement she had been waiting for: she was to attend an interview for the job of waitress at the Trocadero.

Chapter Thirteen

After an interview with the manager and head waitress Lucy was informed she could start work the following Monday. She was presented with two navy blue frocks trimmed with pale blue to wear and felt glad to be getting out of the house.

The Trocadero was the largest and poshest cinema in Liverpool and that fact alone pleased Lucy. The hours were long and she spent most of them on her feet but she was enjoying herself despite the hard work. She earned fifteen shillings for a six-day week, working from ten in the morning to ten at night with two hours off each day, and was allowed to keep ten of them.

'God only knows what you'll waste it on,' said

her mother, who still looked unwell.

'That's unfair! I've never had money to waste. If anything, I think I could easily be a skinflint,' said Lucy with a smile.

Out of her first wage packet she bought her mother some flowers. Maureen thanked her but it was Lucy who put them in water, placing them on the dressing table in Maureen's and Barney's room. Lucy was determined to save money. She walked to work, and the only thing she regretted about her working hours was that she had to give up her dancing lessons. They were in the middle of learning the Charleston, the Black Bottom and the Shimmy. Lucy loved to shimmy and would like a dress with fringing from top to bottom, but that would have to wait. She was lucky at least that she didn't have to pay to see the best and newest films in town.

The Trocadero was situated in Camden Street, off London Road. It had an imposing frontage of white faience tiling in which the cinema's name was carved. Running the entire width of the frontage was a glass canopy with electric lights which sheltered the queues which formed every evening.

Every time Lucy walked through the main entrance into the large foyer with its marble wall panels she experienced a thrill of pleasure. Sometimes she was given the job of watering the potted palms dotted here and there among wickerwork settees and chairs, but most of her time was spent upstairs. A staircase to the rear of the pay-box led to a lounge and it was here she helped serve tea and coffee, Welsh Rarebit, sandwiches and the daintiest, most delicious chocolate eclairs and vanilla slices she had ever tasted. They came from a high-class confectioner's in Bold Street.

Lucy loved it up there. Sometimes if she had a minute she would pull back the velvet curtain dividing the lounge from the balcony. It provided a bird's eye view of the screen and stage. She not only saw what was happening on the screen but could also watch the audience's reactions. The auditorium had seating for over thirteen hundred people. To either side of the apron of the main stage were miniature stages in which scenes were painted throughout the year by an artist from the Liverpool Playhouse. During the interval these were illuminated and much enjoyed by all who saw them. Lucy wouldn't have minded a couple on her bedroom walls.

It was just before Christmas, when she went through the door behind the display unit and cash desk she found the head waitress talking to the manager. The other girls were washing their hands, knowing they would be inspected before they started work. Lucy went to join them.

'Anything up?' she whispered.

'Some Irish singer's coming in a fortnight's time. He's been on the wireless so they're expecting us to be even busier up here than usual that Saturday.'

Lucy's hands stilled on the soap, thinking her mother would enjoy that. Now that her daughter was working Maureen only had Timmy and Agnes to keep her company. Lucy decided she would get tickets for Timmy and her mother to see the show. She doubted Barney would take time off from yet another cinema he had an interest in and where he played, but she would ask him what he thought. It just might get husband and wife talking again.

'"Roses are blooming in Picardy..."' Lucy felt a wrench at her heart as the Irish tenor's voice soared. She was aware of the head waitress dabbing her eyes. She wasn't the only one moved to tears. Lucy could see wisps of white all over the auditorium. Was her mother crying? Were all those other women who'd lost husbands, sons, brothers or fathers? It was seven years since the guns had fallen silent at the front but it could have been yesterday. So much sadness, so much grief, so many families having to cope without a father. So many men crippled or damaged in some way or other. She thought of her grandparents in Yorkshire and was certain they still grieved for their son. One day she would go and see them. She must ask her mother for their address and write to them.

'Luv'ly, ain't it?' murmured a voice behind her.

Lucy turned and looked at one of the other waitresses. 'Don't you find it sad?' she whispered.

'Oh, yeah! But luv'ly with it. A good cry does you good. A good cry, or a kick at the cat and smash a few plates! It does yer the world of good.'

Lucy giggled. 'Poor cat!'

She received a disapproving stare from the head waitress and immediately sobered. The song finished and there was a hush before a burst of rapturous applause.

249

'Action stations, girls!' cried the head waitress.

Lucy let the curtain drop and hurried to her post.

They were rushed off their feet and it was a good twenty minutes before demand slackened and she was able to draw breath and look about her. It was then she caught sight of Aunt Mac. She wasn't alone but with a man, but he was not Uncle Mac. This one was as skinny as a rake and had a bushy brown beard streaked with grey which concealed half his face. He inclined his head towards Aunt Mac as she said something and Lucy stared at him so intently she thought her eyes would pop out of her head. Surely, surely it couldn't be Callum sitting there, drinking tea for all the world as if he didn't have a thing to worry about?

She looked away in case she was caught staring and gazed about her for Timmy and her mother. They had been sitting in a corner by a potted palm but she could no longer see them. When she looked again for Aunt Mac and Callum, they too had disappeared. Was it a coincidence or had they seen each other? Lucy had no way of knowing and had to wait until she arrived home before being able to speak to her mother.

'So was he good?' Barney sat down heavily in his leather armchair in front of the blazing fire. He had to repeat the question before Maureen answered.

'He sang better than any bird!' Her eyes glistened as she cupped her hands and held them against her breast. 'He had the audience in the palm of his hand.'

250

'That good?' Barney looked at Lucy. 'What do you say?'

She eased off her shoes and stretched her artificial silk-stockinged feet towards the hearth. 'There wasn't a dry eye in the house. He sang "Roses of Picardy" and "It's a Long Way to Tipperary". Your brother was killed in the war, wasn't he, Uncle Barney? I'm sure you'd have been moved.'

He said something softly in Welsh.

Maureen frowned. 'I don't know why you do that. It's a waste of time when we don't know what you're saying.' She rested her head against the back of the chair and closed her eyes.

'I don't want you to know. It was rude. I can't be doing with all this sentimentality about the war. It's over. It should be forgotten.'

'We should never forget,' said Lucy, shocked and unable to stop herself. 'When I see a man with no legs pushing himself about by his hands on a trolley and playing the mouth organ for a few coppers, it breaks my heart.'

'I know it's terrible but it's not my fault so don't vent your anger on me!' said Barney, pursing his lips. 'Change the subject.' He glanced at his wife. 'Tell me, did the rent collector call while I've been out?'

'Yes. He'll hand the books over to you on Friday morning.'

His brows drew together in a V above his nose. 'Fine, fine. I'll get young Owen to be here. I want him to take the work over. He's strong and tough and woe betide anyone who grapples with him. He can come to the bank with me.'

Maureen and Lucy stared at him. 'Is that wise?' said his wife. 'I could have gone to the bank for you or with you, but I suppose you don't trust me.'

There was silence and her words seemed to echo around the room. Lucy felt annoyed that Owen had managed to worm his way into her stepfather's good books this far. She darted a glance at Barney and was surprised to see him smiling. 'Don't be silly, sweetheart. You have enough to do – and, as I said, young Owen is tough and strong and will keep any unwelcome attentions away from me. Why don't you go along to the women's group at the church and get involved in good works like I've suggested before, if you've got time on your hands?'

Maureen said, tight-lipped, 'I'm not one of them and I have enough to do. Thanks very much but you can stick that idea where Paddy stuck his ninepence!'

'Don't be common.' Barney looked pained. 'There's nothing wrong with showing charity. It's the Christian thing to do.'

'Christian? Christian! I'm a bloody Catholic, I don't need telling what's the Christian thing to do so leave me be!' Maureen jumped to her feet and rushed out of the room.

'What did I say?' said Barney, with a helpless spreading of his hands. 'I only want her to have friends. You talk to her. Find out what's wrong.'

That was exactly what Lucy intended to do. Although she was worried that Maureen's outburst might be due to her having seen Callum at the Trocadero and she was unsure how to

252

handle that. Should she bring it up or wait for her mother to mention it? Lucy was worried about her mother and stepfather. She didn't know what to do to ease the mental anguish they were obviously suffering and they seemed unable to help each other.

Her mother refused to talk to Lucy, told her to go away and leave her alone. The girl had no choice but to go.

The following morning she decided before going to work to see if she could catch Aunt Mac in. She was in luck and it seemed the old lady had mellowed a bit since last they met. Lucy asked after Callum.

Aunt Mac snorted. 'A fat lot you and your mother care! He's suffered has my boy.'

'Is he still in Ireland?' she asked innocently, accepting a cup of tea and stretching her legs towards the fire.

The old woman did not look at her. 'Where else would he be? He's not doing too badly now since he came out of prison.'

Prison! thought Lucy.

'You don't have to say anything. I know what you're thinking,' said Aunt Mac hastily. 'But you'd be wrong. You mightn't have noticed, busy as you and your mother are living in the lap of luxury, but there's been a civil war in Ireland and he was caught up in it and ended up in prison with that Shaun O'Neill's brother. It's over now, of course, but...'

Lucy almost shot out of her seat. 'Shaun's in prison?'

The old woman's mouth worked and a few

specks of spittle appeared on her chin. 'You got flannel ears, have yer, girl? I said his brother. I wish the other one bloody was! If you'll excuse my language. Trouble, that's all he is. Him wanting my Callum to do things was what got him into trouble in the first place!'

'What d'you mean? Are they both over here?'

'Now why should you think that?' Aunt Mac glared at her and folded her arms across her bosom. 'I haven't forgotten, Lucy, you're in cahoots with a policeman.'

She flushed. 'I haven't seen him for ages. All I'm interested in, Aunt Mac, is whether Shaun O'Neill's alive or dead.'

The old woman was silent. Lucy waited and after several minutes Aunt Mac said, 'I remember our Callum telling me he was in a car crash with his brother. Daniel was arrested but the nasty piece of work was badly injured and taken off somewhere by the Free Irish Troops.'

'Perhaps he's dead?' said Lucy hopefully.

Aunt Mac stared at her with sudden understanding. 'You're scared of him, and I don't blame you.'

'Me and Mam know things about him. If he isn't dead and he decided to come over here, he just might...' Lucy's voice trailed off.

'It's a pity we can't pin that woman's death on him,' Auntie Mac muttered.

'I'd like nothing better,' said Lucy eagerly. 'Only I don't know how we can do it. I'd really like your Callum off the hook.' Her tone was utterly sincere.

'Aye, well,' Aunt Mac said grudgingly. 'I never

did believe you wanted him dead because you did tell the truth about that there pipe of his not being a gun. So tell me, how is your mother? Yer realise she's living in sin? A Catholic, married in the Proddy church. By all that's holy! Your gran would never have got over it,' she tutted.

Lucy decided not to mention her mother's having lost a baby. Aunt Mac might have more harsh words to say about that so she just asked after Uncle Mac and soon afterwards she left.

She realised there was no walking to work for her today. She was late and would have to catch the tram. She ran and as she turned the corner on to Netherfield Road came face to face with Rob. Maybe it was because she was thinking of what Aunt Mac had said that she took a step back and tripped over her own foot. She would have banged her head against the shop window behind her if he had not seized her arm and jerked her upright. It came as a pleasant shock to feel the warmth of his body and the strength of his arms around her. She felt all of a dither and when his grey eyes quizzed her, she blushed.

'Have you been up to something, Lucy? You're looking guilty.'

'Me? What could I have done? It's you being a policeman! You're always looking for someone to arrest,' she babbled.

'Not true! I have another life, but of course you don't know anything about that.'

'I know you've a girlfriend called Blodwen.' She was conscious of his arms still about her and although it was a lovely feeling and made her feel secure, she thought it only right to point that fact out to him.

His brow clouded and he removed them instantly. 'Guilty, m'lud.' Lucy looked questioningly up at him. 'She thinks what I do isn't respectable.' Rob sounded hurt.

Lucy thought the girl needed locking up. 'You stand for law and order! Take no notice of her.'

'That's what I told her but it won't wash. She says the people I have to mix with are the lowest of the low and it's brushing off on me. You wouldn't say I'm a disreputable character, Lucy, now I've told you that?' His eyes twinkled down at her.

'Oh, definitely,' she said boldly. 'You probably take bribes and turn a blind eye to out of hours drinking. Has Blodwen signed the pledge? I bet she has! And I bet if she saw you talking to me right now, knowing I was once a slummy, she'd be terrified that I'd be a bad influence on you.'

'You've changed.' There was a surprised expression on his face. 'You sound like you've more confidence in yourself.'

'I have. That's a good thing, don't you think?'

'Of course.' His smile caused her to catch her breath and for a moment she felt a happiness she had never felt before. Then someone jogged her arm and she blinked and found herself asking him whether Blodwen had suggested what he could do instead of being a policeman.

Rob didn't answer immediately and she wondered with a lift of her heart whether he had felt what she had felt, but that had to be wishful thinking. He said tersely, 'Take over my aunt's timber yard.'

'Your aunt must have been talking to her.'

'It wouldn't come as a surprise.' Rob frowned. 'And will you?'

He did not answer but she could see he was unhappy with the idea. Yet if he loved Blodwen as much as Dilys seemed to think he did, perhaps that was why he looked so unhappy? Maybe he would do as she wanted because he wanted to please her. Lucy felt so angry with the girl. She felt angry with Rob, too, for even thinking of giving up a job which he obviously found interesting. Still he did not answer her and she was aware that time was passing. 'I must go,' she said, moving away from him. 'I'm going to be late if I don't move myself.' She raised a hand in farewell and raced across the road to the tram stop.

It was only when she reached it that she realised she should have told him what Aunt Mac had said about Shaun O'Neill. She glanced across the road and saw that he hadn't moved, was still gazing in her direction. She signalled frantically and when he began to head towards her, breathed a sigh of relief. Then, frustratingly, a tram rattled up and she knew if she didn't take this one she would be late. There was nothing for it but to jump aboard.

It began to move before Rob reached the stop. He ran after it but it was obvious he wouldn't be able to catch it. 'What is it you wanted?' he shouted.

'I can't say it here!' yelled Lucy, above the clatter of the wheels as she stood on the platform. 'Can you meet me in town outside the Trocadero at half-past two?'

She saw his lips moving but could not hear what he said, could only hope he would be there. She wanted this business of Shaun O'Neill sorted out. Though she wasn't going to lie to herself by pretending it was her only reason for wanting to see her favourite policeman.

Lucy found it hard to concentrate on her tasks during the next few hours. She was restless, thinking about that moment of pure happiness. Had she imagined Rob had felt something too? She must have. He was engaged to be married to a woman more his own age and far more beautiful and assured than Lucy was. She had no right to be thinking of him in such a way. If he came it would be purely business. Police business! It was more likely that he had been remembering that with her he was keeping bad company. The company of a murderess! How could she have forgotten? He probably wouldn't come at all.

He was there. Hunched in an overcoat with the collar turned up against a biting wind which immediately found the gap between coat and hat. Now they were face to face Lucy found herself tongue-tied. He spoke brusquely. 'So, what is it that you couldn't shout about?'

She had been right. He had no special feelings for her. 'Shall we move away from here?' she muttered. 'Perhaps we can walk in St John's Gardens?'

His gaze swept her face. 'I didn't come here for a walk: I'm on a case.' Even so he fell into step beside her as she moved away from the cinema entrance.

'I should have told you when we first met,' she said miserably.

'I was right then, about you looking guilty?'

A sharp laugh escaped her. 'You were wrong!'

'You came flying round that corner straight into my arms.'

'Not intentionally. I didn't expect to see you. It gave me a shock.'

'Guilty conscience, like I said.' There was a smile on his face this time, though.

Relieved, Lucy returned his smile. 'I was worried about being late for work. I'd been to Aunt Mac's. We were talking about Shaun O'Neill.'

Rob stiffened. 'You've seen him?'

She shook her head, digging her gloved hands deep into her pockets. 'She told me Callum was in prison in Ireland with Shaun's brother. I don't know what prison but apparently Shaun was badly injured in a car crash and taken away somewhere by the Free State troops. I'm hoping he's dead. Could you find out if he is for me?'

There was such an expression on Rob's face that it made her feel good. He grabbed her by both arms and kissed her hard on the mouth. 'Thanks!'

It gave Lucy such a thrill she touched her own mouth. 'What were you thinking of? There's people around.'

He placed his hands firmly in his pockets. 'I got carried away. Look upon it as a brotherly kiss.' Oh, that hurt, thought Lucy, but he was still talking. 'I really want to nail him! I believe he's responsible for almost killing a police mate of mine. We got into a fight in the Sebastapol area a couple of years back. Tony has never worked again and he's lucky to be alive. I hate knives.'

Lucy felt a shiver down her spine. 'You never mentioned that to me before.'

'I didn't want to worry you but by the sound of it there was no need. He must have scarpered to Ireland straight after the fight. Where did you get this information? Does Barney know McCallum's back in town?'

'He's not,' said Lucy hastily, not wanting Rob tying himself up looking for Callum. 'Unfortunately I don't know the name of the prison.'

Rob smiled grimly. 'I shouldn't have any trouble finding out. That's if I can persuade the officers over me to let me go to Ireland.'

She glanced at him. 'You'll be careful?' Then she blushed.

His expression altered and he said seriously, 'Don't worry about me, Lucy. It makes it more difficult.'

'I won't!' She increased her pace, not looking at him. 'I'm sure you can take care of yourself, a big bloke like you. Just remember, though, the bigger you are the harder you fall.'

He easily kept up with her. 'You're doing it again. You *are* worrying.'

'I'd worry about a dog if it came up against Shaun O'Neill, so don't flatter yourself,' she said in a hard voice.

'That's right! Put me in my place.' She could hear the smile in his voice and looked at him. 'Don't expect to see me for a while,' he said, and walked away.

When Lucy arrived home late that evening she had decided to keep quiet about what she knew of Shaun O'Neill, knowing it would only stir up unpleasant memories for her mother.

Maureen continued to be moody and Lucy did what she could for her. Often she wouldn't get up until lunchtime and this worried Lucy. It was obvious Barney was concerned about her, too, because he fussed over her, telling her to rest as much as she could.

It was Owen's mother who bluntly told Lucy that she was handling her mother the wrong way. 'You're spoiling her soft. The same for you, Mr Jones,' she said, turning to Barney. 'The way you're behaving won't help her get better because it won't bring the baby back. Your wife needs to get out of this house and get some of God's good air into her lungs. The devil finds work for idle hands. What she needs is something to do.'

'Thanks very much for the prescription,' said a harsh voice.

They all turned and saw Maureen standing in the doorway. She must have come down on one of her rare visits to the kitchen. She did not come in but turned and went straight back upstairs. Lucy rose, intent on following her. Barney limped after her, closing the kitchen door behind him. 'Leave her, girlie. It had to be said. Mrs Davies is right. Maureen needs something to do.'

'But what?' said Lucy, wracking her brains. 'Would you allow her to work in the cinema again?'

But he was still adamant about not letting her mother do outside work of any sort. 'You've still

261

got that working-class mentality, Lucy. What would the neighbours think if my wife went out to work? They'd assume I was on my uppers. Her job is to be in this house, looking after me. It's time we put the past behind us.'

Lucy bristled. She was working class and not ashamed of it. 'I agree we have to put the past behind us, Uncle Barney, but if you owned a shop your wife would be working alongside you.'

His jaw set rigid. 'I know you mean well but suggesting I now buy a shop is ridiculous. Your mother would have to handle money and she could spend it on drink.'

Lucy could scarcely believe what she was hearing. 'You can't think that! She hasn't touched a drop since she got married. I thought she might have been tempted when she lost the baby but she hasn't. I'd have smelt it on her breath.'

'Well, we don't want her to start, do we?' said Barney jovially. 'Keep temptation out of the way, hey?' He squeezed her shoulder. 'And talking about money, Lucy, what are you doing with your earnings? Have you thought of investing some of your money?'

His change of mood and subject matter caught her offguard and she almost blurted out that she'd already been persuaded to invest some of her hard-earned cash in an exciting new venture. 'No,' she lied, and smiling brightly added, 'I'm a bit of a spendthrift, Uncle Barney.'

He tutted. 'Shame on you, girlie. I thought you'd have the sense to put a bob or two aside.'

Lucy pulled a face. Why keep her pennies all in one basket? And if it would please him she would take his advice. 'I have a bob or two but not pounds. Perhaps you could invest ten shillings for me? What do you suggest?'

He perked up. 'The electrical goods market is a surefire winner. You won't go wrong there.'

She smiled. 'OK. You can buy me some shares in that.'

'I'm sure you won't lose by it, Lucy,' he said earnestly. 'Even Collins' Ecclesiastical Supplies have broken new ground by going into the production of electrical kettles, toasters and irons.'

Lucy tried to look impressed. They were marvellous things, although Agnes and Mrs Davies were wary of using the kettle and iron Barney had brought into the house. The thought of investing in such things didn't excite Lucy one little bit but she'd committed herself now and her stepfather did seem to have a knack for making money. 'OK, I'll go and fetch my ten bob.' She wanted to get away and see how her mother was.

'You really mustn't fritter money away, Lucy. I'm surprised at you. I thought you were a sensible girl,' Barney called after her.

'There's so much to fritter it on,' she retorted frankly.

Once upstairs she tapped gently on her mother's bedroom door. 'Mam, can I come in?'

'Not now, Lucy. I'll see you in the morning.'

'You are OK?'

'There's nothing for you to worry about,' Maureen said firmly. 'Goodnight.'

Lucy was relieved. 'Well, if there's anything you want – a cup of tea?'

'Goodnight!'

'Goodnight, Mam.' Relieved, Lucy went into her bedroom and took a darned stocking from under her mattress. There was more than ten bob inside it but she didn't intend to leave herself with no money in hand. She'd given the rest to the manager of the Trocadero's broker after a fascinating discussion about an almost revolutionary new development in the music industry. But it would be hopeless talking about that to Barney because where some things were concerned he was bigoted and short-sighted.

She counted the money. There was a little more than she thought so she decided to invest fifteen shillings in electrical goods. She took it downstairs and gave it to her stepfather. 'There's fifteen shillings actually,' she said.

He smiled and promised to do what he could for her.

The following day was Sunday and Lucy was just turning over to go back to sleep when she heard Maureen's footsteps going past her door. Lucy stared bleary-eyed at the window. It was only just getting light. What was her mother doing up so early? Perhaps she'd taken what Owen's mother had said to heart and decided to surprise them all by going for a walk ... or even cooking breakfast for them because Mrs Davies never worked Sundays.

When Lucy eventually got up there was no sign of Maureen in the kitchen but Timmy was there heading for the back door with a ball under his arm. 'What are you doing?' asked Lucy.

He looked round guiltily. 'Shhh! You'll have Uncle Barney down here!'

'What's wrong with that? He wouldn't stop you going out.'

'Not in so many words. He'd smile at me and say, "Not going to church this morning, boyo?"' The boy imitated the man's voice and wide smile perfectly.

Lucy smiled faintly. 'He can't make you go. He's not violent like Uncle Mick was.'

'No! But he'd go on and on and take all the pleasure out of me skiving off with his nagging. He's worse than a woman!'

Lucy laughed and didn't persist. 'Have you seen Mam?'

'She went out.' He sounded pleased.

'Where?'

'She didn't say.'

'What kind of mood was she in?'

Timmy pursed his lips, bounced the ball and caught it. 'She's up to something. She had that look on her face that I remember from when we were younger. She was kinda excited but not wanting to show it.'

Lucy wondered what her mother was up to and debated whether to go in search of her but at that moment she heard the heavy sound of Barney's boot on the stairs. 'You'd best go!' she said, shoving her brother out of the back door.

He had no sooner disappeared than Maureen appeared in the doorway to the yard. She looked furtive and was carrying something wrapped in newspaper. 'Where've you been?' said Lucy.

Just then Barney called down to the kitchen, 'Are you there, Lucy? Have you seen your mother?'

'I'm here, darlin'!' Maureen placed the parcel on the table and almost skipped up the steps to him. 'How about bacon and eggs for breakfast?'

'Mrs Davies put the saltfish in soak,' he said. 'You're up early. Feeling better?'

'I'm fine. I've been and got you some mushrooms. They're pink and tender as a baby's bottom.' She kissed his cheek.

He glanced at Lucy and smiled. 'See, Mrs Davies was right.'

Maureen's smile slipped a second. Then she placed a hand on his arm. 'You're right. I've taken to heart what she said ... but don't you be coming down into the kitchen right now and getting under our feet.' She led him into the music room and sat him down on the piano stool. 'You play us some music and I'll bring your breakfast up on a tray. We've missed your music, haven't we, Luce?'

She agreed and stood in the doorway, waiting to see if he would play. Barney sat there for several minutes, an expression on his face that made her realise anew just how much he'd denied himself since the loss of the baby. Then he unlocked the piano lid and ran his fingers over the keys. Maureen winked at Lucy and left the room.

She followed her mother downstairs into the kitchen. 'You are in a good mood. Is it really down to what Owen's mother said?'

Maureen took down the cast-iron frying pan and placed it on the range. 'Ask no questions and I'll tell you no lies.'

'I think she really riled you,' said Lucy, going over and taking the bacon from the meat safe.

'She roused your fighting spirit. You sound like your old self.'

Maureen hesitated, then smiled. 'I've been to church.' She put lard in the pan.

It was the last answer Lucy had expected. 'St George's early communion? You do surprise me.'

Her mother did not answer but began to sing very softly, '"Ave Maria..."'

Almost instantly Lucy realised where she had been. 'He'll hit the roof,' she whispered.

The singing stopped and Maureen said, tight-lipped, 'Then we won't tell him, will we?' She resumed singing again, louder this time.

Overhead came the sound of Barney vamping on the piano. The fat hissed as Maureen placed several rashers of bacon in the pan. 'But what if he finds out?' whispered Lucy.

Maureen glanced over her shoulder at her daughter. 'He's not a violent man is Barney. Now, no more questions.' This time when she began to sing it was 'When Irish Eyes Are Smiling'.

Lucy gave up. It was a relief to see her mother cheerful after months of misery. She only hoped it would continue.

Chapter Fourteen

'Can I have a wireless or a gramophone as a little present this Christmas to cheer me up?' Maureen's teeth crunched on a slice of toast as she looked across the table at her husband.

'I didn't hear that,' said Barney, without lowering the newspaper.

Lucy's eyes went from one to the other of them and she wondered how long her mother could keep secret her visits to her old church. So far she had managed it by attending St George's on Sundays and St Anthony's in the week. Maureen had managed to pull herself together so much she had even dispensed with Mrs Davies' services. Barney had protested, saying she was an excellent cook, having a way with leeks he particularly liked, but Maureen could be just as stubborn as he was and reminded him in honeyed tones he had told her it was her task to organise the running of the household. There was no need for a cook now she was her old self again. He had given in, but with unaccustomed ill grace.

Maureen rose and went the other side of the table to loop her arms round her husband's neck. 'Don't get prickly, darlin'! Most people have one or the other these days. I could listen to music while you and Lucy are out at work. Liverpool's had its own station for over a year, and if the Lord Mayor of Liverpool's in favour of it I don't know why you have to be against it?'

He sighed heavily and, gripping both her hands, removed them from his neck. 'I credited you with some sense. I'm a musician and the wireless and the gramophone are death to musicians.'

Maureen straightened and her eyes glinted. 'That's a lie! I've been told Jack Hylton and his orchestra are relayed all the way from London on

268

the wireless. It's a miracle, so it is, like aeroplanes being able to stay up in the air!'

Lucy couldn't resist tossing in her two penny-worth. 'Musicians can make a fortune performing on gramophone records these days. Music you can dance to.'

'Jazz!' said Barney, exasperated. 'That's jungle music, and from what I've read about the bright young things I'd say it's not decent. There'll be none of that dancing in this house.'

'What about singing?' said Maureen, resuming her seat. 'There's the Great Caruso – George Robey – Harry Lauder!'

'I've heard their recordings. They're rubbish, all crackly. Don't do credit to them. I prefer them live!'

'The latest recordings aren't like that,' said Lucy, pouring herself another cup of tea. 'They're electrical and are lovely and clear. I've heard them at Dilys's aunt's.'

Barney sighed. *'"Et tu, Brute?"'* He raised his newspaper.

Lucy and Maureen looked at each other and then pulled faces at the newspaper. '"Charleston, Charleston,"' sang Lucy.

Her stepfather lowered his newspaper again. 'American! It has no style. The waltz at least has grace and a decent tempo but these others crossing the Atlantic...' He shuddered. 'Men and women dancing at each other, not with each other. It doesn't seem right. Not that I've ever done much in the way of dancing.'

'You should try,' said Maureen, winking at her daughter. 'What about a clog dance?'

Barney's face stiffened and his nostrils flared. 'That's not funny.'

'Sorry,' said his wife meekly.

Lucy wondered what had got into her but perhaps Mam was right and it was a pity Barney had never tried to dance, even though she guessed it would be tremendously difficult and not at all graceful. Lucy's mind wandered to the other Thursday when she'd had one of her rare nights off. She and Dilys had attended the penny hop at St Polycarp's church hall on Netherfield Road and had great fun. Owen had turned up and despite a barbed remark about her mother sacking his, he'd asked Lucy to dance during the Gentlemen's Excuse Me. She'd accepted because he was a natural dancer and despite Dilys' moody expression had accepted another invitation to foxtrot.

'Well, Lucy?' said Barney.

'Well what?' she said cautiously.

He laughed. 'You're in a dream, girlie. I said at least you'll hear good music at the Trocadero.'

'Definitely,' she agreed hastily. Although Palm Court wasn't her style at all. 'And it's always a pleasure to listen to you play, Barney.'

He folded his newspaper and, standing up, gave her a little bow. 'Thank you.' And he added that they were going to be late for church if they didn't hurry.

Lucy made haste. She was hoping Rob might make one of his rare visits to St George's. He hadn't been there last week but Dilys had made no mention of his being away so Lucy could only think he hadn't managed to get to Ireland.

Unless he'd gone this past week. Sometimes she imagined again the feel of his kiss on her lips and his arms round her and she'd have to remind herself that it had only been meant in a brotherly way.

They slipped into a back pew at St George's because they were late. It wasn't until the second hymn that Lucy noticed Dilys and her aunt were missing from the choir. She did not spot Rob and Blodwen until she herself had slipped out of church as soon as the service finished and stood waiting for Barney and her mother who were being sociable with other members of the congregation. Lucy wandered over to the graveyard. Some of the stones were extremely large and lay flat on the ground. One had fancy wrought-iron railing rounding it, a reminder of mid-Victorian times when St George's had been *the* church for people with money. Barney had told her how his great-uncle had moved out when the influx of Irish escaping the potato famine had sent the population of Liverpool soaring. Everton, which had once been a pretty village, had been swamped by housing for the poor. The really wealthy had then built themselves houses at the south end of Liverpool or out Bootle way.

Suddenly Lucy noticed Rob and Blodwen standing in the doorway, talking to the vicar. Lucy took up a strategic position near one of the standing monuments to the dead so she could watch them. It seemed to her that Blodwen was doing all the talking while Rob stood around like a spare part. He glanced about him and Lucy lifted a hand. He saw her and began to walk towards her. She darted behind the gravestone.

He peered round it, a smile on his face. 'What are you up to?'

'I thought you mightn't want the girlfriend seeing you talk to me,' she whispered.

With an incredulous sigh he pulled Lucy out. 'I'm not wearing a ball and chain, you know.'

'She doesn't like me ... and I thought she might be talking to the vicar about your wedding arrangements.' Lucy was having trouble keeping her hands off Rob. He was looking really smart today in a charcoal suit and a pristine white shirt. The silver-grey trilby he wore was pushed to the back of his head and a lock of dark hair curled on his forehead. His mouth looked soft and inviting.

'No. She wants a big do and for us to buy a house first. So no wedding plans yet.'

Lucy felt weak with relief, thinking there was hope for her yet. 'Could you buy a house on your wages?'

'If we can put a big enough deposit down, so I'm saving hard.' He nudged the edge of the gravestone with the toe of his shoe, hands in pockets, a frown puckering his brow. 'I'd rather marry sooner.'

Lucy's heart sank. It sounded like there was no chance for her but she rallied. 'She still wants you to change your mind about being a policeman?'

He lifted his head and smiled faintly. 'She's working on it, if that's what you mean. She's forever going on about me being my own boss and how good that would be.'

Lucy glanced over her shoulder to see if Blodwen was still hogging the vicar. 'She's very pretty.'

272

Rob nodded. 'She has a good heart but she lost her first fiance in the war and that's made her a bit hard – perhaps even desperate to have something extra in our marriage to compensate for not having him.'

Lucy wondered if anything could ever compensate for losing the man you loved with all your being. Was second best ever good enough?

'I haven't been to Ireland yet,' said Rob. 'The case we're working on at the moment is big. A doctor accused of poisoning his wife ... a man of influence, with friends in high places.' He grimaced.

'Never mind,' said Lucy lightly. 'It can't be helped.' She searched for something else to say. 'Dilys? Your aunt? Nothing wrong, is there?'

A grin lit up his face. 'They've been summoned to Wales. My great-aunt's on her last legs and she has money. They'll be back tomorrow.'

'So you're all on your own? Who'll cook your dinner?'

He jerked his head in the direction of the church entrance. 'Blodwen's mother's invited me to Sunday lunch.'

'What a pity,' Lucy said forlornly. 'I'm quite a good cook.'

He stared at her and there was a look on his face that caused her pain. 'Don't, Lucy! I don't want you getting hurt,' he said in a voice so low that she could only just catch the words. 'I'm in love with her. I'm not worth it. I should never have kissed you. Find someone your own age, love.'

She wanted to say, But you're not that old and

I don't want anyone my own age! Then she heard Barney say, 'Lucy! Rob!'

They both spun round and there was her step-father with Blodwen. She was looking daggers at Lucy and, brushing past her, the older girl slid her arm possessively through Rob's. At the same time Barney put his hand on Lucy's elbow. 'Time to go, lovey. Your mother's gone on ahead to see to the dinner.'

'Right, I'm coming. I was just asking after Dilys,' said Lucy, pinning on a bright smile. 'Rob. Blodwen.'

The other girl inclined her head and Rob raised his hat, his face expressionless. Lucy watched them walk away and disappear round the back of the church. 'I wouldn't get too fond of him,' said Barney, sounding slightly embarrassed. 'Blod's a lovely girl and she has suffered.'

Lucy nodded but made no comment and they walked home in silence.

To her surprise, and Barney's obvious annoyance, there was no sign of Maureen when they arrived home. 'Now where's she gone?' he said, throwing up his hand. 'I want my dinner!'

'I'll see to the dinner,' offered Lucy, checking the oven and noting the roasties were in. 'Mam can't have gone far.'

He drummed his fingers on the table. 'There's something wrong with her. She's getting very forgetful. Her mind isn't what it was since she lost the baby.'

'Perhaps I should go and look for her?'

'No!' he said firmly. 'She might have nipped to the corner shop for something she's forgotten.

It's getting a bit foggy. She'll be back soon.'

Lucy suggested, 'Why don't you go and play some music? I'll hear it down here. It'll be nice.'

He took her up on the suggestion and after she had set the table Lucy raced down the yard and along the back entry into Devonshire Place. She did not get as far as the recreation ground before spotting her mother and Timmy coming towards her. She linked her arm through her mother's to hurry her along. 'He's worrying about you. Said you're getting forgetful,' she told Maureen in a low voice.

Her mother drew herself up to her full height. 'There's nothing wrong with my mind. I know exactly where I've been.'

'And where's that?'

Maureen tapped her nose and smiled. 'Some things you're best not knowing, girl.'

'So you've remembered where you live?' said Barney, sharpening the carving knife on the steel as Lucy and Timmy sat at the table. Maureen was standing across from him with the tureen of roast potatoes in her hand. 'I'm sorry, darlin'! I went and forgot I'd promised to drop a knitting pattern in on an old friend.' She went over to him and kissed the top of his head, afterwards pressing her cheek against his.

Timmy and Lucy exchanged glances. If that was true, thought the girl, why hadn't she said so when first asked? But she couldn't really work up any enthusiasm for finding out where her mother had been. Her own heart was sore. Why did Rob have to fall in love with Blodwen?

Barney began to carve, talking at the same time about the new Rudolph Valentino film *Son of the Sheik*. 'The Trocadero will be packed,' he said, smiling happily. 'The profits from my shares will go up. Remember when *The Sheik* was on, Lucy? Women were swooning all over the place.'

Timmy snorted. 'They're daft!'

'What do you think of him?' Barney shot the question at Maureen as she dished out roast potatoes. She made no answer. 'Didn't you hear me, Mowie?'

His wife looked at him. 'What was that?'

He looked exasperated. 'You're in another world. What's up with you? You should be listening when I talk to you.'

'I *was* listening. I was thinking about it.' Maureen flashed a look of entreaty at her daughter. Lucy mouthed 'Rudolph Valentino'.

'What's your answer then?' pressed Barney.

Maureen smiled. 'I think he wears make up. I don't think that's very manly. It's like wearing smelly hair lotion. I think it's effeminate.'

There was silence. Lucy held her breath. What had got into her mother? Barney had reddened and a slice of beef slid from the fork on to the table cloth. 'There's nothing effeminate about me,' he muttered.

Maureen's lovely eyes smiled at him. 'I like a man to smell like a man. It's something you should take notice of, Barney. Now, do you want another roastie or is five enough? You're getting a bit fat.'

Lucy's stomach quivered as Barney stabbed the beef. 'There'll be no wireless or gramophone in

276

this house for Christmas!' he thundered. 'There'll be no money for new fashions either. You've enough clothes in the wardrobe to last you a lifetime and that's how long they're going to have to last, Maureen.'

She sniffed and dropped a boiled potato on to his plate.

'And another thing,' he snapped. 'You'd be better keeping your eye on Lucy than looking up old friends. The girl has a fancy for Rob Jones and that way can only lead to heartache for her.'

Maureen put down the empty tureen and picked up another of carrot and turnip. She smiled at Lucy. 'I thought you were never going to get married? I thought you had plans?'

'I have, Mam. There's nothing for you to worry about,' said Lucy hastily, wishing Barney had kept his mouth shut.

Silence reigned while they all ate. Afterwards Lucy dashed upstairs, needing to get out of the house, to walk and walk until she was exhausted. Her brother entered her room, grinning like a hyena. 'His face when Mam said that about the hair lotion!' he choked, dropping on to Lucy's bed and rolling about.

'I don't know how she dared,' said Lucy, taking a coat out of the wardrobe. 'She must have been mad. I'd love to know where she'd really been.'

Timmy looked up. 'I followed her,' he blurted out. 'I've been worried about the way she goes off. You wouldn't know about it because you're at work but she goes out some evenings, too.'

'I know where she goes,' said Lucy with a shrug. 'St Anthony's.'

Timmy sat up on the bed. 'How d'you know?'

'She told me.' Lucy stared grimly at her own reflection as she brushed her hair. 'Anymore secrets?'

There was a pregnant pause.

'Well?'

He cleared his throat. 'I saw that Irishman, the one Uncle Mick used to knock around with and invite to our house.'

Lucy dropped the hairbrush. So he was alive! Without Shaun O'Neill's name even being spoken her stomach quivered and she felt sick. 'Where?' she croaked.

'He was in a car with another man. They were driving along Mere Lane in the direction of the picture house.'

'Did he see you?'

Timmy's blue eyes were thoughtful. 'I've grown, haven't I? I doubt he'd recognise me.'

She nodded in agreement. He was almost as tall as she was now, would be twelve next birthday. She'd be nineteen.

'What are you going to do?' asked Timmy.

Lucy picked up her green velveteen cloche hat and drew it over her hair while she thought about what he'd said. Her heart leaped inside her. 'Visit Rob Jones. He said the police want Shaun O'Neill for a different crime than the one I have in mind.'

'What about Mam? Should we tell her? The way she wanders about ... what if O'Neill spots her and hurts her?'

Lucy thought of what Rob had said about hating knives. She gnawed on her lip and came to

278

a decision. 'I'll tell her.'

She went downstairs and found her mother in the kitchen and told her what Timmy had said. Maureen went very still and did not speak for several seconds. Then she shivered. 'I don't know what there is to be scared of. He doesn't know where we live.'

'But he might, Mam,' said Lucy earnestly. 'There's something I haven't told you. I went to see Aunt Mac and she told me Callum was in an Irish prison with Shaun O'Neill's brother. Callum might have mentioned where we live now.'

Maureen stared at her and then laughed. 'Like mother, like daughter! We are ones for secrets, aren't we?'

Lucy felt uncomfortable. 'It was when you were ill. I didn't want to rake up the past and upset you.'

'The past – we can never forget it,' said Maureen slowly. 'I think I'll go to bed and lie down.'

'I'll do you a hot water bottle,' said Lucy eagerly, thinking her mother had received a shock. 'Mam, you've to stop wandering around in the evening on your own. You will, won't you?'

Maureen smiled and patted her cheek. 'Of course. Don't you worry. I'll see to the hot water bottle. You've got your coat and hat on. You get off out, but be careful. Where are you going, by the way?'

'Not far.' After what Barney had said to her mother about her having a fancy for Rob, she wasn't going to confess that she was off to his aunt's house. He mightn't be home yet after having lunch at Blodwen's mother's but Lucy could wait until he arrived home. She kissed her mother and left the house.

The fog swirled about her but it was not so thick that she couldn't see where she was going. She pulled up the fur collar of her coat and shrouded her mouth and nose in it and headed along St Domingo Road in the direction of Mere Lane. A figure loomed up out of the fog and she jumped out of her skin. He passed and she laughed at herself but was shaken because it had just occurred to her, that Rob's aunt's house lay in the very direction where Timmy claimed to have seen Shaun O'Neill. Was she completely mad to be going there? What would Rob say when he came home and found her on his doorstep? Should she go back?

She stopped, gripped by indecision. Her heart told her to go on but her mind said, Go back! You're making a fool of yourself. More footsteps muffled by the fog. Her stomach ached with the effort of trying to steady her nerves.

'Lousy Sunday afternoon,' said a woman's voice.

Lucy agreed and walked on. The fog appeared to be thickening and it was becoming difficult to get her bearings. She listened intently for any sound of traffic before taking her courage into her hands and crossing the road, feeling for the tramlines beneath her feet. Pale yellow light gleamed from the odd shop window and she followed that line of light with confidence. Then she heard a man coughing and tried to see where the noise was coming from. What if she was right to be scared and Shaun O'Neill was in the vicinity? She trembled as she listened to the coughing. Then it stopped. She walked on but could no longer see the lights. Was she even going in the right direction? She was no longer certain and was cold, really cold. She stretched out a hand but there was only space in front of her. Panic seized her and she began to run, her feet making a slapping noise on the ground. She stumbled off a kerb and then on to another one and was about to slow down when she ran slap bang into a wall. She clung to it. Perhaps she would die here?

Lucy did not know how long she rested against the wall but eventually was shivering with cold and so forced herself to keep close to it and carry on walking. She came to a flight of steps and instantly realised the wall belonged to a cinema. It must be the Mere Picture Palace. Relieved, knowing St Domingo Grove was just across the way and having got her bearings at last, she allowed a tram to rattle by before crossing the road.

There was no answer when she knocked at Miss Griffiths' door and she was disappointed, having hoped Rob would come home earlier because of the fog. She huddled on the front step, praying he would not be long. There was no way she would head back through that fog again on her own. She closed her eyes and allowed herself to drift.

'Lucy! What are you doing here?' Someone was shaking her shoulder. He sounded fed up.

She forced up her eyelids and tried to move her limbs but they were stiff with cold. 'Shaun O'Neill,' she said through chattering teeth, accepting Rob's helping hand to get up. She clung to the front of his overcoat. 'T-Timmy's seen him! He-He was in a car going along M-Mere Lane.'

'What!' Rob's hand covered hers and his voice changed. 'My God, you're freezing! How long have you been here? You shouldn't have come in the fog.'

'I-I f-felt I had to tell you.' She peered up at him. He looked worried and that made her feel better. He did definitely feel something for her. 'I'll g-go now. I d-don't want to b-be a nuisance.'

'You *are* a bloody nuisance,' he said, sounding exasperated. 'But I can't let you go home like this. Let me get the door open. You'll have to come in and get a warm.'

'No! Y-You don't want me!'

'Shut up!' He shoved her inside and switched on the light.

Lucy stood in the lobby, shivering, looking up at him. 'You're angry,' she said, trying to smile but failing miserably.

'Of course I'm angry. What'll your mother and Barney think of your being here alone with me? What'll Blodwen and my aunt think if they find out?' Rob loomed over her, ushering her into the big kitchen where she had sat the day Mick had died and eaten strawberry jam and cream scones.

Rob put a match to the newspaper and wood in the grate and then sat back on his heels, watching the whole lot catch fire before placing lumps of coal in its centre. Lucy looked at him and her heart swelled with emotion. She wanted to reach out and kiss the back of his neck but managed to control herself.

'Nobody'll know. I won't tell them and in the fog nobody'll have seen me come in. Are you going to tell them? I think you're pretty good at keeping secrets.'

He glanced at her and she noticed once more that his eyebrows were set in straight, uncompromising dark slashes. 'You've got it all worked out, haven't you?'

She shook her head, gazing at the fire, and shivered. 'Sometimes I can look into a fire and not see the smoke and Uncle Mick unconscious on that burning bed. Other times he's there in my head and I almost can't bear it. I want to run, fetch water and dash it over the fire in the grate.'

Rob was silent. Then he got up and went out of the room. When he reappeared he was carrying a blanket which he threw at her. 'Put that round you.'

She did as she was told, almost wishing herself out of there. He left her alone again but the next time he entered the room he was carrying a tray and placed it on her knee. He took one of the steaming cups and a slice of bara-brith and sat on an easy chair to her left. 'You never did tell me exactly what happened that day,' he said. 'Perhaps it's time you did ... laid a few ghosts. Time I knew what I've got myself into with you. I never asked before because I was worried I might have had you all wrong.'

Lucy warmed her hands on the cup and took

several sips before placing it on the saucer. She made herself consciously think of the day Mick had died. Of course the trouble with her uncle had started long before then. Could she tell Rob about the things she had not even told her mother? Hopefully it would help him understand why she had snapped that day.

'Well?' he said softly, his grey eyes intent on her face.

'I'll have to go back before then,' Lucy started in a low voice. 'It all began when he came back from Ireland. He had been wounded over there in a gun battle and afterwards was no good to the Cause. That didn't please him. He was angry and frustrated. The war ... he once spoke to me about rotting corpses ... about flesh ... and mine being so soft.' Her voice was barely about a whisper.

'He didn't...?' Rob's voice sounded like he was being strangled.

'No!' She stared at him, her eyes wide with pain. 'But might have if ... I don't know!' She lowered her head and gulped at her tea before continuing in a trembling voice, 'He said he was so lonely ... an-and that's what I remember when he-he comes back to haunt me.' Her eyes filled with tears.

Rob put down his cup and came and sat beside her. 'Don't say anymore if you find it too up-setting.'

She got a grip on herself. 'I've never even spoken about this to Mam.' Lucy tried to laugh but her voice broke on a sob. She wiped her wet face with the back of her hand. 'The violence she experienced for herself. It was so hard accepting he had changed from the way he used to be. He used to act daft and play games with me when I was little.' She paused, the tears rolling down her cheeks.

Rob took the hand nearest to him and lifted it to his face; he held it against his cheek before pressing a kiss on her palm. He kept hold of it. 'Do you want to go on?'

Lucy nodded, touched to the heart by the warmth of his gesture. His just being there was a comfort to her and she felt a lovely sense of wellbeing. She cleared her throat. 'The day Uncle Mick died he'd hit me with his fist in the face because I wouldn't tell him what I knew about you and Barney. I almost cracked then but instead I ran. But after he knocked you out there was nowhere for me to run but upstairs. In the bedroom, when he touched me, something exploded inside me! He liked that, though! I managed to knock the gun out of his hand. He-he threw me on the bed, was laughing and calling me a wild cat...' She paused to ease her throat and Rob picked up her tea cup which she had put down and held it to her lips. She took a drink. 'I think then he would have ... you know. But-but I rolled off the bed and picked up the gun. I remember I wanted to say something daft like, "Reach for the sky, Uncle Mick!"' She gazed at Rob. 'Isn't that stupid?'

'I'm amazed you could think of anything to say.' And again he kissed her hand.

Lucy took a deep breath. 'But of course, I couldn't pull the trigger. He lunged at me and I was so scared that I just hit out ... he collapsed on the bed. He'd lit a cigarette and it fell out of his hand and – poof! He'd had paraffin under there.' She stopped, gasping, feeling she couldn't breath.

'It's OK! That's enough! Take deep breaths – slowly now!'

She did as Rob said and began to feel better. He went and refilled their cups and handed hers back to her. His fingers brushed Lucy's and she lifted her eyes and looked at him from beneath her eyelashes, saying shyly, 'You've been so kind.'

He shook his head. 'I should have got all this out of you earlier. You had no way of telling whether he was dead or not at that point. He didn't kill me when he hit me with the gun. You wouldn't have hit him as hard as he hit me. You wouldn't have had the same strength. You didn't kill him. He dropped a lighted cigarette. He stored paraffin. The explosives he had too could have killed even more people.'

Lucy sighed. 'I've told myself all that but I feel better for hearing it coming from you. Still, I'll never be able to forget it all.'

'You have to try and put it out of your mind.'

'I do, but sooner or later it comes back.'

'We all have things we have to live with. I was responsible for a bloke losing his job. I caught him stealing. Later he committed suicide because he couldn't look after his family. We all have regrets.' Rob took the cup from her and placed it carefully on an occasional table. He pulled Lucy to her feet. 'Will you be all right now?'

'I feel heaps better.' She slid her arms about his waist and rested her head against his chest, listening to the hurried beat of his heart. 'Thanks. I love you,' she said quietly.

'Don't say that!' He held her away from him. 'What will I do with you, Lucy?' he said in despairing tones.

She smiled up at him and with a groan he lifted her off her feet and kissed her. It was a long, hungry kiss and when they drew apart for breath, she said on a sigh, 'Nice.'

'Too bloody nice,' said Rob huskily. 'If only *she'd* kiss me like that.'

'She doesn't love you like I do.' Lucy pressed her lips against his with a touch of desperation. She could feel the outline of him through their clothing and wondered if he was as aware of her breasts, stomach and thighs as she was of his body. She strained towards him. Animal magnetism, she thought.

'We shouldn't be doing this,' he muttered against her mouth. 'Not after all you've told me about your uncle.'

'You're not like him. Besides, I want you to love me.' She drew his head down and kissed him again.

The next moment they were flat on the sofa, kissing each other greedily, hands exploring the contours of each other's body. He pulled up her skirt and stroked her thigh. 'Mam said I should run if a man or boy did that to me,' Lucy murmured.

'Then you should run,' rasped Rob, unfastening the buttons of her bodice now and tearing off the binding that gave her figure the fashionable boyish outline. He buried his face

287

between her breasts.

Lucy sighed as he kissed each rosy point. 'Will you do it to me?' She longed for him with a desperate urgency. Rob stilled. She held her breath. He pulled away and she wanted to cry. His face was soft with desire and his eyes looked dazed. He was tearing at his tousled hair. Wincing, he said, 'What the hell am I doing? I-I love Blodwen.' His mouth trembled.

'No!' cried Lucy, scrambling to her knees and fastening both her arms round his legs. 'Would you feel the way you do right now if you really loved her? You love me!'

He shook his head as if to clear it. 'She wouldn't let me go so far. I'm using you, Lucy. I should be whipped.'

'No!' she said, clinging to his arm as he got off the sofa. She was dragged to her feet. Standing on the sofa she was able to stare straight into his eyes and hated the pain she saw there. 'Blodwen wants to change you! If you let her she'll spoil your life. I like you the way you are.'

'Don't say that! It's not true.' He put a hand to Lucy's face and she rested her cheek against it.

'Honestly,' she said in a low voice. 'I'll give you more than she ever will.'

'You must go.' He removed his hands and placed them in his pockets. 'I'm going to marry Blodwen. She needs me and I love her.' He sounded desperately in need of reassurance.

Lucy wasn't about to give him it. Her heart felt like a lump of dough inside her. She felt like screaming, 'She doesn't love you! She wants to be married that's all!' but guessed he might know that already. Thinking such an unpleasant truth yourself was one thing; someone else saying it could hurt unbearably. Didn't she know it! Where was her pride? She wasn't going to beg him to take her.

Slowly Lucy let her hands fall and stepped down from the sofa. She reached for her coat and hat and put them on. She walked out of the room, half expecting him to follow her, but he didn't and that angered her. Where were his manners?

She opened the front door and slammed it behind her. The fog seemed to swallow up the sound. She'd forgotten about the fog and Shaun O'Neill. Perhaps he was lurking just round the corner... For a moment fear gripped her and then she laughed out loud. 'Stupid! That's what I am, stupid!' How would he find her in the fog when she was going to have trouble finding her own way home?

Lucy set off in what she knew was the right direction. It was when she was passing the Mere Lane Picture Palace that she became aware of footsteps behind her. A familiar fear made her stand still for a moment then she tilted her chin and carried on walking. The footsteps followed her but after a while she was convinced there was something familiar about them. Still she did not turn round, just kept on walking, convinced it was Rob making sure she got home safely.

Chapter Fifteen

It was New Year's Eve and Maureen and Barney, Lucy and Timmy, had been invited to spend the evening at Rob's aunt's house before going on to the Watchnight Service at St George's to welcome in the year 1926. Lucy would have liked to have given the visit a miss but the atmosphere at home over Christmas had been so peculiar she needed to get out of the house. She felt torn two ways about being in Rob's company, knowing Blodwen would probably be there too, but to attempt to make excuses to stay away would only invite questions from her mother and Barney. Besides Lucy had made herself a daring new frock and it might be worth going to see Rob's reaction.

Loving someone who said they didn't love you was a painful emotion. She wondered if Barney felt the same as she did, but perhaps she was misjudging her mother and she loved Barney still. No presents worthy of the name had made their appearance under the decorated tree for Maureen from her husband. Only a new apron, frilled at hem and bib, a frying pan and a jar of bright blue bath crystals.

Lucy thought it was terrible of him after the extravagant presents he had bought her in the past but it showed just how deeply his wife's words about perfumed hair oil and his being effeminate had hurt him. Only briefly had Maureen's expression revealed her innermost feelings on opening the presents.

Afterwards, while Lucy and Agnes prepared the Christmas dinner, Maureen had behaved like she didn't have a care in the world, singing the latest Ivor Novello songs and being charm itself to Barney once they were all seated round the table. He appeared gratified by this and Lucy wondered if he believed that by being so stingy to his wife he had produced this effect. If so, she could only wonder how well he really knew her mother.

It was a crisp, clear night and they caught a tram along St Domingo Road because Barney said his hip was giving him pain, but walking along Mere Lane they fell in with Owen and his mother. It seemed to come as no surprise to Barney that they, too, had been invited to the party at Miss Griffiths'.

'She's a very kind woman,' said Owen's mother, her head tilted a little to one side like a bird's as she smiled at Barney.

'You won't find us arguing with that,' he said jovially. Then he sighed. 'I'm sorry you had to leave us. Nobody makes a leek and ham pie the way you do.'

'Well, it wasn't my choice, Mr Jones!' And Mrs Davies glanced in Maureen's direction.

Lucy was surprised to see her mother was smiling. Perhaps she hadn't heard? Was in a little world all her own.

Owen sidled up to Lucy. 'What are the odds there'll be dancing?'

She thought he must be making money over and above the Davies' daily needs because the suit he wore appeared to be brand new. He looked smart but even so still had that devilish air about him. 'Some hope,' she murmured, and mimicked his mother's voice. 'She's a very kind woman – but I can't see us shimmying and doing the Charleston in her parlour.'

'You never know.' Owen grinned. 'Miss Dilys Jones has a way of getting round people.'

'Tried getting round you, has she?' teased Lucy. 'You must tell me what you've got that's so attractive. At the moment I can't see it.'

He didn't appear a bit put out by what she'd said. 'That's because you go round wearing blinkers, Midget.' His arm brushed against hers. 'I rather fancy you, though. I always have.'

Lucy looked at him with a mixture of amusement and amazement. 'My Uncle Mick said you did but I couldn't understand why and I still don't. It's not as if I've ever given you any encouragement.'

'I don't know why I do myself ... all the trouble you've given me.'

Lucy's smile deepened. 'Don't come that! You've caused me a helluva lot of bother in the past.'

'Sod the past! Couldn't you give me a chance to prove it might be worth cultivating my friendship right now?' His eyes gleamed in the lamplight.

Unexpectedly she felt sorry for him. 'Give me one good reason why I should?'

'Because if you don't, I'll really take up with

Dilys and that'll be a shame because then you'll miss out on me getting rich and being some-body.'

'Will you buy me a cinema?' Lucy asked, laughter in her voice.

He hesitated before saying cautiously, 'How much do they cost?'

She laughed. 'Forget it. I was only joking.'

Lucy walked over to her mother, who had fallen behind Barney and Mrs Davies, and slipped her hand under her arm. 'How are you feeling?'

Maureen patted her daughter's hand and looked up at the moon. 'See that? Isn't it just perfect?'

Lucy lifted her face. Not only was there a silvery moon but billions of stars too piercing the black velvety sky. 'Beautiful!'

'So what are you doing coming over to me?' whispered Maureen. 'That lad needs an eye keeping on him. Look how he got round Barney to give him the rent collector's job. You play along with him. You don't want him and his mother getting away with what's ours.'

Lucy was aghast. 'Barney wouldn't!'

'He likes her leek and ham pie,' said Maureen seriously.

Lucy giggled, thinking food was a bit different from S-E-X. She couldn't imagine Barney and the prim and proper Mrs Davies being carried away by unbridled passion, and besides surely he still loved her mother?

Maureen shook her head. 'You might well laugh – but you take my words to heart, my girl.

No man's impervious to a woman's adoration. You just look at the way she's gazing up at Barney, and Owen's far from soft.'

Lucy remembered what he had said about getting rich and decided to heed her mother's words. She rejoined Owen and asked him to tell her just how he was going to get rich. It had also occurred to her that it might be no bad thing to have him paying her attention in Rob's and Blodwen's company.

It was Dilys who opened the door to them. Light flooded out, temporarily blinding them. Lucy and Owen clutched each other, blinking up at her. 'Oh, you've come together!' Dilys didn't sound pleased.

'The mams and Uncle Barney are just behind us,' said Lucy, her eyes adjusting to the light. She stepped over the threshold and took off the fur cloche hat Barney had bought her for Christmas, smiling at her friend who was wearing an amethyst-coloured crêpe-de-chine frock. 'You look great!' said Lucy.

'Thanks!' Dilys flashed her a quick smile before saying to Owen, 'What d'you think?'

'Smashing!' he said, but already his attention had strayed to where Lucy was removing her coat. 'Wow!' His eyes were popping out of his head.

Dilys turned quickly and her lower jaw dropped.

Lucy shook out the fringes of the shimmy frock and looked anxiously at Dilys. 'D'you think it's a bit too much? Only I don't get to go to parties often and I did so want to wear it.'

'It's-It's...' Dilys appeared lost for words. Then she took a deep breath. 'Has Barney seen it?'

'Nobody's seen it,' said Lucy, sweeping her hair up off her neck and adjusting a strap. 'I copied it from a photograph of American fashions in one of the dailies.'

'But it's a shimmy frock! You didn't really think Aunt Gwen would let us shimmy here?' cried Dilys, hands on hips.

'I hoped,' said Lucy, on the defensive. It had helped somehow making the frock in secret while she yearned for Rob. 'Besides, isn't what you're wearing more suitable for dancing than an at home?'

Before Dilys could answer Lucy heard her name spoken by three different people and suddenly the lobby appeared crowded. She looked at Rob and felt almost gleeful. Then her eyes slid to the girl at his side and Lucy despaired.

'You look...' Words seemed to fail Rob, too.

'Lovely?' she prompted, her spirits lifting.

Before he could say anything Lucy's shoulder was seized by Barney. 'What the heck is that frock you're wearing?'

'It's a shimmy,' Maureen answered for her daughter and her eyes were damp as she looked at Lucy. 'You look a treat,' she said huskily. 'Times are terribly hard for millions, and who's to say they won't be again for me or you? You make the most of your life right now, darlin'. I bet the bustle was frowned on in its time. The waltz certainly was! It was considered scandalous, a man putting his arm around a woman's

295

waist in public.'

'That's all very well,' said Barney, 'but...'

'But nothing,' said Maureen firmly. 'Now it's considered shocking for a couple not to touch, but how many of the women who dance today don't have a man to hold? Eleven years it is since we all thought the war would be over by Christmas. How many hearts have been broken in those eleven years?'

There was silence.

Then Owen said with a grin, 'Does that mean we get to dance?'

Blodwen laughed but his mother cuffed him across the head. 'There'll be none of that jungle dancing while I'm around, boyo.'

For a moment he looked really annoyed. He flicked back his hair and took out a comb. 'Don't be a spoilsport, Mam. I'm a man now, not a boy. So don't be telling me what to do?'

Mrs Davies' face crumpled but before she could answer, Rob said, 'Shall we move into the large kitchen? There mightn't be any dancing but you'll all be expected to do a turn. Perhaps Lucy'd like to step into the spotlight and show us how to shimmy?'

'No, no! There'll be none of that,' said Barney, his voice harsh with anger. 'She won't be doing anything so shocking!'

Rob's eyes glinted. 'Double standards, Barney? I bet you see a lot worse up on the silver screen.'

Was Rob championing her? wondered Lucy, her treacherous heart skipping about inside her chest.

Blodwen spoke up next. 'That's uncalled for,

Rob! Mr Jones is only thinking of the girl's reputation.'

'Who's arguing?' said Rob, flushing. 'But you're only young once and I'm not going to be here to see it. I'm on duty in half an hour.'

'You're working?' Lucy looked at him and his eyes met hers. For a moment it felt as if there were just the two of them, and her heart pounded in her chest. Then he moved away and walked into the large kitchen. She realised everyone was watching her and was suddenly angry and near to tears. 'What are you all staring at?' she snapped. 'I'll go home if you like?'

Barney dropped her coat over her shoulders. 'You keep that round you, girlie. There's no need for you to go home.'

'There certainly isn't,' said her mother, giving him an exasperated look. 'My Lucy's a good girl. She knows what's right and wrong. Come on, girl, let's go in.'

Lucy followed her, knowing the rest of the evening would not match up to its beginning for excitement. Rob kept his distance. There were turns as he'd said: singing, poetry and even a tap dance, but he had left by then.

Refreshments were served at ten-thirty. It was then that her mother came and sat next to Lucy who was sipping lemonade. 'See that one,' said Maureen, smoothing her dark green taffeta skirts.

Lucy's eyes followed her mother's to where Barney was talking to Blodwen. 'He feels sorry for her,' muttered Lucy, hating her with every fibre of her being. 'Says she's suffered.'

'Tush! Haven't we all?' said Maureen, sounding vexed. 'You don't want to believe all you see and hear. Young Owen ... you stick close to him. Dilys is making a play for him – see! Over by the refreshments table. You go over there, say you're bringing me an egg sandwich.'

Lucy shrugged off her coat. She was fed up of sitting there clutching it about her – and all because Barney had, as Rob said, double standards.

'So, no dancing,' commented Owen as she went over to the table. He looked at her greedily as if he could eat her.

She thought of what her mother had said, and of Rob saying he was in love with Blodwen. She smoothed Owen's sleeve and smiled. 'You're stating the obvious, Owen lovey. I should have had more sense than to wear this frock here.'

Dilys drawled, 'You said it! I don't know how you had the nerve.'

Lucy felt cross. 'Oh, shut up, Dil! It *is* New Year's Eve. The time to have a bit of fun ... but if I can't have any here then I'll have to hope someone will take me to the Grafton on my next evening off. I'll wear it then.' She gave Owen what she hoped was a sultry look. 'I'll need a partner.'

He didn't disappoint her. 'I'll take you,' he offered immediately, his gaze resting on the swell of her breasts which no amount of binding could quite flatten.

Dilys's cheeks flamed. 'What about me?' she cried, forcing herself between Owen and Lucy. 'I want to come as well.'

298

'I'm sure you can find someone to take you,' he said, grabbing Lucy's hand and drawing her away.

'You're making a mistake,' snapped Dilys, thrusting her face in front of Owen. 'Just like Barney Jones made a mistake by marrying her mother!'

'Hey!' said Lucy, startled and annoyed. 'Keep my mother out of this.'

Miss Griffiths appeared suddenly at Dilys's shoulder. 'What's going on between you three?' She eyed Lucy up and down with obvious disapproval. 'Really, Lucy, hardly a frock to go to church in.'

Lucy had just about had enough. 'That's it!' she said, tight-lipped, pulling her hand out of Owen's. 'I'm going home.' She walked over to the sofa where she had left her coat and picked it up. Timmy sidled up to her, a sandwich in each hand and cheeks bulging. 'Where are you going?' he said in a muffled voice.

'Out of here!'

His face brightened. 'I'll come with you. The food's good but now the turns are over there's nothing to do.'

'Right!' She looked around for Maureen and Barney to let them know they were leaving but both of them looked to be deep in conversation with different people so she and Timmy left without saying goodbye.

Lucy had intended going straight home but once outside she changed her mind. It was New Year's Eve after all and there were plenty of people out and about. Brother and sister wandered aimlessly, not caring where they were going, but found themselves on Scotland Road when the ships' hooters sounded on the Mersey and the church bells rang out. There was dancing and singing on the streets and they got caught up in a conga line. Complete strangers shook their hands and many a drunk aimed a kiss in Lucy's direction while several women took Timmy's face in their hands, told him he was luv'ly, kissed him and pressed a coin into his palm. 'They're all crazy,' he said with a grin, pocketing the money. 'It's just like when I was a kid. So where next? Do we head for home?'

'Might as well,' Lucy agreed cheerfully, feeling much better for the fresh air, the walk and the unashamed enjoyment of the crowds.

They were silent as they made their way to Great Homer Street and were just thinking everything was quietening down when they walked into an enormous brawl. Lucy did not doubt it was of sectarian making, there being plenty of orange and green on view. Men, women and children were swapping punches, kicking and scratching, pulling hair. Some were rolling over on the ground. A police whistle sounded somewhere. Then there as a positive flurry of them. The fight began to break up as the whistles grew louder. 'Let's get out of here,' said Lucy, taking her brother's hand and making a run for it.

They didn't get far before being seized by a burly bobby. 'Come on, you two. What have you been up to?'

'We haven't been up to anything, Constable,'

said Lucy, struggling in his grip. 'Will you let go? You're pinching my arm.'

'I'll do more than that to you, girl, if you don't keep still.' He frowned down at her.

'Are you going to take us to gaol?' said Timmy, his expression lively. 'I've never been in a lock up before. It'll be something to tell the boys at school.'

'It's no laughing matter, my lad,' said the constable sternly. 'Now, the pair of you be good and you might get off with a caution. You look clean enough and I guess you're only kids.'

Lucy fired up. 'I'm no kid. Look!' She unbuttoned her coat and shook herself. The silver threads in the fringes of her frock shimmered in the lamplight.

'Good Lord! That's indecent that is,' the constable said, eyes protruding from their sockets. 'I see what your game is but you shouldn't have involved the lad. I'm arresting you for soliciting.'

'What?' Lucy stared at him. He couldn't believe that she was... Her mind refused to finish the sentence. 'Listen, I've got friends in high places! They'll tell you the sort of girl I am.'

He closed his eyes briefly as if in horror. 'You ought to be ashamed of yourself, girl, and so should they. Fasten your coat! I don't want to be looking at you.'

Lucy stared at him and suddenly found the whole thing ridiculous. As she buttoned up her coat she began to laugh. 'You're making a mistake. I'm just a girl wanting some fun like the bright young things. You ask Detective Constable Rob Jones about me. We're friends.'

He shook his head, his expression severe. 'I don't think that's anything you should be telling me, miss, if you don't want to get him into trouble.'

'It's the last thing I want to do,' Lucy said good-humouredly. 'So why don't you let us go? It'll be easier all round. I'm not what you think.'

He was silent for a moment and then looked at Timmy. 'I'd best see you home.'

Lucy decided it was easier not to argue but as they walked up towards St Domingo Road she began to feel apprehensive, wondered what Barney would say when they arrived home.

At first she thought there had been no cause for her to worry because he was charm itself when he opened the door to the policeman, listening patiently to what the man had to say. It was not until the door had closed behind the bobby that his smile vanished and he swore at them softly. It was so shocking to hear such words on his lips that Lucy and Timmy froze in their tracks. Then, in a voice like the crack of a whip, Barney ordered Timmy to bed.

The boy refused to move and stood with his arms close to his sides, his chin up. His cheeks were pale but he looked determined. 'I won't let you hit her! Where's Mam? She won't let you hit Lucy either.'

Barney had raised his hand but now he dropped it. 'I'm not going to hit her,' he roared. 'But you, Lucy!' He turned on her. 'You do realise how much you've embarrassed me this evening? I didn't know where to put my face when you took your coat off at Miss Griffiths' –

302

and then to go off the way you did without a thank you or a tarrah – and now a police officer coming to the house! I never expected you to turn out like this. I must warn you, I won't allow you to go from bad to worse.'

Lucy had an overwhelming desire to defend herself, to argue with him in an effort to make him see that she hadn't done anything wrong, but she decided it just wasn't worth the effort. What had Owen said about her wearing blinkers? She wasn't the only one. On some things her stepfather's opinion would never alter but she didn't want to fall out with him. He'd been good to her and given her so much. If he wasn't the saint she had once thought him, he could be a lot worse, as she knew from experience.

'I'm sorry, Uncle Barney. It won't happen again,' she said quietly, and placing a hand on her brother's shoulder turned him gently in the direction of the stairs. 'Goodnight,' she called over her shoulder. 'And a Happy New Year.'

The next morning before Lucy rushed off to work she expected something more to be said about the events of last night but both her mother and Barney were strangely silent on the subject. Maureen saw her out on to the street and, to Lucy's surprise, took her head between her hands and kissed her forehead. 'I hope God gives you a good year, darlin.'

Lucy was touched. 'The same to you, Mam.' She hugged her before taking the steps two at a time and running for the tram.

She enjoyed her day. The film was a light romantic comedy starring Mary Pickford and

Douglas Fairbanks. Everything felt normal. She did a stint as usherette and the manager had suggested she might like to have a go at the cash desk, an idea she had floated to him when she had asked his advice on where to invest her money. He knew her ambitions, and although he'd laughed at them, he hadn't completely discouraged her.

Lucy entered the foyer after the last evening performance, dragging on her gloves. She stopped in her tracks at the sight of her brother sitting on one of the sofas. 'What are you doing here? It's late! Does Mam know you're here?'

Timmy stood up, throwing down the *Boys' Own* comic he'd been reading. 'I saw him again!'

For a moment Lucy couldn't think who he was talking about. She'd pushed everything to do with her private life to the back of her mind today. 'Who?'

'Him. That O'Neill fella. He was in a car again but this time it was going along St Domingo Road and he was with a woman. She was driving.'

Lucy stiffened. St Domingo Road! That was really close to home. 'Have you mentioned this to Mam?'

Timmy looked chagrined. 'She was out when I got home. I waited for ages. Agnes didn't know where she'd gone. So in the end I decided I'd come looking for you.'

Lucy was worried. She hoped her mother would be home when they got there. Too impatient to walk and save money, she decided to take the tram.

Barney opened the door to them before they could even knock. He looked worried. 'So there you are, Timmy. Have you seen your mother?'

Lucy stared at him in dismay and pushed her way past him. She was remembering what Timmy had said about seeing Shaun O'Neill along this very road and her fear escalated. She ran upstairs, thinking maybe Barney hadn't thought of looking in the bedroom, but Mam wasn't there. Lucy went downstairs again.

'What d'you think you're doing?' Barney asked, sounding exasperated.

'Looking for her, but she's not there.'

'Of course she's not upstairs! Agnes and I have already looked.' He turned and clunked his way into the music room and went over to the fire. 'You're no idea where she is then?'

Lucy took a deep breath and laced her hands together in front of her. 'Not really.' It was one thing to have believed for years that Shaun O'Neill might be out to get her and her mother, but now the idea seemed suddenly fantastic. Things like that didn't happen, not in real life. But then she thought of Mick and the terrible things which had happened the day the house went up in flames. She cleared her throat, gazing up at Barney and trying not to sound scared. 'I can't remember or not if we ever mentioned a man called Shaun O'Neill to you?'

Barney's expression became alarmed. 'You don't think he's been here ... that he's got your mother?'

'I don't know.' Lucy made a helpless gesture. 'Maybe not here ... perhaps he saw her along the road, shopping.'

There was silence as Barney took a cigarette case from his pocket and lit up with a silver lighter. She noticed his hand was shaking. He inhaled a lungful of smoke before saying, 'We can't do anything this evening. But in the morning, if she still hasn't turned up, we're going to have to do something.'

Lucy agreed. The police! She remembered how she'd told Rob about the Irishman when Timmy had first mentioned him, but he couldn't have done anything about it and for a moment she was angry with him. She felt a chill at her heart, hoping it wasn't too late. A knife in a dark place ... a gun... Bang, bang! She felt she would suffocate just thinking about her mother lying dead in some filthy back alley. It seemed unreal. This couldn't be happening. She would make hot drinks and maybe her mother would come through the door as she was pouring them out.

Lucy made four steaming cups of cocoa but Maureen wasn't there to drink hers. Barney suggested they should go to bed. 'I'm a light sleeper. I'll hear if she's forgotten her key and has to knock.'

Lucy thought there was no way she would sleep that night and she doubted Timmy would either but it was no use staying up. At least in bed they would be resting. But as soon as she lay down, her imagination kept throwing up pictures of Shaun O'Neill looking mean and dangerous. She must have drifted off eventually because she woke sweating and frightened from a nightmare. It was light in the room.

She dressed hastily and ran downstairs, hoping despite the nagging anxiety pulling her down to discover her mother in the kitchen. Instead she found Timmy, Barney and Rob.

Her brother came over to her and jerked his head in Rob's direction. 'I went for him. Uncle Barney was in a bit of a state, clumping about the floor, smoking like a chimney. It's a wonder you didn't hear him.'

'I dozed off for a while.' Lucy was painfully conscious of Rob staring at her. Why did her brother have to go for him? She found herself inconsequentially wishing she had taken the time to brush her hair and wash her face. 'You OK?' said Rob softly.

She did not want him to be nice to her because she was angry with him. 'You promised to get O'Neill! I depended on you to keep us safe!'

Rob stiffened. 'It's not that easy, tracing someone. An Irishman in Liverpool is easily lost. Besides, we don't know for certain that he has anything to do with your mother's absence. She hasn't been missing twenty-four hours yet. She could still turn up.'

Lucy hoped he was right! She sank on to a chair opposite him at the table. 'I'm sorry. I just feel sick with worry. It's not like her.'

He nodded briefly. 'I'll pass on her description to the men on the beat so they can look out for her.'

'Thanks! Although if *he* got to her last night she could already be—'

'Stop it!' shouted Barney.

She stared at him in astonishment and then

307

before her eyes his face crumpled, his shoulders shook and a huge sob broke from him. Lucy was completely taken aback. Didn't know what to do. She darted a glance at Rob who looked embarrassed, ran a hand through his hair and mouthed, 'Can't you stop him?'

She got up, went round the table and put an arm round her stepfather. 'It's OK, I didn't mean it. Of course she's going to turn up. Rob's right. She's been missing hardly any time at all.'

'She can't be dead! I don't want her to be dead,' cried Barney brokenly, resting his head against Lucy. She felt awkward standing there, listening to a grown man cry, but she could understand his feelings. She wondered if they'd had a row after the party in St Domingo Grove but her mother had seemed perfectly calm and undisturbed the next morning. So Lucy continued to pat his back and whisper soothing words, aware that Rob was watching them. She remembered him saying Barney had double standards. Why had he said that?

'Is there anything you can tell me, Lucy, to add to what your brother, Barney and Agnes have said about your mother's daily routine?'

'I don't know what they've told you.' She hesitated, unsure whether to mention Maureen's attending St Anthony's church? If ... *when* – she was going to, be positive – her mother returned, it could cause problems between husband and wife.

'But you're her daughter. She might tell you things she wouldn't mention to anyone else.'

Lucy could see there was something in that but

Timmy knew about St Anthony's so maybe he'd already told Rob. There was nothing else she could think of that her mother had said or done out of the ordinary. 'I can't think of anything.'

He nodded and stood up. 'Then I'll be on my way. I'll drop in this evening and see whether she's turned up.'

'You see him out, Lucy,' said Barney, who had control of himself now.

She did as he said. Rob paused on the doorstep and looked her straight in the eye. 'There was something you'd thought of, wasn't there? Something you don't want Barney to know.'

Lucy was impressed by his perceptiveness. 'You're too smart by half, Mr Detective,' she said lightly. 'I wasn't sure if Timmy had told you but Mam's been dropping in at St Anthony's on Scottie the last few months. Old haunts!' There was a catch in her voice. 'It seems she missed them after all.'

Rob looked interested. 'I'll get the bobby on the beat down there to have a word with the priest. There might be something else she's hiding.'

'You're forgetting the sanctity of the confessional.'

'I'm not talking about sin.'

'Then what could she have to conceal?' said Lucy softly, remembering those moments on the sofa at his aunt's. Perhaps he was thinking of them, too, because he couldn't take his eyes off her and there was a flush on his cheeks. Then, with a sudden swift movement, he turned on his heel and ran down the steps.

Lucy closed the door and went back into the

kitchen. Barney was still sitting at the table. Timmy was standing over the cooker, frying pan in hand. 'I thought you might like some breakfast before going to work.'

'I'll do that. I'm not going to go to pieces.'

'You're not going to work, are you, girlie?' asked Barney in a trembling voice, reaching out a hand to her.

'Aren't you?' She took his hand, thinking she would rather be at the cinema than here, listening, hoping, waiting for her mother to come in. She would rather be occupied out of the house, come home and find her mother waiting for her.

'I'm feeling poorly.' He sounded much older than his years.

'Agnes'll be here to look after you.'

'I prefer you.'

Lucy hardened her heart. This sudden dependency made her feel uncomfortable. 'You've got to pull yourself together. What'll Mam think when she comes home and finds us both skiving off work?'

'She should feel flattered. I promise if she comes back we'll get a wireless.'

'She'd like that,' said Lucy diplomatically, wishing he'd seen fit to buy her one for Christmas.

The day at work dragged on interminably and at the end of it Lucy could not wait to get home to see if her mother was there; but she wasn't.

Barney must have been chain smoking because the ash tray in the music room was overflowing with cigarette butts. Of her brother there was no sign. 'Has Timmy gone to bed?' she asked.

'I don't know where he is.' Barney sprawled in the leather chair, an empty cup at his elbow, a cigarette dangling from the corner of his mouth. He wore a morose expression. 'I've lost count of the times he's asked me if his mam is back yet. He's been in and out of the house until it drove me mad.' Her stepfather stretched out a hand to her. 'I'm scared, Lucy. What if that O'Neill fella has got her? Or what if she's gone peculiar again like she did after she lost the baby and has done something – terrible?'

Lucy's eyes dilated. 'You mean taken her own life? No!' she cried. 'Mam wouldn't do that! Not her! It's not in her nature. She'd got better, wasn't miserable any longer.' Lucy wasn't even going to consider suicide as a possibility. 'Right. I'm going upstairs to see if Timmy's there.'

He wasn't. She took the stairs two at a time on the way down. 'He's not there! Think, Uncle Barney! Did he say anything to you about where he was going?'

Her stepfather shook his head. 'I wasn't taking things in, girlie. I can't get your mam out of my mind.' He looked so woebegone she couldn't be too annoyed with him but she did not want to be in his company and walked out of the room. It was getting on for eleven-thirty. Where could Timmy be? Could he have gone to Aunt Mac's? Maybe he had gone up to Daniel Street to see Owen? Or even along to Rob's aunt's?

Lucy decided to try Owen's house first but she had barely walked halfway along St Domingo Road when she saw her brother and Rob coming towards her. She pounced on Timmy. 'You've had me worried sick. What are you playing at?'

'I got sick of *him*,' said Timmy, his expression mutinous. 'He's only thinking of himself.'

Lucy's eyes met Rob's over her brother's head. 'Any news?'

'Not a whisper. Timmy's been telling me your mam and Barney fell out over a wireless a few weeks ago. I know they disagreed about you on New Year's Eve.'

'What are you getting at? All husbands and wives fall out at times. You don't think *he's* murdered her?' A laugh tripped off Lucy's tongue.

'You'd be surprised at the reasons people kill,' Rob said seriously.

'I don't believe it!' She was angry with him. Barney might be some things, but a murderer?

'Most murders are committed by a family member.'

Her cheeks blanched and for a moment it looked like Rob was going to say something else but instead he turned and walked away. How could he say that? How could he hurt her in that way? She'd started to forgive herself but now... She seized Timmy by the arm and hurried him in the direction of Barney's house.

Her brother protested. 'Why are you so rough? I've done nothing wrong. It's Uncle Barney you should be cross with. What if he *has* killed Mam? He was real mad with her, remember?'

'He wouldn't kill her for that! And you're not to say a word to Barney about this. He wouldn't kill Mam in a hundred years. You've seen what he's like! It's Shaun O'Neill we've got to catch.'

Barney had gone to bed when they arrived home, which disappointed Lucy because she'd thought he would have shown some interest in Timmy turning up. Even so she made excuses for her stepfather. He must be frustrated, unable to go looking for his wife like any able-bodied husband would. Maybe he blamed himself for not being able to protect Maureen from the likes of Shaun O'Neill.

In the morning Owen turned up to dig over the garden. He made no comment about New Year's Eve or her mother being missing. Maybe he couldn't think of the right words, thought Lucy.

Several days later a couple of policemen turned up. They had a warrant to search the house. Lucy was dumbstruck and rushed round to Rob's aunt's to see what he had to say about it but received no answer at the house. Having no time to return home, she went straight on to work. During her two-hour break she wrote a letter to Rob and posted it. When she arrived home it was to discover the front garden had been freshly dug over.

'They were looking for Mam's body,' whispered Timmy as she stood in the hall removing her coat.

Lucy felt the colour drain from her face and gripped the newel post. 'I can't believe Rob's done this. Where's Barney?'

'In the music room.'

Lucy went in and found her stepfather sitting in his large leather chair, smoking and gazing into the fire. 'Timmy's told me what the police have done.'

'They didn't find anything, lovey.' He smiled wearily. 'I told them they wouldn't. As if I'd hurt a hair of your mother's head. It was all down to her clothes being in the wardrobe. They said if she'd gone off after a quarrel or anything of that sort she would have packed a suitcase. A lovely lot of clothes she's got in there, they said. I said to them, "Why should I kill her? I've got nothing to gain by it. Now if it was me who'd gone missing... Well now, she'd come in to something then, wouldn't she?"'

Lucy had to agree. 'Didn't they say anything about Shaun O'Neill?'

'I did mention him, despite Rob's already knowing about him, and they made no comment. So he must have told them.'

Lucy paced the floor, arms folded. 'It's maddening! I could kill Rob. This is all *his* fault.'

'No, lovey,' said Barney, getting to his feet. He put an arm about her. 'You mustn't blame the lad. Seems it was the Chief Constable who made the decision to search this house. Remembered Winnie being killed. A woman killed, another going missing from the same address.' He nodded his head gravely. 'Suspicious, Lucy. But I swore to them on the Bible I hadn't hurt a hair on your mother's head.'

'You don't have to keep repeating that, Uncle Barney. I believe you!' She rested her head against his shoulder. 'I'm just so tired and worried.' Her voice trembled.

'There, lovey, you go to bed and have a good sleep.' He caressed her cheek. 'Sunday tomorrow, you can have a good rest.'

314

But Lucy couldn't rest and the next morning was up early. She ate a solitary breakfast, went into the music room and put a match to the fire before curling up in the leather chair. She watched the flames, emotionally and physically exhausted after another restless night. Her eyelids drooped and she dozed to awake to the sound of Rob's voice. 'Where is she?'

'Keep your voice down, Mr Jones.' It was Agnes. 'She's in the music room, having a little rest.'

The door was flung open and Rob entered. Lucy put her feet down on the floor and straightened herself. 'What is it?'

'You!' She could see he was very angry.

'I suppose it's the letter I sent you.'

'The letter?' He snorted, turned his back on her a moment and then faced her again. 'If that was all! What were you thinking of telling Constable Rankine you were a girl wanting a good time, a bright young thing, and mentioning me by name as if I could get you out of trouble? You've no idea the ragging I've had and the things people are saying about us.'

She had to force herself to think back. All week her mind had been filled with only one thing, her mother's disappearance. Finally she remembered New Year's Eve and all that had happened that evening. 'It was the shimmy frock. He was going to arrest me, thought I was a woman of the streets. I had to do something! Your name worked a treat and he saw us home. After he saw Barney he must have known I wasn't what he took me for at first.'

'No, he decided you were something else! God only knows how but it's got back to my aunt *and* Blodwen. I assure you they both seem to have no trouble in believing something has being going on between you and me.'

'You mean...' Lucy's face brightened and for a moment she forgot her mother could be lying dead at the bottom of the Mersey or buried in some dark place. 'Blodwen's broken off your engagement?'

'No! She's given me an ultimatum. Either I give up my job and take over my aunt's timber yard within the month or it's all over between us!'

Chapter Sixteen

Lucy stood on the front step, hugging herself and gazing down at the garden. It was a week since Rob had told her about Blodwen's ultimatum and since then she had felt physically wounded, convinced he never wanted to see her again. She told herself she had to face up to the fact he really did mean it when he said he loved Blodwen. What was she going to do now? Along with the worry about her mother she felt as if her heart was breaking.

'Hello, Midget!'

She lifted her head and stared at Owen from lacklustre eyes. 'What d'you want?' Her tone was unfriendly.

'That's a nice welcome.' He came up the steps

and stood beside her. 'A pity the police didn't come a week earlier. They'd have saved me a job.'

'Barney told them they were wasting their time. They could have made an effort and checked that you'd recently dug over the ground. I can't credit it that they didn't think how difficult it would be for a cripple like Barney to get digging. They've dug up all the spring bulbs you put in last September.'

'He's stronger than you think, you know,' said Owen, taking out a packet of Woodbines and lighting up. 'Could dig a grave even if it was a struggle.'

'Don't!' she snapped.

'Sorry.' Silence. Then: 'You're not at work today?'

'Yes. I nipped home to see how Barney was... I'll be heading back in a minute.'

Owen rested a shoulder against the door jamb. 'I'm real sorry about your mam being missing. I suppose there's no chance of me taking you to the Grafton now?'

Lucy felt like hitting him. 'You've got that right,' she confirmed, her eyes glinting. 'Take Dilys – you'll make her day.'

He didn't deny it. 'At least someone loves me and there's a lot about her I like. The trouble with Dilys is she wants too much of me.'

Lucy could understand that if Dilys was really in love with him because she herself wanted all of Rob. She buttoned her coat, thinking it was time to get back to work. 'Is he in?' asked Owen, straightening up and nipping out the glowing end of his cigarette before placing it back in the packet. She nodded and without saying goodbye walked slowly down the steps.

Waiting at the tram stop on the other side of the road she noticed several people dawdling past the house. Neighbours had taken a ghoulish interest in their goings-on since her mother's disappearance had hit the headlines of the local newspapers; a rerun of the details of the sensational murder of Winnie Jones and the fact that her murderer had never been found meant that Maureen's going missing was more than a five-day wonder.

Lucy was working at the cash desk now but although the work was much easier on the feet she found it less interesting and was glad when she could head for home.

As she entered the house she was aware of the sound of music. She froze as the Third Movement of Beethoven's Moonlight Sonata, all passion and anger, flooded the place. She wrapped her arm round the newel post, feeling the need for an anchor, and waited for the music to stop before entering the music room.

Barney lifted his head. His face was blotchy and still showed signs of strain but his eyes looked clear and focussed readily on her. 'You all right, girlie?'

'It's been a long day.' Lucy walked over to the piano. 'You must be feeling better to be playing?'

'I am. I've decided I can't stay home anymore. Tomorrow it's back to my place at the piano and entertaining people. So many have sent messages saying they're thinking of me.'

'The police will allow you to go to work?' she

318

said tentatively.

He looked amused. 'They've got nothing on me – and I can hardly skip the country. I wouldn't be surprised if they put a tail on me but that doesn't worry me. I've nothing to hide where your mother's concerned.' His hand covered one of Lucy's where it rested on top of the piano. 'I'm worried about that Shaun O'Neill, though.'

A nerve throbbed at the corner of Lucy's eye. 'I wish they could find him. At least then we'd know if...' She could not finish the sentence and, freeing her hand, walked out of the room. Upstairs she found Timmy reading a book by candlelight. She sat on the bed. 'What are you reading?'

'*Lost up the Amazon!* I tell you, Luce, I wouldn't like to meet an anaconda.' He sounded deadly serious.

'What's that?'

'A giant snake. It could eat you whole.'

'Cheerful stuff,' she said in a teasing voice.

He lowered his eyes to the page. 'It helps to take my mind off things.'

Tears filled Lucy's eyes and she wanted to take her brother in her arms and comfort him. But what was there to say? She wanted her mam as much as he did.

'Luce?'

'Yes?' She averted her face and brushed away the tears.

'You don't think Mam's gone off somewhere to get away from *him?*'

Her head swivelled. 'No! She wouldn't leave without telling us. Mam loves us!' Lucy saw the

319

hope die in her brother's eyes and felt terrible. 'Well, that's to say, in her right mind she wouldn't leave us,' she stammered. 'You've heard Barney say she went a bit peculiar after losing the baby.'

'That's ages ago.' Timmy sighed. 'No, you're right. She wouldn't leave us of her own free will.' He bent over and laid the book open on the floor. 'You can go now. I'll have to get some sleep. I'm doing OK with my firewood. Somehow people seem to know it's my mam who's missing and they're buying more and bringing me all sorts of treats.'

'You can't miss out on them then, can you?' Lucy watched him snuggle down. Then she kissed his thatch of fair hair, blew out the candle and left the room.

She dreamed that night of diving under the murky, oily waters of the Mersey and finding her mother's violated body, made heavy with chains, lying on the sandy bottom. She woke, gasping with the effort of trying to rescue her, and lay feeling the silence and the darkness around her like a weight.

Perhaps even now O'Neill was watching the house, a sneer on his face, thinking of doing the same thing to her. How could she ever feel safe again? Rob wasn't going to keep her safe. He hadn't said as much but it seemed to her he had no choice but to forget any promise he had made to her because of Blodwen. Which was how it should be, she supposed. She sat up, hunching her knees and resting her chin on them. Damn Blodwen! As if worrying and grieving about her mother weren't enough to have on her mind!

Lucy pushed a strand of hair from her eyes with a weary gesture. Surely there must be a clue to her mother's disappearance somewhere? Somebody must have seen something. If she was on friendlier terms with Rob she would have asked him... She told herself sternly to stop thinking about him and tried to sleep again but it was hopeless so she slid out of bed, dressed and went downstairs.

She put on her coat and hat, unbolted the door and slipped outside. Soft-footed, she went down the steps and out on to the pavement. An early tram rattled by and she caught the sound of the milkman's horse clip-clopping up the road. The lamplighter would soon be round, extinguishing the lights, and there would be the knocker upper soon, too. She liked being out in the early morning when she could.

'Where are you going, Lucy? You're out early.' She almost jumped out of her skin. Whirling round, she saw Rob. He was dressed all in black so maybe that was why she hadn't seen him leaning against the soot-darkened sandstone gate post.

'I couldn't sleep. What are you doing here?' Her voice sounded truculent.

'Just keeping an eye on you.' She caught the gleam of his teeth and remembered the feel of his mouth on hers.

'Why?' she said bluntly. 'I thought you weren't on this case. Haven't I made your life difficult enough? I thought you'd want to be shot of me!'

'That doesn't stop me feeling sorry for you. I like your mother as well as you. I can't just turn

321

off those feelings.'

She wanted to cry. Dear Jesus, she was turning into a right watering can! She forced herself to speak. 'What's this? Confession time, Mr Detective?' No response. Had she gone too far? She peered into his face and wished she could read his expression but his features were indistinct, just as they'd been the first time they'd met.

'The priest at St Anthony's said your mother had a strong sense of having sinned in marrying out of her own church,' he said abruptly. 'D'you think Barney knew she didn't feel married to him in God's eyes?'

Lucy laughed despite herself. 'I doubt it! I told you, he had no idea she was going to St Anthony's.'

'You only think that. What if he did know and got angry?'

Lucy's heart felt as if it jolted to a stop before rapidly resuming its beating. Not again! 'You're jealous of him, aren't you?' Rob looked at her as if she'd run mad. 'He's a very popular person. The police aren't, are they, Rob dear? I suppose that's another reason why Blodwen wants you out of the force.'

He grabbed hold of Lucy by both arms and brought her against him. 'You've said enough! Keep off that subject.'

She brought up one hand and caressed his jaw, ran a finger over his lower lip. 'Don't do that!' His voice was angry and he swept aside her hand. 'Let's stick to your mother's disappearance. I'd ask you to do something for me but it might put you in danger.'

Lucy wanted to rest her head against his shoulder and feel safe again, not do something that was dangerous. 'What are you talking about?'

'Our men searched the room where your mother slept – how about you having a look round to see if there's anything you might consider unusual that our men have passed over as unimportant?'

She pulled away from him. 'You're seeing Barney as a killer again. I can't understand you. You were the best man at his wedding. He's family!'

Rob scowled. 'Don't do it then.' He turned and walked away.

Lucy went back into the house, angry with him. Yet later in the day when she had time off and knew the house should be empty except for Agnes, she returned home.

The maid was in the kitchen, drinking tea and warming her feet by the range. 'Don't get up,' said Lucy, and poured herself some tea, buttered some bread and carried it all upstairs. After a gulp of tea and a mouthful of bread she opened the door of Barney's and her mother's bedroom. She hesitated in the doorway, feeling a mixture of guilt and grief. Then, telling herself she was here now so might as well get on with the job, she pulled open a drawer in the dressing table.

She had a struggle holding back the tears at the sight of her mother's gloves, scarves and hand-kerchiefs. Her scent clung to them and was so evocative of her presence that as Lucy searched through them, tears rolled down her cheeks. It was at the bottom of that drawer she found the framed photographs. She took them out and marvelled at the way she had forgotten about them. Here was fresh cause for tears as she gazed down at the young, happy faces of her parents on their wedding day. She supposed Maureen couldn't have displayed the photographs here but there was no reason why Lucy shouldn't have them in her bedroom.

She went on to search the whole room, feeling ashamed and a little embarrassed as she flicked through Barney's underwear. Then she hurried out, glad the task was over and convinced Rob was making a big mistake.

She placed the photograph of her parents on the table next to her bed before gobbling down the bread and draining the cup of lukewarm tea. Then she hurried back to the Trocadero.

The following evening when she arrived home she was seized upon by her brother, who was in his pyjamas. 'Guess who's been here?' he whispered.

'I'm not in the mood for guessing games.'

'Owen's mam, Dilys and her aunt, and that one Rob's going to marry.'

Lucy dragged off a glove and threw it on the floor. 'I wondered when one of them would show up! Didn't expect all of them at once, though.' She shrugged off her coat and hung it on the stand. 'Was Barney here when they came?'

Timmy nodded. 'I heard him putting on the voice, telling them he's not playing at every performance at the moment because he doesn't feel up to it but he's doing his best.' Timmy's voice couldn't conceal his disgust.

'Where is he now?'

'Went up ten minutes or so ago. I was upstairs and heard him so I came down to see you.'

'Let's go into the kitchen. It'll be warmer there and you can tell me what you heard.' A grim smile played round Lucy's mouth. 'I bet they had something to say about me!' She hadn't been to church or seen any of them since her mother went missing.

'That Blodwen thinks you're a right madam,' said Timmy. 'She thinks Barney's a dear.' He put on a falsetto voice. '"We feel so sorry for you! It's a scandal the police persecuting a cripple who's such a good man."'

Lucy grimaced. 'It's true about Barney.' She wondered if Blodwen felt the way she did about her because of the rumours she had heard about Lucy and Rob. 'I suppose they had something to say about Rob, too?' She put on the kettle, sat down, unfastened her shoes and wriggled her cold toes.

'Miss Griffiths is mad to sell him the timber yard so she can retire to Wales now some old aunt's died and left her a house there. Says he could get something called a mortgage for the yard and rent the house where she lives. He could be married in a few months' time.'

Lucy felt as if her heart was being squeezed by a nutcracker. So that was the plan! Had they spoken of this deliberately in front of Timmy, knowing he would tell her? A subtle way of saying: 'Keep off! Don't rock the boat!'

Her brother had gone over to the bread bin. Now he faced her, holding a half-eaten loaf of bara brith. 'They brought two of these, scones, and a big meat and potato pie. They must think you're a lousy cook, but they think I'm a dear, too.' He grinned.

'Kind of them,' she murmured, half-closing her eyes, feeling depressed and drained of energy. 'Anything else you want to tell me? Did Dilys have anything to say?'

He shook his head and said through a mouthful of cake, 'She looked pale and kind of sad. Mrs Davies offered to come back and cook our dinners and Barney took up her offer.'

'How could he?' Lucy was indignant, remembering what her mother had said about Owen and Mrs Davies. How long would it be before she was buzzing in and out of the house like a blue bum fly, all day and every day? Lucy did not like that idea at all but what could she do? It was Barney's house. Tired out and wishing she could get away from it all, she had a cup of cocoa and went to bed.

She woke the following morning having slept heavily for once after a good cry. Realising how late it was she scrambled out of bed and caught the framed photograph of her parents with her elbow. It fell to the floor and with a soft cry of distress she picked it up. To her relief the glass had not broken but the whole lot had come to pieces. She noticed a clip was faulty at the back and as she attempted to fix everything together a slip of paper fell out. It was a letter.

Lucy read the signature at the bottom of the sheet. It was a letter from her grandmother Linden.

She sank on to the bed and began to read:

My dear Maureen,
I know it is a while since I have written to you but I pen this short note in the hope you will be kind and do something for me. Six months ago my beloved William died leaving me with very little. His elder brother has been kind enough to take me in but I am very lonely and would dearly love to see my grand-children.
You've always ignored my letters in the past but please, please, do not ignore this one. I have the money to pay for their fares as well as your good self if you wish to come for a holiday here in Bridlington. If you can see your way to doing what I ask I will be forever grateful. Please reply to my new address at the top of this letter.
My very best wishes to you,
Myrtle Linden

Lucy looked at the address at the top of the page and noted the date the letter had been written: spring 1921. The blood seemed to rush to her head and the backs of her eyes ached. She re-read the letter. There was no need to ask herself why her mother hadn't shown it to her. Maureen had never concealed her feelings towards Lucy's paternal grandparents. So why had she kept the letter? It was a question Lucy could not answer. She could only guess her mother had thought Myrtle Linden might be of use to them one day.

'One day,' murmured Lucy, going over to where she'd left her handbag. 'Today?' Placing the letter inside her bag, she decided to tell her brother about it after she'd given its contents some thought.

She re-read the letter when she had a free moment; heartsore and weary, fed up with working at the cash desk, of waiting for news of her mother but dreading it at the same time in case it completely killed the mustard seed of hope she nursed that somewhere Maureen might still be alive. She decided the letter couldn't have come at a better time. If her grandmother were still alive – if she still wanted to see them – if her grandfather's brother would accept them as guests in his house now they were no longer children, then she would go and visit them.

During her meal break Lucy went to the Post Office and when she arrived home that evening she wrote a letter to her grandmother and went out and posted it. She did not after all tell her brother about the letter but decided to wait and see if their grandmother replied.

Lucy did not have long to wait. Three days later she received an answer to her letter.

My dear Lucy,

It was wonderful to hear from you. I will not say anything about your mother. I think all that needs to be said is that Stan and I are married and you and Timmy are very welcome to come and stay with us for as long as you like. I enclose a postal order for the train fares and look forward to hearing from you with the date of your arrival.

Your loving Granny Myrtle

Immediately Lucy went in search of Timmy.

She found him in the yard with a catapult, taking potshots at one of the neighbouring cats. 'I hope you hit the right one,' she said. Yuk—

'The one which keeps dirtying in the garden? You bet!' He returned her smile and shoved the catapult into his trouser pocket so that the elastic hung out. 'You're cheerful this morning?'

'I've received a letter.' She saw the sudden hope in his eyes and hated disappointing him. 'It's from Dad's mam. She wants us to go and stay with her.' Lucy told him everything and afterwards handed their grandmother's latest letter to him.

He read it swiftly, looked up and said, 'Let's go!'

She laughed. 'I thought you'd say that. I know you're finding it difficult here.'

'Barney doesn't like me now I'm almost grown up, and I don't like him.' Timmy kicked a stone, his brows knitted together in concentration. 'I don't like the way he behaves to you, either. His face droops like a blinkin' bloodhound when you're around. He wants your sympathy all the time.'

Lucy realised her brother was jealous of Barney but he was also right. In the last few days, when she and her stepfather were both home together, he'd expected her to be at his beck and call; in much the same way he'd expected her mother to be. The attitude was not unusual between father and daughter but he wasn't her father and she felt uneasy about getting too close to him now her mother was no longer in the house. It wasn't that she felt endangered as she had with Mick.

Maybe it was down to the way Rob had spoken about Barney. She'd dismissed Rob's suspicions, still half-believing Shaun O'Neill had something to do with her mother's disappearance. Yet she felt Barney could easily smother her own will and sense of freedom if she didn't escape from under his roof, at least for a while.

Lucy wrote to her grandmother, handed in her notice at work, cashed the postal order, purchased their train tickets, wrote to the headmaster of Timmy's school and packed their suitcases before confronting Barney. She had a good idea of what to expect.

It couldn't have been much worse. He was obviously stunned. Then he recovered and called her ungrateful, heartless, a Jezebel! She presumed the latter referred to the shimmy dress which she had never worn again. Lucy put up no defence. She had seen other sides to Barney in the last few months and no longer thought him the perfect man. Even so she disliked hurting him.

'I will be back,' she said, standing straight as a ramrod in front of him, hands clasped together, trembling inwardly. 'I am very fond of you.'

At that his expression altered and he seemed to have trouble controlling his mouth. He got up from his leather chair and stumped over to her, holding out his arms. She submitted to his embrace, only to have trouble breaking away as he wept on her shoulder. Lucy called her brother, who was waiting in the lobby with their luggage. He came striding in and helped her disentangle herself. 'Goodbye, goodbye,' cried Barney, waving both hands.

'Oh, God,' muttered Timmy, and hurried out of the house.

Once on the train Lucy regained enough presence of mind to write a letter on the long journey. She had decided days ago it would be less painful if she didn't see Rob before she left. That she was leaving part of herself in Liverpool she had no doubt. She'd intended to be brief but in the end she told him all about finding the letter and what her grandmother had said, of the scene with Barney and how she hoped Rob would be happy with Blodwen (which was a lie), and pleaded with him to continue to try and find what had happened to her mother. She signed it 'Love, Lucy' and wrote her aunt's address on the top of the first page.

She had intended writing separately to Owen and Dilys but after a few false starts and crossings out she decided not to bother. She would send them a postcard each. Having decided that, she settled down opposite her brother, who was reading another adventure book, and opened the magazine she had bought at the station.

It had been a long journey over the Pennines and across the Wolds of Yorkshire. They'd had to change at Leeds and now Lucy felt tense and excited but convinced she had done the right thing. Listening to the snatches of conversation she could hear around her she felt as if she was in a foreign country. How was she ever going to understand what these people were saying, and how would they understand her? The voice over the tannoy spoke perfect English but he wasn't saying anything she wanted to know. Would she have difficulty in recognising her grandmother? She had brought the photograph of her parents on their wedding day with her and now clasped it in her hand.

Lucy need not have worried. Within minutes an elderly woman wearing an old-fashioned long black skirt and black-beaded jacket, as well as a very large hat, came hurrying up to the newspaper stand where they'd arranged to meet, letting out cries of recognition.

'The spitting image of his father!' She seized Timmy by the shoulders and gazed down into his face with tears running down her plump, rosy cheeks. 'Such a good face! So like our Larry's!' She ran a lace-mittened finger down the youth's cheek.

'Hello, Granny Myrtle.' Under his lazy lids Timmy's eyes glinted with a mixture of embarrassment and amusement as a deep flush came up under his skin. He removed his cap and gave her a small bow.

She beamed down at him. 'You can't imagine how grand it is to be called that. Granny Myrtle,' she repeated, as if by saying it aloud she gained more pleasure. 'We're going to have a smashing time. Stanley is so looking forward to meeting you. He said you can call him Uncle Stan – Great-uncle being too much of a mouthful.' She turned to Lucy. 'And you, lass, you're glad to be here?'

'Oh, yes!' agreed Lucy. 'I wasn't absolutely sure

332

how you'd feel when you saw us but I can tell you're pleased.'

'A handsome grandson and a nice-looking grand-daughter! What more can I ask?' Myrtle's eyes were a faded blue but their gaze was penetrating as it met Lucy's. 'I'm sure you're both strong, and I know you're both used to work, so let's get off home and as soon as you've had something to eat I'll show you to your rooms.'

Lucy wasn't sure why she'd mentioned them being strong but it didn't matter. She supposed she would find out soon enough. Myrtle led the way along the road, informing them Stan's health wasn't too good and she hoped the pair of them were prepared to help entertain him. Lucy had a vision of herself doing the Shimmy and bit back a giggle. This grandmother was very different from the way she remembered her and also different from the sad pleading woman who had written that pathetic letter.

They did not have to walk very far before turning up a road full of large houses. They passed several hotels and guest houses. 'Not much business for them at this time of year,' said Myrtle, 'but come Easter they'll be busy. I've been telling Stan we should take in lodgers but he said he doesn't need the money and besides he'd have to be polite to people – that when he dies *then* I can turn it back into a guest house.'

'Is he rich?' said Timmy, looking surprised.

Myrtle chuckled. 'You wouldn't think so to look at him and me. He made his money in the wool trade ... married young but his wife died when she was only a lass, leaving him with a son to rear. The woman who looked after him decided she'd had enough when she heard about Stan and I getting wed so now Wesley lives with us.'

'Wesley's Uncle Stan's son?' asked Timmy.

And what kind of name is Wesley? thought Lucy.

Myrtle gave a brisk nod. 'Aye! And you'll understand all about him when you see him, Tim, although that could be today or tomorrow. He's difficult to pin down is Wesley.' She stopped in front of a house with bay windows to either side of a green door. It didn't have much in the way of a garden and what there was didn't amount to much. Myrtle opened the door and ushered them inside a narrow dark lobby.

'Do you have electricity?' asked Timmy, peering for a switch.

'Good Lord, lad, no. That would cost money to put in and there's only one thing Stan'll spend money on. Come on and meet him.' She passed a door on their right and then another on their left before opening a third door and flinging it open.

'Stan, they're here!'

The room was at least as large as the music room in Barney's house but lit by several gas lamps on walls and ceiling. There were several small tables in it but very few chairs. The tables all had something on them but Lucy couldn't make out what exactly. She could hear music.

'Stan, turn off that wireless!' ordered Myrtle. 'You're going deaf in your old age. Say hello to our Larry's children, Timmy and Lucy.'

Lucy looked over to a man sitting in a chair in front of the table nearest the fireplace. He turned his white head, which was wreathed in smoke from a large-bowled pipe. She approached him and noticed the chair he was sitting on had wheels. 'Hello there, Lucy and Timmy! Come and tell me what kind of journey you had. Did the train break down?' he said loudly.

'No,' said Lucy, unable to resist a smile.

'The last train I went on broke down.' He held out his hand. The sleeve of his jacket slid back to reveal a bony wrist and frayed cuff. She looked into his face and his eyes seemed very bright, reflecting the firelight as they did. His whiskers were streaked with nicotine stains while his neck had the appearance of a turkey's.

She shook his hand and he winked at her, tapping his cheek with one finger. In a flash of recollection she remembered her father and grandfather doing the very same thing so she kissed Stan's cheek. 'I'm sorry to hear you're poorly.'

'It's just my legs, lass. They let me down just when I need them to hold me up. I'll be wanting you and the boy to be taking me out for a ride now and again while you're here.'

'It'll be a pleasure,' said Lucy and Timmy at the same time. The youth had brushed his way past Lucy to shake the old man's hand.

'The fresh air does him good as long as the wind's blowing in the right direction,' said Myrtle, taking off her coat and hat. 'Now you sit down and talk to him while I see to the supper.'

'D'you want any help?' asked Lucy.

'No, lass.' Myrtle smiled. 'It's all prepared.'

'I remember you used to make lovely cakes.'

Her grandmother nodded. 'I still do.'

When the meal was served, Lucy had never tasted fish like it and said so. She was told it had been caught that morning, and informed if the pair of them were early risers and it wasn't raining or blowing a gale, tomorrow they could take Stan down to the harbour and watch the fishing boats come in. The old man said he would be their navigator.

Washing the dishes, Lucy found herself in a dreamlike state. She had not imagined it being like this. She could hear Stan's loud voice explaining to her brother about Standard Dragon loudspeakers and battery valve receivers. Both apparently had only recently been developed and the loudspeaker enabled a whole family to listen to the wireless at the same time. She now knew that on the other tables were packs of cards and board games: Snakes and Ladders, draughts and chess. A gramophone stood in one corner of the room and there were lots of records. She wondered what her mother would have made of it all and felt near to tears.

'Stanley used to be such an active man,' said Myrtle as she wiped a dish. 'That wireless took a lot of brass but it's made my life more bearable. He was that down in the mouth when we first came to this house. He had a factory in Bradford but a doctor'd told him if he didn't take it easier and retire he'd pop off in no time.'

'But he's OK now?' said Lucy, glancing up from the sink.

'Well, he's not going to get better, lass, but then he hasn't gone any worse for a while.'

When all the dishes were put away Myrtle took Lucy and Timmy upstairs. 'You can have your pick of rooms. This used to be a guest house so they're all furnished. Only the room at the top of the house is taken up by Wesley and he doesn't like anyone going up there uninvited.'

'What about the beds being aired?' asked Lucy.

Her grandmother told her that was easily done. Plenty of hot water bottles and several cupboards full of bedding. As Lucy went into one room after another she couldn't help thinking there was money to be made here if Stanley could be persuaded. At last she and Timmy made their choice and her grandmother fetched hot water bottles and helped her to make up the beds.

Then the old woman watched as Lucy unpacked her suitcase and hung her clothes in the wardrobe. Myrtle asked if Barney was a warm man.

Lucy stared at her uncomprehendingly. 'Has he brass, lass? A bob or two.'

'Oh, yes. He owns property.' She shook out a frock.

'Your mother fell on her feet then. Has nice clothes like yours, I suppose? Big house?'

'I don't think inside it's quite as big as this,' said Lucy, wanting to change the subject. She hadn't told her grandmother Maureen was missing, only that she had remarried.

'Well, whatever your mother's got she should bottle it,' said Myrtle, a mite tartly. 'Wanted you out of the house, I suppose. New husband and a nice-looking girl like you.'

Lucy only smiled, thinking it wasn't surprising her grandmother should feel a touch bitter about Maureen. After all, she had stolen Myrtle's only son and kept her grandchildren away, too.

Lucy had not expected to sleep well that first night but in fact slept better than expected. Even so she was up early, remembering what her grandmother had said about seeing the fishing boats. She pulled back the curtain and gazed out on the street below. It was quiet, no hustle and bustle like St Domingo Road, only a marauding seagull picking at something on the road.

There was a bowl and jug on a stand in her room. The water was cold but she didn't let that bother her. She washed quickly and dressed in several layers, guessing it was going to be cold outside. Then she knocked on her brother's door and hurried downstairs.

Chapter Seventeen

Stan slept on the ground floor and when Lucy tapped on his door he shouted for her to put the kettle on and make porridge and bring it to the recreation room where they'd sat last evening. Then she could send the lad to come and wheel him in. There was a gas stove in the kitchen which was simplicity itself to work and in no time at all Lucy placed three bowls of steaming porridge on one of the tables. She called upstairs to her brother but need not have bothered because Timmy was on his way down. His hair was tousled but he looked bright-eyed enough.

She told him what Stan had said and as she sat at a table and picked up her spoon, heard their great-uncle saying behind her, 'Go test the wind, lad! Although if you haven't heard it rattling the windows then I think our little outing's on.'

A few minutes later Timmy was back. 'It's fair to middling,' he said with a grin.

'You'll have to speak up, lad,' said Stan, holding a hand behind his ear. Timmy repeated his weather report and the old man said, 'Then I'll wear my hat with the earflaps. You'll have to be having one, too, if you're going to be staying here long.'

Timmy looked like he'd rather die than wear the head gear which was produced ten minutes later; hat, gloves, muffler, a thick overcoat and a rug to cover Stan's legs and they were ready to go. It was a bit of a performance getting him off the step but soon they were heading for the sea and already Lucy was realising why her grandmother had wanted to know how strong they were. It was no easy task getting the wheelchair on and off pavements and it took both Timmy and Lucy to manage the thing, especially as one wheel seemed to have a life of its own.

'Easy now, don't let me fall! Stick to the road. This early we shouldn't have any trouble with the traffic,' said Stan.

They didn't, but on being directed to cross the road they went and got a wheel jammed in a tram line. 'Oh, hell!' groaned Timmy as they struggled to free it.

'Watch your language, lad,' gasped Stan, gripping an arm rest of the chair as it tilted sideways. 'You'll have me over if you're not careful.'

Lucy was about to suggest he should get out and lean on her while Timmy freed the wheel when a man appeared and without saying a word did the trick somehow. Before she could thank him he ran off.

'He's got no shoes and socks on,' said Timmy, staring after him. 'I thought you only saw children like that in Liverpool.'

'He must be freezing,' said Lucy, not having expected to see such poverty in Bridlington.

'That's my son Wesley,' said Stan gloomily. 'He has perfectly good shoes with rubber soles but he won't keep them on. I can't comprehend it at all.' He shook his head dolefully.

Lucy couldn't understand it either but after exchanging puzzled glances with her brother over Stan's head, she continued down the road towards the parade. Soon the sweep of the bay lay before them and they came to a halt to take in the view. The sun had not long risen and the surface of the sea was touched lightly with gold.

'Time to get moving,' said Stan loudly after a couple of minutes, rubbing his gloved hands together. 'Head north along the parade. In 1888,' he continued, 'Prince Albert Victor, our King's elder brother, opened the Alexandra Sea Wall. I was there, you know ... with your granddad. Prince Albert would have been king if he hadn't caught inflammation of the lung.'

'Wasn't he going to marry the queen?' said

Lucy, remembering something from a history lesson at school.

'That's right, lass. Instead his brother married her. It was remembering that which gave me the idea of marrying Myrtle, her being my brother William's widow. She's a good woman and it meant I had someone to help keep an eye on Wesley. It's worked out all right. We both had something to give which the other needed.'

Lucy didn't know whether she was expected to say something in response to that but she couldn't think of anything. There was silence except for the lapping of the sea against the shore and the screeching of gulls. She wondered if that was the secret of a happy marriage, having something to give which the other needed? She wondered what Blodwen had to give to Rob besides a pretty face and a nice body. Surely he couldn't be happy with just that? So she must have something Lucy knew nothing about, she thought enviously.

'Now look at Wesley!' Stan's voice startled Lucy out of her reverie. He pointed to the shore where a man was throwing bread up to the gulls. 'Go down and see if he'll come here, Timmy. He needs to know who you two are. It was no use trying to explain before you arrived and he was out off somewhere last night.'

Timmy dropped down on to the beach and ran across the sands. Lucy wondered what was wrong with Stan's son. She couldn't remember her father ever mentioning him.

Wesley came bounding towards them with Timmy running to keep up with him. Now Lucy had a chance to look at him properly. He was only a few inches taller than her but with a strong, bullish neck and shoulders. His face was ruddy and his nose like a large round button. His hair was the colour of old rope and straggled about his ears. He stood in front of them, chest rising and falling, looking at her with the unwavering yet incurious gaze of a child.

'Wesley, these are my nephew's children. Do you remember your cousin Larry? This is Lucy.' Stan placed a hand on her arm. 'And the lad is Timmy.'

'Lucy!' said Wesley, pointing first at her and then at her brother. 'Timmy!'

So he wasn't deaf and dumb, thought Lucy. 'Hello, Wesley!' she said, smiling and holding out her hand.

He seized it and swung on it. 'Like to play with me?'

'No. Wesley! Not now, lad,' said Stan hastily. 'I'm showing them the harbour.'

'Want to play on the sands,' said Wesley, scowling and keeping hold of Lucy's wrist. 'She can come with me. I'll show her things.'

'No, Wesley,' repeated his father firmly. 'Let her go!'

'No,' he said, shaking his head. 'Won't be long.'

Lucy decided to intervene. 'Five minutes,' she said. 'Understand that, Wesley?' she said, looking straight at him, thinking, Tuppence short of a shilling, poor thing.

He laughed gleefully and off they went. They hadn't gone far when he stopped, pulling her down on to the sand where the tide had left its mark in a sweeping line of shells and debris. He picked up a handful of cockle shells and dropped them on her palm. 'Mary, Mary,' he said.

'Quite contrary,' responded Lucy with a smile.

'Garden grow?' He gave her a look of enquiry, head tilted to one side. She nodded. He laughed and, still on his hands and knees, began to crawl and pick up more shells.

Convinced he would soon forget about her, she rose to her feet and made her way back to the promenade.

They resumed their walk. 'You see what's wrong with Wesley?' said Stan gruffly.

'I'm sure he's harmless,' said Lucy.

'Has the brain of a child of five but the body of a man,' muttered Stan. 'It's not easy. I've worked hard, and for what? I had to sell the factory instead of having my son take it over. I worry about who'll take care of him when Myrtle and I go. I don't want him put in an institution. He enjoys life as he is now.'

'No use in worrying about it,' said Lucy, not quite sure what else to say. 'He might die before you. Lots of people die young.'

'Not Wesley. He's as strong as an ox.'

Lucy did not argue but she had seen TB destroy a fifteen-stone docker in no time at all.

The fishing fleet was already in and the harbour was alive with activity. Stan directed them to a spot where they wouldn't be in the way and they watched as keels of gleaming silvery fish were unloaded along with crabs and lobsters. Herring gulls wheeled overhead, staining the quayside white with their droppings. Lucy thought how

343

different it was from being down at the Pierhead watching the liners and steamers coming and going. Quite a few people came over to have a word with Stan, speaking so fast in their Yorkshire dialect that Lucy understood only the odd word. With a smile she realised her great-uncle, like their grandmother, was bilingual, speaking the local dialect while also able to converse with Lucy and Timmy so they could understand them. She was warmed by people's smiles and just as Stan said he was ready to go, was handed a newspaper parcel and told it was for their breakfast.

They arrived home to find Myrtle up and about. 'Did you enjoy yourself?' she asked, fussing over Stan and taking off his hat and muffler.

'Yes!' Lucy told her about being given the fish and about seeing Wesley.

Myrtle darted her a glance and as soon as Stan and Timmy were settled in chairs and the wireless switched on, the old woman beckoned her to come into the kitchen with her. 'Wesley's not a bad lad,' she said, as she washed the fish before sprinkling flour on a table and putting on the frying pan. 'He's just difficult at times like any child. He's partly the reason why Stan won't let me take in paying guests.'

'I'm sure he'd be no trouble,' said Lucy, wanting to reassure her grandmother. 'You should try and persuade Uncle Stan. I'd help you with the guests. I had to give up my job before I came away and so did Timmy. If you want us to stay for any length of time we'll have to find work. I've a little money but it'll soon go if I start spending it and I don't want to sponge off you.'

'Get away with you!' said Myrtle, flouring the tiny whitebait before lying them side by side like sardines in the sizzling fat. 'It's not sponging when I've asked you here. You and Timmy'll be entertaining Stan and taking him out, and you'll be helping me in the house and with the shopping. If you really want to do something extra then you can help me on my stall on market day. I used to do all the farm baking years ago and I pride myself on my range of cakes and scones and bread.'

'I'd love to do that,' said Lucy enthusiastically, gripping the table. 'Perhaps I could make some sweets and toffee apples to sell? I haven't mentioned yet but I did a bit of that to make money a few years back.'

Myrtle looked pleased enough at the idea. 'You can give it a try,' she said. 'Now butter some bread, and I don't want to hear any more nonsense about sponging. What's family for if it's not to help each other?'

No more was said on the subject and Lucy got on with buttering the bread.

Later that day the weather took a turn for the worse so Lucy and Timmy stayed indoors and played card games with Stan. She was concerned about Wesley and asked where he might be.

'Don't you be worrying about him, lass. He likes to be out as much as he can and never seems to come off the worse for it,' said Stan.

Wesley did not arrive home until teatime and was then soaking wet. He began to strip off in front of the fire in the recreation room. 'Not here, lad,' cried Myrtle, seizing him by the shoulders. 'Ladies present. In the kitchen with you now. You can undress in front of the stove while I go upstairs and find you some dry clothes. Look at your feet – they're blue with cold!'

'Girl come with me,' said Wesley, pointing at Lucy. 'I want to show her something.'

'That you won't,' said Myrtle, her colour high hustling him out of the room.

The rest of that week the weather was foul and Myrtle didn't bother setting up a stall when market day came. The wind blew from the east, bringing hail and sleet. Except for excursions to the shops and the methodist church nearby, where Myrtle introduced her grand-daughter to everyone they met, they were stuck indoors. Lucy took time to write to Barney, Dilys and Owen and was sorely tempted to write to Rob again but as she had not received a reply to her previous letter she did not, hoping Barney or one of the others would write and bring her up to date with any news on the wedding front.

After several drenchings Wesley seemed to accept he would have to stay in until his clothes were dried. He wasn't happy, though, and threw a tantrum, upsetting the chess board when Stan was in the process of explaining the rules to Timmy and Lucy. On another occasion he demanded Lucy's attention, producing a book of fairy tales and asking her to read to him.

He sat next to her at one of the tables, so close she could feel his breath on her cheek. She found it unnerving being the object of such rapt con-centration from a man while reading the story of the 'Three Billy Goats Gruff'. Especially when he asked her to read it again and this time he did the goats' voices.

One day he insisted on Lucy and Timmy going up to his bedroom. She was curious, not sure what to expect. His room contained all the usual things and was surprisingly tidy. The clockwork train set didn't come as a surprise, neither did his box of treasures filled with shells, rocks, sweet wrappings and silver paper. But the book on stars of the silent screen did.

'You like going to the cinema, Wesley?' Lucy asked.

He nodded eagerly. 'You like?'

She nodded and sat on the floor, turning the pages of the book, remembering *The Perils of Pauline* and how she'd wanted to be like her. Some hope, she thought now.

At last, to the relief of all, the weather changed. The wind veered to the south and the sun shone. Lucy and Timmy wanted to explore and to their surprise both Stan and Myrtle said Wesley was the man to guide them. 'He mightn't have much in his cockloft but when it comes to the great outdoors there's nobody who knows the area better,' said Myrtle.

'Only don't be middering him with questions! You'll only confuse him,' said Stan. 'And take note – he has no sense of danger.'

Wesley took them round town, pointing out buildings: the New Spa, the Opera House and its gardens, the Floral Pavilion where to their surprise he laughed uproariously, holding his stomach. From which Lucy deduced he had seen a funny show there. And, of course, the neighbouring cinema. She noticed that they were showing a Rudolph Valentino film and was tempted to go inside. Perhaps it was the thought of sitting in close proximity to Wesley that put her off.

He took them to the Priory church in the old town and inside knelt down and put his hands together. He closed one eye and peered up at them from the other. He looked so comical Lucy almost laughed but instead she knelt herself but once on her knees was unsure what to pray for. The two things she wanted required a miracle: to see her mother alive and safe, and to have Rob wanting to marry her. So she just knelt, wishing devoutly her dreams could come true.

When Lucy arrived home she asked if there was any post for her. 'Yes, lass,' said Myrtle, dusting flour off her hands. 'I put it on the mantelshelf in the games room. I must admit I thought your mother would have written to you by now, but better late than never.'

Lucy flushed. 'Mam was never one for writing letters.' She was about to go into the games room when her grandmother called after her, 'If you want to make those sweets of yours do it today. You can come with me to the market tomorrow.'

Lucy's spirits lifted. 'Great! I'll read my letter, then I'll go and get the ingredients.'

She hurried over to the fireplace and grabbed the envelope addressed to her – gazing at the handwriting. It was unfamiliar so it was not from Barney. Could it be from Rob? Perhaps he had found out something about her mother? She tore the envelope open and drew out two sheets of paper covered in neat copperplate. It was from Dilys. Lucy quashed her disappointment and began to read:

Dear Lucy

Thanks for the postcard and I truly hope you'll continue to be happy living with your grandmother. I'm so sorry I never got to see you before you left for Yorkshire. I'm sorry, too, that I didn't come and see you before when your mother went missing. It was partly because I didn't know what to say to make things better for you but mainly because I was angry with you for flirting with Owen. I love him and was scared you would take him away from me. I see now that I was stupid. He's asked me to marry him and I've accepted. We'll be getting married very soon. Aunt Gwen is delighted because we're in the process of buying the timber yard from her. My great-aunt, who left her a house in Wales, also left me some money so everything is working out marvellously.

Rob is in Ireland at the moment. My aunt received a letter postmarked Dublin. She was very secretive about it so I think she must have written to him about Owen and me buying the timber yard. I can't say I'm pleased about that but she might have still thought she could persuade him to buy it. I know Blodwen's not very pleased with us but I could have told her if she'd bothered to ask me that she'll never change Rob's mind about leaving the police force. I think she's feeling a bit fed up. Maybe she'll bring their wedding forward now she realises she's not going to get what she wants. I don't expect you'll be able to come to our wedding but I hope we can still be friends.

Love, Dilys

Lucy folded the letter. Her heart was beating fast and she gazed unseeingly into the fire. Would Rob agree to an early wedding? Perhaps it would be better if he did? Once he was married she would have to force herself to forget him and put him out of her heart.

What was he doing in Ireland? Had he found something out about Shaun O'Neill which had taken him over there? He would surely write to let her know if he'd discovered what had happened to her mother.

She tapped the letter against her teeth. Crafty old Owen, marrying money! She hoped the marriage would work out. It was obvious that Dilys did not want her at the wedding and Lucy could understand why, but really the other girl had no need to fear there would ever be anything between Owen and herself.

As Lucy counted the money in her purse to buy the ingredients for the sweets, she felt restless, realising it was going to be even more difficult now to wait to hear from Rob. She thought seriously for a moment of writing to him again. She dithered then decided he had to make the first move. She had her pride, and besides she had to get on with her new life.

She decided not to bother with toffee apples because it meant spending money on sticks. Instead she found herself relaxing as she set about making toffee and peppermint creams and coconut ice.

It was fun at the market. There was so much going on and her grandmother being well known meant Lucy had no trouble at all selling her sweets. She remembered how she'd dreamed of having a sweetshop before wanting to own a cinema. It was a pity she couldn't persuade Stan to put money into such a venture, although she still had hopes of getting round him to open up the house to paying guests.

The following evening he brought up the matter of Timmy and school. 'If you and he are happy living with us we should write to your mother. If she agrees, he could finish his schooling here.'

Lucy glanced across at her brother and decided that perhaps it was time to come clean. 'We don't know where Mam is. She disappeared a few weeks before we came here.'

Myrtle and Stan stared in astonishment first at Lucy and then Timmy. 'Why didn't you tell us?' said their grandmother, her hands still on the sock she was darning.

'It was too painful to talk about. We – we think she might have been murdered,' said Lucy.

'Don't, Luce,' said Timmy gruffly, lowering his head and staring at the floor.

There was silence. Then Stan said, 'If it's too painful to talk about then we won't. I remember when my first wife died I didn't want to talk about that. I'll just say this is your home now and so Timmy'll have to go to school and afterwards find work here if he can. Do you agree with that, lad?'

Timmy lifted his head, relief on his face. 'I'll go along with that.'

'Right,' said Stan. 'We'll sort it out.'

Within the week Timmy was enrolled at the local elementary school. For the first few days he came home looking fed up. 'They all skit my accent,' he muttered. But within a fortnight he had settled down and was making friends.

Lucy had not received any replies to her other letters and came to the conclusion that perhaps she wasn't going to get any. With Owen's mother to cook his dinner and Agnes to keep the house clean for him, Barney might have decided to cut Lucy out of his life completely because of her choosing to come to Yorkshire. As for Rob, Lucy did wonder if her letter had never reached him but still could not bring herself to write to him again. If he had found out anything in Ireland he would surely have been in touch. She had to forget him!

But Lucy couldn't forget Rob despite throwing herself into all kinds of activities. She had always considered herself a good walker (after all, she'd often walked to the Trocadero and back) but Wesley thought nothing of walking five, six, seven or more miles a day when he was persuaded away from beachcombing or feeding the birds or going cockling with the cocklewomen.

More often than not he took Lucy along the coast, too – she'd long since realised he was far from stupid – he could beat her at Snakes and Ladders and played a mean game of Snap but once Timmy was in school he developed an unerring instinct for getting her alone in places where she was off her guard. The first time was by the fresh water mere at Hornsea, where ducks and all kinds of wild life gathered. He tried to kiss her there. Since he was much stronger than she was, Lucy found herself flat on her back in the grass with him on top of her. She slapped his face and told him to behave. He hung his head and said sorry and so she forgave him and thought it wouldn't happen again.

The next time he took her north. There lay a fishing village where steam power was used to haul the boats up out of the breakers beneath the breathtaking, awesome beauty of Flamborough Head. Lucy loved its towering cliffs of chalk and the view of the sea from the top. It was a little frightening because of the height and the fierce wind which threatened to pluck her off the cliff but it was also exciting.

Wesley said he would show her a place out of the wind, sheltered by a high bank which ran from one cliff to another. There he not only pulled her down in the grass but his trousers as well. He looked at her eagerly, saying 'See!'

It wouldn't have been so bad if he'd had under-pants on but he didn't. Lucy panicked, reminded of the time Mick had exposed his scar to her and asked her to touch it. She lashed out at Wesley, catching him a blow on his arm. 'No, no, no, Wesley!' she cried, and threw her scarf over his thing. 'You mustn't ever show me that again!'

'No?' he said mournfully, and drew his legs together, dropping his head onto his knees.

After that when she wanted a walk Lucy stuck to pushing Stan in the wheelchair. Even so the way Wesley looked at her made her realise she had a problem that wasn't going to go away. Sometimes she heard his footsteps outside her room at night but fortunately, due to the house once having been a guest house, there was a lock on her door with a big key she could turn and place under her pillow. She felt safe then.

Lucy was reluctant to mention any of this to her grandmother and great-uncle. She thought they had enough on their plate. Stan's physical health had started to deteriorate all of a sudden. His doctor came to see him every fortnight. Stan could walk on sticks at a push and was told he really needed to take more exercise to get his circulation going but he had made the decision it wasn't worth the effort. 'Three score years and ten. That's what it says we're allowed in the Bible,' he commented after the doctor's latest visit. 'I've passed that and feel content knowing you and Timmy are here, Lucy, to look after Myrtle and my son.'

Lucy's former life in Liverpool began to take on a dreamlike quality. Before she realised it several months had passed and still there was no word from Barney or Rob. If the latter had received her letter it might be that he saw her leaving Liverpool as sensible in the circumstances. Maybe even now the banns had been read and he and Blodwen were doing all those things that couples about to get married and set up home do. If there had been any news about her mother, surely someone would have written?

As the days grew longer and the weather warmer Myrtle suddenly broke it to Lucy that she had a brother who was a tenant farmer in Weaverthorpe. 'I thought Timmy might like to go with me to see him on the Easter bank holiday, before we start washing all the blankets, Lucy.'

She agreed he could go while she stayed behind to look after Stan and waved her brother off, never expecting him to return full of enthusiasm to work on the farm. 'I know he likes animals,' Lucy said to her grandmother. 'But farming?'

Myrtle's eyes twinkled. 'It's in his blood, lass. Though it's hard work to be sure and the pay's lousy and lots of men are leaving the land, hoping to find work in factories where they think to earn higher wages. My brother has one of those new-fangled tractors, as well as an old Army lorry he bought after the war. He reckons Timmy has an aptitude not only with animals but machinery as well.'

Lucy looked at her brother, who grinned. 'He likes me. So do his wife and the three girls.'

'I've always known you have charm,' said Lucy, ruffling his hair and laughing. 'If it's what you want, you can do it if he's prepared to take you on but you must finish your schooling first.'

He hugged her and then went and did the same to his grandmother. 'You liked it there, too, didn't you, Gran?'

'I did. It's where I was brought up. I was a farmer's daughter. Then I came to Bridlington on a day's outing and met your grandfather and that was it.' Her eyes were dreamy. 'He was so persuasive. In no time at all we were married and I was a sailor's wife.'

'Can I work there during the summer holidays?' said Timmy, glancing at his sister, one arm still round his grandmother.

Lucy hesitated. She was reluctant to lose him

355

for all those weeks. He would be off to the farm soon enough.

Myrtle said, 'If he does that he'll find out whether he's suited to the life or not. Although it's really winter he needs to be there to see how hard farming is when it's cold and dark and everywhere's full of mud and dirt. I know we'll miss him but if it's what he wants then he should do it,' she said firmly. 'There's a lot of unrest because of unemployment at the moment.'

So Lucy agreed, thinking about the unrest her grandmother was talking about. It was all to do with the miners. The government had lifted the subsidy from coal and their wages were expected to drop. 'Not a minute on the day, not a penny off the pay!' retaliated the miners.

At the beginning of May the TUC called a strike of all the energy and transport workers. They were hoping the rest of the unions would join them in an action which would bring the country to its knees, so the miners would get what they wanted. This was all going on as Lucy decided it was time to persuade Stan to open up the house to summer paying guests. Her plan collapsed just like the General Strike, which was over in nine days.

'We should have put ourselves in the Bridlington handbook,' said Stan, putting a match to his pipe. 'Advertising, lass. Nobody'll know about us now. But I've told you, I don't want anyone else here until I've gone. Then you and Myrtle can hire a few maids and set up in business. Just be patient, lass.'

'But I don't want you to die,' she said, a tremor

in her voice.

He looked gratified but held up one hand. 'We all have to die, lass. Be happy for now. Haven't you got a roof over your head and food in your stomach? Haven't you company and entertainment?'

What could she say? She had all those things so she couldn't tell him that the biggest drawback was Wesley who had taken to asking her to go with him to the pictures at least three times a week. He was not going to go away! If she looked into the future, to when Myrtle died, it looked dark. Lucy rebelled against the whole idea of having to take care of Wesley but how could she speak of it without hurting two old people of whom she had become very fond and who depended on her? It was a worry.

Summer brought not only crowds of holiday-makers who changed the whole atmosphere of the town but also the news that Rudolph Valentino had died of a perforated ulcer. Lucy was shocked, remembering that conversation with Barney and her mother, and also reminded of Dilys and the way they had spoken of dancing with him.

She went with Myrtle and Wesley to see his funeral on the silver screen. There was mass hysteria and Lucy wept but soon pulled herself together when she felt Wesley's arm snaking round her and his hand touching her breast.

Summer passed and the holidaymakers went home. Timmy came back from the farm, full of how he could milk cows, dig potatoes and drive the tractor.

It was the day after he returned to school that Lucy received another letter from Liverpool. To her amazement it was from the maid, Agnes, and was written in cramped letters in pencil. She had obviously laboured over it.

Dear Miss Lucy,

I hopes you don't mind my writing but I thinks you should come home. The master's been behaving real queer ever since we had a couple of people here asking after you. He said I was to keep quiet about it but I asks meself why. One was an old lady who came a few weeks ago. The other was a man with an Irish accent who pushed his way into the house. He only was here the other day. I thought the master was going to have an apoplexy but he finally left after seeing for himself you wasn't here. So if you can see your way to coming home soon I think you'd be able to sort things out. He's been stumping around a lot and I suspect he's been drinking.

Your obedient servant,
Agnes Walsh

P.S. I remember him being like this a few months ago after there was a letter addressed to you and your brother from Ireland. I don't know what was in it but I found the envelope and it was postmarked Dublin.

Lucy could feel herself going hot and cold. Had Shaun O'Neill written to her and Timmy, threatening them? That was the only kind of letter she thought he would write to them. Maybe it had contained the truth about her mother and Barney wanted to keep it from them? Was it

O'Neill who had called? He had a nerve, forcing himself into Barney's house when he was wanted by the police. Poor Barney! It must have been a terrible shock to him. Why couldn't he have written to her and told her, though? Lucy couldn't understand it. Unless again it was because he didn't want to upset her? And yet hadn't he upset her enough by not writing? Suddenly the need to know what this was all about overwhelmed her. Yet how could she go to Liverpool when Stan and Myrtle depended on her? She needed time to think.

She finished what she was doing in the house and put on her outdoor clothes before going down to the seafront. There was a north-easter blowing and the beach was a desolate place. She had often heard it said that Liverpool was ⌐protected from the worst of the weather by the mountains of Wales and the hills of the Pennines. Now she believed it and found herself longing for her native city with a fierceness which amazed her. She wanted to wander its bustling streets, to press her nose against the shop windows. She pined for the nasal accents of her fellow Liverpudlians, to hear a shawlie asking, 'How are yer, girl?'

But what about Myrtle and Stan? With the change in the weather his chest was bad. So Lucy returned to the house, still undecided what to do. A week passed and she was still dithering. Then one evening she was sitting with Wesley and Timmy, playing a game, when a foot wrapped itself round hers beneath the table and a hand fell heavily on to her lap. She looked at Wesley. 'Stop that!' she ordered, removing his hand and wanting to wipe off his inane grin with her finger nails.

'Not doing anything,' he said, trying to look innocent.

'Liar!' Anger made her eyes sparkle. 'You're always trying to do something and I'm sick of it!'

Timmy looked at her in surprise. 'Ease up, Luce. What's he done? You know he can't help himself.'

'Shut up!' she glared at her brother. 'Even kids remember what's right and wrong when they're told often enough.'

The room was suddenly silent and she was aware of Myrtle's and Stan's eyes on her.

'What is it, lass?' gasped Stan. 'It's not like you to get so worked up.'

Lucy wished she hadn't spoken. She hated to hear him gasping for breath, didn't want to worry about how ill he was right now. She wanted to say she didn't trust his son, was scared to death that one day he'd defy her and have his wicked way with her. 'I keep thinking of me mam,' she said.

The relief on their faces was worth the untruth. 'That's natural,' said Myrtle, getting up from her seat near the fire and coming over to her. She rested one hand on Lucy's shoulder. 'What would you like to do? I know we've never talked about Maureen going missing and your fears about her. Perhaps now is the time.'

'No!' said Timmy.

Lucy looked across at his tense face and then up at her grandmother. 'I want to go back to Liverpool. I felt sure at the beginning that if there

360

had been any developments someone would have written to me – there's been nothing, as you know. But I had another letter recently and I need to go and speak to someone about it. The police maybe.' She dropped her cards and gripped her hands together tightly. 'I can't bear not knowing any longer. I have to try and find out for myself what's happened to Mam.'

'Then you'd best go,' said Myrtle, pressing her grand-daughter's shoulder. 'Isn't that right, Stan?' she called over to her husband.

Lucy looked at him and thought his face looked grey. He nodded. 'Money,' he gasped. 'I'll pay.'

She got up and went over to him, kneeling beside his chair and putting her hand on his bony knee. 'I'll go tomorrow. I'll be back within a few days.'

He put a hand on her hair and gasped, 'You see you are, lass. But Timmy?'

'I'm staying,' said the youth, getting up and putting an arm around his grandmother. 'Someone's got to look after you two.'

Chapter Eighteen

It was raining when Lucy arrived back in Liverpool. She had left Bridlington bathed in sunshine on a cold, crisp day but the sun had disappeared somewhere over the Pennines where there had been a storm. It was evening and Barney might be working but Agnes was bound to be at the

361

house to let her in, she thought.

Lucy caught a tram and was soon climbing the steps to the front door. She put down her suitcase and lifted the knocker. The noise echoed up the lobby but there was no immediate response so she wielded the knocker again. This time a voice she did not recognise called, 'Hold your horses, I'll be with you in a sec.'

It was more like a minute before the door opened to reveal a complete stranger. 'Yee-s! What can I do for you?' said the woman.

Lucy checked the number on the door. She had come to the right house. Had Barney got rid of Agnes? 'Is Mr Jones in?' she demanded. 'I'm his stepdaughter.'

The woman twitched a strap and smoothed her apron. 'Doesn't live here any more, dear. I'm surprised he hasn't told you ... but then the move was sudden.'

Lucy was stunned. 'Could you tell me where he's gone?'

'Now you're asking me, dear, I can't say for sure. He didn't leave a forwarding address.'

For a moment Lucy could not think what to do. Had Barney moved because of the man who had called on him? Maybe he had been frightened. If that was so, why hadn't he called the police? But maybe he had called them since she had received Agnes's letter.

'Is that it?' said the woman, her head cocked to one side. 'Mind if I close the door? Shocking evening!'

Lucy murmured something and, picking up her suitcase, descended the steps. Perhaps she should go to the police station? She set out to walk to the bridewell in Athol Street. Thinking of policemen, naturally she thought of Rob, wondering whether he had married Blodwen yet. She had to prepare herself for that eventuality. If only she could believe he would be happy with Blodwen, she might not mind his marrying her so much. No, that was a lie! She hated the thought of any other woman having him.

Lucy shifted her suitcase from her right hand to her left, rainwater dripped from the brim of her hat on to the tip of her nose. She was going to be soaked before she got to the bridewell the way the rain was coming down so relentlessly. It was a soft gentle rain but very wet nevertheless.

She stepped off the pavement and crossed a street, only to walk into a lamp post in the dark. She bumped her nose and it brought tears to her eyes. She looked up at the lamp but not a glimmer of light shone from it. The glass must have been smashed by a ball or stone and the mantle broken. Putting down her suitcase, she wiped her eyes and checked her nose gingerly before resuming her walk, only to trip over a brick and go stumbling across the street.

She thrust her suitcase to the ground and the action stopped her from falling. She had stubbed her toe and it hurt. Suddenly coming home to Liverpool seemed a bad idea. She was starting to feel cold. She dragged her bedraggled fur hat right down over her ears and covered her mouth and nose with her scarf. She swapped her suitcase to the other hand because her arm was aching, turned right and headed in the direction of Scotland Road along the wet pavements of the deserted streets.

Suddenly out of the rain loomed a man. She almost jumped out of her skin but there was no need for her to be frightened. He was big and burly, uniformed, wearing a police helmet and was carrying a light. It was like seeing a boat coming towards you when you were about to go under for the third time. Lucy stumbled towards him and clutched his arm. 'Could you help me, officer? I'm looking for someone.'

He stared down at her. 'Don't I know you, miss?'

'I don't think so,' she said, surprised.

The policeman gave her a closer look. 'Yes, I do. I never forget a face. You're the girl whose mother went missing.'

Lucy sighed. 'You're right. There hasn't been any news about her, has there?'

'No, miss. I presume it's not your mother you're looking for right now?'

She shook her head, scattering raindrops from her hat.

He brushed his arm. 'You're really wet – and what's that you're carrying?'

'I've been living in Yorkshire for the last six months or so,' she explained with a smile. 'I've come back to see my stepfather but he's moved and I don't know where to.'

The policeman stroked his chin, looking thoughtful.

'That'll be Barney Jones. He's related to Rob Jones, isn't he? Now Rob might know where he is. He's moved, too, you know, but I can't give you his address off the top of me head.'

Lucy's heart sank. Rob had moved! Did that mean he had married Blodwen?

The policeman took her suitcase from her. 'Come on, luv. You look like you could do with a cup of tea and a nice warm.'

He took her to Athol Street bridewell where there was warmth, voices and laughter. She was ushered in front of a fire and within minutes a steaming mug of tea was placed in her hands. 'Here yer are, girl, get that down yer.'

Lucy thanked the man in a gruff voice because truth to tell she felt like bursting into tears. Her rescuer had disappeared but a younger bobby had taken over from him and stood watching her sip the strong, sweet tea. Suddenly he grinned. 'You're that girl who had a fancy for Rob Jones.'

Lucy reddened. 'I don't know what you're talking about.'

'Gerraway with yer! Barney Jones's step-daughter, mother went missing then you did. We would have had him for that if Rob hadn't said he'd had a letter from you.'

So Rob had received her letter! Lucy's hopes were dashed. She'd thought his aunt might have got to it first and on seeing a Yorkshire postmark, destroyed it. She cleared her throat. 'I believe he's moved. Is he married?'

The young bobby gave her a knowing look. 'Naw! You want his address?' He leaned back against a table and folded his arms. 'He was involved in a fight with some real bad 'uns, you know, and was knived.'

Lucy's heart seemed to stop beating and she

felt as if all the blood had drained from her head. 'He's not dead, though?' she whispered.

The policeman smiled slyly. 'Took it in the shoulder. He's on sick leave. If you were wanting to see him I could take you to the bakery where he has rooms over the shop. It's not far from here.'

'I'd like that, please.' She put down her mug.

'I thought you might,' he said, still smiling.

On the way Lucy wondered what Rob was doing in rooms over a bakery. Had his aunt gone to Wales, having sold the timber yard to Owen and Dilys? And why wasn't he married to Blodwen?

Within a short space of time Lucy found herself in a back yard. 'There's an outside iron staircase,' explained the policeman, leading the way and starting up the steps.

Suddenly a door opened above them and a voice shouted down, 'Don't come any further! I've a red hot poker here.'

'It's Peters! I've a young lady here wanting to see you.'

'Is this one of your jokes, Peters?' The staircase began to vibrate as Rob started down towards them.

She called up, 'It isn't a joke! It's me, Lucy!'

There was silence. She realised she was holding her breath again and thought with a sinking heart that if he hadn't seen fit to answer her letter then he probably didn't want to see her now. Then Rob said, 'All right, Peters. I'll take it from here. I suppose it's no good asking you to keep quiet about this?'

'No, Jonesy. It's like one of those serials at the picture, see? The men'll be dying to know what's happening next in your love life.'

'But it's not like that,' said Lucy swiftly. 'I just need some information from him.'

'If you say so, miss,' said Peters, grinning as he saluted her. 'I'll be off.' He brushed past her and soon Lucy could neither see him nor hear the sound of his boots.

She would have turned tail and run if she hadn't been so desperate to see Rob, and wet and cold into the bargain.

'It's no good standing there like a frightened mouse,' he said, frowning down at her. 'Come on up!'

Relieved he wasn't going to chase her away, Lucy clattered up the stairs as fast as she could. Rob shot a glance at her as he took her suitcase but did not say anything. She followed him into a large room. There was a smell of cooking and a fire smouldered in the grate. Stretched out on a rug in front of it was a ginger cat.

'Love your moggy,' she said, as a way of breaking the silence.

He looked at her as if he knew she was speaking just for something to say and told her to take off her coat and hat and sit down. She sat on the plump, comfortable-looking sofa and watched as he brought the poker down on a large lump of coal. It cracked open and there was a hiss of escaping gas which spurted into flame.

Lucy slipped off her shoes and rested her head on the back of the sofa, noticing how his dark hair had been cut away at the back where there was an ugly wound. Why hadn't Peters mentioned that? She felt a peculiar lurch in the region of her heart and wanted to get up and kiss the wound better. She had to force herself to look away and gaze about the room, noticing the gramophone first and then the pile of records on top of a crammed bookcase. There was a table and some upright chairs and a wooden dresser and a comfy armchair.

Rob straightened up, dusting his knees and brushing his hands. 'What are you doing here?' His voice sounded cold and she knew he was angry with her.

'I shouldn't have come,' said Lucy, feeling wretched. 'But I was found by a big, kind policeman who took me to the bridewell. He disappeared and that man Peters, offered to bring me here. I should have realised it wouldn't be what you wanted but I needed some answers ... and to see you after he said you'd been hurt in a fight.' She stopped and waited for him to say something but the silence lengthened until she couldn't bear it so in an attempt to lighten the atmosphere she blurted out, 'You wouldn't have a hot water bottle, would you? Only I'm cold and wet after walking for what seems like ages.'

He surprised her by kneeling in front of her and taking one of her hands in his. He peeled off her glove and chafed her hand between both of his until it hurt and the circulation got going again. Then he took her other hand and did the same thing. 'Does your shoulder hurt?' she asked.

Rob smiled slightly. 'Of course it hurts but I'm on the mend now. I'm hoping to get back to work in a couple of weeks.'

'You're still a detective?'

He nodded and got to his feet. 'I'll get you that hot water bottle.'

'Thanks.' She watched him leave the room and immediately rose and went over to his record pile, curious to see what music he liked. She read the labels and noted they were HMV and Columbia, which were the two best-selling companies in the world. She smiled; that was where she had invested some of her money. Most of the records were of popular music – *The Student Prince*, for instance, had sold more than two hundred and seventy thousand copies – and surprisingly orchestrated versions of jazz numbers were also amongst his collection. He had a recording by Paul Whiteman and his band.

Rob reappeared with the hot water bottle. She took it and curled up again on the sofa. He left the room and reappeared, this time carrying a casserole dish. 'Hungry?' he said.

She put down the hot water bottle and stood up. 'Yes! can I help? Your shoulder–'

'Cutlery and plates from the dresser,' he said, and left the room once more.

Why was he cooking for himself? Lucy wondered. Having set the table, she lifted the lid of the casserole. Where was Blodwen?

He reappeared with a plate of bread and Lucy took off her coat and hat and sat down. They ate in silence. It was only when Rob cleared the plates and asked if she'd make the tea that she asked him if he'd found out anything about her mother.

'I would have written.'

'Yes,' she murmured, 'but you could at least have answered my letter and told me you had been to Ireland and what you found out there.'

He looked surprised but said nothing, going over to fetch a tin from the dresser. 'Your letter read like you knew what you were doing. I decided it was best to let you be.'

'Best for whom?' She stared at him and then looked away.

He slid a slice of fruit cake on a plate across to her. 'I need time, Lucy, and even then I don't know if I'll have anything to give you.'

She stared at him, only to be shocked by the misery she saw in his face. 'What happened?' she whispered.

'I wouldn't have thought I'd have had to tell you.'

'I know Owen and Dilys bought the timber yard and Blodwen was annoyed. Dilys wrote to me.'

'There was more to it than that.' He took a bite of cake and kept Lucy waiting. She wondered what more there could be. Eventually he said, 'Blodwen started taking a big interest in Barney, going round there with cakes and stuff. He was invited round to her mother's for Sunday dinner. Owen's mother got the sack.'

'What!' Lucy could hardly believe that. 'He loved Mrs Davies' cooking. Perhaps Blodwen was just trying to be Christian?'

Rob choked on his cake. She got up and banged him on the back. He spluttered out, 'I caught him with his hand up her skirt!'

Lucy was truly shocked. 'She must have tempted him. What was she after?'

Rob gulped down a mouthful of tea and said wrathfully, 'What was *he* after, you mean! Trust you to take his side.'

'I'm not taking his side,' protested Lucy. 'You said yourself she started taking an interest in Barney.' She frowned. 'I wonder why Agnes didn't tell me about that?'

'Agnes? Barney's maid? You've seen her since you've been here?'

'No. She wrote to me. Said he'd been behaving peculiar. Perhaps it was because he was lonely after I left. I mean, he'd lost Mam.' Rob opened his mouth and Lucy added hastily, 'Don't say it! Nothing of that sort ever happened when I lived there. He was like a father to me.'

'Right!' said Rob, breathing deeply. 'A father, hey?' His tone was scathing. 'Then why did you leave him? Not scared of him one little bit?'

Lucy was unsure how to answer that and instead said, 'You read my letter. I left because my grandmother wanted to see me and Timmy. So what was in the letter you wrote to your aunt from Ireland?'

Rob looked puzzled. 'What's this about a letter? What are you talking about? And how did we get on to this from Barney?'

'Dilys said your aunt received a letter postmarked Dublin when you were in Ireland.'

'I sent no letter.'

They stared at each other. 'You did go to Ireland?' said Lucy, surprised.

He nodded. 'I traced one of the prison guards.'

She felt a stir of excitement and leaned towards him. 'What did you find out?'

'That O'Neill's brother was a ship's engineer and in love with the wife of a shipowner whose business is in Liverpool.'

'Did you find out the shipowner's name?' she said excitedly.

'There's the rub.' Rob reached out and took Lucy's hand. 'The guard overheard the conversation between McCallum and Daniel O'Neill but didn't catch the name of the woman.'

'You haven't been able to find out what it is?'

He dropped her hand. 'Lucy, your mother's case has been put on file! The trail's gone cold. I've been put on other cases and I'm glad to say we managed to nail the sods who stabbed me. I'm hoping to be made Sergeant soon.'

Lucy was pleased for him but still confused as to why Dilys should believe her aunt had received a letter from him while he was in Ireland. 'Is there anyone else your aunt knows in Ireland?'

He shook his head. 'Dilys must have made a mistake.'

Lucy had to accept that. 'Agnes told me that a man with an Irish accent called at Barney's wanting to see me. It can only have been Shaun O'Neill.'

Rob shook his head. 'I don't get it. If that was so, why didn't Barney get in touch with the police?'

She shrugged. 'It's a mystery.'

'I'm going to have to speak to him.' He glanced at the clock on the mantelshelf.

Lucy's eyes followed Rob's. 'But not now. He'll be working, I guess. I presume you know where he's moved to?'

Rob looked surprised. 'You know that, too?'

She nodded, and refrained from telling him she had already called at the house in St Domingo Road. 'Going back to Daniel O'Neill and this woman he was in love with,' she added. 'Couldn't you check up on all the shipping lines and see if any of them have ever employed a Daniel O'Neill?'

He stared at her as if she'd run mad. 'Do you know how common a name O'Neill is in Liverpool? And that there are at least sixty shipping lines I'd have to check up on?' He looked moody. 'I bet that trail has gone cold, too. The pair of them could be living in Ireland for all we know.'

She rested her elbows on the table and leaned towards him, saying softly, 'But Shaun's been seen over here so what are the odds his brother's been over here too? I've got a feeling they've family in Liverpool. There must be a way of finding the brother or the family and through them getting to Shaun.'

Rob got up and went over to the fire to put on more coal. Then he came back to sit on the sofa. 'We've no proof Shaun O'Neill killed your mother, but I must admit I still want to nail him.'

Lucy moved over to the sofa and sat next to him. Picking up the hot bottle, she hugged it. 'So you'll do something?'

'Maybe.' He put one arm along the back of the sofa.

There was silence. She glanced at him and noted again the cut on his head. She touched it lightly. 'Did you get this in the fight?'

'No,' he said grimly. 'I got it when I punched Barney. Blodwen smashed a plate over my head and broke off our engagement.'

Lucy couldn't help it. She laughed with delight. 'You're well rid of her!'

'I'm starting to believe that myself. She said I was a savage for hitting a cripple.' He scowled. 'You do see, Lucy, why I feel I can't offer you anything?' he said earnestly. 'I'm questioning my own judgement when it comes to love. I thought loving someone meant you were prepared to do anything to make the other person happy but that's not true in Blodwen's case or mine. I wasn't prepared to give up my job, and although she changed her mind about that rather than lose me, and I thought everything was going to work out – she was still seething about it. That's why she started making a fuss of Barney. He apparently made her feel more wanted than I did.'

'And as well as that he's got money,' added Lucy helpfully.

Rob whistled through his teeth. 'She wouldn't be able to marry him, though. Without a body to prove your mother's dead he won't be free to marry for years. She must have realised that by now.'

Lucy could only agree and hope Blodwen wouldn't change her mind and want Rob back. Still, there were other things to think about. 'We need to find Shaun O'Neill.'

Rob nodded. 'But for now let's forget him. So

how was Yorkshire? Are you happy living with your grandmother?'

'It's sad,' said Lucy, resting her head against the back of the sofa so that her hair brushed Rob's arm. 'My Great-uncle Stan is dying. I've promised to go back so I've only a few days here.' She suddenly saw a way of making Rob jealous. 'He's been very good to us and that's why it's difficult to refuse the thing he'd really like to see before he dies.'

'What's that, and what's so difficult about it?'

She glanced surreptitiously at him from beneath her eyelashes. 'Wesley! He's Stan's son and he fancies me.' She let the words hang in the air before adding, 'I've spent a lot of time in his company this summer.'

Rob looked as if he couldn't believe it. 'You can't mean he wants you to marry his son?'

'He needs someone to take care of him,' she said truthfully.

'You can't marry him!' Rob sat up straight, his eyebrows twitching.

'Why?'

He hesitated. 'Because you'd only be marrying him on the rebound from me.'

Lucy heaved a sigh. 'You could be right but what can I do?'

'Don't rush into anything,' he said firmly. 'Marriage is for life and you don't want to make a mistake. I intend staying a bachelor.'

She could have screamed at him but instead stood up and said coldly, 'Really? Time I was going then. Where's my coat and hat?' She glanced about her.

Rob shot to his feet. 'Where are you going?'

'To Barney's. I called at the house in St Domingo Road earlier and found he wasn't there. You'll give me his new address?'

Rob's expression hardened. 'I should have known you'd look him up first.'

She was angry. 'You betcha! You made it plain you wanted me out of your hair long ago.' She spotted her coat and swept it up in both arms.

He went over to the window and drew back a curtain. 'You'll get wet.'

She made no answer, determined to see if he'd let her go out there. Hat! Where was her hat? She found it and put it on, and then her gloves. 'Where's my suitcase?'

Rob looked her up and down and said frostily, 'You'll get your feet wet. You've got no shoes on.'

So she hadn't. Having found them she had no choice but to continue the game. She put them on. He handed her the suitcase with a grim smile. Lucy wanted to spit nails at him but limped out of the room, hoping he would stop her. He didn't. The swine, she thought. He didn't care if she drowned in the rain.

Lucy opened the outside door and stepped on to the platform at the top of the steps before realising she had forgotten her scarf. She turned and he was there with it dangling from his hand. 'You forgot this.'

She snatched it from him and swung it round her neck, picked up her suitcase and clattered down the stairs. If he calls me back now I won't go, she thought.

As she walked down the yard, he called, 'What

d'you think of my motorbike?'

The words stopped her in her tracks. What motorbike? He had a motorbike? She gazed wildly about her, trying to make out a shape that was in any shape or form a motorcycle's. Then she heard his feet slapping the iron staircase. She turned and watched as he lifted a sheet of tarpaulin to reveal a condensation-misted motorcycle.

'It's a brand new Rudge,' Rob said with the pride of possession in his voice. 'I didn't get round to telling you the great-aunt who died left me some money, did I? Not a lot but enough to buy this and the gramophone and to furnish the flat. I could run you to Barney's on it tomorrow. And by the way, I didn't tell you where he's living.'

'What about your shoulder?'

He smiled lazily. 'I told you, that's on the mend. You can have my bed. I'll doss down on the sofa. Your virtue's safe, honest.'

Pity, thought Lucy, going back to the flat with him.

They sat on the sofa and he told her his aunt had moved to Wales when Dilys had married and Mrs Davies had gone with her to keep her company. Then he made two cups of cocoa and left her a moment to tidy his bedroom. He returned with a blanket.

'I hope you'll be warm enough with just one blanket,' Lucy said.

'It's warmer in here than my room,' he said with a grin. 'You'll need that hot water bottle heating up again.'

'I don't have to go to bed already, do I?' Lucy was dismayed. 'How about some music?'

Rob flung the blanket on the sofa and went over to the gramophone, searched through his records and placed one on the turntable. He put in a new needle, then wound up the gramophone. *'Swannee! How I love you, how I love you, my dear old Swannee. I'd give the world to see–'* He jiggled about in front of her, matching the music to his actions. She laughed and joined in before collapsing on to the sofa when the record came to an end.

He put on another and wound up the gramophone again. *'Ma, he's making eyes at me! Ma, he's awful nice to me. Ma, he's almost breaking my heart...'*

'"I've decided,"' sang Lucy, *'"Mercy, let his conscience guide him."'* Her voice trailed off as she looked at Rob. For several seconds they stared at each other. Then he went over and took off the record and put another on, jazz this time which made Lucy's feet want to dance.

'Do you still have that frock?' asked Rob casually.

How he thought she'd automatically know which one he meant she didn't know, but she did. 'Somewhere at the back of my wardrobe,' she murmured.

'No chance of seeing you in it tonight then?'

A giggle escaped her. 'No chance.'

'Then I might as well switch off the music and you can go to bed.' He suited his action to his words. 'I'm sure you're tired.'

'No,' she said softly. After the music the silence

378

seemed to press in on her ears: a cinder dropping on the hearth sounded loud. She was aware of him sitting a few inches away and thought it incredible that it was less than twenty-four hours since she had left Yorkshire and here she was, about to spend the night in Rob's flat. She shifted a little until she felt the warmth of his thigh against hers.

Minutes passed and she was starting to doze off when she felt his arm go round her and his lips against her neck. Immediately, and with her eyes still shut, she turned to face him. Her hands felt their way up and around his neck. He kissed her with a strength of feeling that forced her flat on the sofa. Kiss followed kiss. His fingers felt for the openings on her blouse and she pushed his hands away and looked at him. He smouldered like a damped down fire. 'Let me do it,' she said.

He dragged off his pullover and unbuttoned his shirt.

So there was going to be no stopping him this time, she thought, and dropped her blouse and camisole on the floor. He was taking off his vest when Lucy saw his wound for the first time. She let out a little cry of distress and fingered the healing scar, which still looked painful. She kissed it. He wrapped his arms round her and gazed down into her face. 'You care,' he said, the words slurred with emotion.

'Of course I care.' She pulled his head down and stood on tiptoes so her lips could meet his. He was trembling and so was she. He swept her off her feet but before she could cling to him he dropped her.

From her position on the floor she looked up at him, laughter in her eyes. Only for the expression to change as she saw that he was in real pain. 'You'd best come down to me,' she said.

He lowered himself on to his knees, his hand still covering his shoulder. 'It's not going to be tonight, Josephine,' he said. 'Which is just as well because those sods at the station will be laying bets. I'd like to look them in the face and say your virtue's intact.'

She reached up and stroked his cheek. 'Another time,' she whispered.

Chapter Nineteen

Lucy gazed across the table at Rob. Last night she'd insisted on his having the bed and the hot water bottle while she slept on the sofa. This morning she had prepared breakfast, having been down to the bakery for fresh bread. 'It's a smashing place to live over,' she said. 'The smell of baking is worth a bob extra a week.' She spread strawberry jam on another round of bread and added, 'Will you be able to give me a lift on your motorbike with your shoulder so sore?'

'You still plan on seeing Barney?' There was an edge to his voice.

She nodded. 'I've got to. I want to find out who this Irishman is. I don't think I've got anything to fear – although if I'm honest, I'd rather not see Barney alone.'

Rob's expression lightened. 'Then go to the cinema and see him there. I'll go with you if you like? They're reshowing *The Sheik* and an old Stone-face film called *Daydreams*. We could go to the afternoon performance.'

She accepted his offer gratefully. 'What'll you do this morning?'

'I thought I'd catch a bus to the Pierhead and do some detecting.' He smiled lazily. 'Pleased with me? Plenty of shipping offices down there. What about you?'

'I could come with you,' she said tentatively, although an idea had surfaced while she lay awake thinking of those moments on the sofa.

Rob shook his head and said firmly, 'I'd rather go alone. If you're with me my whole approach will have to be different. You could go and see Dilys.'

Lucy accepted his rebuff meekly. 'Is she living at your aunt's old house?'

He nodded. 'I'll meet you back here at lunch-time.'

She thanked him, swallowed the last of her jam butty, and prepared to go out.

He went one way and Lucy went another, to Aunt Mac's house. She was feeling a little unsure of her welcome. After all, it had been months since she had last been in touch with the old lady and Lucy felt guilty for not having written to her and told her she was now living with her grand-mother.

She hesitated in front of the door, then, taking a deep breath, she rapped a tattoo on it with her fist. Would Aunt Mac tell her to beat it or would she be prepared to give her more information?

The door was opened somewhat furtively and then flung wide. 'Now here's a nice surprise,' said Callum sarcastically.

His presence came as something of a shock but Lucy recovered quickly. 'When are you going to shave off that beard? It makes you look ten years older. Is your mam in?'

'No, she isn't. You've taken your time calling round, haven't you?' He glowered at her, keeping his hand on the door and blocking the entrance.

'I'm sorry. But Mam disappearing the way she did came as a terrible shock. I still haven't got over it. I admit, though, I should have written to Aunt Mac and told her I was living in Yorkshire with my grandmother.'

His eyes hardened. 'So that's where you were? Maureen always said you had a yen to live with them. You grabbed your opportunity and don't care a sod anymore about your mam.'

Lucy went white. 'That's not true! You've no idea how Timmy and I have suffered. We still feel terrible about everything! I don't know how you have the cheek to speak to me like this. You've caused nothing but trouble to our family!'

'Oh, yeah! I bet those are your stepfather's words.'

'No, they're not! They're mine. And if you had any conscience at all you'd do something to make amends. I need the name of the shipping line Daniel O'Neill worked for before he got involved in the troubles.'

Callum stared at her as if she'd run mad. 'What bee have you got in your bonnet now, girl?'

'Shaun O'Neill! You want Mrs Jones' murder clearing up, don't you? He could have done it. You're still wanted for questioning, you know! It must worry Aunt Mac.'

'It does. But you're crazy thinking...'

'Oh, I'm crazy, am I? Well, I told the truth when I was asked whether you had a gun or not. You might have been strung up by the neck by now if I hadn't. Right now I'm wishing I'd told a lie!'

He scowled at her. 'OK, OK. Danny once worked for Green's but he left after an accident at sea when the boss did the dirty on him and stole his girl. Funny how life repeats itself, isn't it?' His upper lip curled and his eyes narrowed. 'The thing is, Green got his comeuppance and ended up dead on his estate in Ireland. Interesting if it happened to the real guilty party in the Winnie Jones case, too.' He slammed the door in her face.

Lucy let out a sigh of relief and patted the door. Callum had given her much more information that she'd expected. It had to be of some use. As she retraced her steps to Scotland Road she had another idea and headed for Maggie Block's refreshment house on Athol Street.

The eating house was just as steamy, smelly, smoky and noisy as she remembered it. The last time she had entered its portals Mick and Shaun O'Neill had been sitting in a corner plotting mayhem. Even now the thought of that day clouded her spirits. Would she ever forget? She ordered a mug of tea and sat down in the muggy atmosphere, prepared to eavesdrop on any conversation that caught her interest. Maggie's was popular with many a seafarer and docker and that was why Lucy was here. In no time at all she was listening to a heated discussion on conditions at sea and the money creamed off by the shipowners to line their own pockets while the men worked their guts off. True.

'D'you mind if I butt in?' said Lucy, getting up and smiling at the two men. 'I need some information. There's another cuppa and a wet nelly in it if you can help me.'

They eyed her up and down. One sniffed and wiped his bulbous nose with the back of his hand. 'That's a nice piece of cat you've got on your head, girl.'

'It's rabbit actually.' Lucy grinned and pulled her chair up to their table. 'What d'you know about a shipping line called Green's?'

The other sailor looked at her sharply. 'He was murdered over in Ireland. He was a tight-arse to work for. His widow's much more reasonable and so's her new hubby. Used to be one of us.'

Lucy could have kissed him. 'Have they changed the name of the company?'

'Naw. Still Green's.' He cocked an eyebrow. 'Do we get the tea and wet nellies now?'

'I'll get them myself,' said Lucy, picking up their empty mugs.

She left them eating the wet nellies, dripping in treacle, and bought some spare ribs, having them wrapped to take out, before she returned to the flat. She reached the top of the staircase only to find the door locked and when she hammered on it there was no reply. Rob must still be out, she thought, and sat down on the platform at the top of the steps. She opened the newspaper, took out a rib and bit into it.

It seemed like she had been there for ages when Rob finally arrived. By then she had eaten most of the ribs and immediately felt guilty. 'You found out anything?' she called.

He came up the stairs towards her. 'Have you been eating?' He touched her cheek and they both looked at the gravy on his finger.

'Sorry! But I was hungry. I did save you some.'

He took out a handkerchief and wiped round her mouth. 'I thought you'd have been longer at Dilys's.'

She quivered slightly at his touch. 'I didn't go after all.' She was uncertain whether to tell him she had seen Callum.

'Was that because of Owen?' Rob's eyes were slightly anxious. 'You don't feel something for him, do you? I know Dilys was jealous of you for a while.'

Lucy wondered if it was a good idea for Rob not to take her love too much for granted until she was sure of him. 'Owen's good-looking and a lovely mover and he did fancy me... If you don't want me...'

Rob was silent as he unlocked the door. She followed him inside. Then he said, 'You can't want Owen. He's married to Dilys now.' He frowned at her.

Her heart jerked in her breast and she wanted to wipe the frown away. 'Why not? I wanted you when you were engaged to Blodwen.'

'I wasn't married to her! Besides, what about last night? I thought we were getting somewhere.'

Lucy said in an amused voice, 'Love's strange, isn't it? We often want what we shouldn't or can't have.' She changed the subject. 'Did you find anything out?'

He shrugged and went into the kitchen. No more was said until they were sitting across from each other at the table.

'About last night. I'm glad you stopped when you did or you might have had to marry me.' She softened the words with a smile. 'Now are you going to be long eating? We'll have to be going soon if we're going to catch that matinee.'

Every seat in the auditorium appeared to be occupied. Rob and Lucy sat near the back. He held her hand and she found it difficult to concentrate on the screen. She kept getting Valentino confused with him. Both had a way of looking at the object of their desire with an upward sweep of narrowed eyes which set the heart aflutter. She remembered Valentino dancing the tango in another film when he'd unashamedly used his body in a way that was – well, it caused the breath to catch in the throat. A girl yearned to find a man who would desire her in such a way. He was strong, graceful, passionate, virile, and on the screen submissive only to the heroine's power.

'He's dead, you know,' whispered Rob in her ear.

Lucy smiled. 'You're tickling my ear.'

He nuzzled her neck and she would have been putty in his hands if they were at his flat.

A woman in the row in front of them turned

and glared at them. Rob trailed kisses down the side of Lucy's face. 'It's disgraceful in public,' hissed the woman.

'You'll be getting us thrown out,' whispered Lucy. 'And I must see Barney. He's got some shares of mine.'

Rob apologised to the woman and subsided in his seat. He did not speak again until the interval when Barney came clumping up the aisle, an unlit cigarette dangling from his mouth. Lucy could hear his breathing before he reached them and she felt a rush of sympathy and warmth at the sight of him, remembering all he had done for her.

'I wonder what his first words'll be and if he'll cry?' murmured Rob.

Lucy pretended she hadn't heard that and stood up as Barney drew level with them. 'Barney!' she said in a low voice.

He heard her and looked in her direction. She saw his mouth quivering and, excusing herself, squeezed past people to step into the aisle. He came towards her with hands outstretched and she took them. 'Oh, girlie, you've come back! I thought you might for Christmas but I'm glad you're here now. I've missed you terribly.'

Lucy thought he looked awful. His eyes were bloodshot and he had put on weight. She became aware they were now the centre of attention and suggested moving to the foyer. 'I've missed you, too. But why didn't you answer my letter?'

'I'm not a letter writer, lovey. But not a day went by when I didn't think of you.' He looked at her and nodded several times.

Lucy couldn't help thinking, When you weren't messing with Blodwen. 'I often thought of you,' she said truthfully. 'But I never thought I'd come back and find you'd moved.'

'Yes,' he sighed. 'That house had a curse on it. I couldn't bear it any longer. D'you know, they even thought at one point I was responsible for you going off. I was living on a knife edge. I kept seeing Irishmen with knives and guns everywhere. I sometimes thought of doing away with myself.'

That last sentence shocked her. Barney was someone she had always considered a lover of life. 'You mustn't think like that.'

He squeezed her hand. 'I wouldn't if you'd come back and live with me?'

She hesitated. 'I've promised my gran I'll be back in a few days. I came hoping to have news of Mam.'

'There's been none!' His face crumpled. 'I'd do anything to have you back, girlie. I've got rid of some of my property and my shares in the Trocadero and I've bought a cinema of my own. If you come back you could manage it. Isn't that what you used to dream about?'

Lucy was aware of a sensation similar to that she'd felt when Barney and her mother had married: the joy of a dream come true. Then Rob's voice dropped like a fishing weight into the pool of silence. 'Why don't you jump at it, girlie? It's the kind of happy ending you see on the screen in there. You can be an old man's darling!' He jerked his head in the direction of the auditorium.

She looked at him, unable to believe he could say such a hurtful thing.

'He's jealous,' said Barney, giving Rob a venomous look. 'His sister's married and his aunt's gone off to Wales. Even that young woman he was engaged to finished with him. He's got a violent temper.' He tugged on her arm. 'Listen to me. There's nothing wrong with your coming to live with me. I'm your stepfather and your mother would have approved. She didn't like your father's mother! You shouldn't have gone there.'

Lucy did not know what to think. What if Shaun O'Neill turned up again? No, she mustn't worry about that. She would find his whereabouts and have him arrested but would keep quiet about him to Barney for the moment, not wanting to upset him further.

Barney was leaning heavily on her and she couldn't take his weight anymore so steered him to a sofa and told him to sit down. She didn't look to see if Rob had followed. 'Barney, I can't live with you,' she said in a trembling voice. 'Gran needs me. Her husband's dying and I have to get back. He's crippled too, you see?'

Barney shook his head. 'I don't believe it. How can he be more crippled than me? He's got a wife. My wife's gone. It's me that needs you most.'

'But Barney...' She tried to explain again why she couldn't stay with him.

He interrupted her. 'You're a fool to yourself! Think of the future. You'll end up with nothing if you stick by them. It's a lovely kind act, your

389

wanting to help your gran, but families can stink! They'll leave you empty-handed and I know how terrible that can feel.'

'You're wrong!' said Lucy, feeling as if she was being pulled apart. 'I'd like to help you. Perhaps if Gran came and lived here in Liverpool – but then there's Wesley,' she added doubtfully.

'I don't care who there is,' said Barney, lighting a cigarette. 'You think over what I said, Lucy. Come home with me after the performance and we can talk properly.' He looked at her with a hound-dog expression. 'I need you. There's no one like you, girlie, whatever Rob's told you. You're a sensible girl. Think about it. Promise?'

She promised and when he'd finished his cigarette saw him back to his seat at the piano. Rob seemed to have vanished and Lucy had no desire to take her seat in the auditorium again. She needed fresh air and to think. She left the cinema only to come face to face with Rob. His expression was strained. 'I'm sorry,' he said, straightening up from against a wall. 'I'd rather have put that look on your face, that's all. It was like a boat had come in, full of your dreams.'

'It had!' she snapped. 'But it didn't mean I was about to climb aboard and jettison other people I care about!' Her cheeks were the colour of wild roses.

He said abruptly, 'You look lovely when you're angry.' And took hold of her hand.

She dragged it away. 'You made me sound not just a money grabber but a whore!'

'I said I'm sorry!'

'I heard you.' She began to walk in the direction

390

of the tram stop. 'I need to go back to your flat and fetch my suitcase.'

He fell into step beside her and said irritatingly, 'You're going to Barney's? You're an idiot!'

She compressed her lips and didn't answer.

'It's not wise, Lucy. He can't be trusted.'

She turned on him. 'Is staying with you any smarter? I was going to leave tonight anyway.'

She had silenced him and he didn't speak again until they arrived back at the flat. As Lucy picked up her suitcase she was near to tears with anger, frustration and disappointment. He could have trusted her not to be tempted by wealth and material things, but there was another dream down the Swannee!

Rob refused to let her carry her own suitcase and dragged it clean out of her hand. 'I want to see you get there safely.'

'I thought it was after I get there you were worried about,' she snapped.

He brought his face down close to hers. 'Don't get smart with me, Miss Linden! Fortunately I've thought again and I don't actually believe you're in any danger from Barney. I just don't like the idea of your staying under his roof. I'm sure he cares about your opinion of him.' Before Lucy could respond to that Rob said, 'Do you want to go on the 'bike?'

She drew her head back and tried to look haughty. 'Your 'bike! Now if you'd offered to drive me in a roadster I might have said yes.' There was a pause and she could tell he was trying to decide if she was joking or not. Then she smiled. 'What about your shoulder? Will you be

OK? Will it be safe?'

He looked relieved and said cheerfully, 'I'm not going to swing it or you over my head. Besides, it's not that far.' He put down the suitcase and left the room, returning with a cushion, helmet, long mackintosh, gauntlets and goggles, and then ordered her downstairs.

She felt a stir of excitement and thought it was a good job her skirt was of the new pleated kind. He threw the cushion at her and donned his gear before wheeling the motorbike out of the yard and telling her to put the cushion on the carrier and climb aboard. He placed the suitcase in front of him. 'You'll have to put your arms around me. Think you can bring yourself to do that?' He pulled down the goggles and kickstarted the engine without waiting for an answer.

Her heart seemed to melt like toasted marshmallow. Placing one foot on the wheel hub, she swung her other leg over, adjusted her skirt and put her arms round him, looping her fingers through the belt of his raincoat. She pressed her lips against the back of his neck. They were off!

Lucy yelped as they narrowly avoided scraping a wall, expecting to come a cropper at any minute as the motorbike roared up the entry. Rob slowed down as they approached the street but as soon as they were out of the entry they were off again. She let out a whoop of excitement and then clutched him tightly as he came to a stop. 'You OK?' he shouted, over the noise of the engine.

'Just fine!' she called. 'Carry on, James!'

It was a journey full of stops and starts but enough speed to thrill. It wasn't until they came to a sudden halt in front of the house she and her mother used to live in on Northumberland Terrace that she fell off.

He looked over his shoulder and lifted his goggles. 'What are you doing down there?'

She rubbed her bottom and rolled her eyes. He grinned. 'Perhaps you'd like another ride to-morrow? You could help me find Daniel O'Neill.'

'No, you refused my help this morning,' she said sweetly. 'I've my own plans. I have to see my man of business. I do have some money of my own. I'm not dependent on sugar daddies.' She looked up at the house. 'So this is where Barney's living?'

Rob nodded. 'I believe he has the ground and first floors.'

It seemed a strange choice for her stepfather to make, thought Lucy, taking her suitcase from Rob. She thanked him and hurried up the steps.

The front door was open so Lucy walked straight on in. 'Anyone at home?' she called.

A door opened on the ground floor and a woman came scurrying out. It was Agnes and she let out a cry of delight. 'Miss Lucy! So you've come! I am glad.'

'How could I not after your letter? Are my things here?'

'They are, miss. Mr Barney made sure every-thing you left was packed carefully and they're in a room on the first floor.' She beamed at Lucy. 'Give me your suitcase and I'll take it up. Then I'll make you a nice cup of tea.'

'I can carry it myself. You lead the way.'

'I'm sure now you're here you'll soon get to the

bottom of things,' said Agnes, throwing open a door.

Lucy hoped so. She went round the room lifting up things she had bought or Barney or her mother had given her, which included a porcelain figurine from Bunty's and a beautiful glass paperweight and several books and games. The curtains she and her mother had chosen before the wedding hung at the windows. Fortunately they fitted. She felt a deep sadness, remembering how they had planned to put the past behind them and looked forward to happier days. But the past wasn't so easy to get rid of.

Lucy opened her suitcase and took out her soap, flannel and towel. Her nightdress she hung over the foot of the bed. Two nights she would stay and then back to Yorkshire unless something happened – such as Rob proposing – to stop her. She had decided to go to the registrar's office in the morning and see if she could find the marriage certificate of Mrs Green and Daniel O'Neill.

Lucy did not take long getting washed and changed. In no time at all she was downstairs, finding out Barney no longer had a separate music room. He had got rid of most of the parlour furniture and just kept what had been in the music room. He had bought a dropleaf table and another comfy chair. The fire was lit and she curled up in an armchair and attempted to forget her worries for the moment by reading Conan Doyle's *A Study in Scarlet*, but it wasn't easy. There were too many unanswered questions in her mind. When she heard Barney outside in the lobby shouting for Agnes, Lucy got up and went out to welcome him.

His face was a picture. 'So you came, girlie. I thought Rob might put you off ... but I always knew you had commonsense. You know which side your bread's buttered on.'

Do I? thought Lucy, helping him off with his overcoat and hanging it up. 'Come and sit down by the fire and I'll make you a cup of cocoa.'

He patted her arm. 'No, I have Agnes to do that. You come and sit with me. Agnes!' he shouted.

The maid appeared, carrying a tray. 'It's all ready, Mr Jones. I've put a cup on for Miss Lucy, too, and a nice big slice of meat pie.' She placed the tray on an occasional table and left them.

Barney reached over to the display cabinet in the alcove next to the fireplace. From it he took a silver flask and into his cup poured a measure of liquid. He took a gulp of the mixture of cocoa and what Lucy realised was whisky, having caught a whiff of it. It came as a shock despite what Agnes had said in her letter. 'For my nerves,' he said, smiling at her. 'Isn't this cosy, lovey?'

It was. The firelight flickered on the furniture and the curtains were drawn against the cold dark night. A lamp glowed in a corner, but Lucy didn't feel at ease. What had gone on between him and Blodwen was very much on her mind but she knew bringing it up was beyond her. 'I can't stay more than a couple of days, Barney. I've explained why so I won't repeat myself.'

'Bring the old people here,' he surprised her by

saying as he poured more whisky into his cup. 'Can't live much longer can they? You ask them. If they won't come then you've done your duty and can wash your hands of them. If they come and they die, your problem's solved. Life and films are full of problems with people. You think you've got rid of one and another pops up. I'll show you the cinema tomorrow and you can tell me what you think.' He began to beat out a tune on the arm of the chair, humming to himself.

He's ignoring what I've said, thought Lucy, and could see what Agnes meant. It was pointless trying to explain further. In the morning she would get up and be out before he was moving – he seldom got up early – visiting the Register Office.

'A Mrs Green who married a ship's engineer called Daniel O'Neill, you say?' The clerk looked up from the open ledger on the table before him.

'Yes,' said Lucy wearily. She had been searching for ages but had found no marriage registered in the last few years between a Mrs Green and a Daniel O'Neill. Perhaps she had it all wrong and was wasting her time. 'I've been to Gambier Terrace and found nothing. That's why I've come here.' She had looked back as far as 1923 and even asked herself could they possibly have been married in Ireland but she didn't want to consider that. If Mrs Green had lived in Liverpool it was more likely she had married in this city.

'Sailors sometimes get married at sea, you know,' said the clerk.

Was that possible? Lucy groaned inwardly. It sounded plausible for a woman whose husband had owned a shipping line and whose would-be husband was a rebel and a sailor and probably of no fixed abode. But how was she ever to find out where they lived if they had married at sea?

'What d'you need the information for?' asked the clerk.

'An address,' she said, pushing back her hair from her forehead. 'I need to find out where Mr and Mrs Green once lived. He was a shipowner.'

'*Kelly's Directory*,' said the clerk instantly. 'It'll give you names, occupations and addresses of private individuals, as well as business addresses.'

Lucy leaned towards him and gave him a dazzling smile. 'Where will I find one?'

'Try the library. They'll probably have back years as well as the latest one.'

Yippee! She wasted no more time but thanked him and left.

Every table in Everton Library was occupied. Maybe that was because it was freezing outside and although not exactly hot in the library, it was better than being at home for people needing to conserve precious coal.

Lucy balanced the heavy directory for 1923 on her braced arm and chest as she turned the pages. Eventually she found what she was looking for: Joshua Green, shipowner, address in Newsham Drive. She wanted to jump up and down with excitement but she didn't, and of course the ex-Mrs Green might not be living there now. Lucy had discovered while perusing the directory that names of streets and roads were given in alphabetical order, as well as people's names being listed separately. If she looked up the address in the latest directory she should be able to discover who lived in Joshua Green's house a year ago. She could feel her heart beating as she found the latest directory and turned to Newsham Drive. Her finger ran down numbers and names – and yes! There it was: Mr Daniel O'Neill, ship's engineer. With a sense of jubilation she slammed the book shut.

'Shhh!' A man put a finger to his lips and then pointed to a sign that read SILENCE. She mouthed 'Sorry!' and replaced the directories in their proper places and hurried out.

Lucy felt like rushing off to Newsham Drive immediately but was hungry so decided to go back to Northumberland Terrace and have something to eat first.

'So there you are, girlie,' said Barney as she entered his apartment. 'Where've you been?' There was yolk on his chin. He was having an extremely late breakfast of bacon, eggs, sausages and fried bread. She thought several children could have dined on half of what he was eating. It was no wonder he was getting fat. 'For a long walk, having a look in the shop windows,' she said casually, pouring herself a cup of tea.

'I should get an automobile,' he said, speaking with his mouth full and spitting out bits of food. 'I've seen women driving. You could drive me around.'

Now driving a car would be fun, thought Lucy wistfully, but he'd only get fatter if he had no exercise. Still, no point in arguing with him. She had discovered that yesterday.

'You given anymore thought to working for me? Like to manage my cinema? Come and see it once I've finished breakfast. There's work needs doing on it, but for the price the owners were asking that's to be expected.'

Lucy hesitated and then decided to tell him what she had really been up to, but before she could speak he pointed his fork at her. 'You've been up to something! You haven't seen Rob again, have you? That young man's got it in for me,' he growled. 'Suspicious! That's what comes of being a policeman. They never take people at face value. He's always taken an interest in you. I remember when you were a kid and lost your cart. He made sure you got wood and found the cart for you. I don't want to go losing you to him after all this time.'

Lucy's heart lifted. Hadn't she wondered not long after she had recovered the cart if Rob was the mysterious policeman who'd delivered her it. But right now that thought had to be put aside. 'I haven't been with Rob. I've been trying to discover Shaun O'Neill's whereabouts. It bothered me you wanting to kill yourself because of him.'

Barney put down his knife and fork, his mouth working. 'So what have you found out?' He looked scared.

'He has a brother and I've found out where he lives,' said Lucy triumphantly. 'I'm hoping he can tell me where Shaun is.'

Her stepfather looked even more scared and, reaching into a pocket, pulled out his silver flask and took a swig from it. 'You can't go looking for him unarmed. He's dangerous.' There was a pause. 'I know where there's a gun.'

What! Lucy stared at him, dumfounded.

'Nothing for you to worry about,' he said hastily. 'It was Winnie's. It belonged to her father who fought in the Boer War. She felt safer having it with her when she collected the rents. And I'd feel happier if you had it with you while looking for that swine who killed your mother.'

Lucy did not know what to say. Her mind was in a whirl. What he'd said about Winnie sounded believable, but even so...

Barney's bottom lip jutted out. Picking up his knife, he dug it into the tablecloth. 'Don't you care about your mother's death anymore? Don't you want justice for her? Perhaps you'd rather go to the police – run to Rob – but that Shaun's a crafty one. They haven't managed to catch him so far. You do it, girlie. They've made a mess of it so far, haven't they?'

Lucy couldn't deny that but why hadn't he mentioned Winnie's gun before? Where had he kept it? The police must have searched the house.

Barney pushed himself to his feet, startling her. 'I'll get it,' he said, breathing heavily. 'You can make the decision what to do with it yourself.' He left the room.

Immediately Lucy breathed more easily. What was she scared of? He wasn't going to hurt her. Even Rob believed that.

Barney returned with a gun. 'Hold out your hand!' he ordered. Reluctantly she did so. The gun was heavy and her hand shook as she remembered holding Mick's gun and threatening him with it. If she had left it alone he might still be alive. 'I don't want it. It frightens me.'

'It's no use being frightened.' Barney's voice trembled. 'You must take it with you.'

It occurred to her that her stepfather was as frightened of it as she was. 'No!' She held it out to him but he refused to take it back, crossing his arms and tucking his hands beneath his armpits.

'You must! It'll make me happier if you have it with you. Think of your mother. I don't want what happened to her happening to you.'

Lucy cleared her throat. 'Is it loaded?'

He barked a laugh. 'Of course it's loaded! What use is a gun if it isn't loaded?'

She nodded and decided to take the gun with her. She would go to Rob and tell him everything. 'You be careful now,' said Barney as she made for the door. 'Just take off the safety catch and point it at O'Neill then pull the trigger. It's as easy as that.'

No, it wasn't as easy as that, thought Lucy, swallowing a lump in her throat. It hurt to be thinking what she was about Barney and it didn't make sense. There seemed no reason why he should have killed Winnie.

Lucy went to Rob's flat but there was no answer. She was so disappointed that for a moment she just stared at the door, wanting to cry. Then she went back down the yard and noticed this time his motorbike was missing. Where had he gone? She thought for a moment, wondering if perhaps she should go to the bridewell and hand the gun over to the police.

401

Tell them of her suspicions. For a moment she gave it serious consideration but then a little voice in her head said, Barney trusts you. He gave you the gun. He's never hurt you. Besides, do you want to have to speak to Peters with his sly smile or any of the others? He'll have told them about taking you to Rob's flat.

She made up her mind to hand over the gun only to Rob. She would find Daniel O'Neill and his wife first and see what she could find out about Shaun. Surely she wouldn't be putting herself into any danger by doing that?

Chapter Twenty

The house fronted the expanse of Newsham Park. A gravelled path flanked by rhododendrons wound round the side of a large red-brick porch where a ship's bell swung from a wrought-iron hook. Lucy rang it and when there was no immediate response, lifted the knocker and banged it.

There were hurrying footsteps and the door was opened by a grey-haired, bony-faced female of indeterminate age, dressed in a maid's uniform. 'Who are thee? I'm busy. If thee's come to ask how Miss Rebekah – or should I say Mrs O'Neill these days – is, then she's been delivered of a girl and both have survived the ordeal!'

This torrent of information was so unexpected Lucy did not know what to say, but as the maid went to close the door Lucy jammed her foot in it. 'Hang on! It's her husband I want to see.'

The maid glared at her and said grimly, 'Thee doest, dost thee? I knew it! He's been up to something. Too good-looking for his own good. Thee's not expectin' are thee?'

Who is this dragon? thought Lucy, amazed. 'I've never met Mr O'Neill in my life!'

'Then why dost thee want to see him?' She sniffed and looked down at Lucy as if she'd crawled from out of a stagnant pond. 'We don't generally have young women calling here.'

Lucy drew herself up to her full height. 'That's none of your business.'

'It is if you want to get past me.'

Lucy had never thought she'd have any difficulty in getting into the house. Five years ago she might have, she thought, when she was desperate and broke, but not these days! She looked respectable now even if she wasn't really. 'Is he in?' she demanded.

'Who's asking?'

'My name won't mean anything to him but you could mention Callum McCallum. They were in Ireland together and we-we're sort of related.' Not quite true but it would do.

'And your name, miss?'

'Lucy Linden.'

The maid slammed the door and Lucy shot back as it threatened to take off her nose. Then she crept forward again and put her ear to it. She could not hear anything so leaned against the door, looking across at the park where there were kids playing football. A horse-drawn coal delivery

403

truck was making its way up the road and she could hear the putt-putt of a motorcycle engine nearby.

The door opened and she would have fallen backwards into the hall if she hadn't been steadied by a hand to her back. She gasped a thank you and once firmly on her feet looked at the man who'd caught her. He seemed vaguely familiar and she presumed he was Daniel O'Neill. He didn't look particularly pleased to see her. 'What can I do for you, Miss Linden?'

She straightened her hat and cleared her throat. 'I wonder if you could tell me where your brother is?'

He hesitated. 'Why do you want to see him?'

'He was a friend of my uncle's. I-I wouldn't be disturbing you if it wasn't important – and congratulations by the way on the baby – but I need to sort something out with Shaun. Something only he has the answer to.'

Shaun's brother stared at her and she felt uncomfortable beneath his scrutiny. 'You say you're sort of related to Callum McCallum?'

Lucy nodded. 'I know you were in prison in Ireland with him. I spoke to him only yesterday.'

'Is he well?'

Lucy smiled. 'He looks it. And your brother?'

Daniel O'Neill did not return her smile. 'Come in, Miss Linden. My brother's staying with us at the moment.'

The gun in her handbag felt extra heavy as Lucy followed the Irishman. Her heart was racing as he led her along a passage and into a room at the back of the house. Warmth hit her and her gaze went first to the gas fire set in the fireplace and then to the man lying on a sofa reading a newspaper. 'That's a helluva draught, Danny,' he said, looking up.

Lucy recognised him and was swamped by a tide of emotion: anger, fear, disbelief. She needed air and moved over to the french windows.

'Who's this?' said Shaun, eyeing her up and down.

'You might have forgotten me but I've never forgotten you,' said Lucy in a low, impassioned voice. She opened her handbag and took out the gun, pointing it at him.

Both men froze. 'What is this?' said Daniel, eyes fixed on the gun. 'You're not really going to use that, are you, Miss Linden?'

She swung the gun in his direction. 'I don't know yet but you'd best not make me nervous. I just want to know what your brother's done to my mother, and if I'm satisfied with his answer I won't shoot him.'

Shaun gabbled, 'I haven't done a bloody thing to your mam! Why should I? I don't remember anyone called Linden!'

'Is murder so easy that you've forgotten us?' Lucy's voice trembled. 'Look at me! Remember my Uncle Mick? The house in Court 15 off Bostock Street?'

The sound of the ship's bell rang through the house but none of them heeded it.

Lucy saw the sudden realisation in Shaun's face. 'I haven't bloody touched your mother, girl. Why should I?'

She was baffled. He sounded genuinely surprised but then he could be putting on an act. 'Be-Because we knew things about you that could put you in prison. Mam disappeared at the beginning of the year and–'

'Miss Linden, my brother is not responsible for your mother's disappearance,' said Daniel, cutting through her words ruthlessly.

She swung the gun in his direction, could see he was tensing himself, ready to take a chance and spring on her. 'I wouldn't try it, Mr O'Neill, if I were you. Uncle Mick taught me how to shoot,' she lied.

'I'm not going to do anything,' said Daniel softly. 'You see, my brother finds it difficult getting around since his leg was amputated.'

Was this some trick? thought Lucy, and shot a glance at Shaun's legs.

'You can come and knock on wood if you like,' he sneered. 'Think you're so clever, don't you? If your mother's gone missing then look elsewhere. Now put that bloody gun away, you're making me nervous.'

Lucy would have enjoyed firing off a round in his direction for all the times he'd made *her* nervous but she might scare the new mother and her baby overhead, and besides there were no bullets in the gun. So instead she went over to Shaun and did the next best thing. She hit first one leg with the gun – he yelped – then the other. There was a thunk. So it was true. She placed the gun in her handbag and looked apologetically at Daniel O'Neill. 'I'm sorry to have disturbed you. I really shouldn't have threatened you.'

'How about a cup of tea?' he said, taking her

406

arm. 'Or something stronger if you like? We could wet the baby's head.'

Lucy was amazed by his calmness. She was shaking like a leaf in autumn. If Shaun hadn't killed her mother, then Barney must have.

Daniel took her into the kitchen where there was a woman and a little boy. A batch of drop scones stood on a wire rack cooling. 'This is Janet our cook and my son David. This is Miss Linden.' Daniel must have noticed her eyeing the scones because he said, 'Are you hungry?'

Lucy nodded.

Daniel's eyes twinkled. 'Hungry work gearing yourself up to kill someone. Not that I think you'd have done it. Help yourself.'

At that moment the back door burst open and Rob stood there in motorcycle gear, goggles pushed up. 'Lucy!' he said, staring at her.

'Yes. What are you doing here?' She would have gone over to him and flopped into his arms if the room had been empty.

'Who's this?' said Daniel, frowning.

'Name's D.C. Rob Jones.' He inclined his head. 'I'm looking for your brother. He's wanted for questioning over an attack of a policeman in Liverpool two years ago.'

Daniel stared at him for several moments, an impatient expression in his eyes, before saying, 'My brother couldn't have attacked anyone in Liverpool that year. He was in Ireland.'

'You can prove that?' said Rob.

Lucy decided to take part in the conversation. 'He's had his leg amputated, Rob.' She glanced at Daniel. 'I presume it was in the car crash you

407

were both involved in?'

He nodded. 'I suggest, Miss Linden, you forego the tea and scones and take your policeman friend with you. My wife giving birth is enough excitement for me for one day, along with you bursting in waving a gun about.'

'A gun?' Rob looked at Lucy.

She put her hand through his arm and whispered, 'I'll tell you all about it when we get outside.'

Neither of them spoke until they had closed the front gate behind them. Then Lucy took the gun from her handbag and handed it to Rob. 'Barney gave it to me – said it was Winnie's and had once belonged to her father.'

He took hold of it, shaking his head in disbelief. 'Why didn't you come to me with it?'

'I did but you weren't there. I was going to tell you everything about how I found out this address and what Barney said.'

'You looked up O'Neill's name in the directory, I take it?' She nodded. 'Me too,' he added. 'It seemed the simplest way in the end. I don't know why I didn't think of it in the first place.' He smiled faintly. 'I suppose I got distracted.'

She squeezed his arm, feeling a great warmth inside her. 'What are we going to do?'

Rob inspected the gun and then pocketed it. 'It was a dangerous thing to do, coming here waving a gun about. That charming man in there was a rebel, too, remember.'

'The gun's not loaded.' She dug in her pockets and brought out the bullets.

He took them from her. 'Even dafter,' he murmured. 'What if he'd had a gun and called your bluff?'

'Better than being responsible for another man's death.'

He leaned forward and kissed her lightly on the mouth and she knew he understood. She smiled. 'Besides, I don't think Daniel O'Neill would have let his brother kill me. He seems a sensible man.' Her smile faded. 'I'm worried about Barney. He said Winnie had that gun with her when she collected the rents so she must have had it with her the evening she was killed.'

Rob nodded. 'But it doesn't make sense Barney killing her,' he said. 'Perhaps she pulled it out from wherever she kept it and threatened Mc-Callum with it. There was a struggle—'

'No!' said Lucy, heaving a sigh. 'I don't believe it. You said you didn't believe Callum would kill. Barney, maybe, in a fit of anger, but not Winnie.'

He eyed her sad face. 'Then you'd rather believe Barney did it?'

'No. But I've got a funny feeling he did.'

Rob looked as unhappy as she felt. 'We'd better get going. There's no cushion. It'll be a bumpy ride.'

What did that matter? thought Lucy, when the other option was being left behind to walk or take a tram which would delay her arrival at Barney's. She wanted to be there when Rob confronted her stepfather. She still had a seed of hope in her heart that he'd be able to come up with some other reason for having Winnie's gun.

It would have been a terrible anticlimax if Barney had left for the cinema but they found

409

him still at home. Agnes looked relieved to see them. 'There you are, Miss Lucy. Mr Rob Jones!' She nodded her head towards the sitting room. 'He's in a right tizzy. Can you hear him playing? He's been at it non-stop since you left. Folk have been complaining but he takes no notice. Can you do something with him?'

'I'll try,' said Lucy, glancing at Rob. She opened the door to Barney's sitting room and they went inside.

He did not appear to have heard them and it was not until Rob put his hands over the keys that he stopped playing and looked up. 'Don't ever do that again when I'm playing! I am the Great Supremo!' he bellowed and smacked Rob's hand away before smiling at Lucy and saying in an almost normal voice, 'So you're back. Did you shoot him?'

'No.' Lucy's skin crawled. 'He-he doesn't know what happened to Mam. He can't have killed her anyway because he's had a leg amputated and must find it harder to get around than you do.'

Barney stared at her. His face had gone a peculiar colour and then he laughed. 'You believe that? He's having you on.'

'He's got a wooden leg,' insisted Lucy.

'A trick!' Barney ran his fingers along the piano keys.

'The gun, Barney,' said Rob, taking Lucy's hand and squeezing it gently. 'Why didn't you tell us about it?'

'Didn't want to,' he growled. 'You'd have jumped in with your big feet and put a stop to everything. It was going so well. Then she had to

410

go and spoil it!' He began to play again.

'Who? What did she do?' Rob was obviously having difficulty keeping the irritation from his voice.

'Winnie. She threatened to have me put out of my home and to go North and live on the income. She couldn't sell the property, mind. She knew that. But she could use the money and choose the tenants and give me orders.' Barney smiled up at Lucy and his eyes weren't quite focussed. 'It was in my brother's will, you see? You came into the music room one day when I was re-reading his solicitor's letter. I dropped it and you went to pick it up. I was terrified in case you saw what was written on it. My brother got his will drawn up before he went back to the front. If they didn't have any kids, when Winnie died all the property would come to me. Everyone believed, though, that it was already mine because I was the elder brother. I didn't say otherwise. If they'd thought I was my brother's pensioner they would have pitied me, and I didn't want their pity. I'd counted for nothing long enough!' His expression turned ugly. 'Father left everything to my brother. He was the blue-eyed boy! And I was dismissed out of hand because I was a cripple. Even my music Father looked on as cissy ... but he never foresaw the war that would take so many healthy young men.'

'So you shot Winnie to get the property?' said Rob.

Barney did not answer but started playing again. He was smiling but looked ghastly. Lucy felt dreadful. 'Did you kill Mam, too? I thought

411

you loved her.'

His fingers faltered and he glanced at her. 'I did love her. I wanted us to be a happy little family, and we were for a while, weren't we?'

She nodded, a lump in her throat. He carried on playing.

'Barney, where did you put Mam? Tell me so I can give her a christian burial?'

'She wanted more than I could give her but I got my own back on her in the end.' He carried on playing, louder and louder, swaying backwards and forwards. The perspiration was running down his face. He looked ready to explode.

Lucy could bear it no longer. She brought her fist down on the keys. 'Stop it!' she screamed. 'Tell me where she is?'

'Don't do that!' roared Barney, and hit Lucy so hard she overbalanced.

Rob stopped her from falling and half-carried her to the big leather chair by the fire. They exchanged looks and he touched her face with a gentle hand. Then he turned to Barney.

He had risen from the stool and was staggering towards them. 'Sorry, girlie,' he gasped. 'Sorry! I didn't mean to do that. Didn't mean to kill Winnie but she waved that gun about and went on and on about getting rid of your mother and you. Wouldn't listen to me. She wanted you out of the apartment, said you'd both give the place a bad name.'

Lucy could barely bring herself to look at him. 'What about Mam?' she whispered. 'What have you done with her?'

'I didn't kill her!' he yelled, waving his arms

412

about. 'You ask that Callum McCallum where she is. He's the one who knows what happened to her. He's the one who ... the ... one ... who ... spoiled everything!' Barney was suddenly gasping, clutching at his collar. His face twisted. He was clumping around in circles. He fell against an occasional table and brought a vase crashing to the floor as he collapsed in a heap.

For a moment neither Lucy nor Rob moved. Then he went over to Barney and got down on one knee and felt for a pulse. 'Is he dead?' Her voice quivered.

Rob's face was tight with concentration. She waited until he looked up and nodded. 'I'll have to go for a doctor. Will you be OK?'

She nodded. Tears were pouring down her cheeks. 'Right to the end he was still blaming Callum,' she said in a choking voice. 'He was always jealous of him.'

'Perhaps it was more than that,' murmured Rob, putting an arm about her shoulders. 'I'll get Agnes to make you a cup of tea.'

She tried to smile but couldn't. He kissed the tip of her nose and left. She curled up in the big leather chair. Her face was throbbing and she couldn't take her eyes off Barney's body, scared all of a sudden in case he should come back to life. She wanted to shout at him: *I once depended on you to make Mam and me happy! You were someone I believed in so much!*

Agnes came into the room, visibly trembling and twisting the hem of her pinny round and round one hand. 'Oh, dear! Oh, dearie me! I knew something like this would happen one day.

413

He's been so up and down this year. You'd have thought he was on a roller-coaster. He'd get so angry and then he'd be weeping. He's been burning papers and letters.'

Lucy said sharply. 'This Irishman that came to visit – had you ever seen him before?'

Agnes shook her head. 'He did say his mother had called earlier and got no joy from the master.'

'He did?' Lucy frowned.

'Maybe they had something to do with them letters addressed to you,' said Agnes. 'The master got angry about them. I remember he mentioned your mother's name and when I asked was he going to send the letters on to you, he threw a paperweight at me.'

'Letters,' murmured Lucy, wondering who could have sent them letters from Ireland who knew their mother?

'Will you be all right, lovey, while I make you a nice hot sweet cup of tea? Perhaps you'd like to go to bed and I'll bring it up to you there? The master never did that to your face, did he?'

Lucy touched her jaw. 'I don't want you blabbing about it, Agnes.'

She looked indignant. 'Why, miss? It'll be all over the neighbourhood in no time that he killed his brother's wife! If I hadn't needed this job I could have told everybody he wasn't the plaster saint they all thought him. Not that he wasn't a lovely man at times, generous and kind. Still, you can't go around killing people without it affecting you. Conscience, you see? It won't leave you alone.'

'You mean, you knew he killed Winnie?' said Lucy in disbelief.

'Not know exactly. I didn't have any proof or anything. It's just as I said,' muttered Agnes, 'he was no angel.'

Lucy nodded. A fallen angel perhaps? she thought miserably.

'Shall I get you that cup of tea now?'

'Yes. I'll have it here in front of the fire.' She had decided to stay where she was until Rob returned with the doctor. She spent the time waiting, thinking about Callum and Aunt Mac and her mother.

It seemed a long time before Rob reappeared and when he did, he had not only the doctor with him but a uniformed police constable and a detective inspector. The doctor duly pronounced Barney dead and arrangements were made for the removal of his body to another room. Lucy was asked to verify what Rob had said about Barney's confessing to the killing of Winnie Jones.

When she had finished making a statement the inspector said, 'I suppose we'll never know where he hid the gun but at least now we can close the case.'

'There's still my mother's disappearance,' put in Lucy.

'DC Jones has an idea about that,' said the inspector gravely. Lucy glanced at Rob, a question in her eyes, but he wasn't giving anything away. 'I suggest you return to Yorkshire,' continued the inspector. 'Once all this gets out you'll be plagued by the newspaper hounds.'

Lucy saw the sense in what he said and agreed with it. Some things would have to wait. She had promised her grandmother she would be back in a couple of days and intended to keep her word. Besides, she had to speak to Timmy. Even so she could not wait to hear what Rob had to say. As soon as they were alone she asked him what it was he was so keen to follow up.

'I'd rather not say.' He was slumped in a chair and looked at her from beneath drooping eyelids.

'That's mean,' she protested.

He smiled and said softly, 'Who didn't tell me what she was up to, finding out Shaun O'Neill's brother's whereabouts? You go off to Yorkshire. I'm not sure what'll happen about a funeral for Barney yet. It could be that he might have got off with manslaughter. He said he didn't intend killing Winnie and yet he knew he'd get the property if she was dead...'

Lucy saw what he meant and shuddered. 'I know what he felt like. What he suffered! Not meaning to kill someone.'

'I know you do but you've got to put it behind you.'

'I was living on ill-gotten gains.'

'That'll teach you to have delusions of grandeur.'

She shook her head at Rob. 'You've never been really poor so you don't know how tempting it is to do things for money.' She paused. 'I'll go to Yorkshire. Hopefully I'll be back within the week.'

'I'll tell you then if I'm right or wrong about my idea.'

416

If he was thinking along the same lines as herself then he could be right, she thought, and that heaviness which had been in her heart for so long lifted. 'You are a pig, Rob, about that!' She got up and went and sat on his knee. He groaned and pulled himself higher in the chair before putting his arms round her. 'Aren't you worried what I might get up to with Wesley?' she said with a smile.

Rob licked the side of her face which was swollen. 'I trust you won't go marrying him before returning here. Barney's will might prove interesting.'

'He might have left everything to Blodwen,' she muttered, frowning.

'I doubt he was taken in. Anyway we've unfinished business to discuss.'

'You really fancy your chances with me, don't you?' she said, exasperated because he wouldn't be drawn.

He kissed her before pushing her off his knee. 'I'll have to be going if I'm to get back as quickly as I want to.'

Lucy knew she wasn't going to get anymore out of him but that didn't really worry her; she was feeling better by the minute. 'Then I might as well see you out and pack my suitcase,' she said, trying to sound cheerful but knowing she would miss him terribly. She would have to come back even if Stan and Myrtle were depending on her to be there for them.

Chapter Twenty One

Lucy sat beside the bed, gazing down at Stan. On her arrival he had still been conscious and they had talked a little but since yesterday he had been in a stupor and she knew that he only had a couple of days to live. Her grandmother had gone out for some fresh air but had been missing for hours. Lucy was worried about where she could be. Myrtle had been delighted when she'd arrived back from Liverpool but had asked her no questions about her time there. Lucy presumed it was because she was so concerned about her husband.

It was to her brother that Lucy had unburdened herself. Timmy hadn't sounded a bit surprised that Barney had done away with Winnie or that he had not sent on letters addressed to them. Lucy's suspicions as to why she was keeping to herself for the moment, not wanting to raise any false hopes in case she was wrong.

There was a sound at the door and her grandmother entered the room. 'No change?' she said, tiptoeing over.

Lucy shook her head, noticing Myrtle's cheeks were rosy and her eyes serene. 'Your outing's done you good.'

'I went to the farm with Timmy to see my brother. I'll sit with Stan for a while. You go and get some fresh air.'

Lucy hesitated. 'Have you seen Wesley? He's been missing for hours, too.'

'He's nothing for you to worry about, lass. You go and have some fresh air,' urged Myrtle. 'There's nothing more you can do for Stan.'

Lucy went but didn't go far. With an invigorating wind in her face she stood on the parade where they had stopped that first day with Stan in the wheelchair and seen Wesley on the beach feeding the gulls. The waves were fierce today, crashing on to the shore as if they were angry. She thought of Barney and Stan. So different, yet alike in so many ways. Both had been kind to her and both had wanted something from her. Barney had failed her and she suspected had lied to her as well. Was she going to fail Stan? If Rob asked her to marry him, could she say no? Having people depend on you was a difficult thing to cope with when you loved more than one person.

'Luce!'

Hearing her brother's voice, Lucy turned and guessed from his expression that Stan had gone. Timmy put his arm round her. He was bigger than her now. 'Come on. Granny Myrtle needs you right now. Wesley turned up at the end and he's howling the place down, but don't you worry,' said Timmy firmly. 'Me and Gran'll sort him out.'

Lucy hoped he was right but wondered what the pair of them could do to keep Wesley in check now his father was dead, not that Stanley had been able to do much anyway.

She found out after the funeral when her grandmother told her to sit down as she wanted to speak to her. Myrtle was making lists and Lucy presumed it was to do with getting rid of some stuff and setting up the house as a summer boarding house.

'You can have the wireless if you can get someone to take it to Liverpool for you,' said Myrtle.

Lucy put down the record she was dusting and sat at the table opposite her. 'What would be the point in that?' she said carefully, pleating the duster between her fingertips. 'You need me here.'

Myrtle smiled and said briskly, 'I don't want you being unhappy, Lucy. Timmy's told me what's been going on in Liverpool and as I've other plans you might as well go home to that young man of yours.'

Lucy's emotions were suddenly in a worse muddle than they had been. 'Why don't you want me? You're going to need help to run this place.'

'I have no intention of turning this house back into a guest house,' said her grandmother firmly. 'That was Stan's idea and I allowed him to think I'd fall in with his plans because it was easier than arguing with him and making him unhappy.' She removed the duster from Lucy's hand. 'I'm getting shut of the place. I'm going to buy a smallholding near my brother's farm – there's one just come up on the market – and Timmy and Wesley will help me run it.' Lucy went to interrupt her but Myrtle held up her hand. 'Wesley might be backward but he's strong and I reckon half his trouble is he needs a proper job to do. Stan would never allow it. He believed him incapable, you see.'

Lucy's spirits soared and so did her admiration for her grandmother. 'You're probably right. I hope everything works out for you.' She jumped to her feet. 'I'd love the wireless! I'll think about Great-uncle Stan every time I use it. Although,' she hesitated, 'nothing's settled yet back in Liverpool. There's something else that needs sorting out – but whatever, I'll be back to see you before too long.' She smiled. 'Life's never dull, is it? The unexpected's always happening.'

Myrtle nodded. 'You could say that. I'm sure things'll work out for you. That young man would be mad not to snap you up. You go off as soon as you like. Keep in touch.'

It was not easy for Lucy saying goodbye to Timmy, especially as there was so much more she could have said to him. As for Wesley, now she knew he wouldn't be pestering her again Lucy could show him affection. Her brother hugged her until her ribs felt as if they would crack. Then he told her to beat it and, taking his grandmother's arm, walked away.

Lucy was exhausted by the time she arrived in Liverpool. Having heard nothing from Rob she didn't know what was going on. At least it wasn't raining this time, she thought, looking up at the stars pricking the night sky. She had a key to the rooms in Northumberland Terrace so took a tram there. Hopefully there would be a welcoming fire in the grate, food in the larder and the news-hounds would have given up and gone home.

As Lucy turned the key in the lock the door was opened from the other side and her mother stood there. Lucy dropped her suitcase and the colour drained from her face. 'So I was right,' she said.

Maureen seized hold of her. 'Now don't you go and faint on me, darlin'! You're not seeing a ghost.'

'I know! But even so...' She clung to her mother, gazing into her beloved face. 'I did guess right then in the end. You wrote to Timmy and me and Barney destroyed the letters.'

'I'm sure that's what happened.' Maureen caressed Lucy's cheek and kissed her. 'I wrote to Miss Griffiths when I didn't hear anything from you. It didn't occur to me at first that Barney wouldn't tell you but eventually it did. So I wrote to you, not knowing you'd left Liverpool. When I didn't hear from you after the second letter, that's when I wrote to Rob's aunt.

'I didn't tell her the truth, of course – that I'd run away with Callum. I was convinced Barney would have kept quiet about that. In fact, I suggested to him that he tell people I'd gone to Ireland for the good of my health. He had to know the truth, of course, and so did you and Timmy. I had no idea you'd left Liverpool and gone to live with your grandmother. No idea that you thought Shaun O'Neill had done away with me. Aunt Mac might have told you if she hadn't been in Ireland. As for Uncle Mac, we kept it from him and he only reads the sports pages in the newspapers.'

'But why didn't Miss Griffiths tell me about the letter?' said Lucy, bewildered. 'She must have known what it was like for Timmy and me?'

'Rob thinks it was just plain cussedness. He said that she'd called you a hussy after you'd appeared at her New Year's Eve get-together in that shimmy frock – and what with the rumours going round about you and Rob, she decided to destroy the letter.'

'But-but she must have been mad!' cried Lucy, putting a hand to her head. 'The police had dug over Barney's garden! What did you put in the letter?'

'I only asked her if you and Timmy were well and could she see her way to persuading you two to come and visit me in Ireland.'

'That's all?'

'Yes!'

Lucy gnawed on her lip, still finding it incredible that Rob's aunt could behave in such a way. 'What about Barney? Did she tell him about the letter?'

Maureen grimaced. 'Perhaps she did ... maybe he told her the truth. Rob said if he did that would only reinforce her opinion that we were women of loose morals. A pity because she could be a kind woman.'

'Both those things are true, of course.' Lucy found herself, as she had once before, wondering if she had wandered into a lunatic asylum. The whole thing was incredible. 'I wonder if she ever had a fancy for Barney herself? I mean ... she was a few years older than him, I know, and he never showed any interest in her but even so...'

Maureen said soberly, 'We'll never know. Because we'll never ask, will we?'

Lucy shook her head. 'I don't know what to say next.'

Her mother led Lucy unresisting into the sitting room and lowered her into a chair. 'Hot sweet tea,' she said, smoothing back a lock of her daughter's hair. 'Or maybe you'd like a drop of the hard stuff?' She took hold of one of her daughter's hands and chafed it. 'My, you're cold, darlin'. Did you have a good journey? How is the old man Rob spoke about?'

'He's dead.'

'I am sorry. It was good of him to take you and Timmy in.'

'It was.'

'And how is Timmy?'

'Fine. Although he's sad about Uncle Stan's death.' Lucy cleared her throat. 'I need a drink.'

'I'll get you one,' said Maureen. 'You just stay there. There's not a thing for you to worry about.'

I suppose there isn't, thought Lucy. As long as Mam doesn't expect Timmy to live with her. He'll be thrilled, of course, and want to see her, but it could tear him apart if she puts pressure on him and would spoil his and Gran's plans. Her mother had to see their lives had carried on and taken a different direction when they'd believed her dead... Something exploded inside Lucy then and she shot to her feet and stormed after her mother. 'Why couldn't you tell us to our faces you were leaving? A letter isn't good enough, Mam. D'you know how much we've suffered? The tears we've shed?'

Her mother turned, looking upset. 'I know! But I told you, I was a little crazy. I knew you

424

wouldn't approve of what I was doing. You looked up to Barney so much, had wanted me to marry him so badly. To be honest, though, I didn't think he'd lie to you, bury the whole thing and act the way Rob said he did. He must have been as crazy as I was.'

'Yes. I can believe he was more than a little mad,' said Lucy, some of the anger draining out of her to be replaced by anguish and a sense of loss. 'But he was also deeply unhappy and full of guilt.'

Maureen looked downcast. 'I know. I suppose I should never have told him I planned on marrying Callum in the letter.'

Lucy's expression froze. 'You couldn't marry Callum. You were married to Barney.'

Her mother took a deep breath. 'But I did marry Callum and we've just had a darlin' little baby,' she said, putting several feet between herself and her daughter. 'That's why Aunt Mac and then Callum came here in search of you. I wanted so badly to see you and Timmy and for you to know about your little brother.'

Lucy had to lean against a wall. 'How could you marry Callum?' she wailed.

Her mother took a deep breath. 'Once a Catholic, always a Catholic. Despite my marrying in Barney's church and saying "I do!" I never felt married to him.'

'You had a baby by Barney, Mam! You were married in the eyes of his church and the state!' Lucy really *had* wandered into a lunatic asylum now. 'You're a loony!'

'No, not a loony,' said Maureen, rolling her

425

shoulders as if she had an itch between her shoulder blades. 'But I was terribly unhappy. I knew I'd made a mistake.' She pointed at her daughter. 'Just you pray you never make the mistake of marrying the wrong man.'

'So how did it happen?' said Lucy, trying to keep calm.

Maureen smiled. 'I met Aunt Mac at St Anthony's and she told me Callum was visiting – how well he was doing in Ireland. So I went home with her and as soon as I saw him, I knew I should have married him.'

'So you did! Conveniently putting aside your own husband and children.'

Scarlet flamed in Maureen's cheeks. 'I never conveniently put you aside. I know I would have to face you with the truth sooner or later.'

'Later rather than sooner!'

'You'd only have stopped me if I'd told you. Perhaps thrown all the times I'd talked morality to you in my face. So I went to Ireland with Callum and there I married him in my own church.' Her face softened. 'It was a lovely service.'

'You committed bigamy,' squeaked Lucy.

Maureen hung her head and then almost immediately lifted it again. 'I'm a widow now. I can get married again and you and Timmy can come to the wedding this time.' Her lovely face shone. 'We'll have a big do. Barney's left me all his money.'

'What!' Lucy could scarcely believe it. 'How could he do that?'

'Probably didn't like thinking about death so

426

kept putting off altering the will he'd made when we were first married. Everything's been left to his dearest wife, Maureen Mary Jones.' There was a rueful gleam in Maureen's eyes.

For a moment Lucy could have killed her. It wasn't fair! Barney had been going to give *her* a cinema! Now it belonged to her mother! It wasn't bloody fair!

'I can guess what you're thinking,' said Maureen, leaning forward and touching her daughter's arm. 'I'd want to kill me, too. But don't worry, darlin'! You won't lose by it.'

Lucy stared at her and didn't know whether to laugh or cry. Maybe later she might laugh but right now she was furious.

Her mother tried to put her arms round her. 'I'm really sorry you and Timmy suffered but I didn't know how badly you were hurting. I thought you just thoroughly disapproved of me. I wouldn't be here now if it weren't for Rob.'

So he had worked it out, thought Lucy, and wondered what he'd made of it all. 'I don't know what Timmy's going to think about all this,' she muttered. 'You won't get him back. He's going to live with Gran. She's got money and property. I've been left a wireless.'

Her mother looked sad. 'I suppose I'll have to accept I can't have everything the way I want it. I was hoping the pair of you would come and live in Ireland.'

'No,' said Lucy firmly. 'I have my own dreams.'

'Your mother could make amends a little,' said Rob, entering the kitchen, hands in pockets.

Lucy looked at him and her heart lifted. 'It's

going to have to be a lot,' she said.

'She could give you that cinema Barney left,' said Rob.

Maureen's eyes twinkled. 'Have you seen it? Two old houses knocked into one. Lucy's welcome to it.'

'There you are, then,' said Rob, grinning at Lucy. 'Your own cinema, love.'

For a moment Lucy struggled to hold on to her anger, then she let go of it. Today hadn't two of the miracles she had prayed for in the Priory church in Bridlington been answered? 'Thanks, Mam.' Lucy smiled. 'Barney did warn me, though, the cinema needs doing up – and when talkies come I'll have to have sound fitted.'

'Talkies! Sound! Now who's a little crazy?' said Maureen, returning her daughter's smile.

'I'm not crazy at all. It'll happen,' said Lucy confidently. 'I'll have to sell my shares and see if the bank will give me a loan.'

'You've got a hope,' said her mother. 'Banks aren't keen on lending money to women.'

Rob said, 'I could sell my motorbike and I've got a little saved. I'd be happy to invest in you, Luce.'

She gazed at him and a warm glow suffused her whole body. 'But you love that 'bike and it could come in handy. I like it, though, that you have that much faith in me.'

'There are conditions,' he said, putting his arms round her. 'If we're in this together you'd better marry me.'

Am I hearing this right? thought Lucy, a bemused expression on her face.

Maureen glanced at them. 'Well, if he's prepared to marry you and put in his pennyworth, I suppose I could lend you some money at nil interest. Right now, I'd better go and see if my baby's awake.' She left them alone.

'What would you do with a mother like that?' said Lucy, lifting her hands in a hopeless gesture.

Rob clasped them both and brought them against his chest. 'At least she knows what she wants and goes after it. She's seen to the funeral by the way so you don't have that to face.' He kissed her fingers and gave her a quizzical look. 'You're not unlike her, you know.'

Lucy protested, 'I wouldn't commit bigamy! You can depend on that.'

'I should hope not!' Rob hugged her tightly. 'I want someone I can trust not to run out on me or slug me across the head when we fall out.'

'I'm glad we can both agree on that,' Lucy murmured, thinking he had long ago proved himself trustworthy. Reaching up, she brought his head down to hers. 'And the answer to your proposal is yes.'

The publishers hope that this book has given you enjoyable reading. Large Print Books are especially designed to be as easy to see and hold as possible. If you wish a complete list of our books please ask at your local library or write directly to:

Magna Large Print Books
Magna House, Long Preston,
Skipton, North Yorkshire.
BD23 4ND

This Large Print Book for the partially sighted, who cannot read normal print, is published under the auspices of

THE ULVERSCROFT FOUNDATION

1	21	41	61	81	101	121	141	161	181
2	22	42	62	82	102	122	142	162	182
3	23	43	63	83	103	123	143	163	183
4	24	44	64	84	104	124	144	164	184
5	25	45	65	85	105	125	145	165	185
6	26	46	66	86	106	126	146	166	186
7	27	47	67	87	107	127	147	167	187
8	28	48	68	88	108	128	148	168	188
9	29	49	69	89	109	129	149	169	189
(10)	30	50	70	90	110	130	(150)	170	190
11	31	51	71	91	111	131	151	171	191
12	32	52	72	92	112	132	152	172	192
13	33	53	73	93	(113)	133	153	173	193
14	34	54	74	94	114	134	154	174	194
15	35	55	75	95	115	135	155	175	195
16	36	56	76	96	116	136	156	176	196
17	37	57	77	97	117	137	157	177	197
18	38	58	78	98	118	138	158	178	198
19	39	59	79	99	119	139	159	179	199
20	40	(60)	80	100	120	140	160	180	200

201	216	231	246	261	276	291	306	321	336
202	217	232	247	262	277	292	307	322	337
203	218	233	248	263	278	293	(308)	323	338
204	219	234	249	264	279	294	309	324	339
205	220	235	250	265	280	295	310	325	340
206	221	236	251	266	281	296	311	326	341
207	222	237	252	267	282	297	312	327	342
208	223	238	253	268	283	298	313	328	343
209	224	239	254	269	284	299	314	329	344
210	225	240	255	270	285	300	315	330	345
211	226	241	256	271	286	301	316	331	346
212	227	242	257	272	287	302	317	332	347
213	228	243	258	273	288	303	318	333	348
214	229	244	259	274	289	304	319	334	349
215	230	245	260	275	290	305	320	335	350